XOCOMIL

The Winds Of Atitlán

David Mohrmann

LastWord Books

Copyright © 2016 by David Mohrmann
LastWord Books
1827 27th Street
Arcata, CA 95521

All rights reserved. No part of this book maybe reproduced or transmitted in any form or by any means, electronic or mechanical, including photocopying, recording, or by any information storage system, without written permission from the publisher, except for brief quotations in a review.

Printed and bound in the United States of America

Library of Congress Cataloging-in-Publication Data
Mohrmann, David.
Xocomil, the winds of Atitlán : a novel by David Mohrmann

ISBN 978-0-9969922-0-6

Front and Back Cover Paintings by David Mohrmann
Cover design by David Mohrmann and Jesse Ostrowski

Author's Note: Xocomil is a work of literary fiction. Certain historical, geographical, and cultural details have been either slightly adjusted or subjectively interpreted for the sake of the story. As for the characters, any resemblance to actual people is purely coincidental.

ACKNOWLEDGMENTS

Before I begin thanking specific individuals, I must say how awed I am by the countless people--mostly indigenous but also ladinos and some foreigners--who have pursued justice, at all odds and at great personal peril, to make sure that Efraín Ríos Montt was brought to trial on charges of crimes against humanity. It was on the day his conviction was overthrown (by a secret court on a minor technicality) that I began this novel. That was almost three years ago, and I have been working on it every day since.

First, and forever, I thank my wife, Lee Torrence, as a most vigilant editor on issues of indigenous Guatemalan culture, and for her extreme patience and constant support throughout this long process. Many thanks, as well, to my other devoted editor, John Heckel, who is a master at conceptualization and was a huge help in cleaning up the novel's gaps and inconsistencies. Other essential aid came from John Daniel--that esteemed word guru--and the writer's group TGI (Jim Hight, Tom Leskiw, Nancy Wheeler, Janine Volkmar, Susan Penn).

A special thank you to my dear friends, Marshall Kane, Peggy Anderson, and Steve Ladd for reading the early versions of many chapters and giving helpful feedback and encouragement. Also to Larry Fried, and T, for the continued blind faith in what I was trying to do. And to Robin Retherford and Erik Lindblom for loving my stories and willing me to keep writing. The same to Anando Le Boef, who has gone to my short-story readings in Guatemala and always thoughtfully critiqued my work. Indeed, Anando was the one who suggested that this short story (originally 'Gracias a Dios') grow into a novel.

I am grateful to my other expat friends as well, who came through at key times with bits of historical and cultural information that I lacked: 'Marco Solo' Weinstein, 'Carpenter Karen' Herman, 'Swedish' Tomas, Dianne Celeste, Jan and Sid Eschenbach, Duncan Aitken, Richard Hutchinson, Margarita and Allen Stern. Many thanks to the Panajachel Center (that is: Aimee Guberman and Richard Dekkers) for a wonderful warm space to do readings from the first draft of Xocomil, and to the many who came and offered suggestions or corrections. Especially Anna Walker, Kelly Agnew, and Alex DaHinton. Plus, of course, countless others who I am, unfortunately, forgetting to mention.

Muchas gracias to Ben Urtz (Quetzaltrekkers). Also a loving hug to my late friend, Victoria Stone, for introducing me to Terry Biskovich (editor of The Revue). And thank you, Terry, for your confidence in, and promotion of, Xocomil.

Finally, most important of all, my heartfelt thanks to Miguel and Otilia, who provided the crucial stories that weave through Book One of the novel. Without their willingness to share painful memories, this book would never have been written.

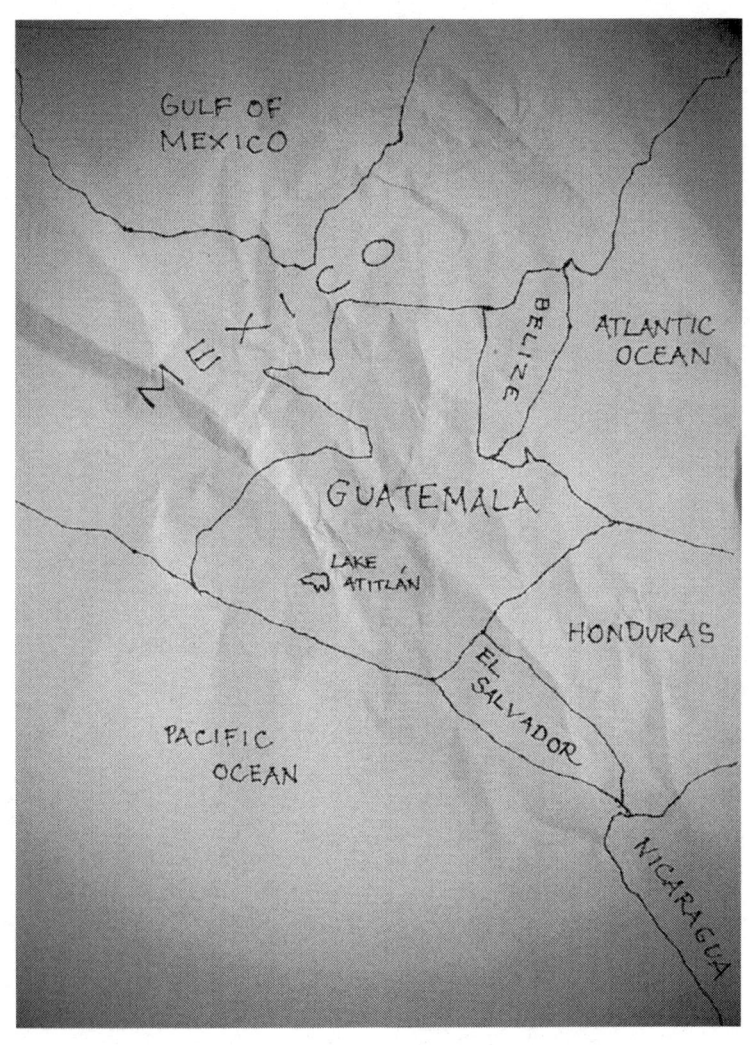

Central America

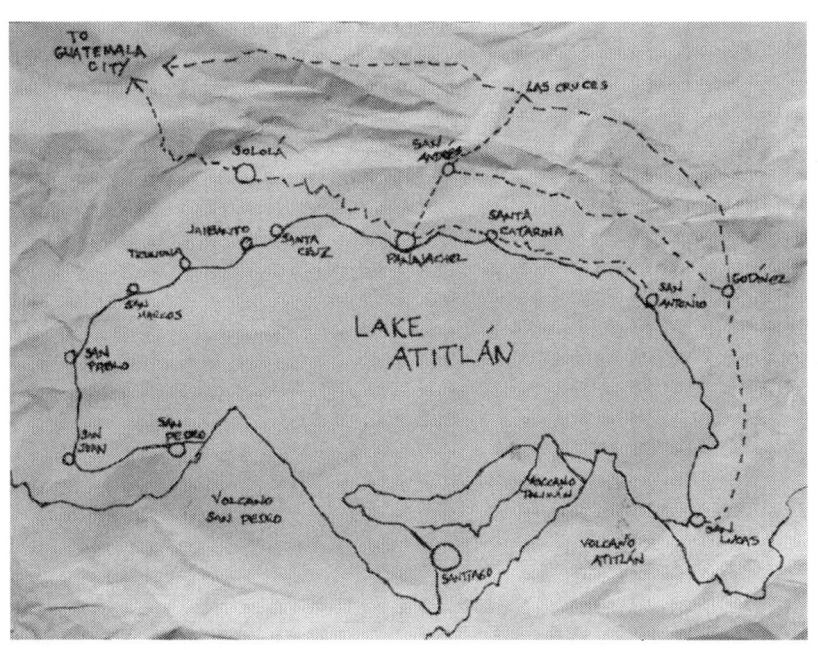

Lake Atitlán

XOCOMIL
The Winds of Atitlán

Eighty five thousand years ago, the eruption of one volcano wiped out nearly all forms of life for many hundreds of miles. The result was a massive caldera in the highlands of what is now Guatemala. Millennium's since, as water levels rose inside the crater--exits closed off by the three smaller volcanoes expanding around its rim--Atitlán was formed.

Atitlán (Ah-teet-**lahn**) is translated by some as *where the rainbow gets its colors;* by others as *the place where water gathers.* In either case. . .a good name for a lake. It is a thousand feet deep. It hides a lot. But its surface reflects a world of human behavior that often taints the beauty of this magical place.

Xocomil (Show-koh-**meel**) is a word unique to Atitlán. It refers to the lake's strong afternoon wind. Originally it meant *the demon's fury.* Since the invasion of Spaniards and Catholicism, however, some converted Maya have taken it to mean *the wind that carries away sin.*

Regardless of meaning, the Xocomil blows nearly every day. Sometimes with fury.

BOOK ONE

Mayazak Pabej

(a Kaqchikel saying that translates as: *Don't fall down on the path.*
Or, in Spanish: *Que le vaya bien*
Or, as we would say in English: *Take care.*)

Corn

Santa Catarina Palopó, Lake Atitlán, Guatemala, 1960

In the beginning there was only corn. That was what the ancients said, and Manuel believed it. Each dawn, before the sun had time to rise, he woke to his grandma straining a bowl of the golden kernels from the *cal* they'd soaked in overnight. For him, it was like the official announcement of a new day. His mouth watered as she washed the softened seeds and hurried them to the *molina*. . .to the one-armed man named Pedro who ground them into *masa*.

This morning the boy misses his grandpa's snores. They always seemed to get louder once she left, the old man's nose and mouth impatient with slumber, hungry for the scent, the taste, of tortillas. Mouths and noses, thinks Manuel, know better than clocks.

He sees his father, crouched down in the far corner of the hut, blowing on a thin strip of *ocote* beneath a bed of tiny twigs. He's trying hard to save the flickering flame, avoid having to use another match. Manuel gets to his feet. He shakes away the cold and last night's fitful sleep. Already dressed in his *traje*, he folds his blanket, rolls up his straw mat, places both against the near wall, and runs outside to the woodpile. Since his mother's death, four years ago, this has been his morning job. Though just six at the time, that was when he stopped being a child. Because his father told him so. Sure as fire. That's how the boy felt it: a hot glowing blaze he could not avoid. Nor did he want to. Of course he was sad about losing his mother, but honored that his need to feel useful had finally been recognized. Yes, he thinks, filling his arms with the right-sized sticks, he's proud to be treated like a man. He wants the responsibility, welcomes the work, and understands when sometimes (for mistakes his father needs him to notice) he gets a thump on the head.

Manuel comes inside with the wood. His father passes by, off to do some job or other that only grown men are fit for. Manuel is expected to keep the fire alive. To succeed, with minimal smoke, he's learned to use the driest sticks, and has never had a problem. Never. So why be worrying today? Because he dreamt about his mother again, that's why. Only this time he could hear her too. This time she spoke to him, woke him shivering in the darkness, and he hates how it made him feel. Unsure of himself. Unsure of everything. "Because I was not supposed to die," she said. "No one understood it any more than you, Manuel. Even if you make no mistakes, son, do everything right, there's no guarantee the sticks will keep burning."

It was the same as when she was alive, telling him not to be so serious, so easily disappointed, that life is a mystery and might not go the way he wants.

"If no one could save me," she says, "is it fair that you, a small boy, is expected to--"

There she is again, whispering in his ear. He drops to his knees by the sputtering flame and forces himself to concentrate. She kept at him all last night, spinning his mind in circles, but he will not let her ruin his day too! He lays down a thicker set of twigs, crisscrossing them like his father taught, to keep the air flowing within. But maybe this time he's waited too long. Maybe this is the day it dies? Heart pounding, he leans in and blows. It's as if his entire life, every bit of it, is held this instant in the loose grip of that tiny failing light. He blows. And blows.

A chicken wanders into the hut. It knows better, stupid bird. Makes fun of him with its selfish strut and cluck. He'd kick it hard were there any chance, but he has to keep blowing. Softer now. Softer. The spark flickers...fades...flickers again...then suddenly, like always, grabs hold of the closest twig, clings by one slim yellow finger, pulls itself up and reaches for more.

Yes...like always. No chance of failure now.

"See!" he shouts, and the chicken runs squawking for the door, running for its life. Manuel's eyes dart around the hut, convinced he has broken his mother's spell, chased her from the shadows. No, he can't be tricked. She cannot make him small and scared and weak.

Freed from her grip, a man once more, he tends the fire, prodding the pile to keep it burning hot. He loves to watch it slowly change: brown sticks turning black; then smoky gray; breaking down and crumbling apart; at last a bed of orange glowing embers.

"Good," says his grandma.

Back with her bowl of masa, anxious to start cooking, she places the *comal* over the three flat stones, six or seven inches above the coals. Manuel arranges the extra branches off to her side, near enough to grab should she need them. He sits down cross-legged on the dirt. His father comes inside and takes the one rickety wooden stool. Then, same as every other morning, the men wait. Manuel watches, mesmerized, while his grandma rolls and pats the sticky mashed corn, like creating the world all over again, rounded and flattened and flipped back and forth between her wrinkled old hands. Though he does not believe that man was made from *maize*, he's not so sure about Grandma Elena. Her sun-baked stalk is withered and brittle, bound to collapse in a heavy wind.

He hopes she will not die today. At least not before he's eaten. He still remembers, with anger and confusion and a sort of numbing sadness, his mother's last tortillas, the horrible sight and smell of them burning to a crisp after she fell and could not get up. By then he'd gotten used to her falling, used to her sickness. Neither he nor his father had known what to do. No one knew.

Sometimes she'd call him to her bed and say, "Don't worry, son, I'll be better soon." But it wasn't true, she never got better. And he did worry. Still does. It was she who put the worry in his mind. He hates her for that. She died, all right, she died. All the worry in the world could do nothing to stop it. Now, if his mother truly loved him, she would know to stay dead, gone, and leave him alone!

Intent on keeping her away, Manuel closes his eyes and thinks about his grandpa, also named Manuel, who at least gave something to his children, something of value, before he died.

The boy remembers sitting in the narrow doorway of their house, quiet as a rock, on the last morning of the old man's life. That was three days ago, but his mind pulls it close.

None of his many cousins were allowed; removed by their protective mothers; spared the smell and sight of certain death. The four sons had been called by old Manuel to hear his last wishes. Young Manuel's father, Hector, sat on the ground. Héctor's three older brothers stood together right behind him. Grandma Elena was off by herself, in the corner--ready, as usual, should the men need anything.

Old Manuel had not eaten for days. He lay on the same straw mat he'd slept on all these years. A light film of sweat covered his face, moistening the white stubble of his chin where a fly sat on its haunches, scratching its skinny black legs together, waiting with the rest. The old man sucked in a long deep breath. Held it tight. Then, unable to stop its escape, he gasped and lunged and gobbled at the used-up air as if trying to get it back. The fly buzzed loud, dodged the gaping mouth, zig-zagged around the room, over young Manuel's head, and out the door.

Héctor touched his father's shoulder. The older sons eyed each other. Everyone, including young Manuel, knew what was coming. His grandpa had long ago inherited three contiguous pieces of land. These *terrenos* were close to the house, on the hillside above Santa Catarina: each measured two *cuerdas*; each was covered with family corn. A full year had passed since old Manuel could help with the crops. He was dying, that was clear, and the day had come to divide the *milpa* amongst his four sons.

"There. . .are. . ." his grandpa said, but the old man's chest was heaving and he could not finish. He closed his eyes and swallowed. Twice. Then tried again. "Three," he coughed. . ."three. . ."

"Terrenos," said the eldest son, José, and young Manuel held his breath. He knew, like everyone else, that warning sound in Jose's voice. From early childhood--or so the story went--he had appointed himself spokesman for each successive sibling. Lean and muscular, he would spark impatient with anyone who did not appreciate his natural ability to understand what mattered and what didn't. This included old Manuel, who had exhausted his minimal tolerance ages ago. "Yes," said José, "three."

His two nearest brothers smiled. Héctor sighed.

Old Manuel exhaled without a cough, which seemed to give him confidence. Eyes brightening, he inhaled slowly and pointed a shaky finger at José. "You, because you were the first, because it. . .is. . .the custom, you. . ." he coughed, "get. . ." he coughed, "the closest."

"Yes father, I know."

"Good," said old Manuel, eyeing him with obvious irritation. "It is good. . .you know. And the second. . .piece. . .by the big. . .flat. . .rock, goes to you, Obrário. And the third, Ramos. . .is yours."

The old man coughed and coughed, then reached out and took hold of Héctor's hand.

The older sons glanced down at their brother. They must have thought it fair that he, being youngest, came last. But what more was there to give? Nothing! They must have thought that too.

"I am. . .sorry, Héctor."

"Yes, Papa?"

"What I've left you. . .here," the old man wheezed, "is our house."

It was not a prideful statement, that was plain. Young Manuel, surprised by his grandpa's tone, looked with fresh eyes around the one room hut. This was his house, too, the only house he'd ever known. Its floor was dirt, its walls of *caña* stalks, its roof of thatched *puja*. Old Manuel had been born here. Had lived here all his life. His parents had died here, and here he raised his own family. Soon as José married, he was permitted to build a house of his own on the same two-cuerda piece of property. In the following years, Obrário and Ramos did the same. Each of them now had children, between the three a total of eleven. Each had his separate chickens, separate stacks of wood, and separate piles of garbage. Héctor was the only one to keep his wife and child in the original house.

Young Manuel once asked his father why they didn't also have a place of their own.

"Because," Hector said, "I like it here."

The boy knew it was because of old Manuel, because his father and grandpa were so much alike. The two of them, it seemed, had always been close, and the older brothers always jealous. So what a strange thing that Héctor, by far the favorite son, was given no tillable land.

How was that possible?

While none of the other brothers were going to complain, they clearly looked puzzled. And, though they tried not show it, pleased.

Old Manuel, still holding Hector's hand, said, "I am sorry, son, your land is not. . .close."

Hearing those words, the three eldest sons shifted from one foot to the other, like the first step of some primitive dance. All traces of pleasure vanished from their faces. Their eyes blinked, their foreheads pinched and crumpled. Young Manuel felt sure they must be wondering, like him, *how could this hut they were in, right now, be any closer?*

Bewilderment bumped and rattled around the room. The boy watched José's body stiffen. His uncle probably worried that the old man had lost his mind, which might call into question his last wishes. José leaned forward and cleared his throat. It looked like he was preparing to confront his father, but all he managed was a burp. Then another. Obrario flinched. Ramos squirmed. Lost without José's normal poise, they bobbed their heads like chickens hunting worms.

Young Manuel had no doubt that Uncle José would soon regain control. A few seconds later he did, his frown changed to a stony smile. Yes, all right, the old man might be crazy. So? Even if it were true, that smile meant, who of them would ever say it? Not José or any of the older brothers. Not the beloved Héctor, right? José glanced over at his mother, perhaps not so certain about her, but seeing that she'd dozed off in the corner made his smile grow wider. Obrário and Ramos smiled too. The boy shuddered at his uncles' sudden confidence. Certain there was no reason to worry, they all relaxed, their steely eyes softening like a three-headed vulture digesting a horse.

Old Manuel had pushed up on his elbows, was hacking out whitish gobs of something sticky. He looked ready to die any minute. Gulping air, he jabbed a crooked finger back behind his head, the words coming in small spurts, propelled by bulging bloodshot eyes. "Your land, son, is. . .it is a . . .sizeable plot, not. . .toooooo. . .faaar." He waved his hand toward Héctor's brothers. "These boys they. . .they . . .could not make it. . .grow."

Ramos and Obrario, from either side, moved closer to José. Manuel strained to hear.

"What did he say?" whispered Ramos.

"Who knows," whispered José.

"What other land?" whispered Obrário.

"Never mind," José said. The boy could tell José was tired of the whispering, the unnecessary chatter, and wanted to get back to work. "There is no other land."

"You. . .may. . .think. . ." old Manuel coughed toward José.

But there was no telling what that might mean. Old Manuel had spent himself and could not go on. At least not with the elder brothers staring down at him.

They left, each happy with their own separate lots, while Héctor waited patiently by his father's side. At one point the old man gestured him to come closer. Héctor leaned in and old Manuel kissed his cheek. "You are a good boy," he said. "A good boy."

Old Manuel could no longer turn his head. From time to time he would wave an angry finger at Grandma Elena, a desperate call for water. To show her shame for not being more attentive, she crawled on her creaky knees and spooned it into his mouth. This was a custom with the older generation. Young Manuel thought it perfectly normal. He knew, of course, that some women complained of being treated like a slave. Thankfully, she was not one of those. For him, as with his father and grandpa, the truth was simple, no matter how it might be judged: a wife's responsibility to serve her husband must never be questioned.

As if to prove it, after getting his fill of water, old Manuel made the exact same gesture--a signal that his woman take it away! And herself too! *Away* his angry hands ordered! *Back to your corner!*

The boy could feel his grandpa's pain, his incapacity to think things through. The old man slapped himself in the head and grumbled with every breath, straining for the right words, the strength to make them say what he wanted. Then, for several seconds, he gazed out into space, blinking, like a barber might at his messy floor, trying to remember where all the hair had come from. Finally, between coughs, he explained, as best he could, how to find the land. It was like trying to follow a leaf during the Xocomil. He reached a shaky hand beneath his mat and came up with a piece of paper. "Official," he sputtered. "Proof." He handed it to Héctor, then slipped into another silence.

Héctor looked at the paper. "I'm sorry, Papa, I don't understand."

All of a sudden, old Manuel's mouth popped open. The intention, it seemed, was to give some final helpful hint. Instead, there came just one long gasp as his head fell back to the mat. His eyes were huge and still. Grandma Elena, seeing Héctor's head turn her way, said, "No, no, he's not dead. He's been doing that for days, sometimes for many minutes, but he always comes back."

So the three of them watched, and waited. After a long time without the slightest change, Grandma Elena sat against the wall and began to snore.

"I'll be right back," Héctor said to Manuel, and hurried from of the hut. The boy also wanted to leave, but knew he couldn't. Then his grandpa's eyes seemed to get bright and glossy. Maybe he was going to cry. Manuel did not want to be alone with him if that happened. He had to do something. Though knowing he shouldn't, he walked over, stood above, and looked down into those wet, staring eyes. A single tear fell, dripping down his grandpa's cheek. Manuel, hoping to wake him up, gave the old man a gentle nudge with his foot, and just like that the eyes went soft and began to close.

"What?" Grandma Elena yelled in her sleep. "What?"

The boy dashed back to where he'd been.

The old woman woke up. Coming to her husband's side, she knelt down and looked hard at his sunken face. Then looked at his filthy bare feet. As if they had the final say, she nodded, sighed, and walked toward the door. Young Manuel scooted back to let her pass. She glanced at him and made a low moaning sound. He expected sadness, but that's not what he heard. Relief, that's what it was. She was happy to have him gone.

Once outside the hut she turned around and glared. Could he really read her mind?

"Yes," he heard her say. . .and then she began to shrink, or somehow create distance between them. *What?* How, he wondered, without moving, could she keep getting smaller and smaller, soon like a puffy little cloud way off in the sky?

The boy blinked, and she seemed to get closer. Though that made no sense either, he kept on blinking, trying to bring her back. But wait, it wasn't his grandma anymore, she'd changed into something else, was now the Xocomil, rushing toward him, her body shimmering red, her eyes burning into his.

"Yes boy," she said, "you heard me right. Life might be easier with one less man to serve!"

He could see her ravaged face again, and the mole on her neck, and the frayed red *huipil* covering her bony frame. He thought he saw his mother floating above her head. But how? None of this could be happening. It couldn't.

The doorframe he was leaning against began to slide backward. Though he tried to brace himself, there was nothing to hold onto. The entry opened up, bigger than the hut itself, deeper than the lake, wider than the endless sky.

He heard his grandma laughing, her breath a foul wind blowing in his face. He saw their three chickens, accustomed to getting breakfast scraps, scramble toward the scarecrow of a woman. He watched as they rushed headlong into her ferocious foot.

Suddenly she turned and started kicking Manuel too.

Kicked and kicked and kicked.

"No," he screams, wriggling away, "stop it. . .stop!" He wakes to a sky of wafting smoke. His grandma is leaning over him, scowling. He covers his head.

"Ay, Manuel," she says, "it's time to eat." She straightens up, not so scary anymore, her pile of wrinkles looking tame. She holds out a plate of tortillas. "Are you back with us now?"

"Yes," he says, spellbound by her widening grin, her abrupt laugh. He hears his father laughing too. Both of them laughing at him.

Small and embarrassed, a child again, Manuel rubs at his tired eyes.

"Boy!" growls his grandma. "Are you hungry or not?"

He takes the plate. How could she ask such a thing?

"Well," she says, "they're getting cold."

"Hurry up," his father says. He gently thumps the side of Manuel's head, then bites into a last tortilla as he walks toward the door. "Today, son, we go to find our land."

Luck

With their paper of 'official proof' (translated by the ex-mayor), and what Héctor thought he'd understood from his father, it took them three separate trips, three long days, to find the inheritance. It was eleven kilometers away, over the near mountain, atop the following ridge: a precipitous knoll covered with weeds.

Manuel saw why it had never been mentioned. Or ever used to grow corn. 'A size-able plot,' yes, more than a cuerda, though laced with jagged stones. He glanced at the huge trees above them to the east, which would block the morning sun. Far worse was the ground itself. "Steep," he said, accustomed to the gentler slopes of loamy soil his uncles had gotten. Manuel knew what a plant needed, and this wasn't it. He knelt, grabbed a stick, poked it at the hard-packed soil. "Rocky."

Héctor gave the boy's head a thump. "It's ours!" he said. "Land for our own milpa!"

"Yes, Papa."

Héctor turned his face to the heavens, clearly hoping to correct his young son's foolishness. "We thank you for this place! We are grateful!" A huge raven screeched overhead, trying to get free of the tiny white bird pecking at its tail feathers. Héctor dropped to his hands and knees and dragged his son down with him. Grabbed a handful of dirt. "This," he said, "is a gift to us." A tear slid from his glossy wet eyes. "We are lucky, son. Very lucky. We must work hard."

And Manuel knew why. To impress his father's selfish brothers. To prove why he'd been favored. Also, of course, because there was no other choice. Day after day they left their hut before sunrise and returned in the dark.

They used the larger rocks to build retaining walls for seven long terraces, each approximately three feet high. That took six weeks. Once the walls were completed, they threw the smaller stones down into the barranca. Then, sharing a single hoe, they took turns digging and scraping at the remaining rubble, filling old frayed burlap sacks with the gravelly mix, hauling it to the land's edge to reinforce the narrow path. The seedbeds took thirteen days of sifting, Héctor not satisfied until every last pebble was gone. Manuel felt sure the land was worthless, but his father had a plan. He'd located an avocado orchard an hour away and they used the sacks to collect its fallen leaves, the owner pleased that they would clean it up for free. Héctor laughed. "Lucky for us, he is not a smart man!" It was as if his father had found a pile of money. The decaying foliage made him smile. The moldy slime beneath it made him giggle. With every trip he seemed to get happier, often beaming up at the empty sky. They dragged the bulging sacks for days, like ants might drag dead beetles. They tilled the leaves and festering rot into their barren soil, along with every trace of organic matter found between the land and their hut: ashes from an abandoned fire pit; dried-out cow patties.

By late April there was nothing to do but sit outside the hut with whoever might pass by and talk about weather, everyone waiting for the first storm. As usual, his father and the older men traded bad jokes and playful insults--no harm intended, or taken--all of them tired of just sitting around. Manuel too. Sometimes he'd play silly games with his friends, like hide and seek, or marbles, pretending to be a kid again, but the truth was, like the other men, he wanted to work.

His father passed each day waiting for the night. "Waiting," he said, "for the sure sign, the old way of knowing: a ring around the moon." It finally came, much later than expected, on the eleventh of May. "Tomorrow, son, there will be rain." Of that he seemed certain. He rose the next morning with a glowing face and whistled as he walked. The clouds were already gathering over the volcanoes, *another good sign*, so Manuel tried whistling too, but it didn't sound right and he didn't want to get laughed at.

Once they reached the land, Héctor stood tall to mutter a prayer at the darkening sky. To Manuel's great surprise, it then began to drizzle. Still, the boy knew, that was not good enough, the earth should be saturated before seeds are planted. But his father only smiled and nodded, satisfied that actual rain was coming. He signaled Manuel to follow as he walked toward the upper terrace, to the far end of the first bed. "Thank you," he said to the dripping sky, "for this needed help."

He kneeled down and poked his index finger into the center of the bed, then untied the sack.

"Here," he said, handing a single golden kernel to his son.

"Me?"

"Yes," his father said. "Maybe you will bring us luck."

Manuel took the seed and held it tight.

"One for each hole," Héctor said. "Say a blessing before you drop it in."

"What is that?"

"Like asking a favor. For the stalks to grow tall and strong. You say it inside, to yourself."

His father left the sack behind and moved away, working down the row, poking holes about an arms length apart. Manuel had never done the seeding. His usual job was to pull weeds--or, when the corn was ripe, help harvest. He leaned over the first hole and took a deep breath. In case Héctor was watching, he closed his eyes. *Please*, he thought, soft as a whisper, *we need a BIG FAVOR.*

He waited a few seconds before dropping in the seed. . .a few seconds before covering it. . . .a few seconds more to make sure his blessing was sufficient.

They did the same for each of the seven terraces. After the final seed, Héctor re-tied the sack with utmost care, then showed how to sprinkle just the right amount of straw over the planted beds--straw he'd found left uneaten by some of the richer cows along their way. For Manuel, like his father, this was not stealing. If something of value sat neglected, it felt wrong not to take it.

Approvechar, that was the rule: one needed to *take advantage* of any opportunity. That was the unspoken law of this difficult world.

It was late afternoon when the ceremony came to an end. Seed planted, prayers given, they watched the muted sun begin its descent. Soon the rain would surely come. Pitch-black clouds swelled above, dense as a breaking wave, and the Xocomil blew hard. Héctor pointed off into the distance where he swore he'd heard thunder.

"Any time," he said. "Any time."

But the time kept passing, the sky grew darker, and nothing happened. Except, little by little, the wind decreased, turned to a pleasant breeze, then stopped. The air became still as a stone, dry as a dusty blanket. Manuel looked at his father's face. The sound of thunder, too, was gone. "What?" groaned Héctor. "I don't understand." Purple clouds turned pink and spread over the volcanoes. Day showed its final fading light. Héctor waved his hands into the sky, as if that might mean something to someone who mattered. Like all the other farmers, his father trusted his ability to read weather, and hated to be wrong. He mumbled to himself and walked toward the steep barranca. He moved with such stiff-legged purpose that Manuel feared he might jump off, disappear forever, leave him alone on this harsh desolate ground. What a thing to think! Instead, not at all surprising, Héctor stopped short of the edge and pulled down his pants.

Squatted to take a shit. After a few good grunts he wiped himself with the old piece of newspaper he'd brought along for that purpose. He tossed it away, pulled up his pants, and walked back to Manuel. Obviously he'd thought things through. Eyes full of superstition, he licked the tips of his fingers and opened them toward the horizon.

"It is close," he said. "Very close."

Manuel also licked his fingers and reached them out, hoping to feel what his father felt.

Héctor laughed, as he might at a poorly told joke, and shook his fist at the sky. "Hah!" he said, then turned to his son, "sometimes rain is lazy."

"Yes, sir."

Héctor pointed at the narrow path. "We will stay here and wait."

Each cleared a spot, one above the other, and lay down to sleep. It was not much colder, nor the ground any harder than back in the hut. Manuel, who had never slept under the stars, felt more than ever like a man. But the night went on and on, a reminder of bad dreams. Over and over, they were forced to throw rocks at the sound of hateful creatures trying to dig up their precious seed. When the big round moon slipped between clouds, Manuel got a glance at the beasts, at their long furry tails. He'd seen them before, or at least their skins, hammered on the side of the butcher's shed, but didn't know what they were called. "What are they, Papa?"

"I don't remember the name. They come from the forest, rats who live in trees. When I was a boy, they were around Santa Catarina too. We used to trap and eat them. Now they're all gone. They taste good if you can catch one, boy. Not like other rats."

Manuel felt sick at the thought of eating any kind of rat. He hated even the sight of them, the skinny tailed ones sneaking between the shadows in their hut at night, scratching at the corn bin. Aside from the tail, yes, he saw the resemblance. "Not as ugly," he said.

"No, son, but also a lot of trouble. We're lucky for this fat moon, and for so many rocks."

While the steady stoning never hit a single one, it prevented the pests from causing real harm. By dawn, their battle over, the humans dozed, relieved of worry until a fresh new sun climbed above the pines and shined into their eyes.

Héctor jumped to his feet and stared at the bright blue sky, his shoulders slumped like a dying plant. Soon, though, he straightened up, and smiled, and looked down at his son. "Good thing it hasn't come yet," he said. "Because we forgot the trenches. Sometimes, if the rain comes slow, you need to help it find the seeds." He took the hoe and dug several shallow channels in the upper path, aiming them into the first bed. Manuel's job was to carve them deeper with a stick and remove the debris while his father dug channels on the paths below, connecting each successive terrace. As they worked, clouds began to swirl above. By early afternoon the sun was struggling to show itself, and the Xocomil returned in force. "I am glad to have had this extra day," Héctor announced, speaking more to the heavens than his son.

To Manuel, his father looked foolish. The boy could not say it, of course, and knew he should not be thinking it, but could not help wondering what good were these endless prayers and constant excuses? Sometimes it was Héctor who seemed the little boy. Why not admit when he's wrong? Or maybe, thought Manuel, it was his mother trying to cause them trouble. Was she haunting his father too? He didn't know. They were exhausted, he knew that much. Neither had eaten since the day before. Neither of them were thinking right.

His father looked at the darkening clouds and covered his heart with both hands. "As you see, we have done everything we can. We are ready for whatever comes."

But in spite of the hopeful words, nothing came. Not a drop. The day passed and again they lay down on the rocky path. Again the tree rats came. Again there was hardly any sleep, followed by another long day of hunger, thirst, and worry.

Then, late on that third night, the sky split open with thick barbs of lightning. Héctor shook Manuel and pulled him to his feet. The thunder clapped loud, echoing above. His father's face was only inches away, closer than he'd ever seen it. "You see boy! See how lucky!"

Within a couple of minutes they were soaking wet, scrambling in the sudden mud to fill in the trenches they'd spent many hours digging. Now they had the reverse problem, an urgent need to stop the torrent from washing away their seeds. Manuel ran along the underside of each terrace, plugging whatever leaks he could find with handfuls of straw, pressing it into the jagged crevices. His fingers were raw, some of them bleeding. He could see his father, above, using the hoe to carve new routes for the water to take. Then the handle slipped and Hector fell face down in the muck. The boy watched him climb to his knees, gagging, close to tears, and spit out what he could of the sloppy grit.

He must be wondering how the gods could still be angry. Manuel blocked a laugh, grumbling to himself and cursing their constant cruelty. For him, the chilling downpour was a punishment he did not deserve.

They worked until daylight without a moment's rest. Neither had ever been so cold or confused.

Around noon the rain finally dribbled to a stop. At last confident that their terraces would hold, Héctor led the way home. They were filthy, exhausted, hungry. And, what mattered more, relieved to have saved the crop. Even Manuel felt a tiny bit hopeful. But not, *definitely not*, lucky.

Avanzado

Months later, Hector tried to explain their meager yield. "Just bad luck," he said. "We lost a lot of seeds when the rain would not stop."

True, thought Manuel, but there was no explanation for the spindly survivors. What was his excuse for that? He knew what his father could not admit. Bad soil. Not enough sun.

Lucky for them, Hector said, there was a company called *Avanzado* that loaned money to anyone who bought its fertilizer. Other farmers were praising the stuff, so he walked to Sololá to find out more. He returned that evening, happy, saying, "The salesman, Señor Martínez, was very helpful. He brought me to the government office, where the company paid for our paper of official proof to be 'notarized' as 'collateral' for the loan."

"What is all that, Papa?"

"Oh, you know, *business words*. Legal things they have to say." Hector produced what he called a 'receipt'. . .then showed Manuel his large bag of *Avanzado Supremo*. "Specially developed chemicals," he said, repeating what the salesman must have told him. "It will make our stalks grow tall."

Manuel remained suspicious. Though all of this was new to him, it sounded wrong, as if he'd heard this story before and knew better than to believe it. In the first few weeks the plants looked the same as always, dry and thirsty and struggling to survive. But, months later, when their second harvest tripled the first, he had to admit it might be because of the fertilizer. Or maybe because the rain came in a normal way this season, and the tree rats were scarce.

Still, it ended up another hungry year since they were obliged to sell most of the corn to pay down the debt. Ah, Manuel thought, so that's the trick. Could his mother be somehow responsible for his father's stupidity. No...this he could not blame on her.

Hector, who had never owed anyone anything, said he was ashamed to not pay the full amount. He went to Avanzado's new office in Panajachel to apologize. Also, if possible, to get another loan.

"I am not the first to have such troubles," he told his son that evening. "Señor Martínez said that on behalf of the company, because of my good character, I could get a discount on this year's fertilizer. Plus another year to pay my debt before they charge 'financial maintenance fees.' He shook my hand and patted my back, son. He wished us luck."

Luck, Manuel knew, would not solve their problems, but each night he watched his father crouch in the corner of their hut and pray for it. Héctor also borrowed five *quetzales* from his brother, Ramos, whom he hated somewhat less than the others. He hired a local shaman to do an ancient ritual with the seed. The man wanted lots more money to go bless the soil, burn copal from the gopher mounds, fill the air with sacred smoke and frighten away the bushy-tailed demons along with every other evil spirit lurking in those accursed trees. Hector said he could not afford all that, but did remember some of the shaman's words. He repeated them with the same grave tone as he dropped each kernel into its hole and covered it with dirt. "Next," he whispered, "we must put our heads to the earth." With a somber face he bent himself over. "We must thank Ix Chel for bringing rain."

Manuel did what he was told. "Thank you, Ix Chel, for--"

"No," his father said. "It is like a prayer, son, in your mind. Only no actual words."

"Yes, sir."

So, for many minutes, Manuel kept his forehead down. Ants and a long-legged spider crawled beneath his nose. Trying not to think with actual words, he silently prayed that Ix Chel, and whoever else might be of some help, would, *this time at least*, listen.

Hector lifted his head to the heavens and made a final request. "If possible. . ." he coaxed, "please. . .try not to wash away the seeds." Then he closed his eyes and bowed his head and groaned. "No," he whispered, "you stupid, stupid man."

Again looking up, with a booming loud voice, he apologized for thinking that gods might ever need advice. His sincerity was obvious, but Manuel had the feeling it would not be enough to appease them. Hector, seeming to agree, kept mumbling, his lips moving with barely a sound.

And Manuel mumbled right along with him. Though he'd never been to a Mayan ceremony, he understood the purpose of prayer. It was for anyone who faithfully believed--or wanted to--and the boy, despite his doubts, realized that the time for trying hard to believe was now.

His father decided to trust that the rain was coming. On the way home, Manuel lagged behind and watched Hector's walk. Not the confident stride his son was used to. No more whistling either, and hardly a glance at the sky. The lake, reflecting a swirl of clouds, spread out beneath the three volcanoes. A luscious cabbage crop was visible on the slope below, next to a ditch of flowing water. There were also fields of onions and beans, but Hector's eyes stayed focused on the steep narrow path. He would not stop to look. He did not want to see what others had. The son could tell he no longer felt so lucky. Good, thought Manuel. What a foolish thing to ever feel lucky in this world.

It was late afternoon by the time they descended the final ridge. The Xocomil was blowing hard. Turning down the path to Santa Catarina, Hector walked faster, never once looking back to see if his son was still behind him. All he wanted was to get back to the hut and hide. By the time Manuel arrived, he had already eaten his rationed ten tortillas and was fast asleep, snoring on his mat.

For Manuel, however, tortillas and sleep were not enough. Tomorrow they would go back to stone the tree rats and wait for rain. Better *that*, he thought, than a day of rest. The thought of doing nothing made his stomach roar like a wild animal. He could not lie around all day feeling its claws.

He remembered seeing men catch bluegills from the shore. If they could do it, why not him? Why not today? A pungent sour saliva filled his mouth. He grabbed his father's spool of line, his single hook, and bolted from the hut, down the twisting narrow *callejones*. He dodged pigs, ducks, chickens, dogs--vaulted their many piles of crap--flew around a final sharp curve, past two drunks trying to hold each other up, and out onto the main road, where he slipped and almost collided with a young girl. She gasped, holding out her hands to cushion his blow. A clay pot fell from her head to the street and shattered, its kernels of corn splattering everywhere. The girl's eyelids were quivering. She was pretty, very pretty, and he'd have no idea what to say were it not so obvious. "I'll fix it," he told her. "I promise." He dropped to his knees and started scooping the kernels into small dirty piles.

An old woman came from across the way and set down a new clay pot.

"You can pay me later, son."

"Thank you, Nan," said Manuel. Her given name, he knew, was Dominga, but when a Mayan woman got old enough she was simply called *Nan*, a term of respect.

He hurried to fill the new pot.

The girl cried out, "This won't work. How can I clean it?"

"At the lake," said Dominga.

"Yes," Manuel said, "I'll go."

"No!" shrieked the girl, "I. . .I have to. . .this is special *maize*, a gift from my mother's uncle. She expects me to be home soon."

"I'll be right back," he said, and ran off with the pot.

People stopped at the commotion and stared, some explaining to others what had happened, some laughing, some shaking their heads. "They will tell my mother stories. I'm going to be in trouble."

"No," said Dominga, "there won't be any problem."

The girl doubted it, aware of how often she'd been warned of shaming herself, and the entire family, by bad behavior. Number one on that long list was talking to boys in the street. Only girls with loose morals would make such a mistake.

"I remember now," said Dominga. "You are Irma's daughter."

"Yes, Nan. My name is Consuelo."

"How old are you?"

"Twelve."

"Twelve? So soon? No, it's not possible."

Consuelo didn't know what to say, could feel herself about to cry.

"A stupid clumsy boy," said the old woman, "but at least he runs fast. It won't be long."

"No, you don't understand, I--"

"Stop it!" said Dominga, as if her wisdom had been challenged. "Look, I know who your mother is. I will go straight there and tell her what happened."

Consuelo let her tears flow. "Bless you, Nan," she said, kissing the old woman's knuckles.

"No, my dear, don't you fret," said Dominga, her hands lingering in the young girl's grasp, "your mother will understand, and in the end she'll have a good laugh."

Consuelo let go and wiped at her eyes. "You must not know my mother well."

"Maybe not," Dominga said. "She is younger, true, though old enough to remember the ways men used to propose."

Consuelo laughed, tears spilling down her cheeks. "What, by being clumsy and stupid?"

"Oh yes, that too, yes. My grandfather broke my grandmother's water pot. Knocked it off her head on purpose. It was how the boy showed interest. If he guessed wrong and the girl did not want him, he had to pay for the pot. On the other hand, if she did. . .well. . ."

"Don't you worry, Nan. That stupid clumsy boy is going to pay you back. Every last centavo!"

"Oooh," said Dominga, perhaps surprised by Consuelo's certainty. The old woman looked around, as if to make sure no one was listening. Satisfied, she smiled and pinched both the girl's cheeks. "Oh my," she said, "yes, yes, yes." Then, as suddenly as it had come, her joy disappeared. She pulled Consuelo closer and whispered, "But please, dear. . .*for your own sake*. . .not so loud."

Manuel, because he could not pay for the pot, helped Dominga carry water and firewood. Whenever spotting Consuelo in the street he went out of his way to say hello. After awhile she started giggling at his approach, knowing what he really meant. This went on for more than a year before she stopped giggling, before they started meeting in private places.

The Jungle   *1967*

The son and his father sat in a stuffy office, staring at Señor Martínez--not the large burly man Manuel had imagined. In fact, he was rather small, with sunken cheeks, a balding head, and a narrow body that matched his thin black tie. Even so, Manuel felt himself stiffen when the salesman closed the door and stood leaning against it. The window too was closed. Latched. An electric fan whirred overhead, the stale air carved into circles, and Manuel gripped the sides of his chair. Sweat dripped down his back. After many difficult years, what Héctor owed the Avanzado company, including 'interest' and 'late charges', threatened to take their land.

"I tried to get you another chance," the salesman said. "I told the owners how much you have improved that rocky piece of dirt. My mistake. It only made them more anxious to sell it."

Héctor leaned forward, wringing his hands. He'd often told Manuel of his trust for Señor Martínez, who had an Indian wife and could speak Kaqchikel. "This year will be better," his father said, hoping perhaps his hope might buy more time.

"It doesn't matter, my friend. These are orders I have to follow."

"Señor, please, we have no other land. Maybe for this year you could--"

"Were it my decision, yes." Señor Martínez looked sad, like the fat man who sold salt in the market, pretending innocence whenever the price went higher. Manuel and his father shifted in their seats. Their eyes followed the salesman, who walked behind his big wooden desk and settled onto a soft leather chair that swiveled his face toward them. "The company will not agree unless I can prove you'll pay it back. All of it. How can I do that?"

"I don't know," said Héctor. "I am sorry. It is not your fault, Señor Martínez."

"Even a good harvest would not be sufficient. Besides, Héctor, you and your son need the corn too. You can't keep giving most of it to us."

"You are right," said Héctor. "Yes, I understand."

Manuel glanced sideways at his father. The proud man was clearly defeated. He looked broken, his head slumped, face collapsed, as if crushed by an internal avalanche. What shame he must be feeling. What a terrible future he must imagine. Without the land they would probably have to work for his brothers. Like begging tortillas on the street. Like dogs. The salesman said something but Manuel missed it, lost inside his own dark thoughts. He looked between the two men, waiting for one of them to speak. His father had still not lifted his head.

"Héctor," Señor Martínez said, "are you listening?"

"What? Oh, yes sir, yes, I am sorry, I realize you are busy and--"

"I was saying that there is a possibility. A client of mine is building a *chalet* by the lake. Close to your village. He is looking for good workers and will pay a fair wage. I told him about you."

The young man sat quietly while the elders talked it through. In the end, his father had to agree. Manuel understood. Working at the chalet would be a way to have guaranteed money, a way to pay his debt, to save their land--not as bad as working for his brothers, no--but, still, a grim solution.

Back home, Héctor sat him down and said, "I have heard of you and the Consuelo girl."

Manuel felt caught. He saw that his father knew what had happened between them. "Yes, sir, I was meaning to--"

"She is strong, this girl?"

"I think so, yes."

"That is good," said Héctor. "A woman has to be strong."

Not like Manuel's mother, he meant, who'd been sick a lot and not much help. Or Héctor's own mother, Grandma Elena, who died a few months ago and left them on their own. What a terrible thing. If a man had to work like a mule his entire life it was only fair that a woman stay healthy and take care of his needs.

"The two of you will marry," Héctor said. "You will have a boy and make me proud." Then a strange laugh jumped out of him. Or not a laugh, really, more like a release of frustration, like when one of their stones found the head of a raiding squirrel. "I'll bet it's already on the way, am I right?"

Manuel wished he could somehow hide his shame. "That is what she tells me, Papa."

"Yes, well, women know these things. No reason to doubt it. I'll go talk with her father tonight. Our house is now yours, son, and the milpa too."

Mine? thought Manuel, who had just turned sixteen. What, was his father leaving forever? Manuel knew he would someday inherit the house and the milpa, but why now? It didn't make sense. His mind was spinning, same as when his mother used to come into his dreams. Was this her again? He stared at his bare feet. Wiggled his dirty toes. Now, for the first time, he felt the fear of having to be a man. How could he possibly take care of everything by himself? He knew he wasn't ready. Instead of feeling wronged, though, the thought made him sad, and deeply ashamed, because it was all his fault. He'd proven himself unworthy. He'd added to his father's troubles, was yet another burden, and must be cut loose.

"Starting tomorrow," Héctor said, "I will live on the grounds at the new chalet, and work hard, and pay off the debt. You will have your own problems, son, and your own family to take care of. You should not have to haul my worries on your back."

"Yes, sir."

"Go tell the girl," Héctor ordered. "She needs to have a husband before it shows."

That evening, a marriage was arranged between disillusioned fathers. The next morning, Héctor went to his new job. The wedding happened a week later, at the church, to please Consuelo's Catholic parents. For them, Manuel knew, it was more an act of repentance than celebration; an ardent appeal for God to forgive their daughter's moral crime; a gesture that might offer her some slight hope of salvation.

Héctor did not attend. Manuel, of course, had to be there--was swept into the whole ridiculous event--first told by Consuelo's mother that he must "Go confess. Repent. Otherwise," she argued through her tears, "the padre might not perform the ceremony." And so, against his useless protests, he was ushered through the big wooden doors of the church, then through a small door into one side of a tall rectangular booth.

He sat down and looked up. It was dark and dank and tight, like a coffin standing on end. From behind the black mesh screen he could hear a voice mumbling some sort of prayer. Then it said, quite clearly, "Tell me son, what are your sins?"

Manuel had heard from others of this strange ritual. Sins? What sins? Was it his fault for being tempted beyond reason by Consuelo's soft breasts, her lips against his, how she made his *tuzakiin* big and hard until he could not help putting it inside her? He was supposed to take the blame. He refused. It was mostly her doing, a trick women played on

28

men to get a baby, get a husband to support them, hold him captive the rest of his life. Yes, she'd pretended to fight him off at first. Another lie. Or, even if it was true, in the end she could not resist it any more than he. So why was that a sin if neither of them could stop it? Was it a sin when the rain did not water his plants? Or when the river flooded? It happened, that's all. That and nothing else.

Certain of his innocence, he said, "I suppose I did not pray hard enough."

"For what?" said the voice behind the screen.

"For not having a baby," Manuel said, and left the stupidity of that dark place behind him.

Padre Mejia must have decided not to embarrass Consuelo's devout parents any further. He hurried through the vows and wished upon them all of God's infinite mercy.

Though Manuel never once thought of it in such terms, he felt abandoned. First by his mother. Now his father. That was the spark of his kindling rage. It burned inside him, undeterred, and cauterized every lingering childhood root. He was alone. No use thinking beyond the obvious.
Not that he was incapable of self-reflection, he simply did not trust it, would not listen to his frightened mind trying to ease his worry, make things seem different than they were. To him it sounded like excuses. It sounded like his mother's voice, a voice he refused to hear. Instead, he worked harder every day--avoiding his neighbors, their laughter and childish jokes--all the while getting stronger, and tougher. . .stricken with a sickness that for him felt like resolve. He would make no excuses, he would not complain. Life itself seemed an enemy out to get him. He was proud to clench his heart like an angry fist and fight against it. His battles, he convinced himself, were necessary. Justified.

Soon as the baby was born, Consuelo started wanting to go to church. Manuel shook his head and walked away. He knew it was her mother's idea and could not be bothered to listen. The old bible-thumper would have to get used to the fact that her daughter was now his.

His wife tried to talk him into other things too. Then one night he slapped her head. That stopped the senseless chatter, allowing him to concentrate on more important things.

He and his father rarely saw each other. When they did, few words passed between them. Once, though, meeting on the main path through town, Manuel felt the need for talk. It was time he should be treated like a man. Not a *pretend-man* anymore, a real one, who'd been left on his own with a heavy load of responsibility. He deserved credit for seeing things through. He didn't need praise, or any sort of sympathy. What he needed was respect. And maybe some interest in how things were going? Not with his family, that was no one else's business, but what about the milpa? It had been another drought year; the rain, and not much of it, had waited until mid May. Despite the troubles, things had turned out well. Wasn't his father interested in any of that?

He should ask if the tree rats had been bad. Yes, Manuel would say, he'd killed four of the furry-tailed devils, and eaten them, and hung their skins on a stick as a warning to others! Héctor would laugh out loud and slap him on the back. Well then, had he needed to re-seed? Lucky for the late rains, eh? How had the plants done?

Instead, all his father talked about was the chalet. For him there seemed nothing else.

"On my first morning," Héctor said, "the construction manager pointed at a huge pile of stones, another of sand, and told me the house would be made to look like a great castle. We walked past the start of a thick stone wall. Then we dropped down to a little creek on the other side. It was barely flowing, clogged with logs and sticker bushes. That whole mess, the manager said, would be cleaned up. It would one day be the young Señora's jungle. *Jungle*, yes, that's what the manager said, and told me it had to be completed before the castle."

"Before?" said Manuel. "Why?"

"Hah!" Héctor said, "why do you think, son?"

Manuel shook his head, not at the question but at the strangeness of his father. It was not a genuine smile on his face. His eyes were angry, his words too, no matter how he laughed them out. Neither father nor son could understand why things had gone so bad. Héctor, best of the brothers, forced from his land, forced to be a slave for rich ladinos.

Héctor did not wait for an answer, just kept talking. "The manager slapped my back and told me it was because a jungle had been *promised* to the pretty young bride! 'Though a King needs his castle,' the manager said, 'more important is to keep the Queen happy! *Very very happy*. . .you understand?' Then, I guess thinking I didn't, he showed me with his hips, you know, the way it's done. Like I'd never done it myself. Like I'd never seen dogs in the street."

Manuel felt unsettled by his father's constant talk.

"Soon the boats started landing. First with masons and their special tools. Then the mortar and wheelbarrows. Right behind came lots of other *peones*, like me, and the man who would end up our boss. He wore a white shirt and black tie, same as Señor Martínez. Could hardly wait to jump onto the dock and start giving orders. 'Ay, Dios mío!' he said at the site where he was supposed to create a jungle. He was a difficult man, full of odd opinions he never explained. It did not matter if we understood anything, only that we did what he said. 'Imperfect rocks' and 'inappropriate plants' had to be removed. The whole creek had to be 're-sculpted.'

"A week later another man came. What they called a 'Plant

Biologist.' Hah! He bent over a few times to take samples of the dirt. He filled little glass tubes with it and took them away. There, done, a full day's work!" Héctor laughed at that, then kept on talking. "Boatloads of topsoil came every day. I tell you, son, that black dirt was beautiful."

Manuel knew his father was thinking of their milpa, wishing he could have put it there.

"And the biologist himself brought many bags of special 'additives' for the soil."

"What's that?"

"Who knows? Something better than our fertilizer, he told us. Things I didn't understand. 'Specific chemistry' for different plants, whatever that means."

Certain plants, Héctor said, he'd known: pineapple and banana and achiote. Others he'd never seen: Floridian ficcus and tres puntas; spiny palms and Swiss Cheese vines and something with huge wide leaves called monsteras. Some needed more drainage, others less. Some wanted lots of sun, others total shade. And, Héctor admitted, after the rainy season it did look like a jungle. Or, that is, the way his boss said a jungle should look. Héctor said he had no idea, but doubted that normal jungles included a walk-in bird-house (what the carpenter called an 'aviary'), where thirteen parrots now lived. It was one of Héctor's jobs to feed them, and clean up their endless shit so the dueña would not step in it. "Ay," he said, mimicking his boss with frantic trembling hands, "Dios mío!"

Their faked laughter at the fake joke led to an uncomfortable pause. Manuel knew his father would take that as a chance to get away.

"May the gods forgive us all," Héctor said. "Well, I should get back to the chalet."

Silly old man, thought Manuel. He felt certain that Héctor had never wanted to be a father, and was glad to be done with it. The truth was, his son felt the same. What a waste of time.

"I understand," Manuel said, and felt a tinge of sympathy. But he did not give a damn about the gods' forgiveness. No, what Manuel wanted was relief. He wanted some kind of payback for his suffering, and envied his father's aloneness. To be alone, for Manuel, would be a blessing. . .a reward. Whenever he passed the Catholic Church and saw poor Christ hammered to the cross, he imagined it must have been the same for him. Painful, yes, but at least he'd finally rid himself of all the worthless people begging for this or that, always wanting more!

What bothered Manuel most was the sadness he now, this moment, felt--a feeling seldom experienced and never tolerated for long--like the dull throb of pain where a tick has sunk into one's flesh. Manuel hated that his father would leave without a decent goodbye. After all those damn words, he couldn't spare a few more? It was as if the man he'd grown up with--the sole person he'd ever, in his own way, loved--had been replaced by someone from another world. A world Manuel could not fathom. Héctor had not asked a single question about his life. No, this was not his father anymore, just another man, a stranger, who wanted no part of him.

Right then, a drunkard wandered down the path to offer his bottle of *aguardiente*. It was Tat Rigoberto, an old Mayan *curandero*--once an esteemed healer--now a devoted drunk. He did not recognize Héctor or Manuel (was long past the point of recognizing anyone) yet truly wanted to share his holy water. Both father and son were necessary to guide the elder out of the sun. They sat him on a stoop in the shade of a protective wall and waited with undue patience as he showered them with sacred blessings. They bowed to the man's pious benedictions and only walked away when his words slurred beyond identification.

After crossing to the other side of the path, Héctor turned to his son and said, "Last month the dueño chose me to be his *guardián*."

"Congratulations," Manuel said, wondering why his father sloughed it off, as if slighted by the great accomplishment. Yet he must have seen the admiration in his son's eyes. That explained the shy smile. That explained why, out of the blue, Héctor asked about the baby. "The woman named him Jaime," Manuel said. "He cries a lot." But the last thing Manuel wanted to talk about were women and babies, so he steered their conversation around to the milpa: the late rain; the higher cost of fertilizer; the tree rats and gophers and swarms of biting flies.

Hector seemed amazed that, in spite of the problems, his son had managed a thirty-kilo harvest. "Good for you!" he said, patting him on the back. "And in less than four years, son, I'll have paid the entire debt. It will be your land, free and clear. Someday I hope to see it again."

"Yes," said Manuel, "I hope so too."

"The problem is, it's hard to get away from the chalet."

"I'll bet there's plenty to do."

"Oh, you know," Héctor said, *"only whatever the dueños want whenever they want it."* He laughed at his little jibe while his face turned serious. And sad. "They built me a concrete house at the top of the land, by the trail to San Antonio. Half the size of ours, with one window that doesn't open. I'm glad they keep me busy because it's an oven during the day. I just go there to sleep. They made sure it's not in sight of their castle, but close enough for their *pinche* cowbell! The good part is, no one bothers me at night. Sometimes I bring a candle and take walks through the fake jungle."

"Maybe," said Manuel, "there are fake monkeys in those trees."

"Ah, yes, maybe."

"At least you can be thankful it's only a fake tiger behind those monster leaves!"

Héctor laughed. "You think so? Then why did they give me a real gun?"

Manuel laughed too. It was genuine laughter, like nothing they'd ever shared before. Both were relieved, and for a few short moments rid of their shame. Neither of them should be so miserable, thought the son. No, they were not lucky men, that was certain. Still, things could be worse than raising corn on a rocky western slope. . .or living in a fake jungle.

Indio
Santa Catarina, 1971

Four-year-old Jaime loves waking at first light, for a small drop of time not knowing who or where he is. He stares up at the grass-thatched roof, its varied texture rippling like the lake during a Xocomil. A diffused glow illuminates the particles of dust that flutter down to him like tiny white butterflies. Then, hearing his father, the boy closes his eyes and the world returns. He wants to go cuddle with his mother and the babies. No, not yet, he has to wait. Manuel decided he was old enough to sleep by himself. Such orders cannot be questioned, but Jaime knows that mornings, after his father leaves, are different. He's sure his mother is also awake, also waiting.

Manuel rises every day at dawn to go water the onions. With so many people coming to the lake, corn is fast being replaced by crops that can be sold to the new chalets and restaurants. Ladinos and foreigners want lettuce and cabbage, cauliflower and broccoli, carrots and tomatoes. Onions, of course, are always in demand. And easiest to grow.

He's taken over the field from a man whose son was accidently sprayed in the face with insecticide. The boy lost his sense of balance, suffered excruciating headaches, and the man needed money to pay doctors, to buy medicines. There was no choice but to sell his land for a low price and go look for work in the city.

Manuel sometimes needs to nod his head and listen to those who go on and on about *the poor family*. 'Such a terrible thing,' they say. 'Such a tragedy.' Yes, well, of course, all of that is true, but still, for the sake of his own family, he had to take advantage of the opportunity. In three years the land will be his alone. The profits too. Until then, he'll be the one taking a risk. A big one! It's not as if he wanted to go into debt. His father had surprised him by arranging a loan through Señor Castilán, *dueño* of the chalet. At first Manuel resisted, thinking back to the Avanzado days and hating the idea of owing anyone money. But, after weeks of worry, he conceded it was the right thing to do, a thing he had to try. Unlike their rocky milpa, this was a good piece of land. Worth the risk.

Now it's up to him to work hard and pay the money back. He has to keep at it, not let anything get in his way.

The field is a twenty-minute walk up the mountain. Though it measures less than a hundred square meters, the watering takes two hours because he only has one bucket. Oh well, he thinks, at least there's a flowing stream close by. Better than with the milpa, where he must beg the clouds for rain! Thankful for what he has, not expecting miracles, Manuel never complains. Not like his fellow farmers. Tomás, on the next plot over, struggles with tomatoes--easier to sell, and for a greater profit, but much harder to grow--prone to strange diseases, a haven for destructive bugs, and always greedy for more and more water! Every day the simple-minded idiot dreams of pumps and sprinklers, wishing against reason he were a rich *chaletero*.

This morning, as Manuel takes a needed rest, his neighbor comes over, bucket in hand, and sits down next to him. "I was thinking. . ." says Tomás, and Manuel sighs. He knows what is coming. "What if. . .if you and I and a couple of the others--"

"No," Manuel says, like a sharp machete chopping off the man's thought. Usually he would say no more. Words, his father taught, were tools. They exist for a purpose and should not be carelessly thrown around. While Héctor often failed to follow his own advice, his son has no such problem. Still, sometimes words are necessary. He likes Tomás, they've always been friendly, but the man has forgotten himself, who he is, and needs to be reminded. "The pipe and fittings alone," Manuel reminds him, "would cost a whole year's harvest. None of us have that kind of money. Or the time to go buy it and haul it here and install it. And what about the pumps and sprinklers? The gasoline? Come on, Tomás, we are *Naturales*. There is nothing wrong with that, my friend, it is simply true, so what good is your dreaming?"

"It does not have to be a dream," says Tomás. "I know Señor Castilán loaned you the money to get started here."

"Mind your own business."

"Everyone knows, Manuel. We know he is a very generous man. A man willing to help. Your father might talk to him, he might--"

"My father is a worker at the chalet."

"He is the guardián! It was his dueño who got you your land! What we're thinking is--"

"You waste my time," Manuel says.

Tired of the chatter, he walks away, fills another bucket, hauls it to his thirsty plants. To forget the stupidity of Tomás he works faster than usual. Hard work makes the mind stop thinking. If he thinks at all, it is about his breakfast back home. The only thing he ever expects is a stack of tortillas, a cup of hot coffee, and maybe, he hopes, a bit of quiet.

After cuddling, then feeding the children, Consuelo balances the basket of dirty laundry on her head and hurries it to the big flat shelf of stone on the edge of the lake. One piece at a time, she leans over and scrubs hard. She has about an hour to get it all washed and laid out on the rocks to dry before she must get home to start cooking. Along with prompt meals and a tidy house, Manuel insists on clean clothes. That goes for his family too. He has no use for people who walk around looking ragged and beaten. "Without self-respect," he says, "there is nothing."

While his parents are gone, Jaime takes care of one-year-old Felipe and the newborn, Erica. Because they usually remain asleep there is not much to do. He loves to lie between their warm little bodies, his mind going wherever it wants. He follows the light coming through the window and watches everything change: the wood-plank counter becomes the mail-boat cruising toward Santiago; a big wooden spoon hangs from the wall like a slender brown bird diving for the water. If one of the babies begins to wake he rubs its stomach and makes a gentle shushing sound. It has always worked before, so he does not understand why today Erica pushes his hands away and screams, her stomach heaving. Jaime kisses her puffy cheeks, thinking that's what his mother would do. He tries to sing one of his mother's songs but cannot remember the words. A yellowish liquid appears around the edges of Baby Erica's mouth. Jaime wipes it off. Within minutes it is back, thicker. Felipe also begins to cry. So does Jaime. He is afraid of being blamed, that his father will hit him.

Consuelo returns to find Jaime in a panic, rubbing at his sister's face, trying to make the crying eyes and sticky yellow stuff go away. She pushes him aside. Not knowing what else to do, she rubs her saliva into the disgusting gunk that seeps from between those tiny parched lips. Within a few minutes it softens and she wipes it off. She rocks the bawling Erica in her arms, using a bit of old *corte* to remove the returning slime. After awhile it stays gone and the baby does stop crying, but not in a way that seems normal. Too quiet now. Far too still. Consuelo is ready to leave, go look for help, when Manuel arrives.

If his tortillas are not ready, which almost never happens, he scolds her. Might even give a light smak to her her head. This sick child, however, and her obvious worry, seem to distract his hunger. He takes the baby and goes outside. . .holds Erica up to the morning light. Seeing no obvious defects, only a general lethargy that for him must not look serious, he shakes her until the tears again start flowing, then hands her back to Consuelo.

She knows Erica should see a doctor. Knows, too, it must be her husband's decision.

"What will we do?" she says to his blank face.

"About what?"

Consuelo closes her eyes and searches her mind for the right words to say. She knows he does not see this as a problem. At least not like the ones he deals with every day. Problems that she has no idea about, he claims, and could never understand.

"Look," he says, perhaps sympathetic to her motherly concern, "if she does not get better, there is a foreign doctor in Sololá where we don't have to pay. We can take her on Friday."

"Yes," Consuelo says, because everyone knows about the foreign doctor. He comes in his van once a year and is there for a couple of months. It is bad to be sick any other time, leaving just the public hospital--also free, but a frightening place. A place where you go to get sicker. A place you go to die. She is glad he knows this too. Glad he agrees.

"I'm hungry," says Manuel, walking back inside the hut and sitting at the table.

Consuelo follows. She is supposed to go start the fire and heat his water and cook his tortillas. Instead she stands there holding the baby, looking at him.

"What?"

"I was thinking," she says, "maybe I should go tomorrow."

"It can wait until Friday."

Consuelo sees the fury in his eyes. Yes, she knows they have to be frugal. Market is on Friday, when he carries the onions to Panajachel, then pays a man to drive him up the mountain. It is a great cost to pay that fare, and unthinkable for any other reason. Yes, all right, she understands, but what does it matter? Today is Wednesday and her baby should not have to wait two more days! She fears making things worse, but has to try and convince him.

"Please, Manuel, I could take the baby by myself."

He laughs. "What," he says, "with a boy in each hand and a baby on your back you're going to walk for six hours up that--"

"No," she says, "I could get Rosa to watch the boys and--"

That's when he hits her. More like a slap. Hard enough, he must be thinking, that she will never again question his decisions.

Baby Erica dies that next market day while Consuelo waits to see the doctor. She sits on the ground outside the van, rocking the infant in her arms, refusing to believe her child is dead. She trusts that a foreign doctor will know how to fix anything. It is possible, she keeps telling herself. It has to be possible.

She spends less than a minute with him. She is not surprised, aware of all the people he needs to see. Even if Consuelo came to the clinic yesterday, he says, the child would have died.

"Next time," he says, "you should bring your child for regular *free* check ups."

She hears the judgment in his voice, blaming her for Erica's death. He is a young white doctor who speaks through a translator. Does not understand a word of Kaqchikel. He knows nothing of her life or the way things work with Indian families.

Against his ignorance she has no defense. After the doctor leaves, one of his assistants stays in order to explain the procedure and costs of a funeral. Consuelo wraps Erica in her *tzute* and runs.

Manuel, frustrated with a customer, pays no attention to her return. Suddenly there she is, sitting on the ground, off to the side, the baby quiet on her back.

Good, he thinks, because this fool is making him crazy.

"Come on," says the man, frowning at the stated price, "you can go lower than that."

Though Manuel does not speak Spanish, he understands. God, how he hates market days! Dealing with such people! He resents having to sit here on the cold ground, surrounded by women's gossip, while he worries about the work he's been forced to leave undone in the onion field, in the milpa, and at home--wood to chop and carry from the mountain, water to haul from the lake. Being a good husband, he was willing to help out after the difficult birth. For many days after! Consuelo suffered with Jaime too, but not like now, with this constant weakness in her belly. Even the baby on her back seems a burden. How could she possibly manage a full costal of onions? She can't. That is plain. Which means he has to do it, what else can he do? Maybe she is sick, maybe she is, but can it really be so bad? Why always the sour face? He sees plenty of other women selling the entire day with babies on their backs, so why not Consuelo? Look at her sitting there, staring at the ground, off in her own world with no idea what he's going through. How did he end up with such a useless wife? And a sick child too? What more could go wrong?

His customer--a thick ladino with a face full of whiskers--again insists on getting a pound of onions for a few centavos less than the lowest price Manuel will go. . .some kind of game the fat man is playing. . .trying to insult him, treat him like a silly woman.

"No," says Manuel, struggling to find the right Spanish words. "Final."

"Too much," the man says. He shakes his head and walks away. Manuel knows how a ladino thinks: *Indios* are not worthy of respect, but at least they should know not to waste a real man's time.

Hijo de Puta, thinks the Indio, struggling not to say it, knowing to keep the Spanish curse words hidden safely inside his head. But the effort overwhelms him and he cannot sit there selling any longer. Not for another *pinche* second. Manuel stands, fists clenched, wishing he could hit someone. He needs to get away. Anywhere. He has to start walking before his head explodes.

"Woman!" he barks at Consuelo. "I need you to work!"

As he passes, not bothering to look at her, she stands and screams and hits him hard on the chest. He gasps--not pained by the blow, but shocked, as are others, by the spectacle of it. A mangy dog jumps out of the shadows and starts barking. Manuel doesn't care about that. Or her tears. What bothers him, and seems to mute the yapping dog, is the sudden silence he hears all around. Sellers and buyers have stopped what they're doing and stare as the small frail woman keeps crying and hitting her man.

He grabs her wrists and squeezes them tight. "What is wrong with you?"

Instead of shutting up, she wails in front of everyone, "God sees what you have done, Manuel! He knows! And He will make you suffer!"

But most of the suffering will be hers. It begins with the ride back.

43

Everyone is quiet in the pickup, mumbling to each other, somehow aware of the dead baby on her back. From Panajachel, it is a long silent walk over the hills to Santa Catarina. Manuel then leads them up to what used to be the family milpa--now Jose's land--to the small portion of it at the northernmost edge that has served for decades as a graveyard.

Consuelo might have gone to her parents. She might have begged their forgiveness and promised to rejoin the church if they would pay for a proper funeral. But she has no strength for that, her sadness and shame and this tiny lifeless body almost more than she can carry.

They pass the many small wooden markers--one of which, she knows, is Manuel's mother--and finally reach those of his grandparents, the last to die. Next to their graves, Manuel digs a small hole. Deep enough, he says, to keep away the dogs. Consuelo wraps the baby tight within her tzute and lays it down inside. She holds her tears until he covers Erica with a mound of dirt, until he places the new marker, until he goes away, knowing he is not wanted there, thinking he's done everything he can. How did she end up with such a man? What did she do to deserve him? Her mother warned that Consuelo would pay for her sins, that she would suffer greatly. Is this what she meant, that God would kill her baby? Yes, maybe she is to blame for letting Manuel stick his tuzukiin inside her, a trick men have to take women's power away, order them around the rest of their lives. So why hadn't her mother ever told her? Why the daily warnings about sin, but not a single word of how it is done?

Now, cursed to be his wife, there is no way to stop it. Manuel does whatever he wants while God just watches. That is what she's forced to live with. That is God's punishment. Beneath her quiet surrender, though, a tiny voice, perhaps baby Erica, screams for revenge.

A Necessary Thing

Manuel began hitting her harder, and more often. Consuelo should have known better than to shame him in public. Soon pregnant again, she felt a constant fear, growing like her belly. Like the baby it twisted, it kicked, it sapped her strength. At times it made her physically sick. She was terrified that one day he might beat her to death. She considered running away, going home to the safety of her family, but that would be worse than dying. Manuel would insist on keeping the boys--a man's right, he would say--and Consuelo cannot bear the thought of leaving them behind, with him.

No, she decided, trying to calm herself. . .*not leave, no. . .just keep my distance. . .do my work. . .take care of my children and try not to make him mad.*

Also, she had to remember it could be worse. Manuel, though a thick-headed, nasty-tempered mule, did work hard every day. He gave them what they needed to survive. He was not a good man, no, but compared to some of the others, well, at least he didn't drink, or gamble on the cock fights, or humiliate her by chasing other women.

The key was to obey his every word, and let him mount her whenever he wanted. She did not need to enjoy the sex, only pretend not to hate it. But as she got bigger he got more and more irritable. Though she tried every day, it was impossible to avoid his rage.

A few days after the baby was born, before the girl even had a name, Consuelo saw something in that miraculous little face and could not take her eyes away. At first it seemed a normal thing, the eyelids trying to stay open, blinking at the morning light. It reminded her of Jaime, how coming out of sleep he still often blinked like a newborn. Only this was different. The baby's forehead was pinched with effort, as if struggling to see her. . .as if looking for her, trying to tell her something with the only language it knew. Consuelo believed this must be a message from God--a warning that it wasn't just her, that all of them were in danger--a sign for her to do something. She could not wait, could not hope their life might get better.

Knowing it never would, Consuelo took the children and snuck off to her parents' house, where her mother hurried them inside, like secrets to be kept from the neighbors.

"I am sorry," she said to her daughter's plea for help, "you cannot stay."

"There is nowhere else to go, Mother. Please, I--"

"Don't beg me, Consuelo. I don't want to hear it. Whatever the problem is, you should beg for God's mercy. He will understand."

Jaime and Felipe sat in the corner, watching. Consuelo held the baby close, hoping the matriarch might relent, and was forced to hear a long list of admonitions that required from her a great deal of apology, and the confession of many sins, most of which she had not committed. She promised to attend mass each and every Sunday, too, but in spite of it all they were told to go home.

"Home," her mother said, "is where a woman belongs. With her husband."

"I am afraid," cried Consuelo.

"Oh. . .well. . .that," said her mother, stepping back from the tears as if they might be catching. "That is a different thing than duty." She took an old cloth napkin from the table and mopped at her daughter's eyes. I've told you from the beginning, girl, church is the only place to take your fear. If there is any peace to be found in this terrible world, it is there. There your sins are forgiven."

Since forgiveness was what Consuelo felt she needed, church was where she went. Every Sunday morning. She got up early to feed the chickens, the children, and Manuel. He'd sit there eating his tortillas, saying nothing, usually hitting her when she came back. It was clear that he did not want her to go, but his fists could not stop her. She was sure that nothing could stop God's promised salvation. Having heard that, many times, from Padre Mejia, her suffering had begun to ease. She'd learned in church (praying and believing, as the sermons taught) how to accept suffering as a natural thing. A necessary thing. Though Consuelo knew she was not wise enough to understand why, the padre's words assured her that Manuel's continual abuse brought her and the children closer to God--their patient torment like a slow, bumpy, truck-ride to heaven.

After several weeks, something changed. Manuel let her go to church each Sunday without punishment. He would sit pouting on his mat in the corner of the hut, eating by himself, and was usually gone when they got back. *Amazing, the speed of providence! Maybe God would finish the job, would cut off his filthy thing and toss it in the lake.*

Well, no, probably not: a hope as yet beyond the power of her prayers.

First and foremost, she must be thankful for Manuel's miraculous tolerance. Was he afraid of what people might say if he kept them from church? If he cared what others thought, then yes, but since he'd never cared before, why start now? What was going on? Why did he look so lonely on his mat, so pitiful, when she went off with the children?

She hoped it was because of God. Maybe, at last, Manuel could feel the eyes of judgment upon him. Or maybe, more likely, it was fear of the government spies. To have avoided Christianity as a reckless young boy, that was one thing. And not uncommon. But to oppose it as a grown man could be dangerous. It could mean he was a pagan. Or, far worse, what people called a *communista*, which was against the law. Consuelo did not know what it meant, only that *communistas* were being hunted down and killed in the mountains. Anyone suspected of anything bad, it was said, could turn out to be one.

Then it hit her, hard as his angriest fist. What if, to avoid that problem, Manuel started going to church? *Oh no, oh no.* Yes, it's true, there was a time she would have welcomed it, but now it seemed a curse, the thought of him wearing a white shirt, like the devil kneeling by her side, singing the same psalms, praying with his eyes shut tight as if to the same God, every bit of it for show! And a waste of time, too, because Jesus Christ could not be fooled. Consuelo knew He would someday make Manuel pay for his constant meanness, for hitting her and the children. For letting Erica die.

Night after night, for months on end, she prayed for the brute to suffer some terrible death, which somehow only increased her fear. Then, one Sunday morning at mass, her mind began to wander. She imagined a long sharp knife. Its blade gleamed of brilliant holy silver and burned away the shadows, making everything clear. Manuel lay asleep on the floor of their hut. She knelt down next to him and lifted the knife.

At that very instant, Padre Mejia called out from the pulpit: "Aleluya!"

Consuelo looked up and saw him glowing with godliness.

"Aleluya!" he shouted again, his eyes now searching the congregation and quickly finding hers.

"Aleluya!" his parishioners shouted back.

Consuelo had never seen him so animated, and she felt trapped by his rapt attention, caught red-handed with her murderous thoughts. But what surprised her most was the look of deep compassion in his eyes. Perhaps God was inspiring him to save her, give her one more chance. Her brand new baby, after all, was a perfect symbol of salvation, and perhaps made him remember that 'No one can see the Kingdom of God without being reborn.'

"To be rid of the devil," wailed the padre, loud as any evangelical, both his hands reaching for the sky, "you must bring Jesus Christ into your heart! Bring Him in, brothers and sisters, let His glory free your soul! Aleluya!"

"Aleluya!" echoed the flock.

"Aleluya" Consuelo whispered into her cupped palm. But her heart was pounding and would not be ignored. It was all just too much for the poor woman, impossible to escape, and suddenly she knew, as if God were calling from her soul, that this was no time to be shy or ashamed.

"Aleluya!" she cried out.

The padre looked surprised by her lonely outburst. His eyes grew wide and wet. "Yes, my child, give yourself to Christ Almighty."

Tears flowing, Consuelo filled her lungs and screamed it to the heavens: "Aleluya! Aleluya! Aleluya!"

"Mama?" said Felipe, looking scared.

She leaned over, baby Flor in her lap, and hugged the boy close. Jaime was sick that day, off being cared for by a neighbor, and Consuelo missed him, wishing he could have been there too, feeling God so near. Then and there she welcomed Jesus into her heart as her personal savior. She dropped to the ground, dragging the little ones with her, and begged the Lord's forgiveness.

Padre Mejia came down from the pulpit and put his hands upon her head. "Bless you," he said. And through his touch she could feel God warming her heart. He took away her fear, her sorrow, her seething hatred. "A baby," Jesus said with the padre's gentle voice, "is our Father's way of giving hope. You are blessed, my child, with three wonderful children, three tender mercies. Never forget how lucky you are."

Consuelo had never before thought herself lucky, but the next week, as if to prove it, God managed to get Manuel further out of her life. Hector found him a part-time job at the chalet. Between that and the onions and the milpa, he was gone most days from dawn until dusk, and too tired at night to bother with her. *Aleluya indeed. Praise the Lord!* There would also be a guaranteed amount of money each month. Now, in addition to tortillas and eggs, they could have beans, plátanos, papayas . . .and maybe for Christmas this year a chicken!

Consuelo felt so grateful, so blessed, that a few Sundays later, when Padre Mejia reminded the congregation "not to take our blessings for granted," she listened with all her aching spirit. Again it seemed the Lord was speaking to her.

"Redemption," the padre insisted, "does not come without sacrifice."

"Amen," whispered Consuelo, who instantly knew what must be done.

Burning inside, like walking through the fires of hell itself, she closed her eyes, lowered her head, and did what her mind kept screaming was unthinkable. Silently, solemnly, she forgave Manuel. She prayed for him, for his salvation. Because Jesus said she must. She pleaded with Christ to take away her husband's constant worry, imploring Him to open the poor man's simple mind to the many joys of a religious life, to make him aware of the glory, the eternal light, which only God could bring to a darkened heart. She dropped to her knees, crying and praying that Manuel might someday, somehow, be a happy man.

For herself she wanted nothing.

Well, she thought, fingering the crucifix that hung around her neck, *just that Manuel have less anger toward me and the children.*

It seemed a reasonable request: fair and simple and, yes, *necessary*. While the sermons had made her very aware that 'The Lord moves in mysterious ways' (His acts, though often bewildering, nevertheless to be accepted and revered) Consuelo never understood why such a small favor could not be granted.

New Castles   *Santa Catarina, 1974*

Manuel never did go to church. The thought had not once crossed his mind. In addition to tending his onions each morning, collecting water and firewood most afternoons, going to the Sololá market on Friday, the milpa on Saturday, the Pana market on Sunday, he worked at the chalet from Monday through Thursday. He worked hard to impress the dueño, to make his father proud, to assure the payment of his onion-field debt.

The dueño, Señor Castilán, had finished his mansion of finely fit stone, the modernized version of a famous Spanish castle where his ancestors, it was rumored, might once have lived. The castle's grounds were magnificent. In addition to the jungle and aviary, there was a swimming pool, a fancy *temazcal*, and a lawn the size of a *fútbol* field. Close to the water stood a miniature castle, a playhouse for the dueño's children.

A place like that, thought Manuel, twice the size of his home, just for children to play in? How were such things possible?

A huge jacaranda tree stood at the center of an exterior spiral staircase that led to the make-believe castle's second-floor balcony. From there, far to the left, one could see the eastern cliffs of the lake. To the right of the cliffs, beside the village of San Lucas, a few palatial chalets were ensconced along the shoreline, backed by the towering volcanoes of Tolimán and Atitlán. Farther right, on the other side of Santiago bay, was the San Pedro volcano. Rising above the glassy sheen, all three peaks reflected across the lake, making everything else look small.

The dueño's children did not seem to notice. As if to protect their mighty castle, they would put on painted cardboard hats and arm themselves with sticks and run in circles around its balcony, warning everyone within shouting distance of *Pirates!*

"Peerahtays!" they kept screaming. "Watch out for the *peerahtays!*"

The Castilán family came from Guatemala City every Friday, if the weather was good, and returned on Sunday afternoon. All the workers planned their week accordingly. Everything had to be perfect before the fancy private boat came into sight. It was Manuel's job, first thing Monday morning, to clean up the little castle. Fighting pirates was a damn messy business. He collected soda bottles, half-eaten burritos, melted candy, and anything else they left behind. He mopped the children's dirty footprints off the floor and wiped their spit off the windows. His most important duty was to keep this a safe and spotless place for them to play.

Back home, he built his own private hut. It had low caña walls with a thin thatched roof. No windows. Just big enough to hold his sleeping mat, with one short shelf to lay his clothes. He did not need a castle, but he did need this. Except for the times he called Consuelo in, the space was his alone. No one dared disturb him. His wife and children slept on the floor in the larger hut. Manuel only went in during meals, or whenever he decided something had to change.

"With so much to do," he told them, "I need help." He put his hand on Jaime's shoulder and looked him in the eye. "You understand, boy?"

"Yes, Papa."

"Good," Manuel said, and without another word went back to his hut.

After he left, Consuelo told five-year-old Felipe that he'd be watching over Flor, almost two, and the newborn, Adriana. That, at least, gave Jaime--now eight--some needed relief. He'd always felt responsible for Baby Erica's death, and the newest girl reminded him of her. . .the same roundish face and dull brown eyes. He didn't want to be there should it happen again.

Manuel rose at dawn to go water the onions. Jaime jumped up the instant his door banged shut. Not being ready would justify his father's rage. The fear of that had kept the boy awake for most of the night. Relieved it was finally morning, he left his mat and blanket on the ground and rushed outside.

Manuel handed him the old banged-up bucket, then took the new one he bought yesterday, and the hoe, and walked off. After a few minutes he looked back. Jaime ran to catch up.

"What," said his father, "you're tired?"

"No, sir."

"Good. Hungry?"

"No, sir."

"Right. Because we eat and rest after we work."

When they reached the onion field, Manuel handed the new bucket to Jaime. The boy now held one in each hand.

His father stared down at him. "What are you waiting for?"

Jaime nodded and moved toward the stream.

"No," Manuel said, and laughed at the boy's confusion. "Here." He pointed to the ledge above it. "This will be faster. You need to have a full one ready whenever I hand you an empty."

Jaime peeked down at the fast narrow flow. He hoped he'd misunderstood.

"Go ahead," his father said, "try."

So the boy set one bucket on the ground, gripped the other, lay on his belly and stretched down toward the water. But he could barely reach it, and the edge was slippery. He could not manage to scoop a full bucket without Manuel having to grab his legs to stop him from falling in. "Never mind," his father said, pulling him to his feet, "come with me."

Jaime did not hesitate when ordered to stand in the stream. He was already cold, and the lazy sun would take another hour to rise over the cliffs, and none of that mattered, nothing to do but do what he was told. He stood waist-high in the icy flow and kept quiet. What he desperately did not want was a whack on the head, the constant threat of it intended to keep him, as his father would say, *always ready*. Ready for what, Jaime was never sure. Always, like now, having to guess, he filled the first bucket. Manuel watched him closely. Handing it off, Jaime did not dare show anger for fear he would be punished. Once his father left, for further protection, he let his mind go numb, and on the break between buckets cinched his eyes tight, struggling to block the shivers.

When they got home that morning he was allowed to eat all the tortillas he wanted. And drink hot coffee, too, with half a spoon of sugar. Only he and Manuel got any of that. He'd hated that bone-chilling water, but liked this part of being a man.

After breakfast, Jaime went with Manuel to the chalet. Was told to rake leaves. Better, his father said, than wasting time at home. "It doesn't help, boy, the way your mother babies you. You must learn how to work."

Right before noon, Consuelo delivered their basket of tortillas, still warm after a twenty-minute walk from the village. She made sure to get there early, Jaime knew, to avoid any chance of being late. Then she ran off again. While eating, the boy stayed silent in case his father and grandfather wanted to talk. After lunch, he filled a costal with the leaves and trimmings he'd raked. As ordered, he dragged it to a large hole at the far edge of the property and emptied the sack. That done, he pulled weeds, and daydreamed, until Manuel was ready to go.

Months later, with the first mild rains, his father surprised him. Instead of dumping the twigs and branches into the hole, he was told to sort the sizes into different piles. Then Manuel showed how to stack them for a proper fire. He handed Jaime a match. "Go ahead," he said, "light it."

Jaime used only one.

"Good," Manuel said, looking proud. "But you need to be careful, son. Don't put on too much. And watch it close. Fire can be a dangerous thing."

Jaime now looked forward to his days at the chalet, off by himself doing a job that mattered. Once he got the hang of it--lighting the fire before it rained, and feeding it, fanning it, watching it burn--he stopped worrying he'd get yelled at and enjoyed his time even more. It was his first real sense of pride. *Yes*, the boy thought to himself, *I am also needed to keep the chalet beautiful.*

It is on one such afternoon that Jaime wanders over to the playhouse castle. He knows he's not supposed to be there, but can't stop wondering about it and is willing to take the chance. Not much of a chance, really, since his father is nowhere in sight, busy planting shrubs on the jungle side of the mansion. It seems a perfect time to take a look.

A quick look, that's all he wants.

Because the door is locked, he peeks through one large window where a curtain has not been closed. The walls are painted a deep sky blue. There are big white clouds floating on it, and a bird with a long green tail that he knows is called a Quetzal, like the money. In the middle of the room is a thick dark wooden table with high-backed wooden chairs. On the table are white plates, silver spoons and forks and knives, and tall glasses.

It reminds him of the old wrinkled magazine he once found by the lake. It had a picture like this, of rich people sitting around the same kind of table. There were other pictures too, of shiny new cars, of men smoking cigarettes, and toward the back a beautiful white woman, almost naked, with long blond hair and bright red lips, and blue eyes looking straight at him. He tore that page out and hid it under a bush behind a large rock. He planned to look at it again the next time he went with his mother, certain he could get a peek while she was washing clothes.

But when the chance came, the picture was gone, and now he's forgotten the strange way that woman made him feel, or why he even cared. He remembers only the rich people smiling and sitting at a table like this, sipping from the same sorts of glasses, their plates full of colorful food. He's sure it means a celebration is going to happen. Soon they will be arriving, handsome men in their shiny dark suits, beautiful women happy to show their chest and legs. It's going to be a party, yes, but why? For him maybe? Really? Yes, yes, why not for him? *For Jaime: the great assistant Guardián!*

Of course he knows he's making this part up, so why not make it good. . .with lots of grilled chicken, and Coca Cola, and buckets of ice cream. There will be musicians in special party clothes playing songs he's never heard. And a piñata. Maybe even a dancing pig!

He climbs the staircase to the upper balcony. Looks out over the water. Though the wind feels light, he sees it pushing hard along the wide sparkling surface, lines of thin dark ripples like the cuts of a sharp machete. He can almost see a huge blade slicing away the calm. The Xocomil, for Jaime, has always been a mystery, its secret code whispered across the water from San Lucas Tolimán--*a warning from God to be a good person*, says his mother, *to be kind to others, tell the truth, and do what is right*. Because it is visible on the lake before it can be felt on shore, he used to think the water brought the wind. And maybe it does, no matter what anyone says.

Maybe that's what Señor Castilán's children were trying to tell him. He remembers watching them one day. They were running around the balcony, screaming Spanish words he did not understand, wearing strange hats and waving sticks, fighting something he could not see.

"They pretend the castle is a boat," his father said.

"Why?"

"To look for *peerahtays*."

"*Peerahtays*?" Could that be another name for waves? "What does it mean, Papa?"

Manuel said, "Who knows?" and walked away.

Thinking of that now, Jaime wishes he could say it back to him. Yes, he would say, *who knows?* Maybe he, Jaime Xuluc, will live in a castle some day. Maybe he'll have lots of fancy parties. Maybe he will have a boat of his own. And fight *peerahtays* too! *Who knows?*

Jaime has no idea how this might happen. Or, for that matter, how anything happens, although sometimes he does seem to know things in advance. Like when he goes to work in the onion field, or drags his sack of leaves to be burned. Everything feels old and already done, like he's living in the past, playing out a story that's been told, and told, over and over again. Other times, like now, he is sure this is new, brand new, and anything might happen, anything at all. Life is whatever comes next. That's how he wants to live--never certain, always wondering--but doesn't know how to do it.

He lets his eyes go blurry and takes in everything at once--the lake, the volcanoes, the sky--the whole world, all of it, glistening in the mid-day sun as if lit by heaven for him alone. *The Good Lord*, his mother says, *speaks to us through visions. That is how we learn to see what matters.* And Jaime believes her. His eyes focus downward to the water. He sees how quickly the waves have come, a fisherman not far away paddling his *cayuco* hard for shore. Before he can make sense of that, a gust of wind slaps his face like an angry hand, *like a warning from God.*

Panicked, Jaime charges down the circular stairway, across the grass, back to the fire. To his amazement, it is still burning. What? Has it really just been a few minutes? Has time passed at all? Has he scared himself over nothing?

In spite of the heavy Xocomil, he throws on another branch. He stirs the glowing coals and tries not to think of rich white people smiling and raising their glasses to him. The wind messes his hair, scrambles his thoughts, and a blurry image of the blonde woman--soft skin and red lips and deep blue eyes--skitter through his mind. Suddenly, surprising himself, he starts to laugh. He feels lucky, certain he's gotten away with something. And learned something too. For who knows how long, he was somewhere else, another person, a happy person, in a whole different life.

The very thought, because of how wonderful it is, makes him nervous. He twists around and looks for Manuel. He knows this kind of thinking can get him into trouble.

No, he can't talk about this day, not to his brother, or his mother either, not to anyone. He has to hold it inside. Keep it secret. Still, he thinks, smiling, no one can ever take it away. It is his forever. He can remember it whenever he wants, and knowing that is good enough.

Hours later, soon as they leave the chalet property and are out on the path, Manuel grabs Jaime by the collar and lifts him high off the ground, his bare feet dangling. He slaps the boy's face, then pulls him closer. Noses nearly touching he yells, "Don't you ever go there! You hear me!" Manuel's eyes are wet with fury. "Never again, you understand!"

Floating Fish   *Santa Catarina, 3:20 a.m., March 3rd, 1976*

Jaime woke to a world of dogs. But first, in his dream, they are a flock of sleek white birds. Lying in his *cayuco*, afloat without aim on the wide glassy lake, he watches them flapping overhead, wing to wing, shouting down their proud hellos, fading into a warm pink sunrise. They look like egrets, only egrets do not sound like this. And would not fly away. Egrets have no better place to be. So where are these strange birds going? Mexico? El Norte? Or, who knows, maybe Heaven? That's what his mother would say.

The birds agree with her and squawk at the boy's surprise.

Sure, he thinks, why not Heaven? Jaime knows better than to doubt a flock of sleek white birds.

Then, without a trace, they were gone, his dream torn apart by the inescapable truth of howling dogs. He bolted upright. Shocked, trembling, he stood there listening, telling himself not to be afraid--it was just dogs. But why so many? Why so crazy? He remembered the other time they'd sounded this way. . .that year it stopped raining. . .that year the milpas shriveled down to nothing. . .that long dry year when everyone went hungry, especially the dogs, who even in the best of times had to fight for scraps. Most had been hunted down and slaughtered for the bony meat they gave. The wild ones, though, were harder to catch. They'd hidden themselves away on the mountain, and at night came back to run in warring packs, scour the *callejones*, attack anything left unguarded. His mother could not sleep until she'd used the heavy wooden maize bin to block the door of their hut. For months, Jaime's dreams had been haunted by hellish mongrels chasing him, razor-sharp claws holding him down, wicked yellow teeth ripping him to shreds.

Though the boy had never heard a siren, the wailing dogs produced the same effect. He ran to his mother's mat. His brother and sisters were already there. Consuelo pulled him close as the earth started rumbling, shaking, shifting back and forth, tossing them from side to side. They slid along the ground, a single lumpy shivering mass, like grains of rice stuck together, spilling from a slick flat plate. The caña walls rattled. There were loud crashing sounds outside, like monsters Jaime could not see, fighting to the death. All around were echoing screams, more frightening than the dogs.

At last the earth stopped rocking. Jaime had never felt anything like it. It was not like the little shakes that came once or twice a year. . .this was something completely different. He and his siblings clung to their mother, the five of them wound in a tight tangled ball, terrified, coughing in the dusty air. Jaime would have chosen to stay that way, face against his mother's breast, but the stillness could not be trusted either and his mother must have known it.

She righted herself and got to her knees. "Please, dear Lord . . .please take us with you."

Manuel rushed into the hut. "Come on, woman! Hurry!" He grabbed the two small girls, one under each arm, and took them away.

Consuelo steered her boys outside, where it was lighter. They watched from their rocky stoop as the nearly full moon showed a stream of people charging down the narrow callejón: tripping, falling, getting up. Jaime saw his many neighbors, but everyone looked different. People who day after day lived side by side, laughing together about all the endless problems, now acting like complete strangers, pushing to get past each other, get away, as if something terrible were chasing them. Auntie Rosa ran by shouting, "Hurry up, Consuelo, the world is ending!"

This must be what his mother had told him about, the day the blessed would be lifted to heaven. People were in such a rush, Jaime realized, because not everyone would be taken. There were lots of barking dogs too, though no one seemed to care. What did a crazy dog matter when the whole world was ending and eternal salvation coming to replace it? His mother carried Felipe from the stoop and the three of them struggled along with the rest. Stingy old Señora Cocalojáy was dragging a huge pig by a rope, apparently worried there might be a lack of food in heaven. Jaime doubted she would be among the chosen. Pushing past her was that big fleshy sow of a man, Carlos Mendoza (son of a Mexican, some people said; *son of a bitch* said others), the man in charge of cock fights, known to pester, and sometimes beat, anyone who did not pay a debt on time. Yelling his ugly Spanish curses he knocked people aside, sure to be one of the first in line. But it didn't matter because he wouldn't get chosen either. Only the poor and weak.

Reaching the main path, everyone turned toward the Catholic Church. If there were any important announcements to be made (*like*, for instance, *who was going to heaven!*) they would certainly come from the priest, Padre Mejia. Jaime stuck close to his mother's side. He assumed, because of her strong Catholic faith and devotion to Jesus, she would be welcomed with open arms.

His father was nowhere to be seen. Probably went the wrong direction on purpose. Jaime felt sorry for his little sisters, who would have to go to hell with him.

The crowd packed into the small square in front of the church. Everybody knew each other, and knew where they were, but they all looked alone and lost. Women wailed--some to the Mayan God, *Ma'am*, but most to Jesus--begging forgiveness for whatever they might have done to cause the world's end. No, it had not ended yet, *but the time*, as Jaime's mother would say, *was near*. On the other side of the main path were two collapsed buildings. Another looked about to fall. The church bell, someone said, had tolled by itself, then slipped off its mount and gone crashing through the roof.

Consuelo managed to maneuver them within sight of the large arched entryway. Padre Mejia, fully robed, stood on the top step, arms outstretched and fingers extended as if straining for something beyond his reach. Illuminated by the brilliant moon, he looked prophetic.

"Padre, please, what does it mean?" sobbed Señora Cototemoq.

"Tell us, Padre," cried Señora Xoj, "is the world really ending?"

The men were more direct: "Is God inside, Padre?" and "Is He waiting for us?" and "When are we going to heaven?"

The padre calmly shook his head, a half-smile on his bearded face. His stiffened fingers bobbed gently up and down. Jaime figured it was his way of trying to quiet the crowd. It didn't work. Hearing that he'd appeared, people squeezed past each other to see what he had to say. They would not stop until they found God's appointed servant, the only man who mattered now. Those in front fought to hold their ground. Consuelo clutched the boys' shoulders and drew them near.

Padre Mejia retreated to the shallow landing, his back against the heavy wooden doors. But the crowd kept moving, pushing, pulsing toward him. He looked scared. Helpless. Finally, perhaps seeing he could be crushed by those determined to get inside (for what good was a man of the church, the people must be thinking, no matter how pious, if blocking the sight God Himself?), he sacrificed his calm and screamed at them, "Stop it! Stop and listen! Stop!"

That worked, for the moment, to stall the panicked advance. Jaime could sense the padre's relief, and prayed for him to do something fast.

The holy man stepped forward, a stare of urgency in his eyes. "God speaks through me!" he shouted. Much of the crowd, though, as he could plainly see, did not hear. While its surge was temporarily halted, the noise had increased, a barrage of fear flying at him like rocks from a slingshot. Most cried out that they had done nothing *truly bad* and called for The Good Lord's promised forgiveness. Others, who sounded desperate, even hateful, threatened the padre's life were he not to get out of the way and let them talk directly to Jesus. Jaime wondered if they blamed the padre for bringing this horror upon them with his constant preaching against 'sin and abomination.'

Once again the holy man held out his arms and bobbed his stiff fingers.

"Let him speak!" someone hollered at the top of his lungs, and the square went silent.

Padre Mejia showed an unconvincing smile. "God has given us a stern warning," he said, "but promises all will be well."

The crowd gave a collective sigh. For the majority of them, as he probably expected, this vague assurance was perfectly acceptable, and for a few short seconds the anger subsided, replaced by mumbled renewals of faith, hopeful whispers, and grateful tears.

"Please tell us why?" Senora Sajvín said between sobs. "Why did this happen to us?"

"As I've told you before," said the padre, "God works in mysterious ways."

"Yes!" a voice boomed out. "I suppose that explains why our Lord Almighty, creator of the entire universe, would destroy His very own church with His very own bell!"

Jaime turned to see the shadowy face of Renaldo Bej. The man's puffy cheeks looked close to bursting, his eyes hidden in darkened sockets. Renaldo was an *evangélical*, himself a budding pastor at his *Church of the Complete Word*, who occasionally, for no apparent reason, might be transformed by a flesh-trembling trance. This did not seem to be one of those, but who could be sure? People said it might happen anywhere, anytime, his body shaking out of control, the words of God spurting, sometimes drooling, from his mouth. Jaime had seen it once, though it had not resembled any kind of preaching to him. More like someone having a convulsion. His mother told him that's what they call it. She was referring to Pedro, the basket maker, who suffered from a disease called epilepsy, his fits so violent that he had to be held down and his jaws kept closed to stop him from biting off his tongue.

"Perhaps God is trying to tell you something!" Renaldo Bej bellowed at the padre. "Perhaps He does not approve of your tall pointy steeple and your big brass bell!"

Padre Mejia looked perplexed as to how he should confront the obvious heresy. The venom in Renaldo Bej's voice had stricken the entire crowd. People stood hushed in a suspended awe, wondering who of these religious giants would prevail.

"The bell has not fallen," said Padre Mejia. "That is an outright lie."

"Is it?" said Renaldo Bej.

"To lie that way is a mortal sin," said the padre.

"You cannot frighten me with threats," said Bej. "Let us inside, padre, let us see for ourselves."

"You *should* come inside sometime, Renaldo. It would do you good."

"I'm ready now, *your eminence*. Aren't we ready?" he shouted at the crowd. "Let's go!"

"No!" screamed the padre. "For God's sake, have some respect!"

"It's because the doors are jammed shut," yelled Jorge Sajvín, another evangélical. "I tried them. He can't get into his own church."

"Well?" Renaldo Bej said to the padre. "What do you say to that?"

Bej had fast become the center of attention. Were it only he and his handful of followers, who knows what might have happened next? The vast majority of the crowd, however, was Catholic, and close to exploding. Jaime knew there was a history of problems with Renaldo Bej. Most people, and especially Catholics, considered him a troublemaker. The boy could feel their collective rage, could feel the excessive strain on their vowed Christian tolerance. A few whispered that the blasphemous dog should be beaten. Someone yelled he should be doused with gasoline and lit on fire! Fortunately for Bej, cooler heads prevailed, choosing reason over violence. That the doors of the church were jammed meant nothing, they said. The same had happened with many doors. And plenty of others agreed, said they'd had to break theirs down or climb out the windows.

Renaldo Bej laughed. "Our Evangélical Church," he said, "was not the least bit damaged."

"What," said a man behind him, "is that supposed to mean?"

"That the Good Lord knows!" shouted Bej. "And makes sure to protect the righteous!"

Someone grabbed hold of his shirt and a shoving match began. It would have come to blows had not the village teacher, a large man called *Profe* Garcia, come to break it up. Though a Catholic, Garcia said his personal choice of religion was not what mattered.

"No," said Renaldo Bej, dusting himself off, "nothing matters except God's eternal truth."

"It was an earthquake," said Profe Garcia. "God had nothing to do with it."

That stunned everyone, and several people objected, including his fellow Catholics. Of course it was a quake, they said. Everyone knew that. But a quake like this could only have come from God Himself, so what did He want of them?

Renaldo Bej--as usual outnumbered and outflanked--must have seen his opportunity to escape before anyone could strangle him. While the crowd surrounded Profe Garcia, the frazzled preacher slipped off into the darkness. Padre Mejia had also disappeared.

"It is a question of nature," said Profe Garcia, "not religion."

Though people did not seem to like that any better, they looked more curious than hostile. Profe Garcia was tall and wide, with enormous physical strength, and, most agreed, indisputable intelligence. Born of a Kaqchikel mother, he was raised as a ladino in the city. Now a certified teacher, he'd returned to the village and married a Kaqchikel woman. While everyone, in truth, thought him a bit strange, his opinions were generally trusted. Or at least tolerated. "We owe the man that," Consuelo told Jaime one day, "because he always treats us *Naturales* with respect."

Indeed, he was known to be an affable man, a generous man. Though school was free, the books and materials cost more than many poor families could afford, and Profe Garcia usually helped out. He had offered to pay for Jaime's supplies, which was why Manuel disliked him. The proud father could not allow it. "My children," he'd told the teacher, "are busy with more important things."

But Jaime knew the real reason. Padre Mejia often spoke of it, and the word he used was *"Envídia."* *Envy.* What it meant, he said, was hating another person for having something you didn't. That made sense to Jaime. He'd noticed how Profe Garcia's wealth of knowledge made his father's eyes narrow, his jaw tighten, his nostrils flare.

Profe Garcia was explaining, as best he could, what caused an earthquake. The moonlit side of his big jowly face rippled with the effort. Though he spoke in Kaqchikel, the words only made Jaime more confused. Something about *earthly cycles*. . .something about *shifting plates*.

"You're wrong!" a young woman shouted at the teacher. "We are doomed!"

"What do you know?" Jaime heard from his left. He turned and saw the ghostly figure of Tat Sando, by far the smelliest person in town. Also the oldest. For that reason alone, according to tradition, in spite of his stink and strange ideas, he must be honored, even by those who went out of their way to avoid him. Though his face was hidden in shadow, the old man's voice was loud and clear. "These things happen," he said to the young woman. "If not this then something else. It won't be the first time. Or the last."

"Tat Sando is right," said Profe Garcia. "I beg you not to make things any worse than they are. An earthquake is. . .well. . .it's like a storm under the ground. Some are much bigger than others, that's all. Really, there is no reason to panic. This is not the end of the world."

"We thank you," said Doña Toribia, wife of Don Miguel, the cayuco maker, "for knowing more than God." She was another of the few who disliked Profe Garcia. But unlike Manuel, who chose to ignore him, she regularly complained of 'the supposed teacher' to anyone who listened. Or even those who didn't. She was the kind of woman whose opinion, like it or not, was impossible not to know.

"There are complicated reasons for an earthquake," said Profe Garcia. "Unfortunately, I am not a trained geologist."

"A what?" said Doña Toribia.

"A geologist is a type of scientist, someone who could better explain it."

Doña Toribia chuckled. "Oh, make excuses you mean. Big fancy words. Schoolbook lies."

"We should only listen to the word of God!" shrieked Basilia, standing at Doña Toribia's side.

There was a look of agreement between the two women, which struck Jaime as odd since everyone knew they hated each other. But maybe, at the end of the world, it was meant to be that life-long enemies become friends. Their main problem, his mother had told him, was that both were great talkers, and excellent at finding fault with others, but neither liked to listen much, or ever be criticized.

"It is clear," Basilia proclaimed, "that The Lord has given us our final warning! Let sinners repent and bow to the grace of glory or reap His everlasting vengeance!" Eyes rolling back in her head, Basilia collapsed to the ground and began to howl. Many others joined her.

Worse, far worse than dogs, thought Jaime, who covered his ears and prayed that God would hurry up and take them first, even if it meant there might not be room for him.

By daylight, two hours after the quake, God had not yet arrived. There were lots of people sleeping on the cold cobblestoned square in front of the church, still waiting. It was evident to anyone who looked that the bell had not budged from its place atop the steeple. But no one noticed, or seemed to care, everyone focused on one simple truth: *Gracias a Dios, the world had not ended!* And, until it did, they told each other, a reasonable person must go on living. There were mouths to feed and fields to tend and damaged houses to fix. *Who knows, maybe the teacher was right about the earthquake. Maybe, like Tat Sando said, what happened was just one more tragedy to survive.*

Manuel, though rejecting their faulty logic, did agree it was time to go home. He led his family back to the hut, where they found an overturned woodpile, some splits in the caña walls, and a few broken bowls. That was the extent of it. Consuelo dropped to her knees, crossed herself and thanked The Lord.

Manuel shook his head and left. In spite of the need to work (because there was always something to be done) he walked past his waiting tools and wandered up the mountain toward his milpa. Like others, like the earth itself, he too was shaken, his mind jolted loose by the quake. While he knew it could not be true, nothing seemed to matter anymore. Nothing. The thought made his head throb, his legs feel like straw. He stumbled over a branch and realized he'd taken the wrong path, had no idea where he was. Drops of sweat, or perhaps tears, stung his eyes. He angrily wiped them away. *What is going on? How can I be lost on a mountain I've known my entire life!*

Suddenly dizzy, he flopped to the ground. . .a few moments later was snoring. His dream, which he would not remember, took him down a long narrow tunnel into the dark brooding earth, past massive roots of unseen trees, to a shallow hole, soft and cool and quiet, where no one could ever find him.

Consuelo brought her children to the lake. "That's where God will be," she said. Others, Jaime saw, had come too, as she said they would. He imagined them spread everywhere along the shore--Kaqchikel and Tzutuhil; ladino and foreigner alike--everyone looking for His sign. Soon the doomsday pastors would arrive to dunk their flock of followers and moan their urgent prayers, but for now everyone was still and silent, staring at the water. The boy could hardly believe it. No one had wisdom enough to explain what they saw: thousands of silver fish floating dead on the surface. They looked to Jaime like little shiny boats sleeping on their sides, as if waiting for God to bring them wings and the Xocomil to carry them away.

Then the ground began rumbling again. The lake rippled and the silver fish shivered and the people ran screaming from the water's edge.

For many days afterward--about every three hours, every time like new--the earth shook and more houses collapsed. No one went inside except when necessary. No one slept much either, just minutes here and there between the waiting, everybody certain the hell would return. When it did, they hurried to some open spot. But the fear never ended. There was no escape. Numerous *aldeas* in the mountains had been destroyed completely. Every day came news of somewhere else. The hillsides above Santa Catarina were strewn with fallen trees, and a person had to stay on guard in case another boulder came crashing down the mountain, or the ground cracked open beneath one's feet. It might happen without any warning. Whole cows, it was said, had been swallowed alive. Many people were missing too. One fisherman, who swore he'd never fish again, saw his cayuco spin in circles, then disappear down a twisting funnel of water.

When the big shakes came, Jaime and his family ran for Jose's milpa. His father's hated uncles, and their wives and children, went as well. Of the many things he was forced to understand, this, for Jaime, was the hardest. Though they lived within sight of each other, these were people he barely knew. But here they were with him. Side by side. Close. It was as if everything had changed, as if they truly cared for one another--the whole extended family, in its many different parts, huddled as one, breathing the same air, sharing the same fear--all of them together, like they never were in real life.

Bare Feet

The aftershocks continued to rattle everyone's life. "Never mind," Manuel said, and went back to work, taking Jaime with him. That was fine with the boy, who felt safer away from the village. They watered the onions every morning, and worked at the chalet as usual, but it wasn't the same. Señor Castilán had stopped coming on weekends because the road between Sololá and Pana was closed. That also meant no pickup trucks going to Sololá on market day, which was bad for the farmers. Most of them chose to leave their fields and take whatever time it took to clear the debris.

At first Manuel refused, said he was too busy with other things. Then, weeks later, he changed his mind. "You'll have to do the onions by yourself," he told Jaime.

The boy, now ten years old and happy to be on his own, was sure not to show it. "Yes, Papa."

It was good having his father gone, but there was a cost. Every night, returning at dusk, Manuel complained, in a bragging way, about how hard the job was, how dangerous, how he strained, along with hundreds of other men, to push aside the massive boulders and remove the fallen trees. This went on for more than a month. Manuel kept talking about all the progress they'd made. Still, the clearing was so narrow that few cars dared to climb the mountain.

Then the rainy season came with a force and the roadwork had to end. It started again six months later, but the bigger boulders could not be budged until the army came with their big machines. Eventually the road was passable for larger trucks, and to everyone's surprise the army kept on going, extending the road from Pana, along the cliffs, to Santa Catarina and San Antonio.

That's when Guicho bought a pickup truck, which promised to make trips to the Sololá market much easier than before.

"No more walking to Pana!" Manuel said at dinner one night. "Guicho will leave at dawn tomorrow morning from the church."

Though told he would be needed, Jaime was not ready when shaken in the darkness. The horrible quake forever imprinted on his mind, he thought it had returned. He gasped and looked for his mother.

"Market day!" his father shouted, "we have to hurry!"

They raced down the steep, narrow, twisting alleys with their bulky costales, out onto the street and up toward the church just as Guicho began to pull away. Seeing them, the driver stopped. The other farmers laughed and shook their heads, their version of grumbling, upset by the delay. Like Manuel, they were in a hurry to get to the market before the good spots were taken.

Sololá, at more than 600 meters above the lake, was often foggy and damp--even in the dry season--a miserable, bone-chilling place unless the sun broke through. Manuel had an old *chumpa* to wear, Jaime just his two cotton shirts. It was a cold the boy had never experienced. He winced at the throbbing numbness of his stiff bare feet against the rough cobblestoned road. Worse, hours later, as his flesh began to thaw, the cuts--full of blood and grime--bit into him like angry little teeth.

By 6 A.M. the bargaining began, and there were lots of people selling onions. Piles of onions everywhere. Manuel gripped Jaime by the shoulder. "Listen," he said.

"Yes, Papa?"

"It is your job to point at our pile, get the buyers to stop here. If it's a *Naturale* you say, Our prices are the best, friend. Come have a look."

"All right."

"But to a ladino you say, *Buen precio!*"

Though he'd heard these Spanish words before, and understood their meaning, it was the first time Jaime would ever use them. "Buen precio," he said.

"Look like you mean it, boy. And smile," his father said, an angry grimace on his face. "You must look friendlier than the rest."

"Yes, sir."

"Oh, and you have to say *Fresca hoy!*"

"When?"

"After."

After what? thought Jaime. "Please, Papa, maybe I don't understand well enough."

"You say it after the rest," Manuel said. "*Fresca hoy!* That means it's fresh today. That's something they want to know. Go on, say it."

"Fresca hoy!" said Jaime, wondering how it could be true since the onions were picked days ago? *Never mind. Do what you're told.*

"Say it all together."

"Buen Precio Fresca Hoy!"

"No," said Manuel. "Not so fast. Watch me. . .very friendly. . .and look them in the eyes when you say it: Buen Precio!. . . Fresca hoy! Buen Precio!. . .Fresca hoy! You see? See the way it goes?"

"Yes, sir."

"Don't forget your smiling," Manuel said.

"All right."

"And stop that silly shivering!"

Jaime nodded, tried to shake away the chill, which made him shiver more.

But his father wasn't looking. He'd stood to get a better view down the row of vendors. "Get ready," he whispered, "here comes one."

Jaime craned his head to see. It was an old Indian woman coming their way.

"Go ahead, boy, say it," Manuel said, slapping him on the shoulder, but it was already too late. She'd stopped and was chatting with a vendor several spots in front of them. It seemed they might be friends. Anyway, she was buying that woman's onions, not theirs, and Manuel gave a low growl. "See what happens if you don't speak up?"

Jaime could tell his father wanted to smack him--was only holding back because it might be bad for business.

"They have to see us before they see the others," Manuel said. "You understand?"

"I understand," said Jaime.

From then on, he called out louder than anyone. It did not seem to make a difference. People might buy their onions, yes, or they might buy someone else's. It was a thing of chance, that's all. And he could tell from the looks he got, no matter how loud he said it, that no one believed their prices were actually best. Some even said so. Said they charged the same. Or more. Manuel shook his head and laughed and told Jaime it was a trick to make him drop his price.

For the next two years, Jaime went to most Friday markets with Manuel. The boy hadn't grown much in all that time, but he did feel older, smarter, and after awhile the job got easy. The smiling, that is, and the proper words. Not the cold. He never got used to that. Or the hunger. Hours dragged on, the endless haggling--a pound here . . .half a pound there--and some days they sold nothing, which meant nothing to eat but the cold tortillas they'd brought from home.

On lucky days, though, like today, every last onion went, sold to a restaurant owner from the city! Manuel laughed and slapped Jaime on the back. They shared a piece of grilled chicken and a cup of coffee. Then big juicy mangos, one for each! Most of the money, of course (what his father earned that day and what he'd already saved) went to buy fertilizer. That was a must because fertilizer was what made the maize grow tall. It was late April, nearly time to plant, and Manuel looked proud walking into the feed store.

He bought a full *quintal* and loaded the heavy bag into the back of Guicho's truck. While the other farmers admired it, patting its back like an old friend, Jaime felt a familiar anxiety. The truck pulled away, the steep curvy downhill road unable to distract him. Like every other year, Manuel would now go work on the milpa. He would take several days to haul supplies and tools up the mountain: fertilizer, seed, and soil amendments; hoe and rake, traps and poison, drinking water. Jaime hated planting time. His father always came home exhausted, always in a bad mood, always looking for trouble.

Not wanting to think about it, the boy stood up and gazed out over the truck's top railing, the wind against his face as the truck sped down the mountain. Soon the lake came into view beneath the setting sun. A chance to let his mind fly. It was the one good thing about going to Sololá, that on the ride back home he could pretend himself a bird, a sleek white egret soaring over the water, watching the tiny villages below, their fields full of people no bigger, or more important, than mice.

Jaime felt a great weight against him. He looked up, saw it was his father. Manuel had also decided to stand, and now his face, with closed eyes and a slack jaw, hung precariously above. His lips were moving, as if trying to tell himself secrets. Jaime shuddered, imagining Manuel's chin dropping lower, closer, settling on top of his head. It reminded the boy of those old wooden masks he'd once seen during a Mayan ceremony.

77

There was a leopard roaring on the head of a priest, and an eagle flying from the skull of a dog.

His father started snoring. The other men pointed and laughed. Jaime could not let that go on, so gathered his strength and pushed Manuel upright. His eyes shot open, looked down at his son, and then he said, as if he'd given it a great deal of thought, "Something has to change."

At supper that night he said it again. He'd strained a muscle in his back, he said, and could not carry what he was used to. "Anyway, starting tomorrow, Jaime will go with me to the milpa."

Manuel said it to no one in particular. Jaime heard it simply as a statement of what would happen, an undeniable fact. He knew his mother could not help. What could she say? Jaime was the same age as her brothers when they began working in their milpa. Their milpa, however, had not been so far away. And her father was not Manuel. The boy saw the worry in her face, but they both knew she could do nothing to stop it.

"Felipe," Manuel said, "you will water the onions this week. You will rake and dump the leaves at the chalet, too, and also clean the playhouse."

"Yes, Papa," said Felipe, a tiny smile sneaking from his serious face.

Of course, thought Jaime, for Felipe this was a major promotion. Soon he would be sipping cups of hot coffee, same as his big brother.

The next morning, at dawn, hearing Manuel stir, Jaime rolled from his mat, fully dressed, and joined him outside. The first load was distributed into two sacks. His father would carry the bulk of it, for him just a bit less than normal.

"Here," he said to Jaime, hoisting the lighter sack to the small boy's back, "how's that?"

Knowing there was only one acceptable answer, the son gave it.

"Good," Manuel said, and off they went.

The first day was really hard. The following two were torture. Fatigue, like an evil spirit, crawled deep into Jaime's muscles, groaned in his neck and shoulders. He could say nothing. Each morning he was expected to carry whatever his father piled on top of him. When they returned at dusk he ate his tortillas, flopped to his mat and fell asleep.

By the fourth day, Jaime had stopped counting. He might have deduced that this would be the last, since there was nothing left except the tools, the water, and a quarter-bag of fertilizer, but he now lacked the ability to reason, dull-headed as the mule he'd become.

He slumped under the final load, following Manuel's footsteps up the long steep slope, his bare toes bashing rocks, roots, or sometimes just the ground itself. "*Pinche cabrón*," he said beneath his breath. He'd learned the Spanish swear words while working at the chalet. He remembered the day a branch had fallen and raked across Manuel's face. "Pinche cabrón!" his father had yelled, over and over, blood streaming from his nose. Having no idea what the words meant, Jaime said them now with the same sharp tone of moral outrage. But he knew his curses must not be heard. "*Hijo de puta*," he whispered. Those were other dirty words, ones his father rarely used. . .so they must be really bad, thought Jaime. . .unspeakably bad. That was why he said them again. "Hijo de puta, hijo de puta," over and over, like a loop of pure hatred circling through his brain. And if there were worse things to say, he would, because how was it possible to keep stubbing his hijo de puta toes! How could he be walking along, staring at the ground, and watch it happen? He felt bedeviled, suddenly certain there was no way to avoid it. What a mean hijo de puta trick. "Pinche cabrón!"

His knees ached too. . .and his head. . .different hammers pounding him with every step.

And there would be no rest until they reached the rim: *El Mirador*. Jaime loved that place, not for its panoramic view of the lake and distant volcanoes, but because of the five-minute stop Manuel would allow, the water he'd get to drink, the three cold tortillas he'd eat.

One step after another, that was his singular thought, until, at last, he made it.

The best way to stretch these moments out was to lie on his back in the shade. He closed his eyes and focused on the wonder of his jaws chewing, his throat swallowing, his stomach feeling not quite so empty. The smell of corn filled his nose. He breathed it deep and his body settled into the earth like a seed sprouting roots. Time, as if its flow had been shut off, came to a welcomed halt.

He chewed. He drank. He swallowed. His mind began to drift away, a windblown cloud. Each mouthful lasted and lasted. Then was gone. All of it, finally, far too quickly, gone.

"Let's go," Manuel said, giving him a shake.

It was an order Jaime dreaded because next came the always too steep *monstro* hill. Up and up they went, a sharp-curved ascent, baked by the sun a fading brown, its path loose with slippery dirt. Dust rose into Jaime's mouth and nose and made him cough. Gritty sweat dripped into his eyes. Knowing he must not cry was, at this place, never enough to stop the tears. He slowed down when he felt them coming, forced to take the chance that his father might get too far ahead. He hoped Manuel would not see or hear his weakness, would only once in awhile, as usual, swing his head around to make sure that Jaime stayed in sight.

They'd gotten past the steepest part of the hill and were moving toward the stand of pines. It was like a bit of magic, this tiny stretch, out of the dreaded heat and up into the cool green trees.

Hunched over by the load, Jaime wiped his eyes dry and opened them wide. On every trip he looked forward to seeing one particular flower, his favorite, a *girasol*--or *sun turner*--given that name because of the way its big yellow face keeps rotating toward the light. He loved how it stood alone, and proud, like the guardián of the forest.

But today it lies broken by the side of the path, as if someone has intentionally kicked it down. *Why? Why would anyone destroy such a beautiful thing?* He stops, the hill sloping down to his right. He looks closer. There are legs splayed out in the weeds beneath dirty bare feet. He drops his sack.

"Come on boy."

His father is standing above, at the edge of the pines, watching him.

"It is a man, Papa."

"There is nothing to be done," Manuel says, and continues up the path.

Jaime knows he has to go. First, though, he takes a final glance. The man is from San Antonio Palopó. That's certain because of his red and white striped shirt and his black knee-length skirt. It is hard for Jaime to believe what he is looking at. He has seen lots of dead dogs. Other animals too. But never a man. The left arm is twisted, maybe broken, behind his back. There is blood caked on his neck. The face is turned away, and the boy is glad, thankful he does not have to look into a dead man's eyes. He spots a piece of paper pinned to the striped shirt. There is writing on it, big bold letters. But what good are big bold letters to a boy who hasn't learned to read?

Jaime lifts the sack to his shoulder, certain of trouble if he doesn't get moving.

Instead he stands and stares. It's the man's bare feet that hold him, just dirty bare feet. The soles are thick and scarred like those of his father. But these are dead. *Dead feet.* Strange, he knows it's strange, to have never considered that feet could be dead. It's like thinking of the mountain being dead. Or the lake. Or the Xocomil never blowing again. Impossible. Of course, he knows that people die. He thinks of Baby Erica, and the old lady who used to sell fruit outside the church, and many others too, their bodies put into boxes and carried to the graveyard, buried in the ground under white painted stones with their names written on them. In his family they get buried at the outer edge of Uncle Jose's cornfield under plain wooden markers. Then they are gone. Gone forever. And none of that seems the least bit strange. So why, he wonders, be surprised by dead feet? If a person dies, like this poor man, the feet have no choice but to go along, right? Right?

But his mind won't accept it.

What's really scary is that he half expects these feet to get up and start walking. . .like they were born to do. . .because it seems so wrong for them to lie there doing nothing.

"Jaime!" screams his father from somewhere up above.

That snaps the boy out of it, and he sees his own bare feet, moving fast as they can up the mountain. He feels like a frightened ant must feel, and for a few fleeting moments there is no pain at all. A relief that surprises him. A relief soon gone.

Having felt it, though, makes him realize that something has changed forever. Oh yes, he is getting used to this. One day he will be exactly like his father. . .hard and unstoppable. . .able to withstand anything. The tough skin of the earth will make the tough skin of his feet. The pain is, and will always be, bearable. This is what it means to be alive.

Pulseras *May, 1979*

When Jaime told her about the dead man from San Antonio, Consuelo's eyes started tearing up. The boy had not expected that, and wished he'd kept it to himself. "The man was killed," she said, "because of his bare feet." Then she ran outside the house.

That night, after coming back from Manuel's hut, she gathered her sons and they huddled together on the floor. Baby Adriana lay gurgling between them. Flor was asleep on her mat.

Jaime said, "Mama, is there something wrong?" but she didn't seem to hear him.

"Listen," Consuelo whispered, "I have an idea for us, a way to earn money."

"How?" whispered Felipe, like it was a game they were playing.

Jaime said nothing, frightened by his mother's serious tone. He felt sure it had something to do with the dead man.

"By making things," she said. "Here, at night. Your father cannot know. You understand?"

She must have seen from their faces they did not.

"Don't worry," she told them, "there's nothing to be afraid of. He doesn't care what we do so long as we don't bother him."

True, thought Jaime--unless they somehow caused him trouble, Manuel ignored them. He only came into their house for food, or to give an order. Otherwise, he was either outside, working, or alone in his hut. Alone except when he called for Consuelo. It could happen now. . .this very minute . . .which was why she looked scared. . .why she was hushing them and whispering. Keeping a secret from Manuel was a dangerous thing. He might smack her for the smallest reason. Or no reason at all. Jaime sometimes heard her cries, and she always looked sad, and smelled different, when coming back from him. Smelled like fish. The boy had never understood. The morning after one of their nights together, his father gone, he'd snuck inside Manuel's hut. Expecting to find a pile of fish bones, he saw nothing. Maybe his father forced her to eat them. Maybe that's what made her cry.

Consuelo ducked underneath the counter, where she kept boxes of household supplies: soaps, lime, and other stuff only she ever handled; stuff that made Jaime's nose burn, his eyes water. At the bottom of the biggest box, beneath a pile of stained rags, was a smaller box. Things had to be moved to get at it. She reached inside and pulled out four shiny black bags. Each was tied with a bow of colored thread: green, blue, red, yellow.

"Pick one," she said to Jaime.

Without thinking, he pointed at the yellow.

She smiled. He could see that she knew he'd choose it.

His mother undid the bow, opened the bag, and pulled out an entire roll of yellow thread.

Jaime let out a gasp and Felipe a joyous little cry, almost a tweet, like a hungry bird might make at the sight of a worm. Both covered their mouths for fear of waking Manuel.

It was not the thread that surprised them. Thread had always been a part of their lives, used by all the village women to weave their *huipiles*, but neither boy had seen a whole roll of it before. It was like a treasure she'd kept hidden. Jaime looked at his mother's huipil. Woven into the basic red background were stripes of green and blue. All the village women did the same. But, like a few others, she was experimenting with different abstract shapes--fish or cats or women reaching for the sky. On the one she wore now, circling around the collar, were tall blue cats with yellow whiskers.

"You like the yellow," Consuelo said, "because it is brightest."

Jaime nodded.

She dug to the bottom of the small box and grabbed another plastic bag, tied with a piece of ordinary string. Out of that bag she pulled three narrow bands, each of different colored threads, each a long series of pointy lines, like arrows.

"These are called *pulseras*," she said.

"Where did you get them?"

"I made them, Jaime. Auntie Rosa taught me."

Rosa was not their true aunt, that's just what the kids were told to call her.

Felipe picked up one of the pulseras. "What is it for?"

"Auntie Rosa says people wear them in El Norte." Consuelo took the bracelet, wrapped it around Felipe's wrist, and tied off the loose ends. "See?"

"Yes," he said, lifting his eyes to hers, "but. . .why?"

"Gringos say they bring protection. Friends give them to each other."

Jaime remembered a few weeks ago, his mother and Auntie Rosa talking on the front stoop when they thought he was out back feeding the chickens. "It was a gringa's idea," Auntie Rosa had said, "because in her country there was also a war, same as ours, with soldiers killing poor people in the mountains." He'd wanted to ask about the war in Guatemala, but knew his mother wouldn't answer, not wanting him to think about such things. As if war was a secret to be kept from children. So he pretended not to know what he often heard whispered about, that Indians were getting murdered by the ladinos for causing trouble. Ladinos and their soldiers were the enemy of Indians, that was all he really knew.

"Auntie Rosa and I work separately," his mother said. "She will sell what we've made to a man in Panajachel. Three quetzales for twelve-dozen pulseras! Yes, it's true. And I think there will be time to make two or three every night. So it will take less than a year for Jaime to get his shoes."

"What?"

"You are almost thirteen, son. Almost a man. You need them."

"Why?"

"Because I said so, Jaime, because. . .because then the ladinos will see you are a serious person, a person who should be respected."

"What about me?" said Felipe.

"Your brother is older. He needs them first."

"All right, Mama."

Jaime smiled. He liked the idea of being respected. "I want to help," he said.

"Yes," Consuelo said, lighting a prayer candle, "you will. I am going to need you both."

"You mean tonight?" said Felipe.

Consuelo tousled Felipe's hair. It was his job, she told him, to stand guard. . .to watch Manuel's hut through a crack in their bamboo. . .to warn her if his father came outside. Once Felipe agreed, and was positioned, she dug into the pulsera bag and showed them smaller bundles of the different colored threads. These bundles, she explained, had strands already cut to the proper lengths. She pulled out one of each color, then turned to Jaime.

"All right, son. . .watch what I do." She laid the four strands on her thigh and made sure their ends were even. Exactly in the middle, she pressed down with her finger and rubbed them toward her knee until the very center--about an inch long--was twisted together. Then she turned the twisted part into a small loop and tied it off. Jaime did not see how, but decided he'd ask later. "This is the beginning," his mother said. She ran a piece of string through the loop and tied it around the leg of their chair. Eight strands of thread now hung underneath. "Next, we start the pattern."

Her hands began working fast. She kept winding the threads around each other, lifting and pulling and tightening them into knots, until the first arrow was finished. Jaime watched closely. She did another arrow, then stopped and looked at him.

"All right, son, now what?"

"I don't know, Mama."

"Yes, you do." She pointed at what she'd already done. "The first arrow is red, the second yellow. Which one next, blue or green?"

"Blue."

"Good." She started a blue arrow, very slowly, showing him how. "Around and through and knot. . .pull it up tight, you see. . .around and through and knot." When finished with that, she made a green arrow. "And now we go back to red, you understand?"

"Yes."

He kept watching, seeing more clearly how it was done, and after an hour could tell her, with certainty, what to do next.

"Go on, Jaime, give it a try."

"Yes, Mama. Which color first?"

"Whatever you choose."

Both of them smiled when he said he would start with yellow.

"Good idea," she said.

He evened the threads, but getting the initial loop was hard. His mother did the rubbing part on her knee, formed and cinched the loop. That done, he ran the string through it, tied the string to another of the

87

chair's legs, and began the pattern. He thought this part would be easy, but it wasn't. Soon he sat there frowning at a slack and jagged arrow. "It's no good. It doesn't look right."

"You have to pull the knots tighter."

"I'm too slow."

"Don't hurry," Consuelo told him, undoing his work. "It has to be done right, Jaime. The man will only buy the good ones. No one cares how long it takes."

Night after night he kept at it, slowly, each knot good and tight, until his fingers started getting the rhythm. Within two months he could do them almost as fast as his mother, and Felipe could not tell which were Jaime's and which were hers. They counted twenty-six that were properly finished. . .much less than they'd planned because Consuelo had decided that the only safe times were after her visits with Manuel. He would bring her into his hut shortly after dinner. Jaime knew by now that whatever happened in there, it never took long. His mother would hurry back, get out the thread, and wait until Manuel began snoring. Then they got to work. The problem was, Manuel might wake up to pee and notice their little candle burning. A constant danger. So poor Felipe had to stay on guard, had to watch, hour after hour, for any sign of him stirring. And how could the boy be sure when there were so many distractions? Dogs barking. Or a rooster going off. Or some drunken man singing, or praying, or yelling at the moon.

Sometimes their mother would take a break to go encourage him.

"I'm doing my best, Mama."

"I know, son. You're doing fine."

But it looked to Jaime like his brother was in a constant panic, perhaps fearing what could happen should Manuel catch him spying. All of a sudden, for no apparent reason, Felipe would say *"shush!"*--a signal for them to put out the candle, stash the thread under their mats, lie on top and close their eyes. It was usually a false alarm, and a lot of time wasted.

On many such nights Consuelo would whisper, "No more, boys, let's go to sleep."

It was strange the way she'd say it, as if this were a time to rest. But for Jaime, more often than not, sleep was the opposite--the most tiring part of his day. Within minutes of lying down he would be in a fast-moving dream. The dreams were unpredictable, yet always familiar. Sometimes he was swimming in the lake, a shiny silver fish; or maybe that flock of sleek white birds flying above the volcanoes; or both; sometimes there were men on shore, with guns or machetes, and he knew they were looking for him; sometimes they sat in cayucos, dangling their sharp hooks in his face; or stood on the tops of mountains, pointing their rifles up at the sky, and firing, trying to shoot him down.

From some dreams he woke up shivering. Those were the ones he remembered best.

Over and over he'd dream of a small boy, smaller than him, with an old man's face and his mother's voice. The boy might be down by the lake, or inside a hut, or out in a smoking field. Usually, though, the boy was standing in their milpa, hiding behind the tall stalks of maize. He was speaking to someone, but Jaime could not see who. *Others*, the boy said, *tried to understand those sounds we never heard before. Like huge growling beasts. They should have run like me. They waited too long, until it was too late. And now what does it matter? With nothing left, not our houses or our animals or our milpas, why should we run anymore?*

The boy seemed real, like someone Jaime knew, someone he'd forgotten. The dream was scary, but not the boy. Jaime knew he was saying something important. Maybe they were supposed to meet each other again? Maybe, one day, they would be friends?

A lot happened in that dream, but the light of day made his memory of it fade, then disappear, and he wondered where the boy was, lost somewhere that Jaime could not find. The thing he did remember, of this and every other dream, were the colors. So many colors. Like endless interwoven threads.

It took them six months to complete the first twelve-dozen pulseras. Rosa, with twelve-dozen of her own, plus the pottery her uncle had made, went to Panajachel for the big Sunday market. That evening she met Consuelo by the church and handed her two quetzales.

"I thought you said three," Consuelo said.

"Yes," said Rosa. "It isn't right. The man told me there are women in Sololá who make them cheaper. He would rather have ours, he says, but only for this price."

"It's not enough," Consuelo said, handing back one of the bills--her debt for the thread.

"I know," said Rosa, taking the money, "I'm sorry about this, I. . ."

But her friend seemed unable to finish the sentence. Something was wrong. "What is it?"

"I feel bad. He liked yours best. If it was only yours, he might have paid three."

"Never mind," Consuelo said, patting her friend on the shoulder. "Hey, without your help I would have no money at all, right?"

"I told him you'd be making more."

"What about you?"

"No, I can't. Little Pablo is sick again and keeps me up most of the night. And I'm sick too."

"What's wrong?"

Rosa smiled. "Oh, nothing. Just the usual. You know."

"Another one so soon?"

"Miguel isn't happy about it. He calls me the baby machine."

"Well," Consuelo said, very serious, "maybe he should quit filling up the tank."

Both of them laughed at that, and hugged, and went their separate ways.

That same evening, after her time with Manuel, Consuelo and the boys got back to work. And, every night they could, they worked hard, even harder than before. She loved being together with her sons in the cool dark stillness, doing something that would help them both--first Jaime, then Felipe. Their persistence, without a single complaint, made her proud. She was tired, yes, but happy.

In seven months they had another twenty-four dozen. But Rosa was ready to have her baby, could not make the trip to Panajachel. Consuelo would have to go. Rosa told her, "The man's name is Francisco. He always comes to the Sunday market and will be looking for me by the front entry, where I sell with the other potters. He knows your name, and knows you've been making pulseras. Don't worry, he will find you."

Late Saturday night, while Felipe watched Manuel's hut, Consuelo dug out the top layer of onions from the costal. She tucked their bag of pulseras in the middle, then piled the onions back on top. Jaime, kneeling on the ground, holding the sack steady, saw how nervous she was, her actions rushed and awkward, her forehead perspiring.

"Can I help, Mama?"

"No, it's all right, it's done."

"You're sure he'll let us go?"

She sighed, crouched down beside him, and smiled. "He wasn't so hard to convince," she said. She no longer spoke to Jaime as if he were a child. He liked that, of course, and also knew he deserved it. "With Rosa watching your brother and sisters," she said, "what does he care?" Then she leaned over and whispered in his ear, making him feel more like an old friend than a son. "He knows I'll be back to cook his dinner. That's all that matters. Besides, any onions we sell will mean an easier day for him in Sololá. He figures it's good training. . .that someday we can sell there too."

The next morning, Consuelo mounted the big basket of onions on her head and Jaime slung the heavy sack of them over his shoulder.

Manuel came into the house and laughed. "Well," he said, "aren't you a pair!"

Jaime still expected trouble. *No*, his father would say, *I changed my mind.* Maybe he would tell Consuelo she was mistaken, that he'd never agreed in the first place. Or he might say that Jaime couldn't go, that he needed the boy here with him to do something--anything--whatever he could think of to ruin their day.

Instead, Manuel just grabbed the tortillas Consuelo had prepared and went back outside, laughing, sounding happy.

Because Manuel would not allow them a ride in Guicho's pickup, it was over an hour's walk to the Pana Market. On the first steep hill Jaime realized the truth: Manuel liked this extra day of rest--at home, alone-- and by making them walk he would not only save money, but have more time to himself. The boy's fear of his father had turned to hatred.

He was surprised that his mother did not seem upset. She sang to herself as they plodded up and down the road. Perhaps noticing his bad mood, thinking him tired, she offered to carry the sack of onions, but he said no, he was fine, and kept on walking.

Once they reached the market she looked for where Rosa sold, on the street across from the main entrance. But today there was no extra room by the people selling pottery, or so they said, so she took Jaime's hand and squeezed between a man selling coconuts and a woman selling flowers.

Jaime saw the two vendors share a look, a wordless objection. Consuelo set her basket down, removed the top third of onions from the costal, and took out the pulseras. Carefully, as if performing a sacred ceremony, she slipped them from the protective plastic bag and arranged the colorful bundles in two separate stacks of twelve dozen each.

The coconut man wagged his head and the flower woman smirked. Both were then amazed, as was Jaime, when a few minutes later a young lady, a foreigner, knelt down and stared at the pulseras. She had a beautiful round face, white and luminous, with long shiny hair as black as night. The boy was mesmerized. He lost all sense of time. It was as if she'd always been there, this lady, shining like the moon, her eyes now slowly lifting toward his mother, her voice gentle as a prayer.

"Cuanto?" she said.

His mother said nothing. Jaime saw she was confused. Why? She could not speak Spanish, and understood very little, but definitely knew that *cuanto?* meant *"how much?"* Still, she looked startled, as if the young lady had just burped in her face. He shook his mother's elbow and now she stared at him, her eyes slightly glazed, and it came clear what she was thinking. . .that this was not supposed to happen. . .that she'd expected a man, the same man who Rosa had sold to before. . .that he would be expecting to buy all of their pulseras. . .that she did not know what to do.

"Well?" the flower woman said to Consuelo. "The lady wants to

93

know what they cost, those things of yours. She is trying to bargain."

Consuelo's eyes opened wide, as if she'd suddenly woken up. She turned to the flower woman and said, "Tell her I do not bargain." She pointed at one stack. "Three quetzales for twelve-dozen."

"Three?" said the flower woman. "Are you serious?"

The foreign lady dug into her purse and pulled out six quetzales.

What, thought Jaime, *she wants all of them?*

At that exact moment, a man crouched down and covered the pulseras with his hand. "Wait," he said to Consuelo in Kaqchikel, "don't you know a woman named Rosa?"

Jaime flinched. From what his mother had told him, he assumed it would be a ladino buying the bracelets. But this was an Indian man--an Indian man *not wearing his traje!* He not only had shoes, but also dark gray pants and a clean white shirt, which made no sense. Why would a Naturale dress like he worked in a bank? The boy looked at his mother, who looked equally confused.

"Rosa is my friend," she said.

"You are Consuelo," the man said, and shook her hand. The foreign lady held out her money, but the man had edged in front of her and kept on talking. "Nice to meet you," he said. "My name is Francisco. Your friend Rosa, you know, promised her bracelets to me."

"Rosa and I both want three quetzales," Consuelo said. "That is what they're worth."

"The lady wants to know if there is a problem?" said the flower woman.

Jaime saw it was true, she did look upset, perhaps believing she'd done something wrong.

"Tell her no," his mother said.

"Rosa and I had an agreement," Francisco said.

"Maybe you did," Consuelo said, "but not with me."

She pushed past him and handed the pulseras to the young foreign lady.

Francisco stood up. "You're making a big mistake. If you cannot honor a contract, I--"

"Sorry," Consuelo said, looking him in the eye, "they're sold."

"This tourist will be gone tomorrow. Then who will you sell to?"

"Whoever gives me the fair price. Today it is her."

"You'll regret this," Francisco said. *"Indios stupidos,"* he mumbled as he left.

The foreign lady handed Consuelo the money, who nodded and shoved the paper notes down the front of her huipil, against her bare chest, then smiled and pointed at herself. "Consuelo."

"Mucho gusto," said the foreign lady. "Me llamo Luanne."

"What?" said Consuelo in Kaqchikel, looking to the flower women for help. "What did she say?"

"Her name is Luna. In Spanish it means moon."

"Ah," said Consuelo. "Luna."

Jaime was not surprised he'd guessed it.

The flower woman knelt beside the moon lady and started asking questions. She'd made herself an essential part of the transaction. Jaime saw the worry on his mother's face, no doubt thinking the woman would want some kind of payment for her service. He didn't think so. She liked the attention, that's all, it made her feel important, gave a needed break from having to hawk her goods.

"She is a rich girl from *El Norte*," the flower woman said.

"Hay mas?" asked the moon lady.

The flower woman's eyes got big. "She wants to know if she can buy more!"

95

"Yes," Consuelo said. "Tell her yes."

"When? She will want to know."

"Of course," Consuelo said, nodding her head--a look of certainty in her eyes--a big surprise to Jaime, who knew she could not be sure. "Tell her I will have this many again in four months."

The moon lady listened to the translation, then answered in a way that seemed to be a question.
The flower woman responded with more questions of her own. They went back and forth like that until everything, it seemed, was properly sorted out.

"Our government," the flower woman said, "will not let her stay. She can come back in six or seven months. And you cannot believe what else."

"What?" said Consuelo.

"Ay, Dios mío!" the flower woman squeaked, crossing herself while shaking her head.

"Tell me," Consuelo said.

"She wants to buy all you can make. She wants you to save them for her alone. She promises six quetzales for every twelve dozen!"

"You told her three, right?"

"Yes, yes, and she told me *six*, amiga, you understand? Six is better than three, *sí?*"

"Oh. . .yes. . .*sí*," said Consuelo. She turned to Luna, smiled and nodded.

"Sí?" said Luna. Then she dug into her purse again. She handed Consuelo two more quetzales and said something in Spanish.

"She is giving you that in advance," the flower woman said. "Not so smart, this girl."

"Sí, sí, gracias," Consuelo said, quickly tucking the extra bills down the front of her huipil. Blushing, she reached out and shook Luna's hand.

The moon lady smiled and said, "Mi placer."

"She says it's her pleasure," translated the flower woman.

Then Luna shook Jaime's hand too. "Hasta luego," she said, her grasp as gentle as her eyes.

Jaime smiled back, holding on as long as he could.

"*Ojalá*," he said. . .a Spanish saying which he took to mean "*Yes, I pray that it comes true*". . .the very best answer, in a world of constant disappointment, for whatever one hoped might happen.

It took the rest of the afternoon to sell a quarter of the onions. One quetzal and ten centavos. Even so, Jaime was certain his father would be impressed. Pleased to have gotten anything.

Before heading home, his mother stopped in front of the stall where shoes were sold.

What? thought Jaime. *Oh. . .oh yes.* How had he forgotten that their many months of work were done for these? For shoes. Well, all right, this might be fun, standing at the counter as if they were ladinos, looking at the many pairs of shoes lined along the shelves against the wall. But it felt like a silly game they were playing, like they were doing something wrong. He gazed up at the top row, at the tall black leather boots with metal tips, like those the soldiers wore who drove through Santa Catarina in their big green trucks.

He hated the look of them. Just looking at those shoes made him want to leave.

"Choose," Consuelo said.

His mother's face was flushed, excited. To please her, he pointed at a shorter, less shiny pair on the bottom shelf.

"How much?" she asked.

The pockmarked man behind the counter looked at her like she was crazy. Or, worse, was dreaming at his expense, wasting his valuable time. "Ten quetzales," he said. "Tell me, *Mamita*, do you know how much that is?"

Jaime, embarrassed, looked up at his mother, at her blank face, unable to read her expression. Then it came to him. *Oh no, she's serious.* He'd never before considered it possible, but now saw she was determined, no matter what, to buy him shoes. *Ten quetzales? Really?* His face went blank too. How could shoes be worth so much? The biggest bag of fertilizer cost far less, that he knew, and it struck him how stupid this whole thing was. Why would a poor Indian boy be looking at shoes?

The shoe man, who must have been thinking the same, was staring at his mother.

Passersby began to gawk.

Shame, that's what Jaime felt. Because it was his fault. It was because his mother worried about his safety. She did all this just to protect him--yes, all right, he understood--but it was a bad idea for her to make them look foolish in front of everyone.

"Please Mama," he said. "Please, let's go."

His mother also seemed to feel the shame. She grabbed his hand and hurried them from the market, away from staring eyes, out onto the street. Jaime still couldn't tell what she was thinking. And didn't ask. He only hoped it wasn't about shoes. Never again about those stupid shoes!

It was seven hilly kilometers back to Santa Catarina. Though obviously exhausted, his mother insisted on carrying a full basket of onions on her head. When close to the top of the final hill she made a strange sound.

Jaime lifted his eyes from the road, where he'd been watching his every step, and looked at her. At first he was worried, but soon realized, by the way she turned her face his direction and pretended a scowl, that she was playing. His mother faked a cry, squeezed her eyes shut, and strained against the heavy load, the unyielding pain, as if otherwise it might push her down forever. Then she stopped, looked at him again, and laughed. . .like her extreme discomfort was a joke.

Jaime stopped and laughed with her, the pain only funny because they shared it together.

Shoes

Portland Memorial Coliseum. . .June 12th, 1980

Back from Guatemala, while staying with her parents in Palo Alto, Luanne located the next Grateful Dead concert on the west coast, and had no trouble finding a friend, with a car, who wanted to go.

She bought tickets in advance and made sure to arrive early. She needed to find the right place to set up, with a parking spot nearby, and decided on a grassy slope within sight of the coliseum's entrance. Her friend, Becky, went off to smoke another joint. Luanne, feeling anxious, laid the first eight-dozen pulseras out on a blanket, but before she could sort them by color, as planned, a crowd had formed.

A girl started picking through one of the piles. "How much?"

"Wait," Luanne said. She wondered where she'd left her sign, then realized she didn't need one. "Two for a dollar," she said to the expectant faces. "All of them, two for a dollar."

She sat down, astonished, as people quickly picked out pulseras and handed her money. She was setting out six-dozen more when a frizzy bleached blonde leaned in for a closer look. "What are they?"

"They're called friendship bracelets. You give them to your friends. For protection."

"Protection from what?" snickered a red-haired guy standing behind the blonde.

That's when Luanne focused on who was buying the bracelets. Females only. Their boyfriends stood behind--yawning or frowning or doing whatever--waiting for the coliseum doors to open. "Probably from you," she said to the red-haired guy, an obvious joke to get the girls giggling. She let out a sigh of disgust and stared into his dull, vacant eyes.

Maybe he didn't know any better. Maybe he'd come from some other planet. *War? Injustice? Genocide? Huh?*

Luanne might have told him about Guatemalan boys his age being hunted down and killed every day. She might have mentioned how lucky he was to sleep in a bed, and not go hungry, and never have to run for his life.

Ah, forget it. Why bother? Besides, there was no time for politics, or therapy, with so much money flying her way. She dug into her satchel and pulled out another six-dozen.

Wow, was this really happening? Telling Consuelo she'd return in six months had been her typical wishful thinking. *Ojalá* was right. Who could possibly guess it would go this well? Luanne smiled at her good fortune, thrilled by the chance she had to actually fulfill a promise.

Qué frigging milagro!

But she did not return in six months, or eight, or ten, and Jaime saw the fear in his mother's face, worried that the moon lady was gone forever. For him it was unimaginable. He felt sure that Luna would come. With another rainy season approaching, however, and most of the tourists about to leave, how much longer could they wait? Francisco had continued to pass them by with his ugly sneer. One time he'd stopped, stared at Consuelo, and raised his hands in the air, whatever that meant. Maybe he was saying she should give up. Jaime was determined not to let that happen.

The boy had worked hard, not for shoes but for his mother. Because it calmed her. Because it lessened her fear. For months after Luna left, they'd worked whenever possible. But then his mother's stomach got bad again, and Jaime was too tired at night because of his long days working with Manuel. They had the first twelve dozen finished, which Consuelo said was enough to buy his shoes, so they took a break. A break that lasted until she started doubting Luna's return.

Though her stomach was still a problem, she got them back to work.

It went slower now because her trips to Manuel's hut were less frequent. On the few nights they could, they worked longer hours, which meant they were often exhausted the following day. All three of them struggled to do their regular chores, and regularly made mistakes. Especially Jaime, whose mistakes were more noticeable because he was so often working with Manuel.

One morning, the two of them expected early at the chalet, Jaime failed to hear the slam of Manuel's door. The boy was fast asleep, dreaming on his mat: sitting tall and strong in his bright yellow cayuco, drifting across the deep blue lake. The Xocomil began pushing him toward San Pedro. No problem, he thought, confident he could handle anything. It was a warm afternoon and he steered the boat with ease. Then, without warning, a huge gust blew the oar from his hands, spun it away, and the wind turned red, hot, dragging him like a loose thread up the green volcano, straight toward its gaping mouth.

He woke, screaming, to fists clenching the collar of his shirt.

"I am sick of it!" Manuel screamed in his face. "What goes with you, boy!"

If he'd been more awake, Jaime would have known what was happening. He'd have apologized for his laziness and begged his father's forgiveness. Instead, still fighting against the fierce imagined wind, he lashed out and struck Manuel under the chin.

The smaller children gasped. Consuelo grabbed Jaime by his left foot, trying to pull him free, but Manuel pushed her away and slapped his face. The boy felt blood spilling from his nose.

Manuel stared at him, then groaned and marched off. "Fix it!" he yelled at his wife.

Consuelo laid Jaime's head in her lap, stroked his hair, and said they were finished making *pulseras*. "Don't worry, everything will be all right."

Jaime smiled. He'd been waiting for this to happen. Aside from a promise of lots more sleep, he saw it as a sign that Luna would be arriving soon. He said so, knowing his mother also believed in signs, certain she was thinking the same, but when she said nothing, just kept stroking his hair, he sensed her doubt. "It's true, Mama, she's coming, I know it."

At the next Sunday market, Francisco suddenly appeared, perhaps understanding that his chance to cheat them was fast slipping away. Like never before, he drank coconut milk, bought a bouquet of roses, and hovered like a vulture. After chatting with the flower woman for a few minutes, he crouched down and pretended to examine their onions.

"Can I help you?" said Consuelo.

"I warned that you'd regret it."

Jaime watched his mother's face go blank, like she hadn't heard him.

Francisco said, "One last time, are you ready to sell?"

"I have promised the bracelets to someone else."

"There is no one else, *amiga*, and there will not be another chance."

Jaime saw he meant it, and that his mother was scared. To his surprise, she shook her head at the man and said, "No Señor. No gracias."

"Your loss," Francisco said. "I won't ask again."

The boy hated him. Truly hated him. God did not approve of hatred, but He must agree that evil people like Francisco, and Manuel, had to be stopped. Unfortunately, He did not help. Another Sunday passed, and another, his mother looking more and more worried, and still no Luna.

The next market day, as they set out the onions, Consuelo said,

"Son, this may be hard to understand, but sometimes God wants us to be humble."

"I don't know what that means."

"It means not being selfish. Selfishness is a sin, no matter who does it. Maybe I was being selfish to wait so long for the gringa. Why put my faith in a total stranger? It was easy for her, living far away, to promise more than anyone else. But we can't wait. You need your shoes."

Jaime said nothing. He could see that his mother had made up her mind, she would sell their pulseras to the vulture. He kept thinking *It's not right, it's not! Why such a hurry for those stupid shoes?*

Angry, disillusioned, the boy stood with a bunch of green onions in his hand, shook them in the air, and shouted at the stupid world as loud as he could, "BUEN PRECIO! FRESCA HOY!"

He sees a pretty girl standing in front of him, staring, laughing soundlessly with her eyes. He is shouting like a fool and swinging his onions. . .there are people talking and moving all around. . .but the space between the two of them is still. . .is silent. It's as if he's in two places at once. The moon lady could stop time too, but with this girl it feels different, like she's stopped it just for him.

Then a woman grabs her hand and leads her away.

The girl looks back at him and smiles.

Jaime quits shouting and watches her disappear into the crowd. She's gone, but in his mind those laughing eyes keep looking at him. The attraction is something he can feel. Something he is certain of. It doesn't matter how, or what it means, he doesn't care, his mind scrambling for any excuse (*I have to pee, yes, that's what I'll say*) to go after her . . .find her. . .see those eyes again.

"Stay here," says his mother, jumping to her feet. She hurries off, in the opposite direction from where the girl has gone. "Señor!" Consuelo yells, "Señor!"

She runs to catch up with Francisco. She tugs on his sleeve. Jaime watches him shake his head and wag his finger in her face, watches her nod and cry. A crowd of people watch too. Finally she returns, the vulture following close behind.

"I have twelve dozen," she says, pulling their pulseras from the plastic bag.

"Good," Francisco says, and examines the work. "Yours are the best, Consuelo."

"Yes, Señor, yes, yes, thank you."

"Too bad you waited so long. The price has gone down."

"Please, Señor, I--"

"I can give you one and a half quetzales." His face has turned to stone.

Jaime looks away, confused. From Luna, he remembers, it would have been six, that's the total in his mind, and it's hard to fathom so much less. He looks at his mother, at her wrinkled forehead. She must be trying, like him, to add one and a half quetzales to what they've already made, then subtract for what they owe.

"No," she says, "I. . .I cannot take less than--"

"That is my final price."

She closes her eyes and shakes her head. *No.*

"Oh, come on, I'm joking," he laughs, as if she's far too stupid to understand the simplest thing. "Of course these are worth two. If, that is, from now on, you only sell to me."

"Yes. . .all right."

"Bueno," he says, handing her the two quetzales and stuffing their months of work into his worn leather satchel. He smiles at her and stands. "I'll take more whenever you have them."

And just like that, he's gone.

"What," says the flower woman, "you could not wait a bit longer for the gringa?"

"Come," Consuelo says, grabbing Jaime by the hand. She leaves the pile of onions behind. He knows where they are going. This deal with Francisco made her feel cheated and she must prove there is a reason for what she's done. In a rush to make that clear, she leads him into the main market, to where those shiny black shoes are lined along the rough pine shelves.

Behind the counter is the same frowning pockmarked man. He looks upset by their return until Consuelo lays down the two quetzales and digs into her huipil to produce the rest. Ten green bills. At that his eyes light up.

He ushers them both inside the booth and sits Jaime down on a low wooden stool. Whistling to himself, the man measures one of the boy's bare feet with a cold piece of steel. Other Indians peek over the counter to see what's going on, amazed it is one of their own going through the strange process. The man gets a pair of shoes from a box under his counter. "My best bargain," he says. Consuelo beams, her eyes focused on Jaime. Then, with a couple of painful twists, like evil magic, the shiny black things have replaced his feet. "There," the man smiles, "what do you say?"

"Stiff," says Jaime.

"Well yes, son, because they're brand new!"

"They pinch my toes."

The man nods and removes them. One at a time, he takes each shoe and bends its rounded end up and down, up and down. Satisfied, he shoves the boy's feet back inside.

"There, is that better?"

"No."

The man raises his eyebrows at Consuelo.

"I've already checked," she says to Jaime. "These are the only ones we can afford." Her eyes have turned sad. She needs this to happen and will not be happy unless it does.

"They're fine," Jaime says. "Just pinch a little."

"No problem," says the man. "You need to wear them for a while, that's all. Work them in."

"All right," Jaime says, and Consuelo hands over their entire savings, all that hard-earned money gone to hide her boy's bare feet.

The coconut man and flower woman hunch down to touch the brand new shoes. Both are speechless. Consuelo keeps quiet too while gathering the onions.

"Envidia," she whispers to Jaime once they've gone, as if proud to be attracting the famous sin.

Walking in them is torture, perhaps less from the pain than from acting like he's happy. "Good," he says when his mother asks how they feel. "I think I'm getting used to it."

"You are a lucky boy."

"I know, Mama. Thank you."

Jaime tries to avoid moving his toes. Much of the pain starts there, like barbs pricking each of their ends and scraping along their tops. Worst, though, is at the rim of his right shoe, the edge of it sawing his ankle. His mother walks ahead, as if to avoid noticing his misery. She struggles, too, with the basket of onions on her head. Her stomach pain has gotten worse. Though she never complains, he sees it in her slumping shoulders, especially now, with the Xocomil pushing hard against them. Neither of them can escape the torment. It seems like some clownish dance they're doing, the boy also shifting around, fighting the relentless wind while trying to better adjust his feet inside these *pinche* things. But it's no use, the agony at last making him stop, just for a second, to catch his breath and will himself on.

Then a thought flies into his head--a crazy, terrible thought. Sharp as an arrow, it sticks fast. "Mama?"

"Yes?"

"What will we say to Papa?"

"Yes," Consuelo says, "I'm thinking that too."

OH. . .GOD. . .NO! the boy screams inside his head. Why, he wonders, has she never thought of this before? Why make a problem that cannot be solved? *Stupid stupid stupid!*

"I'm afraid," she says, "we can't tell anyone."

"No."

"No one, Jaime. Not Felipe either. Not yet. I will find a good moment to tell your father."

At the lookout above the village, their last chance not to be seen, they hide the shoes toward the bottom of the costal he's carrying, where the pulseras used to be, and cover them with onions.

Jaime is glad to have the damn things off his feet. His toes are on fire with budding blisters.

She frowns at the grimace on his face. "Don't worry," she says, patting his back, "I promise, son, you will be wearing them again soon."

It is late afternoon when they arrive at the hut. Luckily, Manuel and Felipe are still not home from the chalet. After putting the shoes in the thread box under the counter, Consuelo quickly starts a fire, then gets out the masa for their tortillas.

"Go to Auntie Rosa's house and bring your sisters," she says to

Jaime. "Hurry!"

Off he runs, his feet screaming with every step. By the time he and the girls return, Manuel and Felipe are there, eating.

"Well," his father says to his mother, "did you sell any?"

"Just a few," she says.

"Like I told you, it's not worth the effort. There are better ways to spend your time."

"Yes, you're right."

"Glad you agree. Because for the whole next week, including Sunday, I need Jaime to help me with the milpa. We start tomorrow morning. All right, son?"

"Yes, sir."

"Really?" Manuel says, a concerned look on his face. "Sure you feel up to it?"

It is a strange question for his father to ask. Stranger still to sound as if he means it.

"Or do your feet hurt?"

A trap. Jaime should have known. But how does his father know about the shoes? Heart pounding, the boy glances at his mother, wondering if she was forced to confess their secret. Her eyes tell him no. *NO!* They warn him to be quiet, but how is that possible with his father expecting an answer? What should he say? What?

Jaime is ready to confess, to beg forgiveness, when Manuel shows a tiny smile, then laughs, then squeezes him on the shoulder. "So. . .fell down again, eh boy?"

Oh, thinks Jaime, catching his breath, his father saw him limping, that's all. . .or maybe saw his bloody toes. "They're not bad, Papa. I tripped over something and scraped them."

"Well," Manuel says, "as the old people love to say, *'Mayazak Pabej!'*

He says it like a bad joke; like there has never been a more ridiculous saying; like such idiotic nonsense is beyond his understanding.

Everyone, including Adriana and little Flor, laughs along with him. Like Jaime, they will do anything to keep him from being mean.

It was lucky for Consuelo and the kids that Manuel had had a great day at the chalet. A day, she knew, he'd been wanting for years. He bragged about it later, in his hut. "Hector finally went to the milpa," Manuel told her. "He saw the new terraces I built and was *shocked*, he said, by the loamy soil. Now he understands how much work I have done, and why my harvests are so good."

"I'm glad," Consuelo said. "You deserve his pride."

"I hope," he said, "that our sons will someday deserve mine."

"They will," she said.

"Well, maybe. With Felipe there's a chance, but Jaime is too dreamy." Then he laughed. "No wonder he keeps falling down!"

She laughed too.

"It's funny," he said, "the way some people trip over nothing."

Like her, thought Consuelo. She was sure that's what he was thinking--that she was a dreamer too, same as Jaime. She knew Manuel felt grateful not to be like them. For him, dreams were meaningless, not to be bothered with. All he needed was his milpa, his onions, his job at the chalet: things he could, because of his good sense and constant hard work, control. Including his wife. Manuel got what he wanted whenever he wanted it. Or else.

She prepared herself as usual, first loosening her *faja*, then lifting her corte and lying on her back. But tonight was different. She could feel it.

Tonight, perhaps because of the special day he'd had with his father, he seemed genuinely happy to be with her. He leaned over, ran his hand through her hair, and kissed her on the lips, many times, like he used to do when they'd first met. He sat her up and unwound the faja. She pulled the corte free. He helped take off her huipil, then took off his pants and shirt and lay down naked beside her. In no hurry whatsoever, he gently fondled her breasts, as if waiting for her to relax, get comfortable, before doing his business. Feeling thankful, she rubbed his back while he pounded away, and made sounds like she enjoyed it.

Afterward, he lay there in the dark, his face striped by the moonlight seeping through the caña wall. He was calm. Noticeably pleased. It seemed the perfect time to talk about shoes. She tied the faja around her corte, put on her huipil, and sat down next to him. "Manuel?"

"Huh?"

"I'm worried what's going on in the mountains. It's dangerous to be Jaime's age. Government soldiers are killing the young boys."

"Also us men."

True, thought Consuelo, though she'd never once worried about him. "The difference," she said, "is that you know how to avoid trouble. Jaime is not so smart."

"Well, I keep telling you that."

"Yes."

"Because you're too easy, woman. You baby him. That's not how he's going to learn."

"I should have listened. I have to teach him, like you, to be smart, to be strong. And there are other ways we can help him."

"What?"

"We have to keep him safe while he's learning."

"How?"

"Well, I was thinking, if he looks like a boy with money, the soldiers might leave him alone."

"Yes," Manuel said. "And if a pig could tell lies, he might become mayor."

"Hah!" she shrieked, pretending to find the old joke funny. They laughed together for a few seconds and it did seem possible he would listen. Maybe she should try another joke?

"Go now," he said, "I need to sleep."

"I bought him shoes."

"What?"

"Shoes."

"What do you mean?"

"Shoes, from the market. I have been making bracelets in my spare time and--"

But he'd grabbed her by the throat and she could not finish. "You did what?"

He pulled Consuelo up with him, threw on his pants, his shirt, dragged her out of his hut, across the narrow yard, and into the house. "Where?" he roared.

All the children were sitting up, at full attention, the moonlight through the window making frightful sculptures of their faces.

"Here," Consuelo said, and dug the shoes out from under the counter.

Manuel grabbed the shoes but never gave them a glance, just shook them at her. "How much?"

"Ten quetzales."

"Impossible! Where did you steal these?"

"No, I paid for them. . .with money I made."

"You? How?"

"See," she said, reaching back down into the box and coming up with the bag of thread. She pulled out one of the rolls. "From this."

He took the roll, and the bag, both his hands now full of things--things which made no sense to him, Consuelo knew, and that only made him angrier.

"Rosa got the thread from her sister," she said, "who knows a man, an Indian man named--"

"What are you talking about?"

"Rosa gave some of the thread to me and I made *pulseras*. . .at night . . .while you were sleeping. I sold them to this man in the market and--"

"Not any more you don't!"

She saw he couldn't hit her because of all the things he was holding onto. He turned, took the lot of it back to his hut, and slammed the door.

The next morning, Manuel came into the house while she was cooking tortillas. Without a word, he slapped the side of her head. Then stared straight at Jaime and yelled, "I will not have my son pretending he's better than the rest of us! The boy is who he is, woman. Shoes cannot hide it."

"I am sorry," she said. "I bought them for his own good."

Those words made him growl and he hit her again. "What's good for my children, and good for you, is for me to decide! Me, is that clear?" He swung around to face all of them, threatening everyone of them at once. "Deceive me again, any of you, and I'll break your pinche heads!"

The following week he sold the thread to one of the weaver women. He wouldn't say what happened to the shoes. Maybe he sold them too. Or just threw them away.

While hating Manuel for hitting his mother, Jaime felt relieved--even thankful--to be done with those horrible things.

LA GLORIA *March, 1981*

The pretty young girl could not stop thinking about that loud boy with the onions. She wondered what made him so mad, yes, but that was only the beginning. Aura, now eleven years old, had always been fascinated by things she did not understand, and was now equally fascinated with the *WHY* of it. Why did she care? She could think all day about that boy, right, but what good would it do? On the other hand, she thought--stuck with her mother in this long, slow-moving line at the bank--what else was there to think about?

Unlike the local Indians, who could easily go off and do something else, Aura and her mother, Dolores, had to wait. It was their *Banking Day* in Pana. They'd come from up beyond Las Cruces and could not return without doing her father's business. They did this once every month, first going to the market on Sunday, staying the night with one of her mother's aunts, then getting into line early Monday morning. The plan, as usual, was to make it back home ahead of the afternoon heat.

But the girl could see that was not going to happen. A group of guerillas had tried to rob the bank on Sunday night. Two of them were killed, one had escaped, and armed soldiers stood at the door. They interrogated every Indian to enter, as if he or she might be the missing culprit. Or might know who it was. Or might have some information, anything, to locate other trouble-makers.

By the time her mother finished it was well past noon. They hurried from the bank and squeezed onto the next pickup truck to San Andrés. From there they found one going to the junction called Las Cruces. Then came another hour's wait before a Rébuli bus showed up. The driver dropped them off seven kilometers later at a large opening, the entrance to the *finca* where they lived. Arching high across its steep dirt road, supported on either side by posts the size of tree trunks, was a sign. It was intricately carved, with birds and flowers surrounding the ornate letters: **LA GLORIA**.

Every time she saw those words the girl felt fascinated. . .and small.

Dolores took Aura's hand and led her across the asphalt street to where the dirt road began. Though the sun had dropped low in the western sky, it was still hot. "Well dear," Dolores said, "if we're lucky, one of the trucks will be coming soon."

Aura let go of her mother's hand and moved back for a better look at those words on the sign. She knew what they said, but wondered, for the first time, how so few letters could possibly describe the great finca. "Papa says it means the biggest and the very best. Is that true?"

"I doubt it," Dolores said, but the girl could see her mother didn't know. Both of them spoke passable Spanish, but the meaning of some words remained unclear. "I think it comes from the Bible. Something about the Christian God. Come on, Aura, let's start walking, the truck can pick us up along the way."

But today there was no truck, which meant a five-kilometer uphill walk in the late afternoon heat. Aura didn't mind. Though slick with sweat inside her heavy huipil, she hardly noticed the discomfort, forever amazed by the deep quiet, the feeling of space all around her. Much different from the constant noise and narrow crowded streets of San Antonio Palopó, where they'd lived her entire life before coming to this place. La Gloria was definitely better than that. But *The biggest? The best?* She knew her father sometimes said things which were not true, like promising to buy them a car, a refrigerator, and, for Aura, because she was his *Princess*, her very own peacock.

Still, about the finca, he could be right. Far up the mountain, on

115

both sides of the road, grew thick rows of coffee. Rows and rows of it beneath tall leafy trees. They'd already walked an hour, and it would take another to reach their house. First they would pass the dueño's hacienda. Aura thought about it as she plodded along: a two-story mansion, made of wood, its private vegetable garden growing food that she had never eaten. There was a barn full of fancy horses, and on the other side of the hill, beyond the workers' huts, a pasture of cows, goats and sheep. At the southern boundary flowed a year-round creek. Downstream from that was a pond with a fenced-off fishery. Her father had once taken her inside. He'd showed off the trout and tilapia trapped within its concrete walls. "Wealthy chalet owners," he said, "pay high prices for our fish. For our livestock too. Because La Gloria has the very highest quality of everything. Especially coffee. The finca is huge, Princess, with thousands of plants and millions of beans. So huge," he bragged, smiling and tickling her chin, "that the rest of the world looks small."

The sun was setting by the time Aura and Dolores arrived at their concrete-block house. Salvador, Aura's father, stood in the doorway. "Well," he said to her mother, "I see you have arrived."

Aura squinted at the odd formality of his language. Things he said often seemed like some sort of criticism. In this case, the girl heard a sharp recrimination for whatever mistake his wife had made that caused them to return home later than expected. Rather, that's how she felt. Her young mind could not quite make sense of his words. He simply sounded odd--on purpose--like he wanted to make trouble.

Salvador dreaded the *Banking Days*. Hated to be left behind. Of course he would rather go to town and get some relief from the endless work, who wouldn't? But it was his job, his accepted duty, to stay on the finca and make sure that nothing went wrong.

An Indian by birth, he was grateful to have been lifted from the peasant ranks by the dueño--a man known for his impatience with mediocrity. Salvador had to prove himself worthy. Señor Alvarez, he knew, assumed that the other workers, also indigenous, would agreeably follow orders from one of their own. A pity they didn't. The truth was, they resented Salvador's authority.

There were more than fifty peones under his charge. The poorest of poor Indians. They'd come from many different places, desperate for a job, and were expected to work hard for very little. *Their misfortune*, thought Salvador, but not his fault. Before the finca, he was sure, they'd had it much worse, many of them with no land, and no hope for a decent future. On some fincas, peones worked for nothing. Just to be fed. Just to stay alive. At La Gloria, however, they were paid every month, got huts to live in, and three meals each day at the communal kitchen.

And Sundays they could sleep as long as they wanted. Or, if they chose--which most of them did--could attend the early-morning evangelical gatherings in the dueño's barn, surrounded by his prized horses. Sometimes the stench was strong, though none of the true believers complained. Quite the opposite, they rejoiced at a chance to worship their Lord, cry away their sins, and pray for a better tomorrow. 'Without Sunday,' he'd heard one man say, 'I could not keep going.'

Even the Catholics attended. *Better this*, they must have thought, *than nothing*.

Salvador agreed, and approved of their faith. Let them have whatever God they needed to exist. It was none of his business. His sole concern was that they work hard and make no trouble, because Salvador had plans. He hoped to one day save enough money for a small finca of his own. Why not? Since childhood he'd been aware of his calling for greatness, had once actually considered being a preacher, but luckily realized in time that he did not believe in God. His desire to preach had been, more than anything else, an enchantment with words. . .the power of words. He believed in his natural ability to lead. He would learn to speak with maximum effect, same as the dueño, and because of his dedication he deserved having a nicer house and a much higher salary than the others. He'd earned his position of trust, no matter what they said behind his back.

On these accursed *Banking Days,* however, he did not feel so special. He hated having to eat in the communal kitchen, forced to hear the silly women cooks with their constant jabber--their soups too thin, their tortillas too thick. Such hardships, he reasoned, must sometimes be tolerated--proof of his character--but not for one damn minute more than necessary! This extra wait had put him in a terrible mood. He knew his wife would have some excuse for her tardiness, but never mind, he didn't care. Her job now was to make their supper. That was what he'd meant by 'I see you have arrived,' and he wondered why she stood there looking so confused. "*Ven*, Princessa!" he said, holding out his arms to Aura. Salvador spoke only Spanish to his children, knowing they would need to learn it.

Aura hugged him around the waist.

"*Hambre,*" he said to Dolores, who should have known he'd been waiting to eat.

She gave a paltry nod and walked to the woodpile.

"I'll do it, Mama."

It was their sixteen year old son, Raul, running through the long purple shadows. The boy filled his arms with dry sticks and carried them to the sheet metal lean-to where they did their cooking. There was a perfectly good kitchen inside the house, with a nice little stove, but Dolores liked to cook on the fire outside. Fine with Salvador because it meant less propane to buy, thus more money he could save to buy their own piece of land.

Raul lit the paper. Blew on the flame. He was well built, tall for an Indian, with big brown eyes and pitch-black hair. A scar across his left cheek marred an otherwise handsome face. He'd fallen trying to climb a boulder above their house in San Antonio when he was eight years old . . .a boulder he'd tried climbing before, many times. . .a boulder his father had warned him, over and over, to stay away from. Salvador had never hit the boy before that day. Nor had he since. And he hoped he never would again. He was not a violent man. He preferred to get his way by using reason. Unfortunately, he reasoned, with some people, like his son, it did not always work.

Raul glowed at the sight of Aura, dragging their father by the hand, running to tell what she'd experienced on her trip to Panajachel. Like Salvador, Raul had to always stay behind at the finca. Since turning sixteen he'd been a regular worker. He'd lived in his own bamboo hut and earned his own money. Just ten quetzales a month, but one day he would have enough to leave the finca for good. He thought about that every day. About El Norte. Right now, though, there was only Aura, and he listened closely, noticing her excitement when she mentioned the loud boy.

"Why?" Raul said. "What was he shouting at?"

"Maybe he was crazy," Salvador said.

"Or in love," said Raul, laughing. "I think he was shouting at you, Aura!"

Aura wrinkled up her face. Raul knew she adored him, and he tried to always say things that would make her laugh.

"No, silly," she said, "he was shouting about onions!"

"Yes, yes, very sly. He had to try and fool the others."

"Oh, Raul, stop," said Dolores.

"Look, look, the truth is in her eyes, Mama. That boy's trick did not fool Aura."

His sister screeched and charged him.

He fended off her soft fake blows. "Yes," he said, "you see, I'm right!"

"Enough," Salvador said. Having lost the hand of his daughter, he'd sat on one of the wooden stumps and now looked eager to change the subject. "How much coffee did you pick today?"

Ah, thought Raul, a chance for his father to be the boss. "Three pounds, sir."

"Always a head above anyone else," said the boss, winking at Dolores, apparently bragging about his son. But Raul heard the sarcasm in Salvador's voice. . .a way of putting him in his place for sometimes thinking he knew more than other people. Even more than his father!

Dolores stepped between them and handed her husband a stack of tortillas.

Salvador stood and said to Raul, "You must keep the others working hard. Señor López comes on Wednesday. He says everything must be harvested by the 15th. Are you listening to me, son?"

"Yes, sir."

"Good," said Salvador. "Well then, tell them."

On Wednesday it took Salvador all morning to build a small stage from the wooden crates and leftover lumber stored in the barn. It had occurred to him at breakfast. A wonderful idea, he thought, and hoped his initiative would be appreciated by Señor López, La Gloria's 'Manager of Operations.'

After lunch he herded the workers out into the yard and ordered them to sit in the dirt and wait. "It won't be long," he promised, aware of their discomfort in the glaring sunlight.

Señor López had said he would be there no later than 1P.M. It was 2:08 when the long black private car came roaring up the driveway. The tall gaunt man sat still in the back seat until his personal driver opened the door and helped him out. Then, with a sense of urgency to his step, he walked past Salvador without a single word for him or the slightest bit of wonder at the platform.

López mounted it and cleared his throat. The man looked worried. Perhaps because he knew that peones from other fincas were leaving to join the army, thinking it a better way to improve their lives. Stupid thinking, but even so, that must be why the manager had come.

"The dueño and I are confident that you will meet the final deadline," he said.

Salvador counted forty-five workers present--all but the eight who were too sick to get off their mats, the woman having a baby, and the three cooks.

"We believe you should be rewarded in advance," López said. "For dinner tonight there will be chicken and rice! And *atole!* Furthermore, we've decided on a special bonus. Anyone who wants to put in extra hours may collect the beans that have fallen from hillsides already harvested. Think of it, how lucky you'll be to make your own coffee with the best beans in Guatemala! Congratulations," he said, and nodded at the short applause. "And there will be other rewards in the future, I promise, if you keep up the good work!"

Señor López left the platform and made a big show of standing by the car's trunk while ten plucked chickens were carried off by the cooks. Then, securely tucked into his back seat, he gave a final wave, rolled up his window, and disappeared in a cloud of dust.

"You heard the man," said Salvador. "Back to work."

How glorious, thought Raul, as he trudged with the others up the eastern ridge. What a wonderful *reward* for us, what a *special bonus*, to put in *extra* time and work *extra* hard to save the fallen beans that none of us want instead of letting them rot, as usual, with the coming rains.

The boy was absolutely certain that no one was stupid enough to be fooled by such crap. Which got him thinking. All those fallen beans out there, if he wanted them, were his. He began harvesting the leftovers that evening, with a flashlight, after all day picking on the slopes, and he did the same every night thereafter, allowing little time for sleep. By April he'd collected ten pounds. By the end of the month, almost twenty.

On May the 3rd, harvest time over because of the coming rain, most of the workers were let go. All that remained was a skeleton crew, including Raul, there to prune the coffee bushes and burn the slash. Meanwhile, he kept collecting beans at night. By mid May, on a Tuesday, finally stopped by a torrential storm, he had twenty-four pounds.

Wednesday morning was clear and bright, but he'd been told that other storms were on their way. A good time to quit.

His idea was to sell the beans in San Lucas. Someone had told him of a vendor there who bought anything of value. He could hardly wait. Though the beans weren't dried, and not worth much, Raul hoped to get eight or more quetzales for the lot. Raul remembered that the vendor sold on weekends in Guate, which probably meant he left for the city on Friday. Which meant he would have to go tomorrow! He explained the situation to his father and asked for Thursday off.

"But tomorrow," Salvador said, "is not Sunday." Then he crossed himself. "The day of our Lord, Raul, is the only day we don't work."

"Please, father, I--"

"I am not your father in this, boy. I am your boss."

"I will work the next two Sundays without pay. Or whatever you want. Please, just tell me--"

"Wait," Salvador said, because it occurred to him that this was a perfect opportunity to pay the government fee, due once a year, to update his legal papers. His plan had been to go take care of it the following week, but then Señor Alvarez decided he'd be coming to ride his horses and inspect the property. "I tell you what," he said to Raul, "you can go on one condition."

"Yes, anything."

"You also go to San Antonio for me. Important business. You must get to the government office before it closes."

"That's no problem," Raul said. "I'll leave at dawn, sell my beans in San Lucas, and be in San Antonio by noon."

"Good," Salvador said, happy that his son could be of some use. Also that the boy would be grateful for this favor and might better acknowledge his father's authority. Salvador arranged for Pedro, one of the truck drivers, to take Raul as far as Godínez. He even helped his son load the costal of beans into the back of Pedro's truck. In the evening, he handed Raul an envelope. Inside, he said, was the signed government form, and the payment. "Make sure it gets there," he said.

Raul walked off, injured by the lack of trust. But there was nothing he could say, and until tomorrow nothing he could do. Soon though. . .very soon. . .his father would be impressed, would be thanking him, would be treating him with the respect he deserved.

123

El Norte

May 18, 1981

Raul sleeps very little that night, thinking about El Norte. He's been thinking about it ever since one of the workers showed him a magazine called *Sunset*. That's what made him certain the place exists. The old crumpled pages had photos of beautiful white people sitting inside their fancy chalets; or outside, under umbrellas, on patios full of flowers; or in bathing suits by deep blue swimming pools. They all looked happy, and rich. So rich that they'd never have to work. Raul imagines having his own truck, his own tools. He will be a great and famous gardener. Everyone will want him to work on their fincas--all of them bigger and better than La Gloria! He will build a two-story house, with bougainvillea climbing up its walls, and a white picket fence like in the magazine. His mother and Aura will each have a room of her own overlooking the pool.

    The next morning he waits for Enrique, the driver, to finish his breakfast. They leave at seven, are in Godínez by eight, and from there Raul catches a pickup to San Lucas. The vendor is in his stall at the far end of town. As expected, they haggle over the coffee beans. In the end, Raul gets his eight quetzales, plus a handful of tortillas that the vendor's wife gives him, she says, because he looks so hungry.

    He jumps on the next truck heading toward Godínez. At Agua Escondido he gets off, runs down the well-worn path to San Antonio, and arrives at noon, just in time for the government office to close its doors for lunch.

No problem, thinks Raul. He can wait. He walks to the lake and sits on one of the docks. It feels good to be finished with that sack of beans . . .good to have money in his pocket.

Clouds are thickening around the volcanoes and the Xocomil has started early. Off to his right, a pretty girl has spread her washed laundry out on the rocks to dry, and now, he sees, will wash herself. He loves how she pretends to be invisible, lifting her corte, soaping her legs. He watches her avoid his eyes, showing more and more. Suddenly bashful, the girl uses her skirt as a curtain and scrubs her private parts. Finished, she leans forward, cleans her face and neck, her armpits, then reaches up inside her huipil to cool her breasts. She wades back to shore, never once looking his way. *Oh yes, you know I'm watching, mija, and you need to see I'm not an easy catch.* Raul stands and walks back to the church. There is no rush, he can find her some other day. He's certain she's not going anywhere.

The boy lies down on one of the church steps, closes his eyes and thinks of her naked body beneath those clothes. The thought of that makes him happy too. And the sun on his face. When he has more money, and a better job, he could ask her to be his wife. He's noticed that girls are attracted to him. Married women too. They have their ways of saying so, like the vendor's wife with that handful of tortillas. On the finca they watch as he walks home from the mountain, his clothes dirty from work, his face covered with sweat. Maybe they like his scar, maybe that's it.

He thinks again of El Norte. Just the name of it in his mind feels warm and good, his thoughts of the place so familiar that it's hard to believe he's never been there. He laughs at how much he can miss a country he knows nothing about. When he does eventually go, it will feel as if he's *going back*--as if it is, and has always been, his home.

Something nudges his shoulder. He squints up into the sun at a group of men standing over him.

"Get up," one of them says. Another takes hold of his arm and pulls him to his feet.

"What's going on?" says Raul.

"You need to come with us."

Raul sees they are soldiers, ladinos wearing camouflage uniforms, camouflage hats, and polished black boots. The two on his right have rifles.

"What did I do?"

"Nothing," says the man holding his arm. He is much older than the others, with long deep lines carved down his cheeks. His face is serious. "You did nothing."

They walk to a big green truck with a brown canopy over it. The old soldier tells him to climb in. There are Indian boys packed onto two wooden benches. More sit crowded on the floor.

"You counted?" the old soldier says to the younger one.

"Yes, twenty-five."

"Enough. That's our number."

The two soldiers with guns shove Raul up against the other boys and climb in behind him. The old soldier closes the tailgate, then pulls down the canvas flap to stop anyone from seeing in or out.

No, thinks Raul, he has done nothing, but what does it matter? Soldiers do whatever they want, which is why Indians avoid them whenever possible. He remembers lots of talk at the finca about villages in the mountains being burned. Worthless rumors, he thought at the time. Now he wonders. Maybe what they said was right, that the government has begun arresting people just for being Indians.

The truck bounces down the cobblestone road. A boy across from Raul has started crying and the nearest soldier pokes him with the barrel of his rifle. The soldier has a red splotchy face, like a pig. He looks happy that the boy cannot stop. "Quiet!" he yells, then pokes him harder. "I said quiet!" The boy clamps his hands over his mouth. The pig-faced soldier smiles, settles the rifle back across his lap, and says, in Spanish, "Welcome to the army."

It's a long drive to wherever they're going, hot and humid inside the tarp-encased truck. The other boys are sweating too. Not a word passes between them. Raul sees that some are from Santa Catarina, some from Panajachel, some from Sololá. The rest wear traje he does not recognize.

The crying boy has slept most of the way, his head bouncing around with every bump. At times it falls to one side or the other, to the shoulder of a fellow captive, who pushes it away. The soldiers seem to like that, and after awhile it becomes like a silly game they're all playing: the two on either side of the boy scowl at his drooping head, push it away, and make the soldiers laugh. Sometimes the other Indian boys laugh too. Even Raul. He knows it's because of the soldiers. With their focus elsewhere, they might not bother him. He feels ashamed. A sharp curve comes and the crying boy falls forward. Those on the ground turn and shove him back. The boy jolts upright on the bench. His eyes flash open to smiles and laughter, stare for a few short seconds at nothing, then slowly close.

"Just like a baby," the pig-faced soldier says.

"Missing his mama's tit," says the other.

"I too," says the pig-face, "miss his mother's tit."

A few of the boys laugh. Raul looks down at his cramped legs. Pretending to rub them, he feels for the money. It is still in his pants' pocket, and the envelope too. He closes his eyes and tries to think. He needs to talk to someone with authority. His father, he'll say, is a very important man. An Indian, yes, but he works for Señor Alvarez at La Gloria, that will make a difference. Realizing their mistake, the soldiers will apologize. Well, if not apologize, at least give him a ride back to San Antonio. He can spend the night on the church steps, or down by the lake. Or maybe the pretty girl will take him to her house. She will be impressed with his bravery. Maybe he'll kiss her. In the morning, first thing, he will make his father's payment at the government office, then head for the finca.

Strange, how good it feels to think about going home. He imagines himself walking that steep twisty road to a place he thought he hated. The work conditions, yes, but he loves the tall trees, the grassy meadows, the flowing creek. . .and what a joy to see his house again, his mother standing in the doorway. Aura runs from the front stoop and wraps her arms around his neck.

Something hits him on the side of his head. His eyes shoot open and he looks around at the truckload of smiling faces. The pig-faced soldier has a pouty look on his face. He says to Raul, *"No mames, chico."* It's a common Spanish jibe that means *Stop sucking tit, little boy.* All the others know it, and know they'd better laugh. Except for the crying boy. Now awake, again he seems ready to cry.

Hours later the truck stops. The two soldiers poke with their rifles and order the boys into a line. A middle-aged man with a stiff green uniform--an officer, Raul supposes--is standing next to a pair or huge black boots with a huge fake army helmet sitting on top. It's a sculpture made of concrete, and much taller than the officer, who points to the metal sign on the wall behind and reads the Spanish words aloud: *"Welcome to*

Chimaltenango, where the people and the army say NO to communist subversion!"

The majority of these boys, the officer must know, do not understand Spanish. Should Raul let him know he does? Should he speak up now and make his complaint? No, not yet. Dizzy from the winding roads, he'd better wait until his head clears.

The officer walks up to a boy from Pana and says, again in Spanish, "Do you understand?"

When the boy shakes his head, the officer slaps his face.

"Not good enough," he says. "Spanish is our official language, son. You need to learn it."

The boy nods, and says in Spanish, "Yes, sir."

"Good. And the rest of you, how many know what I just said?"

Most of the boys raise their hands immediately. A few hesitate, not certain what they've been asked, then raise theirs too. The power of numbers, thinks Raul: the fear of not agreeing with whatever a soldier might say. To be safe, an Indian must pay close attention to what happens in this ladino world. And not complain. Otherwise, he might as well hide in his hut and starve.

"Who is hungry?" says the officer.

They raise their hands faster this time.

"Good," he says. "Very good. Because if you want food, or clothes, or a mat to sleep on, or anything else, you ask for it in Spanish. We speak no other language here. *Understand that?*"

They nod.

"Say it!"

"Yes, sir!"

"Good. So tell me, then, what is a communist?"

The boys glance sideways at each other.

"You," he says to the boy he slapped, "what is a communist?"

"Bad," says the boy.

"Yes," the officer says, giving him a pat on the shoulder. "That is one Spanish word you have to know. Bad. *Very bad.* Which is why we must fight them. To protect our country, right?"

"Right, sir."

"Yes, yes . .good," the officer says. "Now we can eat."

He climbs into the cab while the pig-faced soldier points his rifle toward the back of the truck. That one vague signal is all it takes. The Indian boys know exactly what to do.

The next stop is a large tin windowless building with many mats laid out on the floor. The boys are each given a blanket, *cobija*, then told to choose a mat, *petate*, that is not already taken.

At the mess hall, for them, supper consists of watery beans and cold tortillas. They get their portions and are told to sit at a bench away from the other benches. Because no one else is dressed in traje, the newcomers are easy to identify. They seem out on display and marked with a big stamp of disapproval. Raul is not hungry. . .feels sick. . .just wants to get out of there. He looks around for the old soldier, the one in charge when they picked him up in San Antonio, but he's not in the room. Or his pig-faced assistant either. Probably out looking for more Indian boys to take.

Raul can't wait any longer. He stands and walks to the nearest table of soldiers.

"No," one of them says, "you stay over there."

"I need to speak with the *jefe*," Raul says, not knowing the military term for *boss*.

An officer who's been standing by the door comes to see what's going on. Raul noticed him before, because he walks with a definite limp . . .like one leg is shorter than the other.

"Please, Corporal Belasco," says the soldier at the table, as if asking forgiveness, "he told me he wants to talk with the *jefe*."

"The *jefe*, yes, of course," the corporal says, and smiles, then slams his knee into Raul's stomach.

Doubled over by the blow, Raul retreats to where he was sitting before. No one helps him. Everyone in the mess hall is quiet, waiting to see what will happen next.

"Listen up!" shouts Corporal Belasco. He points at the boys in traje. "You do not talk unless an officer tells you to. You do nothing except what we tell you. Am I being clear?"

They all nod and mumble, "Yes."

"Sir!"

"Yes, sir!" they shout back.

Belasco walks to their table and stands next to the slumped Raul. "Clear enough, *Jefe?*"

"Yes, sir," he says, close to tears. He's never felt so helpless. So alone. He only wants to go home. Not to El Norte--*forget El Norte*--but to La Gloria, to his mother and his sister. His family.

After a week of filling in old outhouse shitholes, and digging others, Raul and his group are issued uniforms. His brown shirt is stained and frayed around the collar, his camouflage pants too short, his boots too tight. All of their traje is tossed onto a fire and burned. Raul is glad that he put his eight quetzales in the envelope, with the government money, and hid it under his sleeping mat.

"The test of a good soldier," Corporal Belasco says, "is to always have a clean uniform."

It's a test impossible to pass. Each day, having failed as expected, they must bend over and get kicked in the ass. The corporal makes sure that "Jefe" stays the dirtiest, and gets kicked the most.

One late afternoon, on his way back to the barracks, Raul looks out at the high chain-link fence that runs around the perimeter of the base. There are, as usual, a group of Indian women standing outside, peering in, and on this particular day, perhaps because of the fading light, he thinks he sees his mother. Though unable to stop and get a good look, Raul glances that way again, and again, trying to be sure. At last he realizes it isn't her. Hopeful thinking, that's all it is. And he misses Aura too. Misses her so much. The truth is, he even misses Salvador. Once he's back home, Raul promises himself, he will try hard to be a better son, to make his father proud.

"What," Belasco calls out from behind, "you want to leave us, *Jefe*? You want to run off with a bunch of old women? Think you could make it over that fence before I shoot you in the back?"

Raul says nothing, just keeps walking. How, after all these weeks, could he be so stupid? So what if Belasco is twenty meters away? What matters is, that bastard never stops watching, does not miss a thing, and will take any excuse to abuse him.

After dinner, as they wait to be dismissed, return to the barracks, Belasco walks up to their table with a big smile. "Well, *Jefe*," the bastard says, tossing Raul the emptied envelope, "maybe now, without distractions, you'll learn to appreciate where you are."

Each Sunday morning there is a church service, led by some local evangélical pastor. Indian soldiers are encouraged, though not required, to step up front and confess their former lives of sin. All they really have to do is learn the songs. The crying boy, Elicio, becomes the loudest singer. Also a regular confessor. Dry-eyed and matter of fact, he bemoans his filthy Indian ways, how he never knew God until he joined the army. "With the Good Lord's blessing and guidance," he declares one day, "I will give my life for the glory of Guatemala!"

Most nights, an old white-haired officer named Colonel Otero lectures them in the mess hall. He is a wide-bodied man with a thin face and a droopy eye. He also has a very soft voice, which makes clear that whoever wants to eat had better listen up. The subject of his lectures never varies. *EVIL*. They all need to learn about *EL MAL*, a world of constant *MALIGNO*.

Once, speaking of the "endangered motherland," Otero gets emotional, wiping away tears while praying they "find the strength to do what must be done!" He speaks of *communism* as a kind of alien germ that has infected Guatemala. "You Indians," he says, "because of your primitive nature, are most susceptible to this disease. You are here," he explains, "to be inoculated with truth. . .to learn about the obligations of civilized society. . .to fight against the sickness in your blood."

Right then, a ladino officer in the back starts coughing. The timing is so perfect that even the other officers cannot help laughing. Otero stiffens and everyone gets quiet, except for the man who cannot stop coughing. The colonel finally has him removed.

Every couple of weeks, more Indian boys are brought into the camp. They sit at the same far table--dressed in their traje, set apart from everyone else--and Belasco is sure to demean them. Since the new boys are last to get fed, someone will be singled out for lagging behind; or for requesting an extra tortilla; or for failing to eat all of his over-cooked beans; or eating them too fast; or not fast enough; whatever it takes to clarify that they are shameful Indians, not soldiers yet, and deserve no respect.

Every time it happens, Raul's hatred of Belasco burns red hot and he has to stop himself from doing something stupid.

In July they are broken into different groups, each a mix of Indians and poor ladino kids, each group led by one of the newly arrived combat officers. At last Raul is free of that bastard Belasco! It's as if there is hope again, and again he starts thinking about the fence. His new commander is a sergeant named Ortiz. The sergeant does not seem interested in abusing him, and Raul is determined it stays that way. He has learned well how to keep his mouth shut, speak only when necessary.

On their third day of advanced training, Ortiz takes him aside. It is the first time Raul has truly looked at the man, the sergeant now giving no other choice, staring him in the face. He is much older than Raul, perhaps in his mid thirties, with reddish hair and freckles, a wide thick nose, and a heavy flattened chin that brings to mind a hammer.

"Is it true you want to leave us?" Ortiz says. His voice is gentle, his eyes calm. If Raul did not know better, he might think the sergeant wanted to help.

"No, sir, I. . .I never--"

"Because I am a hunter," Ortiz says. "You should know that about me. And there is nothing I enjoy more than hunting down a traitor." His eyes stay calm, waiting for Raul to say something, which the boy senses had better be right.

"I understand," he says.

"Ah. . .well. . .we'll see," Ortiz says, reaching over and ruffling Raul's hair. "We'll see."

Mayazak Pabej *July 18, 1981*

This time, when he heard his mother crying, Jaime grabbed a shovel and charged into Manuel's hut. "I'll kill you!" he screamed. "Don't think I won't!"

"Careful, boy."

"No, you're the one who needs to be careful!"

His father lifted the blanket and pushed Consuelo off his mat.

"Get out of here," Manuel said. "Both of you."

Jaime had never seen his mother naked. Her breasts, yes, whenever she'd nursed the babies, but not like this, along with everything else. Not with that bushy hair between her legs. He turned away while she wrapped her waist in corte, pulled the huipil over her head, and left. He took a last quick glance at his father, who Jaime knew had not stopped staring at him.

The following day, Consuelo relayed Manuel's order that Jaime, alone, was responsible for the onions, which included selling them in Sololá. That was no problem. At the chalet, though harder to stay out of Manuel's way, Grampa Héctor found plenty of work that kept him distant from his father.

Jaime was a favorite of his grampa, who had taught the boy everything he knew about flowers. They spent lots of time together in the various gardens, caring for the plants. Jaime had learned their names and what they needed in order to flourish. His grampa trusted him to make decisions on what should go where. "You are a born gardener," Héctor said. "That is what you are meant to be."

Jaime agreed. Yes, a gardener. In spite of the ongoing tension with his father, he was happy.

One morning in August, as another storm threatened, Jaime spotted Manuel kicking at the ornamental palm tree he'd planted the day before-- a tree the boy had been nurturing in the greenhouse for many weeks. It was not the first time he'd found a broken plant. Now he knew why.

"What are you doing?" Jaime said.

Manuel laughed. "This thing is stupid. It doesn't belong here."

"Get away!" the boy screamed, and tried to get between his father and the tree.

Manuel tackled him to the ground. They slid down the embankment into the creek, and Jaime somehow ended up on top. He plunged his father's head underwater and held it down.

"Stop!"

It was Héctor, standing on the opposite bank. Jaime let go and stood up. Manuel sloshed his way out of the water, gasping for air.

The boy walked off, satisfied that his father could never, ever, frighten him again.

The next day, Héctor took his grandson aside. "I will not ask what happened between you two. That's none of my business."

"All right."

"But he is your father, Jaime. No matter what it was, you need to apologize."

"No, sir."

"What?"

"I will never apologize, Grampa. Not to him."

"Then you. . .well. . .you need to go. I cannot have the two of you fighting, you understand?"

"Yes, sir," said Jaime. He saw from the baffled look on his grandfather's face that some better explanation was needed. Instead, he dropped the shovel and walked away.

After another week of silent, tense days around the house, Consuelo woke Jaime in the middle of the night. She'd just returned from Manuel's hut. Her plan had been to stay calm, to keep this just between them, but she could not stop the tears, the sobs, and all the other children woke up too. She hated letting them see her like this, but there was no other choice.

Jaime sat up and clenched his fists. "He hit you?"

"No," she said, wiping the tears from her eyes, trying to show with an emotionless face that he need not worry about her.

"What then? Mama?"

Though Manuel was snoring loud, still she spoke in whispers. "He is a hateful man, Jaime. I'm afraid. . .afraid of what he's going to do."

"Nothing," Jaime whispered back. "He's a coward, Mama. He's scared of me now. One thing is for sure, he won't dare hit you anymore."

"No, he won't," she said. She lied. She wouldn't tell him what had happened a few days ago while he and Felipe were away. Perhaps fearing Jaime, Manuel had warned the girls to keep their mouths shut. If he and his wife were fighting, he'd said, it was no one else's business. To prove it, and make sure they understood, he'd slapped the back of Consuelo's head. Just because he could. And of course he would keep hitting her, Jaime was foolish to think it would ever stop.

But the scariest thing was the brute's constant silence. Even in the mornings, while Jaime was off watering the onions, Manuel stayed quiet, as if any kind of talk might somehow give away his planned revenge. She knew her husband well. Knew how he thought. He would make Jaime suffer for insulting his dignity, for embarrassing him in front of Héctor, she was certain of it.

"Your father cannot be trusted, son. I want you to go away. Somewhere safe."

"Where?"

"Grampa Héctor came to speak with me the other day. He told me about a large finca up by Las Cruces where you can get work. It's called La Gloria, owned by a rich ladino, a man respected by the government and known to protect his workers. It's not so far away."

"If I go, he'll hit you."

"We won't let him," said Felipe, who'd been listening from his mat.

"We won't," said little Adriana, and Flor chimed in, "We won't, we won't."

"Shhh!" Consuelo said, and everyone held their breath until Manuel's snoring could be heard.

Felipe knelt next to Jaime and whispered, "Mama is right. We want you to be safe."

"Listen," said Jaime, grabbing him by the shirt and pulling his face close. "If I go," he said, "it's up to you, you understand?"

"Yes," Felipe cried out, "I know."

Jaime let go. Then tried to smooth his brother's shirt. "I'm sorry," he said.

Consuelo leaned over and kissed Jaime's head. "It's not your fault, son. None of this is your fault." There was another baby coming, maybe that's why she was so emotional, but crying would not help. She had to stay strong, had to convince Jaime he must leave. She got up, went to the counter with his satchel, and packed it with tortillas. A first rooster crowed, there wasn't much time. She sat him down and quickly went over Héctor's instructions. "Remember," she said, "you must stay away from the roads."

The boy nodded, but Consuelo could see it was all happening too fast, he wasn't ready. She hugged him close. Felipe rubbed his back. The little girls sobbed and held on tight to both his legs.

"Enough," Consuelo said, pulling them away.

Jaime grabbed his satchel and went for the door.

As he opened it, taking one final look, Consuelo forced a smile through her sudden tears and whispered, "Mayazak pabej."

New Soldiers

August 13, 1981

Three months after Raul's capture, another group of Indian boys arrived, many of them, as usual, looking beaten, hungry, eyes to the ground like common dogs. Raul could see they were shamed by their shabby condition, were trying to not draw notice. But one boy stood out, and Raul felt immediately drawn to him. Last in line, shortest of the group, his traje was caked with mud, his throat covered with layers of white gauze. Blood was soaking through the bandage.

Soon as they got to their table, Corporal Belasco limped over to stand behind the injured boy.

"Well," he said. That was the signal for everyone to be quiet and witness the coming punishment. "What do you have to say for yourself, Jaime? Your name is Jaime, right?"

The boy said, "Yes," and then, apparently unable to turn his head, tried to turn his body.

Belasco jammed his knee into the boy's back and he stiffened with pain.

"Did I tell you to move, Jaime? Do you think you can move whenever you want?"

"No, sir."

Belasco addressed his audience: "I am pointing Jaime out because he worries me. Because he may never be one of us. Seeing our soldiers, I am told, he tried to run. *A coward? A traitor?* Well, for his sake I hope not, but it's true that some Indians are unable to rise above their race, men, so all of you must keep an eye on him. Another false move and he's dead." Belasco then limped back to his post by the door. "Good," he said. "Enjoy your dinner."

The room returned to its normal noisy clatter of spoons digging for the few actual beans submerged in the brackish broth. Raul was sitting with his own group, gathered around Sergeant Ortiz. As they'd learned (from Ortiz, because he'd wanted to impress them), he was once a Kaibil. Or, rather, had gone through the famously rigorous training to become one. Neither Raul, nor anyone else, had asked why the sergeant was no longer a member of the elite fighting unit. It was wiser to ask things that gave him a chance to brag.

Earlier today, Ortiz had provided them with new Israeli rifles and demonstrated the correct way to skewer a canvas dummy with a bayonet.

"Best under the sternum," he said, glancing at Raul. "Or directly to the heart. If stabbing from behind the enemy, aim below the ribs, on the left side of the spinal column, toward the kidney. For maximum damage, you jerk the rifle butt up, ripping the blade down through the body. Then, *snap*, like breaking a chicken's neck, you yank it to the side."

After the instruction, Ortiz gave each member of the group his own bottle of Coca-Cola. He gathered them into circle to drink their sodas and hear whatever it was he had to say. "Any questions?" he said. Concerning the new Galil rifles, he meant, but did not seem to mind when his men wanted to know more about him.

"Is it true," said the crying boy, Elicio, "that Kaibiles never sleep?"

Everyone laughed, including Ortiz. Then his face turned serious. "We are trained not to need it," he said. "A Kaibil learns to fight no matter what. Sometimes in war there is no sleep. Sometimes no food or water."

"What was the hardest part of the training?" said Miguel.

Miguel, Raul thought, was the boy most likely to be a good killer. Perhaps a Kaibil himself. The sergeant had anointed him 'Our *sharpest* sharp-shooter!' after their first round on the rifle range. He also got a pat on the back for his excellent stabbing and yanking. His question, it seemed, was aimed at setting himself a challenge.

"Oh, we had to do lots of difficult things," Ortiz said. "On the first day, our commander bit off and ate the head of a live chicken. Said we'd all have to do it."

Right, thought Raul, *and you probably swallowed snakes and live scorpions!*

"You did that?" said Pablo, a quiet boy from somewhere near the coast.

"I did. It's easier than it sounds. The hardest thing," Ortiz said, "was giving up my dog. A warrior's greatest test, men, is battling with his heart."

"Tell us," said Pablo, who said it in a way that made clear how much he missed his dog too.

"Well, we were each given a puppy at the beginning of our training. To clean up after. To keep out of trouble. A puppy can be a lot of trouble, you know." He smiled at their serious faces. "I'm joking," he said, and that got them smiling. "I named mine *Chucho*."

Everyone laughed.

"Not very original, I know. I didn't care. To me it was just another thing I had to do. The problem was, I started liking the mutt. I would wake up each morning with him laying on my bunk, staring at me, waiting for me to open my eyes. He'd lick my face. He'd follow me everywhere. I figured I wouldn't have the dog long, so enjoyed him while I could. I was happy when we were ordered to train them. It would be a lesson, our commander said, primarily for us, because if we could not train a dog we could not be properly trained ourselves. And it was fun! I loved it! My Chucho, he quickly learned to sit. . . to come. . .to walk by my side and never run off. He made me proud. Made me happy. And soft. I'd never had a dog, you see, and never imagined it would be so hard to lose him." His eyes began to glaze over. Everyone saw it. *Oh yes*, thought

Raul, *this part is true*. "When they were six month's old" said Ortiz, "the commander ordered us to kill them."

"Dios mío!" cried Pablo.

"Yes," Ortiz said to him, "that's how I felt. I didn't want to believe it. My mind tried to make me believe that Chucho would be an exception. Learning the truth was part of the training."

"You killed him?" said Elicio.

"I did. I killed him and cooked him too. And ate him."

All of them, even the steely Miguel, stared at the sergeant, like at someone from another planet.

"A good soldier must conquer the heart," Ortiz said. "If we fail, evil finds ways to turn it against us. What if my dog had gotten rabies? Would I be able to get past my love, my heart, and kill him before he attacked an innocent child? Or what if your brother becomes a communist? Or if you come to a hut in a village somewhere and a mother cries, begs for your mercy--the whole time protecting a son who waits, behind her door, for a chance to kill you? EL MALISIMO, you see, works against our hearts! In war, we will go to places where people are changed. Changed forever. Revolutionaries, they call themselves. *Communists*. Servants of the Devil is what they are, who will lie to your face, tell you anything you want to hear. You must not let your hearts be fooled, men. There is no saving a tainted soul. You may feel sorry for them and want to forgive their traitorous acts--that's what the Devil wants you to feel. That's how he tricks you!"

During the weeks that followed, Raul noticed everyone avoiding Jaime. He wanted to help the kid, but knew that if he tried it would only make things worse. One night, when Belasco was out of the mess hall, he went up to Jaime in the food-line and whispered exactly that.

"Thank you," Jaime whispered back.

"That's all I can say," said Raul, and walked back to his table, feeling that already they were friends.

In November the Chimaltenango troops were transferred to a base in Santa Cruz del Quiché. The move came with a sense of urgency. Only a few of the trainers, like Belasco, stayed behind. The newer recruits also went, though they lacked sufficient training.

Raul made sure to get his mat next to Jaime's, and before long their friendship was strong. Though he did not say it, Raul felt a need to protect the smaller, less confident boy. As it turned out, however, there seemed nothing to protect him from. For months, led by Ortiz, their squadron patrolled the quiet hills, each of the soldiers tending to be silent, focused on his own thoughts.

Raul kept wondering about the sergeant. Most of the others were in awe of him, actively vying for his respect. That, of course, was what Ortiz wanted--what he'd intentionally made happen--what he seemed to need. But why?

This morning, at breakfast, Raul watched the sergeant's face, all aglow because finally they'd received the order he'd been waiting for. . .to go where there was fighting. They would leave in two days and the sergeant could hardly wait. Joking with Miguel and Elicio, there was that same fragile quivering in his voice as when he'd told them about his dog. It was a strange sound--a kind of tremor beneath each and every word. Whatever it was, Raul didn't trust it: an echo of something not being said . . .an ugly lie trying to stay hidden.

The sergeant's eyes went dull as he returned to gobbling his beans.

Then, all of a sudden, as if bursting through a door in his mind, Raul saw the secret, saw the lie.

Really? Could it possibly be so simple?

Yes, of course. It was not what Ortiz did, Raul realized, but what he didn't do. . .what he still needed to do in order to prove himself. Had he eaten the head of a chicken? Probably. Would he enjoy shoving a bayonet into someone he thought an enemy? Definitely. But could he kill and cook and eat his beloved Chucho? *No.* That's what sounded so wrong the second Ortiz had said it. It was a statement of policy. . .of what was *supposed to happen*. All around his words, though--in the tightness of his throat, his quivering voice, his sorrowful eyes--the truth demanded to be told. No, he could not do that to his pet dog. That's what *did not happen*, and what he cannot bear to confess. That's what had stopped him from becoming a Kaibil, Raul felt certain of it, and he felt certain, as well, of what it meant.

The dog was no doubt eaten in front of its master. What, then, had the disgraced warrior saved? Nothing. He'd lost his dignity in saving nothing. That's the point. A huge mistake, and Ortiz must know it. He was here, now, to convince everyone, and especially himself, how ruthless a soldier must be. He had suffered greatly to understand what mattered, had learned his lesson well. If ever given another Chucho, Raul knew, he would not hesitate to eat him.

Mothers

November 4, 1981

Three months had passed before Consuelo decided she must go look for Jaime. She left early one morning--after Manuel and Felipe went to the chalet--first dropping the girls off with Rosa, then finding her way, via two pickup trucks and a bus, to the great arched sign of La Gloria.

Consuelo walked the final two hours up the steep twisting road. It had been warm when she started off, but now a cool Xocomil was blowing, the air rich with scents of rotted leaves, decomposing wood, and traces of smoke from some unseen fire. Tips of the tallest trees hid in a dense white mist. Dark gray clouds stacked around the mountain rims, promising to bring more rain.

Consuelo stopped often. With a new baby coming soon, she had no choice.

Finally she saw a hut. A worker, stationed there, told her how to find the crew chief's house.

Dolores was sweeping out front when the pregnant woman, panting and disheveled, came into the yard. Seeing her Santa Catarina huipil, Dolores said in Kaqchikel, "Can I help you?"

"My name is Consuelo, I, I am looking for--" But she had to stop and catch her breath.

Dolores took the distraught woman's elbow and sat her down on the stoop. "Wait," she said, and went into the house for a glass of water.

Consuelo drank it down, nodded her thanks and said, "I need to find a man named Salvador."

"I am his wife."

"Then you know my son, Jaime."

"Jaime? No, I don't think so."

"He came here to work two months ago."

"Well then," Dolores said, "my husband will know him. It's nearly lunchtime, he won't be long." Another helpless mother, she thought. A pair of helpless mothers worried about their sons. After re-filling Consuelo's glass she went out back to check the laundry. She folded what was ready, flipped the still damp pieces in hope of a bit more sun, and came around the front of the house.

Consuelo was gone.

Dolores put the dry clothes on the kitchen table, then went looking for the strange woman. The workers in the barn had seen her, yes, and told her they did not know where Salvador was. The cooks in the communal kitchen had said the same.

Walking home, Dolores saw her sitting on the stoop.

"I know I should have waited," Consuelo said. "I'm sorry, I don't have much time."

"When did you last see your son?"

"The day he came here, three months ago."

Wait, thought Dolores, suddenly confused. Yes, he may have come, many did, but three months ago, in the middle of the rainy season, there was little chance of finding work. He was probably sent back home. Less than a day's walk. It made no sense. "He came from Santa Catarina?"

"Yes."

"Please," Dolores said, "come with me."

She felt trapped by the fear in this woman's eyes. It made Dolores scared too. To escape that fear she'd closed herself off since Raul's disappearance, her doors locked and bolted, her back to the outside world. But why had Consuelo come? To bring Raul back into her mind? *Yes, all right, both of our boys might still be found. It is possible.* Is that what she now felt afraid of? Hope? No, she could not let herself believe it. She didn't know how, but maybe, if she could find this other boy, it might lead to her Raul?

She took hold of Consuelo's hand and gave a tender squeeze. They walked together, side by side, up the hill, past the dueño's house, past the barn and the corral and down the narrow path to the orchard. As they moved through the high wet grasses, Dolores listened for orders being given. Hearing the familiar noise, she went toward it. A few minutes later they found him. A worker was in a tree above, pruning, while Salvador told him exactly where, exactly how.

"Now, see, you go to the next split down," he said, his voice gentle yet full of authority. The worker stopped and stared when he saw the two women approaching. Salvador also stared.

"This woman," Dolores said, "is looking for her son."

"Now?" said Salvador.

"Please," said Consuelo, "my boy came from Santa Catarina, he--"

"I am not finished here. You will have to wait."

"He came three months ago," Dolores said. "Maybe you could--"

"Take a break," Salvador said to the worker. The man smiled and dropped down from the tree. "All right," Salvador said, "what?"

"My son," said Consuelo. "I am looking for my son."

"Yes, I understand. And you think he came here."

"To La Gloria, yes, I know it. His name is Jaime. Jaime Xucul."

"Well, I'm sorry, he never arrived."

Consuelo's face went blank, her dark eyes pooled with tears.

Dolores said, "Are you sure, Salvador? Maybe he--"

"Yes," he said. "There is no Jaime on the finca. I am sure."

Consuelo collapsed into Dolores's arms and started sobbing.

"Ay," Salvador said, staring at Dolores. "Lorenzo!" he shouted, and the worker, who'd been sitting off to the side, jumped to his feet. "So, if you don't mind, we have work to do."

"I understand," Dolores said, patting Consuelo's shoulder. "My son is also missing."

Salvador shook his head. "Please woman, not now. Not again."

"Some say the government took them," Consuelo sobbed. "To be soldiers."

Salvador droned, "Yes, yes, a mother's dream. . .good excuses for your lying sons."

"You don't know," Dolores answered back.

"I know Raul stole my money. That is what I know."

Dolores said, "Let's go, Consuelo, this is no help."

"No," Salvador said as they turned to leave, "no help at all!"

Back at the house, Dolores made coffee. She felt better now with someone she could talk to. They each drank two cups and convinced themselves there was hope. Neither of their sons would disappear without a reason. They were good boys; they would have stayed in contact. Yes, their mothers decided, it must have been the army who took them against their will. Though a horrible thing, it was either that or the unthinkable, which neither would dare to mention.

Both were drying their tears when Aura came home from San Andrés. The dueña of La Gloria, a middle-aged ladina named Juana, had kindly insisted on paying for the girl to attend school. Juana made sure that the truck driver, Enrique, took her there each morning on his way to a delivery in Panajachel. In the afternoon Aura took the bus home, and she usually walked the finca road by herself. Today, though, Enrique must have been on his way back.

He parked his truck across from their front door and the girl got out.

Dolores smiled and waved at Aura. "Hi sweetheart!" But her daughter, as usual, was not so friendly in return, giving Dolores a tepid hug and looking at Consuelo with what seemed like suspicion. Ever since Raul's disappearance, the girl had been sensitive to changes of any kind. "Aura," said Dolores, "this is my friend, Consuelo."

Consuelo shook the girl's hand. "I am honored," she said.

Aura said nothing, and Dolores began to worry. She was afraid that Salvador might show up any minute and cause trouble, or that Consuelo might say something to make Aura fret more than usual about her brother. "Enrique!" she called to the truck driver, who was walking away.

"Yes, Ma'am?"

"I need you to drive my friend to the main road."

"Where is Salvador?"

"He's the one who told me. He's off in the orchard and cannot come himself."

"Well," said Enrique, "all right. . .soon as I--"

"No, please, now," Dolores said. She turned to Consuelo. "How can I find you?"

"At the Pana Sunday market. I sell onions next to the flower woman."

"Good combination!" joked Dolores, her hands trembling. "Enrique, take her to Las Cruces."

"Las Cruces?"

It was the end of a very long day and she knew he did not want to take that extra twenty minutes. She had to stay strong. "Salvador would not want our pregnant friend caught out in the rain."

"Fine," said Enrique, and turned toward the truck.

"Go," Dolores whispered to Consuelo.

"But what will we do?"

"You, nothing. You need to get ready for a baby, and take care of your other children. Don't worry, Consuelo, I'll come tell you what I find."

"Bless you," said Consuelo. She took hold of Dolores's hand and bent to kiss it.

"You know," Dolores said, pulling her hand away, "perhaps being mothers is not always such a blessing." Dolores sensed Aura's eyes on her, but could no longer hide how she felt.

"Oh. . .yes. . .it is a blessing," Consuelo said, wiping away tears. "It truly is. We have to remember that, Dolores. That more than anything."

"Now?" Enrique said, waiting by the truck.

"Yes, yes, now," Dolores said, and gently nudged Consuelo toward him. Aura ran off, away from her mother, as if knowing that she must. Again, Dolores was alone.

Consuelo smiled as the big truck rumbled down the steep dirt road. The sun had come out. Wet leaves glistened on the trees. She'd never before sat in the front with a driver, but that wasn't what made her happy. For so long she'd been missing Jaime. Now she felt him close.

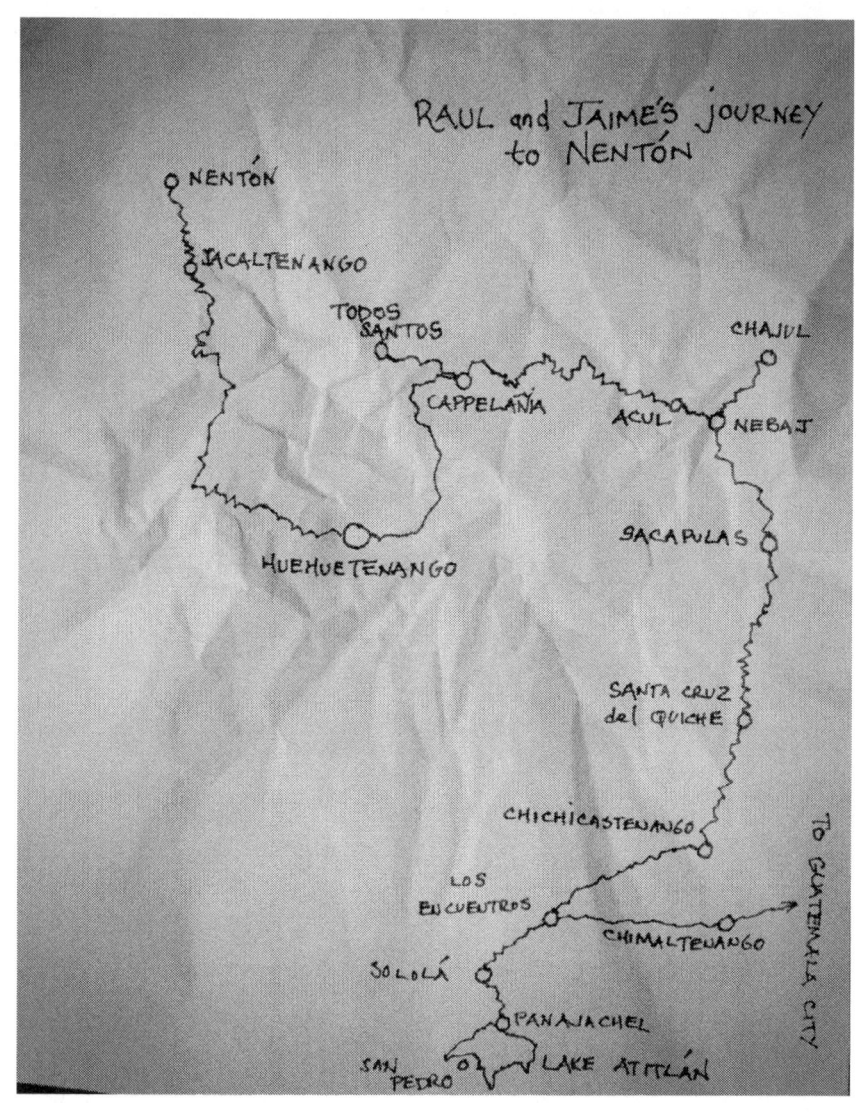

Raul and Jaime's Journey to Nentón

BOOK TWO

Days of the Dead

"Goddamn, well I declare, have you seen the like?
 Their walls are built of cannonballs,
 Their motto is don't tread on me.

Come hear Uncle John's band, playing by the tide.
 Come with me, or go alone,
 He's come to take his children home."

(Jerry Garcia and the Grateful Dead)

Corn

Salina, Kansas, 1960

Jacob, from an early age, hated corn: the long seasons of planting and maintenance and harvest; town boys off to play sports after school as he hurried back to the farm. He had a similar aversion to religion, his weekends filled with mandatory duty to church as well as chores. The only reprieve came Saturday night, for a single wonderful hour, when he was allowed to watch *Bonanza*. His parents permitted little other television in the house. That included the news (an attempt to 'subvert their Christian values'. . .'distract them from what mattered'. . .'poison their minds' with 'modern ideas' they could not, would not, trust). They had bought the TV in order to watch Billy Graham and Oral Roberts. Necessary viewing. Every Sunday it came in strong doses, spooned to Jacob against his will like castor oil.

On the Sunday morning of October 31st, at age ten, Jacob would first contemplate his death. He and his father were watching one of Graham's crusades. The holy man stood inside a huge white tent stuffed with starving souls.

"Sit still, Jacob, and listen."

"Yes, sir."

"You heard what the reverend said there, son? About the slippery aspect of sin?"

"I did, sir, yes."

"Bread's ready!" called his mother from the kitchen. "Anybody hungry?"

"Please, Melie, later!" his father called back. "It can wait 'til the commercial."

This came after the earlier Baptist church meeting and two hours of Bible study. Anything the boy might learn at public school, according to his parents, paled by comparison. By the time he'd turned eight, Jacob was required to have an intimate familiarity with his father's favorite books: Genesis, because it tells the beginning; Exodus, because it lists the commandments; Luke, because it best explains the gospel; and Romans, because it offers the promise of salvation and the blessings of grace. Jacob, fearing his father's tests, spent much more time studying the large leathered tome than he would have wished. For show, he made a point of reviewing it before doing his regular homework. A practice lauded by his parents. The boy knew that their praise was misguided, that they interpreted the sour look on his face as devotional contemplation.

At the commercial, his father went to the kitchen for bread and coffee, then got waylaid by a neighbor who had come to borrow tools. His mother went outside to chat with the man's wife, leaving Jacob alone in the house for a good five minutes. It was assumed he would keep watching Billy Graham. Instead, he flipped through the channels and happened upon a bleach-white skull, with big glossy eyes, staring straight at him. Jacob's hand stayed frozen to the dial. The skull had long black hair, and a crown of peacock feathers. It was a female skull, the rims above her eye sockets sprouting curly lashes, her cheekbones tinted rouge. Because tonight was Halloween, Jacob thought it must be a mask. While his parents did not approve of the custom, or bother to acknowledge it, he knew what he was missing. Kids might wear their costumes to school, or share some of the candy they'd collected by pretending to scare their neighbors. It was a dress-up game, a chance to make believe you were someone different, like Superman or Annie Oakley or Mickey Mouse. Witches and goblins and ghosts were also permitted, but never something like this. No parent he knew of would ever approve of this. This came from somewhere else, somewhere he should probably not know about.

When what he thought was a mask winked and moved backward, Jacob gasped. It had a whole skeleton attached. He saw space between the bones. No, this was no costume. The bones rattled around in the air like a bunch of crazy sticks. The skeleton's gangly right hand held up a burning candle as she swiveled his way, lashes fluttering, her deep dark sockets pulling him in. Then she spoke in a language he did not understand.

"Feliz Dia De Los Muertos!" she whispered in a husky voice.

"What the devil is that?" his father said from the kitchen.

"I don't know."

His father came for a closer look, no doubt baffled by why Reverend Billy would include such a thing in his sermon. Now there were a group of skeletons. Each wore a similar crown. They started dancing in a circle, bones clattering, strings dangling from above, and it was clear that they were puppets. Jacob let out a sigh of relief. One of the puppet skeletons pounded on a drum as it danced. Another played a flute.

"In ancient Mexico," said a deep male voice with a strong Spanish accent, "over a thousand years ago, there were--"

But his father had rushed forward and turned off the set. "Explain yourself," he said.

"I was looking for cartoons."

"That was no cartoon."

"No, sir."

His mother came into the room and saw her husband's angry face. "What happened?"

His father pointed him down the hall. "Go to your room, son. We'll discuss this later."

'Later' meant a short reprieve, a matter of minutes, until his parents had time to consider the appropriate response to Jacob's moral transgression. Waiting in his room, he thought of the skeletons. Could not get them out of his head. That's what was under his own skin, holding him together. Just a bunch of floppy bones. That's how he would someday look once worms were finished eating his flesh. That's what death would bring. He stretched out on his bed and closed his eyes and imagined himself in a box covered with dirt, a box that would eventually rot and let the worms in. *Wow.* But he'd be dead, so he wouldn't know it, right? Like in a dreamless sleep. Unbelievable, to not feel, not be aware of anything, because his spirit would be gone from his body, floating happily above, on its way to heaven. At least that's what he was supposed to believe. Good excuse for not thinking about worms.

There was a knock on his door. In came the parents.

His mother sat on the bed and held his hand. "Were you scared, Jacob?"

"A little. It was a mistake, Mom, I didn't mean to--"

"I know, honey. I only want to make sure you're not still frightened by. . .by whatever you--"

"No, really, I'm okay."

"You disobeyed me," his father said.

"I'm sorry, sir."

"More important, you turned away from the Lord. And," he said, snapping his fingers, "just like that the devil knew it. You saw how fast it happens. That's what the Reverend Billy was explaining when you turned him off. Did you like what it was you saw?"

"No."

"Because that is hell, son. That is *eternal damnation.* You got a good look at it, didn't you, and it was Satan who made you watch. He fooled you into it, boy, was trying to. . .trying to. . .trap you."

"I understand, father."

"Yes, all right, you understand. But will you remember?"

"I'll never do it again, I promise, I--"

"No, you won't. And you won't be leaving your room today either, or watching *Bonanza* until I say otherwise." Jacob knew he was meant to feel a punishing load of disappointment. "That should, I hope, be reminder enough." "Yes, sir."

"Think hard on it," said his father, and his mother rose to join him at the door. "Life is no cartoon, son. Do not be fooled by the tricks of this world." He was quoting Romans. And then came more Romans: "We know how, in all things, God works for those who love him, who have been called according to His purpose." As his father closed the door, he left behind a final note from Proverbs: "Trust in the Lord, son. Lean not on your own understanding."

Jacob did not mind a day alone in his room. There was a lot of thinking he needed to do.

The skull had scared him, sure, but now it made him think outside of himself. Life was way bigger than he'd ever considered. Death was coming, no way around that, but first there was life, mysterious beyond belief. . .life in Kansas, and in other places too. . .places usually unmentioned, like Mexico, Africa, Japan. . .a whole world of other people, other languages, other ways of thinking.

Too bad about *Bonanza*, though. It was hard to imagine his parents watching it without him. But they would. He knew they would. They also loved the show, and looked forward to it from week to week. Aside from the Lord, they only believed in wholesome frontier people like the Cartwrights, trusting in their general goodness and the moral instruction they provided.

Jacob, however, watched for his own reasons. For him, it was the land that mattered: the open range; the trees and creeks; the rolling hills of anything but corn.

It's summer now and he's running fast, away from the house and the sharp eye of his father. With the slightest blurring of his vision everything looks different, allowing him to pretend he's in a strange, exotic place--not Kansas --a place where unknown, unexpected things might happen. "Get 'em Fish! Get 'em!"

Fish is an old brownish Cocker Spaniel. Jacob's mother found the dog at the shelter for his twelfth birthday, and allowed him to name it in spite of his father's objections.

"Not the name for a dog," his father said.

"Is now," his mother answered.

"Get 'em boy!" screams Jacob, and Fish charges toward a big stellar jay. The bird seems not the tiniest bit intimidated. With an annoyed screech it flies off, leaving the dog stupefied, panting in its wake. Pitiful, thinks the boy, and just that fast he's back in Salina, thinking of Frank Renendorf. . .of Frank's Australian Shepard, Molly, who *can* catch birds. Jacob's seen it. Fish, though, never has a chance. It's his big floppy ears that keep getting in the way. The boy takes one in each hand and kisses the top of his head. "Poor Fish," he says. "Poor, poor Fish."

Besides Fish and *Bonanza,* Jacob feels lucky for their pond. Well, not a pond really, more of a long, wide puddle, but he likes it anyway, especially after sunset when the heat dies down and the frogs start croaking. Or on early summer mornings like today--his chores finished--before it gets too hot. He sees the surface gleaming beyond the tall brittle stalks. They run toward it. The dog, as usual, wins the race, splashing ahead while the boy squirms out of his clothes and wades in after him. Slimy grey mud squeezes between Jacob's toes. . .then up inside his butt crack as he flops down next to Fish, the thick copper water settling just below his chest. He looks at the empty sky's reflection and considers what they might do next. No hurry in that. There isn't much to do, after all, so he doesn't mind just staring at the water. Random thoughts flit like blind moths inside his head. Minnows nibble at his legs.

"Tell ya what," he says to Fish. "Whatd'ya say we call this Jacob And Fish's Place?" Yeah, sure, a perfect name, since there's nowhere else for cooling off, or thinking things through, or planning his future. "One day, bud, I'll be someplace completely different." He looks up, trying to imagine it. Stalks stand thick against the cornflower sky like a wall of yellow mountains. He sits still, breathing anise, his mouth watering for a taste of licorice. He watches a black-and-red dragonfly dance through the air. A couple of ravens come squawking down to the lone spindly cottonwood at the far edge, though it might have been a flock of parrots were there any decent trees. Or maybe flamingos! Or at least ducks, for godsakes, if the pond wasn't so darn shallow. Not enough water for real fish either, or for any actual swimming. He remembers his father saying how they would make a full size pond of it some day, full of bass and trout. But, same as any other dream, Jacob knows that's never going to happen, and it's been hard for him to hide his disappointment.

"Quit your sulking," his father said to him the other day. It was at sunset, the clouds blood red from a sweltering afternoon, his father's face thick with grimy sweat.

Jacob had made the mistake, again, of asking about the pond.

"You're not a child anymore, son. You know there's plenty of things to get done around here."

"Yes sir, I know."

"More important than a pond, you understand?"

"I understand."

"All things come as the Lord provides," his father said, and Jacob could hear a sermon on its way. First a touch of Genesis (always the best place to begin), followed by the trusty commandments (the whys and wherefores of every sanctioned rule), before getting around to Romans (the reward for good behavior), which did seem a logical place to end. Key words (*temptation, redemption, salvation*) were filtering through, but Jacob was not listening. More important right then was a pinkish line scratched across the crimson sky: the trail of an airplane off to some foreign place? He wondered what corn looked like from way up there? And what about him? Could he be seen at all?

But his wonder was interrupted by a hard whack to the head. His left cheek stung and his ear was ringing, the pain so sharp he could not stop the tears. Then his head was grabbed like a melon.

"You see what happens when you don't abide the Lord!" his father said. "I don't know where it is you go, boy, but this is where you'll always end up! You hear?"

Sure, Jacob thinks, his mind returning to the pond, his legs scissor-kicking the muddy water. Oh yeah, he hears. Has heard it all his life.

Yeah. . .yeah. . . .so what?

"So what!" he says to Fish, who whines and tries to lick his face. The boy pushes him away. Though not a selfish kid, Jacob is angry at nothing ever happening! Yes, his father's right, for now there's no way to change it. But that can't stop him from growing up, from making his dreams come true. "Sorry boy," he says. He reaches out and pulls the dog close. "You'll see," he says, petting Fish's head. "You'll see."

Jungles

Salina, Kansas, 1968

Jacob did grow up. The summer after he graduated from high school, a full year since Fish had been flattened to a bloody smear on the new Interstate, disappointment seemed to him a natural part of life, a feeling he should get used to. He expected this realization to terminate his endless daydreams. It didn't. And far worse were the dreams that came at night, when he fondled Gail's breasts and stroked the smooth soft flesh of her inner thighs. How deceptively wonderful they were. *How pitiful.* Try as those dreams might to scratch his itching misery, they could not bring his girlfriend back. She would never again be meeting him in the old granary building. Imagination had become an enemy. Dreams, which came no matter what, had to be forgotten, or at least dismissed, so he would not embarrass himself with senseless hope. He had to stop thinking about her and the things that might have happened. Like it or not, he had to be a man.

Jacob focused on Pastor Matthew's Sunday morning sermons, which covered the subject of desire and despair well enough (in a general, non-specific way) to explain his angst. About the rest, though, scripture could not help. It said nothing about his fascination with mountains and jungles, or his dreams of wildness and adventure in strange, faraway places.

That's what got him thinking about Vietnam: a strange and faraway place; a place of mountains and jungles; a place that must be full of wildness and adventure. It had changed from what President Johnson once called 'a political problem' into a full-blown war. Lots of kids were volunteering. And the war felt necessary to Jacob too--in his case, to escape the farm.

His mother cried, holding tight to his arm.

"Please, Mellie," his father said.

"It's okay, Mom, really, I'll be fine."

She let go and slapped Jacob across the face, her eyes burning into his.

"Don't be stupid!" she said. "You don't know! You couldn't possibly know!" Then she grabbed hold again, more fiercely than before, her fingernails gouging into his back.

When his father pulled her off, the crying got worse, coming now in great gasping sobs as she stared from deep dark sockets, same as that Day of the Dead skeleton he'd never forgotten.

"Please, Mom," Jacob said, trying not to cry himself. "Please."

"Mellie," his father said. He held her face into his shoulder and gave Jacob a quick nod. The boy saw it was an order for him to go, get away while he could. Also an acknowledgment. An approval. While uncomfortable with his wife's hysterics, his father looked proud.

Jacob's first letter included this: *Everyone calls me Jake now. My sergeant's idea. Sergeant Roberts. He's kind of old, and a lot shorter than me, but tough. Real tough. My uniform is too small in the arms and legs and he says I look like a scarecrow. He ordered me a new one but I haven't got it yet. He's an all right guy even if he makes us climb over logs and crawl in the mud. The idea is to get us filthy dirty so we have to clean our uniforms. Then he gets us filthy dirty again. No kidding, Dad. And Mom, Mom I swear, they sure don't know how to cook like you!*

He decided against telling the hardest stuff so as not to make his parents sad. The dumb-ass orders he had to follow were bad enough. Worse was the training of how to kill people. You had to stick your bayonet into a straw dummy, and to be a good soldier you had to get excited by it. . .or pretend. .had to make believe the dummies were enemy soldiers who you hated like the devil. "Fucking gooks!" the guys would yell. That was their name for the Vietcong: *Gooks*. It reminded Jake of Halloween, the way his friends dressed up as knights and pretended to hunt dragons, or goblins, or traitors to the king. Some of the soldiers acted like that, like spoiled little kids trying to impress each other with their toughness. It seemed that *they could hardly wait* to start killing gooks.

To his credit, Sergeant Roberts did not encourage such talk. He'd make guys do lots of pushups whenever he heard it. The thing was, these idiots loved to do pushups. The more the better. They took the punishment as proof of their courage and bragged behind the sergeant's back, saying they knew he secretly approved. Jake thought it was just more big talk. Sergeant Roberts had to be smarter than that.

"War is a terrible thing," the sergeant once said, and he seemed to mean it. He seemed a reasonable man. Not always, of course, because being a drill sergeant meant he had to enforce the dumb-ass rules, show his authority, keep things under control.

"What the fucking hell are you doing?" he'd holler at Jake on a regular basis. "Pull that finger out of your shit hole you sorry son-of-a-bitch!"

The sergeant's eyes would bulge out of their sockets when he hollered, veins throbbing in his neck and forehead. Jake understood it was for a good purpose. Basic training, he'd learned, was basically about making a soldier tough, which was the only way to keep him alive.

"I mean now soldier!" Roberts would shout in his face.

"Yes sir!" Jake would shout back.

In the actual jungle, Jake didn't feel so tough. It rained a lot more than he'd imagined. It was full of mountains, yes, but also biting bugs, poisonous snakes, and, someone told him, tigers.

And, for damn sure, lots and lots of gooks! Not the kind of strangeness Jake had hoped for.

He was afraid. They were all afraid. Even their commanding officer, a second-lieutenant named Bill Sanders, was afraid. Sanders wasn't much like Sergeant Roberts, who'd stayed behind, in Fort Benning, to train other boys how to be soldiers. In fact, Sanders was the opposite. For one thing, he was a young guy, in his mid twenties, who'd come to Vietnam straight from college. For another, he liked smoking dope. And liked others smoking it with him.

Jake remembered the night he first got stoned. It was the lieutenant's idea. They were bivouacking at the edge of a little creek when Sanders lit up a joint, took a toke, and passed it on. "Time," he said, "to get a few things straight." He blew out smoke while signaling for the joint to keep moving. "Truth is, quality dope was the only reason I made this trip."

That got everyone smiling. A funny guy, no shit. And they all laughed when Jake started coughing. All except Billy, who must have known he'd soon be coughing too.

Once everyone toked, Sanders said, "Okay, okay, now listen up. I'm warning you guys not to piss me off more than I already am. You need to know I'm not supposed to be here. I joined the ROTC because some asshole told me I'd land somewhere safe, be sitting at a desk sipping sake." He paused, shook his head, then gave it a good smack. "Swear to God, I don't know what went wrong. . .how the hell I end up here, in a jungle, with a bunch of fucking idiots!"

Though everyone was laughing, including Jake, he knew it wasn't funny. But he got good, like the others, at not showing it. Day after day they'd laugh whenever possible at the dumbest things--things so dumb that no one ever remembered afterward what they were. Or cared.

They'd laugh at that too, about how it didn't matter, and light another joint, and laugh that it was about to matter even less.

After awhile the jokes stopped working for Jake, and the fear got worse. He might have felt lucky, how when the fighting came he always made it through--other guys hit instead of him--but that, of course, was where the fear came from, that his time was coming.

He tried to let his mind go. He had a vague recollection of doing this as a small child, before he knew what real fear was. But now it seemed impossible. The closest he could get was remembering those days with Fish, sitting quiet in their pond, staring off into nowhere and thinking strange ideas--anything that might get his mind away from Kansas. *Yeah, asshole, right.* It didn't take long to realize that those were the very ideas that had gotten him here, trapped in this damn jungle.

Rattled and lost, he tried the opposite of letting go. He would find something, anything, to focus on. . .and would stay there, right there, holding on tight, not moving an inch, until he saw inside the thing itself . . .saw it as if nothing else existed. . .not even him. Sometimes it was beautiful, like a young girl smiling as they entered her village; or it might be plain, like an old man smoking a pipe by the side of the road; or ugly, like a big brown rat dragging an empty can of beans away from their garbage pile.

There was something about that rat. Something he could not let go of. Jake had been sitting on a small rise, with undigested beans churning in his belly. It was the final glimmer of another day, the bright orange sun at last setting beyond the nearby ridge, when he spotted it. The rat, perhaps hearing Jake's stomach growl, stopped, let go of the can, and looked at him. It was a few seconds, at most, yet time and space seemed to disappear. Jake focused on the rat's whiskers, which were catching what was left of the sun's afterglow. And the more they twitched the more Jake understood. It was like he had his own set of twitching whiskers, his own instinctual knowledge of the world at that precise moment. He knew the rat was not afraid of him. He could feel it. None of this came to Jake as thought, simply as truth. Then came a deeper truth, which surprised him, that the rat was *not afraid of anything*. Oh, sure, were Jake to make the slightest move, or perhaps even consider it, the rat would slip away into the high grasses. Not out of fear, but the instinct of survival. A natural reaction. An action that was different, completely different, than Jake's stalking sense of fear. As it was, the rat just sat there on its haunches looking curious--not the least bit concerned by any possible danger. Finally, he gave his head a tiny shake, rubbed his paws together, again took hold of the can and pulled it off the trail, down toward the gully below, out of sight.

The next morning, Jake sat with Little Billy on the edge of the trail, close to where the rat had disappeared. They were eating beans. . .again . . .again waiting to start their daily patrol. Jake threw his can into the gully. Easier for the rat. Little Billy, still not yet finished with his beans, did the same, as if Jake were in charge and had decided they should stop eating.

Ah, Little Billy. He'd been given that name to distinguish him from the other Billy, both of them from Arkansas. Though not any bigger, the other Billy was black. Jake figured that no one felt right about calling him Black Billy, so it was decided, as such things get decided in the army, that because Little Billy was a few months younger, it also made him smaller. Or some such shit. Anyway, good for him, Little Billy sucked it up. What other soldiers called him was the least of his problems.

"Hey, Jake."

"Yeah."

"See that nasty-ass gully down there."

"Yep."

"You ever wonder about places like that?"

"Nope."

"I mean places, like that, where no one goes."

"You mean overgrown marshy places full of ticks and leeches and maybe cobras?"

"Yeah, yeah, sure, but not just that, I mean other places too, like say some endless desert, you know, or way offshore, out in the waves on some empty ocean."

"What are you talking about, Billy?" Jake never called him Little Billy to his face, though sometimes, like now, the name did fit.

"Nah, nah, nothin' man, never mind. I'm just trippin', I guess. It's just that when I think about those kinds of places I always think of death."

"Really? Is this really something we want to talk about?"

"Sorry, but yeah, I guess I do." And then Jake saw just the tiniest bit of a Billy smile.

"OK, Billy, tell me why that is."

"Well, I guess because, far as I know, normal people avoid those kinds of places." The smile widened, but it wasn't any kind of happy smile. "Not like us, you follow? I mean who in his right mind goes off into the middle of fucking nowhere?"

"No one I know."

"That's what I'm sayin', man. Right?"

"Yeah," said Jake. "Right."

A few weeks after, as they patrolled yet another trail to fucking nowhere, the lieutenant heard on his walky-talky of a large Vietcong patrol somewhere close by. He gave his coordinates and waited for a response.

Then the thing went dead. With no backup, he decided it best that they hide out in the nearest swampy bog. They sweltered in the shadows for hours, ordered not to make a sound, up to their shoulders in a slimy grayish gunk that smelled like the dead bodies of the village they'd just come from. Checking each hut, his rifle raised and ready, Jake remembered the faces of a woman and a little girl, staring at him from beneath a pile of bamboo. It was like they were seeing the devil himself. They didn't want his help, that was plain, only that he go, *go away, go. . .*so he'd pretended not to see them. . .and left. . . but now could not get their eyes out of his head.

Aaron, the very youngest, started crying. He was mumbling something too. Jake didn't know what. Or care. It was fear, that's all. All of them knew that sound. Being too loud for safety, though, Lieutenant Sanders pulled the eight of them into a tight circle. Sanders and Aaron were in the middle, the others outside, holding on to each other like in a football huddle. Weird that Jake should think of football since he'd never once played it. But nothing really surprised him anymore.

"It's okay to be afraid," the lieutenant said. "Damn stupid not to be. Fear makes you pay attention, men. Fear is what might save your life."

Jake felt confused, but nodded agreement with the rest. Admitting the fear suddenly seemed a good idea. For the first time, Jake felt grateful for the lieutenant, how he'd found a way to bring them together. That, Jake knew, was the most important thing--that they believe the same. Even months later, after Sanders died, they kept believing. Even with the endless killing. Even with all the pot they smoked, trying to forget, they had to remember the good part of their fear. Had to keep believing. Believing was their only chance.

But by the spring of 1973--the war reaching its inglorious end like an unidentified body tossed into a rice paddy--no one was believing anymore. Something had changed, even in places like Salina, Kansas, where once boy-soldiers returned from Vietnam angry, disillusioned men.

Jake was one of them, out of the army now for two years--not counting his eight months in the military hospital. He was staying at his parent's house.

First thing, he tore down the poster of Jimmy Dean from his bedroom wall. Then grew his hair to a normal length, tossed his medals along with his high school books into the garbage, and burned his uniform. He read *Siddhartha*, *The Stranger*, and *Steppenwolf*. None of that helped either. Nothing made sense anymore, not even his anger. He had a hard time accepting that the war was over. But he tried. Tried his best to be normal. He was always polite to his parents. He took a job at a hardware store, and managed to stay a year before he had to quit. He met a girl who was very nice, and pretty, but would not stop asking what it felt like to be *there*, and if he'd *killed* anyone, and if he *really was* OK?

Then she wouldn't leave him alone when he stopped returning her calls.

One night, in a bar, he hit some longhaired guy for looking at him weird. *No*, he'd already told the guy, *I was not proud to be a soldier*. "But what really burns my ass," he said, "is how we get treated by fucking ingrate brats like you." That's when Jake got the snide little grin and decked the asshole. Then got kicked out of the bar. Yeah, well, fuck their condescending peace and love bullshit! Fuck them! Easy to be self-righteous when you're safe, letting others do the dirty work. It didn't matter what these assholes said, or didn't say. It was in their eyes. Jake felt blamed for things being different; blamed that he and other vets had brought some kind of evil spirit back home with them. And who knows,

170

maybe they had. Though impossible to define, Jake also sensed a difference, a mysterious and unsettling change, as if beneath the surface of those rice paddy graves the innocent dead had sprouted root tendrils winding all the way to America's heartland.

He watched a lot of television in his room, smoked a lot of joints, and, whenever possible, did nothing. Days went by, one after the other. Time passed, that's all. It passed.

One day he could not stop laughing at a magazine picture of John Wayne. The great actor's face was made up smooth as a baby's ass. He wore a ten-gallon cowboy hat. *Wow. Unbelievable.* Still laughing, he tore the picture into shreds. Jake's mother knocked, and kept knocking, until he turned up the Dylan to block her out.

Another day the door flew open. He was on his knees, crying, pounding his fists on the floor.

"What the hell!" his father hollered--so loud it made Jake think of Sergeant Roberts. Then their eyes met. The older man, like an embarrassed child, looked away. "It's disturbing your mother," he said, and gently shut the door behind him.

"You want macaroni and cheese?" his mother asked one night, trying to change Jake's steady diet of peanut butter and jelly sandwiches, of eating them alone in his room.

"No, thanks."

"How about my special meatloaf, Jacob, does that sound good?"

"No Mom, really, I'm not hungry."

"Is there anything on your mind, dear?"

"No."

"You sure, honey?"

"Yes, Mom, I'm sure, OK, I'm sure!"

"Maybe what you need," his father said, "is a change of attitude."

Jake shook his head. Said nothing. Went to his room and locked the door.

Attitude? Change of attitude? What the hell did the old man mean? Could a *change of attitude* alter what had happened, what was still happening, and might, if Jake could not come to terms with it, happen for the rest of his life? What he *needed* was to see things as they were. He needed to *change himself*, not his damn *attitude*. He needed to keep looking closer, stick his nose right down into the shit. So that's what he was doing. What he had to do.

Sure, the weed may have skewed his moods, but he believed his perceptions correct.

That same night, watching a *Bonanza* re-run, he saw himself trapped inside the unruly wild stallion who was trapped in a corral by Little Joe Cartwright. Little Joe, Jake's former idol, threw a noose around the proud animal's neck and wrestled him to the ground. While cowboys cheered, stomping their feet and waving their hats, Little Joe forced him to submit, shoving a fist of steel between his teeth, over and past his gagging tongue, smack against the rear of his mouth, to the point where it would, if he did not yield, choke him to death. The beast must be tamed for this high and mighty rich boy; must give Little Joe his ever-bridled assistance; must herd the equally abused cattle around an endless Cartwright estate; must chase after persons of undeniable evil; must sacrifice his life, if necessary, for the sake of his oppressor.

The next day, Jake announced to his parents that he'd stopped believing in religion. And *America*. And, for the most part, everything. He went on and on about lots of things that made no sense, that just kept people stuck and stupid, the list including television, school, and church.

His father sat there stiff, his fists clenched.

"It's just too much," Jake said, "I'm finished," and headed for his room.

"Well," he heard his mother joke, trying to calm her husband, "at least now he's talking." But Jake knew she had no idea what he was talking *about*. She came to his room, burst into tears, and in the end persuaded him--begged him--to speak with Pastor Matthew.

The following evening, sometime after supper, the good pastor arrived. He came to Jake's room and gave the wayward son's shoulder a meaningful squeeze. Jake listened with undivided attention to the wizened old man. The pastor, in his calm, gentle voice, urged Jake back to church, to faith, to the eternal blessings of Jesus Christ and God's infinite mercy.

At last, when it was his turn to speak, the young man said, "Sorry, sir, but I don't believe all that. God exists, I think, but not in any church." These were things he'd been thinking about, things he'd wanted to say for a long time. Then he thought of Joni Mitchell. *Ah*, he thought, *what the hell?* "Religion," he said, "for me, is like chopping down a forest and putting up a tree museum."

Heading out the door, Pastor Matthew repeated the sacrilege to Jake's father, who apologized, saw him off, then cornered his son in the kitchen.

Jake braced himself against the refrigerator. Expecting the predictable onslaught of scripture, he was shocked when his father grabbed him by the neck.

"Boy, I want you out of here."

"Please, Gerald," said his mother.

"No," his father said, letting Jake go and walking away. "Tomorrow, is that clear? You just plain don't belong!"

His mother smiled a sad smile. She ran her nervous fingers through Jake's hair, then left the room to join her husband. Her intention, the son knew, was not to change his father's mind, but to understand and comfort him. His mother couldn't say it, but she also wanted Jake gone.

The Branding Iron   *1974*

With one change of clothes and the eighty dollars his mother had shoved into his pocket, Jake got on a Greyhound bus to Denver. First things first, it seemed a matter of common sense to put Kansas behind him. Why give childhood any more thought? Why slip backward into memories he did not want? Though his mind was not finished with Nam, his body had to keep moving forward.

He spent a few months that winter in and around Phoenix, doing construction jobs and learning, from a Mexican co-worker, *un poco de Español*. In the spring, he found his way to the hills of Northern California. A longhair in Arizona had told him about Garberville. "Free pot," the guy had said.

Yeah, uh-huh. But hey, why not check it out?

Jake camped by the river, and every morning walked up into town to look for work. He took plenty of breaks in The Branding Iron, a bar where locals hung out. It was made to look like a saloon from the Old West. A rattlesnake skin was tacked up just inside the rustic redwood door. There were cow skulls and a Winchester rifle on the wall behind the bar. The bar itself took up most of the space, running full length down the narrow passageway to a small alcove, and pool table, at the far end.

But instead of cowboys, this was a place for redneck loggers. No pot, just lots of drinking.

No problem for Jake. Being from farm country, and a vet, he knew how to drink, and keep quiet, and tolerate the endless stream of swearing, or tits-and-ass jokes, or arguing over sports, or talking shit about some 'prick-tease' woman, or her 'gullible' husband--or niggers, wetbacks, hippies.

Whatever got a groan or a smirk or a slap on the back.

"You fat fuck, Henry, when's the last time you saw your dick?"

"Don't need to, Sam. Your wife's got no problem finding it."

Whatever the hell kept them laughing.

The latest buzz was about all the longhaired 'sissy boys' buying land out in the hills. After tossing around some homo jokes (wondering, you know, *who was it making those hippie fags so goddamn happy?*) they'd shake their bewildered heads like at a riddle with no solution.

Hippies seemed, for these guys, a true problem, and on this particular night they needed a lot more booze than normal to blur their irritation into focus.

Sam shook his empty mug at Bob, the bartender, and said, "Fuckin' Beatles."

"What, you want another?"

"No, dammit, I'm saying it was those fuckin' Beatles started the whole damn deal."

"Yeah. . .well. . .fuck those fuckin' pansies," Henry said. "Point is, who's gonna finish it?"

Some guy Jake didn't recognize said, "Maybe some of them pretty heads need breakin'."

Everyone gave that a solemn nod, then the homo jokes started up again.

They gave Jake an occasional glance, and he, as usual, said nothing. No one seemed to care. The loggers accepted his quietness. They liked him just for being a vet. Once in awhile he'd get a few days of work out in the woods, cleaning up brush after a cut, and burning slash. Those who couldn't provide a job made sure to buy him drinks. Word had gotten out he was some kind of war hero, a lie that worked in his favor. Who knows how many *gooks* the guy had killed, right? Could be why they let him stay quiet and kept filling his glass. Anyway, no one ever dicked around with Jake.

It was soon after the threat of breaking heads and the solemn nod that one of those hippies sauntered into the saloon. Everyone got quiet. The kid sat next to Jake at the end of the bar. His long blond hair was tied back in a ponytail. He had a wispy beard and bright blue eyes. Maybe he'd just turned twenty-one and this was his idea of a birthday celebration? Bad idea.

"Hey," he said.

"Hey," said Jake.

The kid smiled and ordered a beer.

"Someone needs a haircut," Henry said from down the bar. Then a few guys gathered behind him.

The kid said, "What, am I not supposed to be here? Should I leave?"

"Nah," said Ray, dumbest of the dumb. Ray was a middle-aged guy who loved to wag his tongue, like a little snake peeking out of its hole, and brag about all the young pussy he was licking, and would keep on bragging no matter how many times he was told to shut his lying mouth. Jake avoided this guy because he was not only an asshole--lots of them were assholes--but an asshole *on purpose*, who seemed to go out of his way to be one. "No problem," the asshole said, his left hand on the kid's shoulder, his right hand on Jake's. "Hell," he said, looking around, "a man deserves a nice cold beer at the end of a long hot day, am I right boys?"

No one answered.

When the beer arrived, Ray leaned over and spit in it. Then he put his face close to the kid's, almost cheek to cheek, and stared at the glass, as if waiting for it to complain.

Jake had had enough. A rage rose up in him he could not block. He grabbed Ray's greasy hair and slammed his forehead down on the bar, the fucker going limp as an empty hose and falling to the ground. Nobody said or did a thing. Jake took hold of the kid's arm and led him outside. "Oops," he said, "Guess we won't be drinking there anymore."

"No," said the kid. "Guess not."

"Let's walk."

They went around the block, to where Mickey had parked his hippie bus. By then they knew each other's names, and the kid, Mickey, could not stop apologizing. He said he needed Jake to *get* that he regretted the trouble he'd caused. Innocent as hell, thought Jake. And what a talker! He must've been real scared back in the bar, because now he went on and on, admitting he should have known better, shouldn't be surprised by what had happened. The kid explained that for a whole long list of reasons, including asshole loggers, he didn't often come off his land, was himself kind of a reclusive type who preferred animals and trees to people, which partly explained his decision to not eat meat, just veggies and fruit, and why he preferred weed to alcohol except of course on special occasions, such as tonight, when he might, if allowed, have had a beer or two because yes, in fact, it was his birthday, and who knows the next time he'd be back in town?

"Happy birthday," Jake said.

"Thanks," Mickey said. "Sure am glad *you* were at my party."

They drove down by the river, to a small park across from the sand and gravel yard. They smoked a joint and sat looking at the moon. The whole time, Mickey kept talking. He'd inherited money from a dead aunt, had decided to get out of San Francisco, out into nature, away from all the people, the pollution, the *social bullshit*. He'd bought forty acres in a place called Ettersburg. He was, he said, a *Back-To-The-Lander*. Then he laughed. "That's what us hippies from the city call ourselves once we've moved to the country and gotten ourselves a little dirty. In other words," he said, waving the joint, "I'm growing this."

"Good for you," Jake said.

"Yeah, if the deer and rats don't get it first."

"A farmer's life."

Mickey grinned, took another puff, then said, "Ah shit, I should get going. You live in town?"

"Not quite. I got a tent down by those bushes over there."

"Yeah? No one bothers you?"

"Not yet. I've been warned. Maybe after tonight I'll get warned again."

"Hey," Mickey said, "you want to camp out on my land?"

"Hell yeah," Jake said.

So they took down the tent by flashlight and headed up into the hills. It was more than an hour's ride, much of it on a curvy, bumpy road.

Jake was amazed that the Volkswagen could make it. "I thought you'd need a jeep for this."

Mickey asked if he'd ever heard of the Baja Run?

"Nope."

"It's a race they have in Mexico. A thousand miles of sand dunes and cactus and shit. And Volkswagen Beetles win the damn thing every year! They started making these buses in the sixties. A mechanic friend of mine told me to get the '72 because it has a bigger engine, better clearance, and single-piston front disc brakes that. . .*oh shit!*"

Mickey had come around a corner and needed to slam on his single-piston front disc brakes at the edge of a wide creek.

"Almost forgot," he said. He backed up into a flat spot on the right, off the narrow road, and turned off the engine. The water sparkled in the moonlight. "Be able to cross it in a couple weeks," said Mickey. "Someday I'll build a bridge."

They crossed the creek on a few well-placed boulders. It was a ten-minute walk along the rocky shore to the clearing where Mickey had a tent. Jake pitched his on a ledge overlooking a small glassy pool, and spent much of the night watching it reflect the moon.

In the morning, Mickey showed him around. "Someday," he said, "I'll build a small cabin, which I'll turn into a drying shed once I have time to build a house."

"Sounds like a lot of somedays," Jake said.

"Yeah, well, depends on what happens."

"Which depends on the deer and rats?"

"And the Feds. And any slime-ball loser who might want to steal my crop."

"Wow," Jake said. "Risky."

"Risky, yeah, but beats the hell out of growing corn, am I right?"

Mickey had heard that part of Jake's story and knew there was no problem joking about it. He led them up the hill, through a break in the dense manzanita, to a small flat shelf. Behind it, to the north, was a thick wall of Douglas fir. The shelf was full of tiny pot plants in black plastic grow-bags, surrounded by eight-foot deer fencing. Mickey opened the gate for a closer look.

"What's that?" Jake said, pointing at the tiny grayish pellets around each bag.

"Poison. Rats are my worst enemies. At least until these babies get bigger."

"No other way but poisoning them?"

"Not that I know of. There's just too fucking many."

Jake just nodded his head, thinking for a second about the rat he'd met in Vietnam. But he knew better than to get sentimental. After killing people, where did he get off worrying about rats? Time to change the subject. "You pump water from the creek?"

"No, I'm lucky, got a year-round spring up the hill. Here, I'll show you." They walked up into the stand of firs. Mickey had built a little redwood spring box, though a majority of the flow was leaking away. "Pretty cool, huh?"

"Cool for sure," Jake said, "but not very good. If you want, I can make it better."

They went back to town, bought 2x4's and several bags of ready-mix, and lugged them to the site. The next morning, Jake formed up a three cubic foot concrete enclosure. After it cured for a couple of days, he put on a redwood lid.

Mickey was thankful. He bought them a dozen six packs, and food, and made sure there was an endless supply of pot.

For a solid week, Jake helped dig holes in six long lines on a longer, wider shelf. That's where the plants would go once they were big enough. They ran water to the new spot and built another fence, this one with a door they could lock. They topped the fence with barbed wire to discourage any deer, or humans, who might want to steal the crop.

Then they waited. The starts weren't quite ready to plant, Mickey explained, because they hadn't yet been *sexed*. Only females would go in the ground. That's the way it worked. The little boys had to be destroyed. . .could not be allowed to fertilize the girls. Thus the name *sinsemilla (without seed)*.

One night, while they sat around the fire getting stoned, Mickey started yacking about *the mystery of life* and *fate* and who knows what else.

"I, um. . .uh, was thinking. . ." he said, his lungs too full of smoke, forcing him to cough it out.

"Think again," Jake said, taking the joint and another toke.

"No man, hey, seriously now, would you consider sticking around, helping me with the crop?"

"Already am."

"Yeah, exactly. . .so why not make it official, right? With two of us, we can grow a lot more."

"Listen," Jake said, clearing his lungs, "I'm a corn man. Don't know shit about this stuff."

Mickey laughed and started rolling another joint. "Truth is, there's not a hell of a lot to know."

And he wasn't kidding. In one day, Jake learned to identify the slender white hairs that defined a plant as female. Big deal. "Too bad," he said, "that women are not so easy to figure out."

"Yeah," Mickey said.

They spent their days sexing the baby marijuana plants, planting and fertilizing and watering the females, digging more holes and poisoning more rats. Otherwise it was just lots of time being stoned, with many hours for Jake to wander by himself in the woods, or dunk in the creek, or read.

Later, while the plants were growing, they built the cabin that would someday be the drying shed. Mickey had contacted 'an old buddy' from San Francisco to come help.

Her name was Liz. . .a good carpenter who also had connections in the city: trusted ways of unloading their stuff. She was a well-built, redheaded beauty, who Jake kept watching because she reminded him of Gail, his high-school girlfriend. Liz had bigger breasts than Gail. And what seemed to be stronger legs. In fact, the two looked nothing alike. It was something else. . .the way she moved. . .and the way, like Gail, she kept watching *him*.

Then, one fine day, she handed Jake his first hit of acid.

The Grateful Dead

Though it would be five years until Luanne met Consuelo, she first began thinking about friendship bracelets at a Grateful Dead concert. Winterland Auditorium, San Francisco. August, 1974.

She'd just turned sixteen.

Her parents, in order to attend a weekend meditation retreat in Big Sur, had agreed to let her stay with Susie, a friend whose parents they considered trustworthy. Or, as her mother put it, *at least reasonably trustworthy*. Reasonable trustworthiness was a necessity, she'd said, because of Luanne's *flighty* nature. What her mother really meant, the girl knew, was *reckless*, as she made sure to mention the time last summer when Luanne got caught sneaking alcohol from various bottles in the liquor cabinet (vodka, whiskey, rum) and combining them "willy nilly" into a half-emptied quart of ginger ale.

"Or what about this spring," her mother continued, brandishing the receipt, "when you *borrowed* my credit card?" This was, in her mother's mind, Luanne's worst offense: "That you would charge movies, meals and, and what, coffee. . .which you don't even drink. . .and dresses, socks, two pairs of shoes, lipstick and a bathing suit--most of it for a girl you claim to hate!"

After dropping Luanne off at Susie's house, her mother had second thoughts. Then third and fourth thoughts coming in quick succession. "I don't know," she said. "Maybe this is not such a good idea."

She glanced over at Luanne's father, Stu, who was smiling and waving good-bye from the driver's seat of their car. He idled at the curb, perhaps fumbling with his own doubts while waiting for her, as usual, to tell him what they'd do.

"Oh hell," she said, forcing a smile, "I guess it will be all right. I should stop worrying."

He slowly began to pull away.

"Well," she said, "what do you think, Stu? Is it going to be okay or not?"

"I. . .I don't know," he said, and she could feel him beginning to brake.

"Keep going, for godsakes, GO!" she said, outraged that her husband was such a gutless wonder.

Stu said nothing, just kept on driving, and for the next hour they rolled down the road in a dark, stifling silence. Her head ached. Her heart too. Clearly, neither of them had achieved their guru's stated goal of *shining in the light of everlasting oneness.* In fact, were nowhere close. It had been a long rough year with Luanne. They had no idea what to do with the impulsive girl. Still, they could not lose this chance to get away. . .to center. . .*to flush all worldly troubles from their minds.*

And it worked. Being incommunicado for the entire weekend proved a perfect temporary solution. Except that there had been no way for Susie's dad, on Friday evening, to inform them that he and the wife had been invited by his boss, all expenses paid, to the Masters Tournament in Carmel.

He later admitted it was a mistake to go, but explained that there were many reasons he could not refuse the surprise offer. "I tried to call," he said, "but the retreat center wouldn't answer the phone. Being such spiritual people, I'm sure you see I did the best I could."

"Well," Luanne's mother said, "actually no, I don't."

The man was an idiot. She felt no qualms in saying so. His daughter Susie, however, had been much more sympathetic. Appreciating the difficulty of her parents' predicament, the little bitch had calmed their minds and guaranteed their exit by arranging a Saturday sleepover at the house of another friend. She'd even given a wrong number to call, in case of emergency.

Actually, there were several friends. They'd gathered at Jyl's house, whose parents were also gone for the weekend. Jyl said she didn't know where. Nor did she care. Luanne admired her older friend's bold defiance, and sensed that this would be the best sleepover of her life. The sleeping part, for those who eventually did, would not begin until six o'clock on Sunday morning. Meanwhile, they had a full Saturday night ahead of them, which included a lot of complication: their idea of excitement. Because Jyl lived in a neighborhood of Palo Alto, thirty-five miles from the City, the first thing was to hook up with Bob, a college guy, a friend of somebody's brother, who'd already offered Jyl a ride.

"And," said Jyl, smiling, "you know, a joint if I want it." She laughed. "And...you know... whatever else I want."

Luanne saw that handling boys was no sweat for this girl.

Jyl said, "I told him, *Cool*, which seemed to make him real happy." Then she made a stupid pouty face. "Uh...uh, wait, hold on there."

Luanne could see she was pretending to be Bob, showing how his disappointment when the other four girls piled into his car. And she was right, Bob did pout.

"What," he said, "am I the chauffer or something?"

But it must have occurred to him that pouting was not in his best interest, because he quickly lit up the first joint. Sure, thought Luanne, the odds of his scoring had just quintupled, right?

"Hey, you know, why not?" he said.

Getting their way, of course, meant the girls would have to put up with Bob for the rest of the night. Ugh. Still, like he said, you know, *why not? Not to worry* (about anything) was what mattered, right? So they smoked his joints and suffered his bad jokes, and giggled, often, at how crazy they were, how careless, how out of control! Words were rarely required. Luanne sighed and laughed the same language as her friends. Everything seemed possible. Inevitable. Including, as they stood in line, a tall blond glittery woman (a perfect likeness of the good witch, Glinda, complete with crown and magic wand) who asked them, please, to open their mouths. How could they say no?

"Peace," she said, placing like sacrament a tiny pane of acid on their tongues.

Luanne smokes pot often. It is never, though, ever, anything like this. At last the world is opening up, showing secrets she could before only imagine. She marvels at the huge, flashing, translucent eyes. Faces float by like near-to-bursting pink balloons. Random flurries of visible guitar notes zigzag through the thick warm air, ricochet against the walls, and surround her--spidery filaments of pure electricity--while the huge hazy cavern fills to overflowing, throbbing with hoots and chants and stomping feet and *sound check. . .yo. . .check . . .yo. . .*drums *pabum,* like beating hearts, *check pabum check check pabum. . .*her life beginning over again, hands waving *check* bodies swaying back *pabum* and forth *check check* like grass blowing in visible wind, on some other planet, some other time *pabum bum. . .bum pabum. . .*and OH MY GOD, OH MY GOD, when Jerry comes out the chanting leaps higher, a million birds rising into the light, wings across a rainbow sky, flapping together side by side, sounds vibrating through space, oscillating lights and shapes melting into the high domed ceiling.

Years later, Luanne would realize that beyond her private joy, and awareness, it was a night of special celebration for this raucous gathering of self-proclaimed dropouts. Most were older than her, in their early twenties. A good number of them were reeling from Nixon's resignation a few days before. It was yet another chance to affirm their collective faith in a world that could, indeed, be changed by persistent idealism and unconditional love--not to mention easily available drugs--and lots of free (or free as it gets) sex.

Luanne is tall, with a sunburnt nose, two long dark braids, a slim waist, a perfectly rounded ass, and tiny budding breasts. Thanks, also, to her moon-like face, sparkling blue eyes and luminous smile, she gets kissed and fondled several times. Enjoys every second of it. She pulls loose only when touch trespasses some instinctual sense of comfort. Hands unable to hold her, she flits away, beyond the reach of unwanted complication, back into the pulsing throng. . .weaving among the other elated auras. . .fairies in a field of flowers.

Can she stay this happy always? Yes! Yes! Yes! Why not?

Flowing without aim or intention she finds herself in the outer hall, where a vast array of confectionary delights await the crowd's need for something sweet. Luanne definitely has the munchies. But not any money. Even if she did, she would not, could not, stand in a line. She hates lines of any sort. For any reason.

Down from the food booths are what Bob warned her to avoid, what he called the *Downer Tables*. Instead, choosing to avoid him, she's also ignored his advice, and suddenly there she is, bewildered, listening to a very short, very white man, with crooked brown teeth and red blotches on his face, explain why to never eat fish.

Fish? Really? She giggles, which seems to make his blotches get redder, his words come louder and faster. Something about mercury. Something about a farm and immorality and inbreeding and *artificial what?* Holy shit, she'd rather be getting groped by dipshit Bob than listen to this guy. "Sorry," she says, and wanders down the hall, away from the main auditorium. She is thinking of fish, watching her feet swim along the river of a floor.

A sheet of paper blocks her vision.

"Are you registered to vote?" says a woman with a blue painted face.

"No," Luanne says.

"OK," the blue woman says, and pushes past, fighting upstream.

Luanne gives her new world a passing glance. Tables line both walls, the space between them humming with chaotic energy. It reminds her of times she's fallen asleep in front of the television and woken to its crackling fuzz. *Wow, this is too much.* Unfortunately, there seems to be no chance of turning around, the narrow stream carrying her forward, straight into the heart of civil unrest. To her right: contaminated food and water. To her left: nuclear waste dumps and acid rain. Sucked down the line, as Jerry sings in the background, she becomes far too aware of toxic run-off and starving kids in India, mismanaged government agencies and mislabeled medicines and mistreated pets. From all directions, as if there were nothing else, an endless supply of unwanted news: daily assaults on nature and innocence of which, until now, she's remained happily unaware.

"Downer, am I right?"

It's Bob over her left shoulder. Huh? Where did he come from? "Yeah," she says, meaning him. What, is he following her?

"The thing is," Bob says, "these people are never happy."

"Why?"

"Because no amount of hope could ever be hopeful enough."

"Really?" says a guy with glasses and a balding head. He has a handsome face. Luanne looks past it, to the tufts of hair riding his ears. "Still seems pretty bleak to me," he says. "Why, exactly, are you so hopeful?"

"Well," Bob says, "what about getting rid of Nixon?"

"Drop in the fucking bucket."

"Right," Bob says. "My point exactly. The thing is, man, sometimes we need a break."

"Which means?"

"*Which means* I, for one, am sick of the constant complaining." Luanne can see that Bob is trying to impress her. "*Which means*," he says, "enjoying my life, no matter what, as best I can."

"Yeah, I get it," the bald guy says. "Because you're convinced that the best way of changing a corrupt system is to not support it. In fact, to totally ignore it. We should all stay good and stoned and quit our jobs tomorrow."

"Right."

"Lucky for the revolution, most of you idealists don't have to work. I'll bet you don't."

"I'm a student," Bob says.

"Supported by your parents, whose values you reject."

"Hey," Bob says, "none of their choices were mine, OK?"

"Yeah, right, a real *downer*," says the bald guy. "Being privileged, and shamed by it, you feel an obligation, whatever the cost--a cost you simply won't pay--to charge into nothingness."

"Fuck you."

"You'll live off your folks and get stoned every day and begrudge your good fortune until they finally kick you out of the house. No problem because there's always some other house--the house of whoever hasn't yet gotten the boot. It doesn't matter who or where. Or how long it lasts. That's the gist of your revolution, right?"

Bob turns to Luanne. "I'm outta here. You coming?"

"No."

"Whatever," says Bob, and squeezes off into the crowd.

"Sorry," the bald guy says. "Dicks like him just rub me wrong."

Luanne giggles and squirms, trying not to imagine it. "You're funny," she says.

"No. . .actually I'm far too serious. What's your name?"

"Luanne. Yours?"

"Ray," he says, and shakes her hand. "And why, Luanne, are you so stoned tonight?"

"I don't know," she says. "Do I have to know?"

"I suppose not."

"And why, Ray, are you so *far too serious*?"

"Good question," comes a voice from directly behind her. Luanne turns and looks up at a tall willowy man with a short blondish ponytail and electric green eyes. She tries not to stare.

"Oh," says Ray, sounding disappointed, "hey, Jake."

"Hey," Jake says. He looks down at Luanne. "Are you, by chance, an Indian princess?"

"No."

"Could've fooled me. My name's Jake," he says, and holds out his hand.

She takes hold of it. "I'm Luanne."

"It's the braids, I guess. Or maybe--"

"What's up?" Ray says.

"Oh," says Jake, laughing, letting go of Luanne's hand, "yeah, sorry, I'm, uh, looking for Liz."

"Good, *uh*, luck," Ray says. "Last time I noticed she was looking for someone else. Know what I mean? That-a-way," he says, pointing back toward the main hall.

"Peace," Jake says to Ray, and turns to Luanne. "See you later, princess."

He smiles, then is gone.

"What's his story?" says Luanne.

"Jake? Oh, he's the most recent boyfriend of my ex girlfriend."

"Ah."

"Yeah, right. A sordid tale of love. And, of course, peace. Peace and love are what these hippies all believe in."

"Something wrong with that?"

"No, don't get me wrong--peace and love are wonderful things, especially if nothing needs to be sacrificed to get them."

"You're a little *too serious* for me, Ray." Luanne re-shakes his hand, is ready to move on, get back into the hall. "Very nice to meet you."

"Too bad," he says. "I was thinking you might be different."

"Different?"

"Than your college boyfriend." Ray's eyes have narrowed and hardened, as if her intention to leave has injured him somehow.

"Hey," she says, "he's not my--"

"Easy to stay hopeful when your mom's doing the laundry and fixing your meals and the pot keeps flowing for free. Let's see how you feel once you're crashing on a stranger's floor and stealing from the fridge. Then again, if things get rough, you can always go back home."

"Why are you being mean?"

"Am I?"

She sighs and turns to go.

"OK," he says. "Wait. I apologize." He holds up his hand and makes the famous sign. "*Peace.*"

She steps closer, their faces only a foot apart. "I'm not kidding. Why?"

"I don't know." He laughs. "Do I have to know?"

"When you're being mean to someone, yes. I didn't do anything to you."

"OK," he says, his eyes softening. "OK, you're right. Sorry. I don't know, I. . .I um. . ." and he looks away, up in the air, like the rest of his thought might be floating around above the crowd.

"What?"

Ray says, "I guess I don't understand the purpose of our revolution."

"Oh," says Luanne, giving it a few seconds of consideration. "Well, no, I guess I don't know either, Ray." She gets that he is truly sorry and kisses his cheek. "Sorry, I have to go."

And, though she does, a part of Ray goes with her. His voice is in her head now, finishing the conversation. *So we stop cutting our hair. Big deal. Or stop washing our clothes. Or eating meat. What does any of it matter, you know? What is it we want?*

Luanne thinks of the tall guy with green eyes (Jake, is that his name?) and wonders what it is he wants. If she sees him again, she'll ask.

Jake sits in a far corner of the auditorium. He has already put Luanne out of his mind. Tonight he doesn't want a pretty girl. Doesn't want anything. He's not here, like others, to have fun. Fun is irrelevant. But he's not cynical like Ray. Nor does he mind losing Liz.

His intention is to release her, along with all other distractions. He takes a deep breath, drops a second tab of acid, crosses his legs and closes his eyes. The music surrounds him. His earth. His sky. Having no clue what needs to change in his life, he's decided the best he can do is nothing. The idea exists like a distant star, wobbling just within his vision of imagined possibility. The Dead are singing *Uncle John's Band*, a song he interprets as a pleading, in multiplied harmonies, to let the world and its endless concerns go; to follow the music only, the love only; to once and forever surrender and be taken home.

Home, for Jake, is a way of being. No place matters more than any other because every place, in its essence, is the same. He learned that in Nam, where the jungle, the very thing he'd dreamt of as a boy, turned into a nightmare. It's not the place, it's what you bring to it. What you do there. He remembers his long happy days with Fish and the quiet of their shared pond. That is where his fluid mind now flows. . .as if he had never left.

Luanne continues to wander in the outer hallway, looking for an entry to the main auditorium. The band begins her favorite song, *Uncle John's Band*. It seems an omen. She must be getting close. The hallway, however, has ended, and she's faced with the final table.

Stunned, Luanne stops and looks around. *Huh?*

But the truth is, she likes it here. The music comes drifting through the air. . .waves of radiant warmth rubbing silky against her cheeks. Soothing. And the light feels muted, as if tuned to a low humming chord. She closes her eyes and feels that warmth inside her too. Feels how good it feels. Wait, she thinks, she doesn't need to go inside. Doesn't need to go anywhere. Or do anything. Happiness is wherever you are. She could live in a closet, if necessary, and nothing important would change.

She spots a woman sitting behind the final table. There's no one else around. The woman has a somber expression. Calm but serious. Lonely?

Luanne steps closer, drawn by the many rows of thin colorful bands. She leans forward. "What are these?"

"*Pulseras*. . .in Spanish," the woman says. "I call them friendship bracelets."

"Oh," says Luanne, who has the inexplicable feeling that she should have known. Why do these things seem so familiar? What's going on?

The somber woman's face lights up. Not bright, like the ones inside the hall, but with a steady sheen--a light left low on purpose in order to stay burning longer than the rest. Her eyes are soft, a deep amber glow, inviting Luanne to smile. . .to giggle. . .to laugh at her own confusion. The woman picks up one of the bracelets. "They're from Guatemala," she says. Her voice is also soft. Clear. She reaches out and lays it in Luanne's palm like an offering of peace.

"Beautiful," says Luanne. Because it truly is: an intricate pattern of arrow-like shapes, each a different color, the bracelet splitting apart at one end into two threaded braids. At the other end is a threaded loop, where the braids, she sees, are meant to tie together. Luanne knows nothing of Guatemala. Just that it's somewhere below Mexico, somewhere in Central America, along with Panama and Costa Rica and maybe Colombia. She isn't sure. Has never cared. Holding the bracelet in her hand, though, she shivers with a rush of sadness.

"I was down there earlier this year," the woman says. "I work with some indigenous families, and got the idea to have these made."

Luanne does not know what *indigenous* means. "Why?"

"The Indians are being abused. The government steals their land. I'm trying to make people aware of their suffering. Vietnam may be over, but this is our war too. We make it possible. I'm hoping people will get involved."

"How?"

The woman thinks about it for a moment, then laughs. "Well, I. . .I don't really know. For starters, I guess, they could buy these bracelets as a way to show solidarity with the Indians."

"I'm sorry," Luanne says, "I don't have any money."

"Oh honey, that's no problem. At least you're listening. People need to know what we're doing down there, slaughtering innocent peasants just because--"

Luanne starts backing away. She feels like such a little girl. The woman looks confused, is watching her closely. Luanne wants to stay, but is unable to keep listening. She's heard these kinds of stories before and knows where they end up. It would be impossible to understand. She would feel horrible. And the woman's sad eyes are too hard for her to look at. There is a fuzziness in Luanne's head, a buzzing numbness in her ears. Her hands are trembling.

"Are you all right?" the woman says.

"I'm sorry," says Luanne, and turns to go.

She remembers saying *sorry* to Ray. And to the short blotchy white guy talking about fish. Why, she wonders, does she keep saying that? *Sorry? Sorry for what?* And why does it seem dangerous to say it? To think it? Why does she want to run, get away, before this woman makes her say or think anything else?

Then, realizing she's still got the bracelet, Luanne turns back, almost crying, and holds it out.

"Please," the woman says, "it's a gift. I want you to have it."

"No, really, I--"

"It's OK, hon. *Really.* It's OK."

Ruins

Palenque, February 19, 1976

Two years later, Jake found himself traveling with Orph (a small and somewhat sickly black Lab) in the 1967 Volkswagen bus he'd converted to a camper. Or, rather, a sleeper: no stove; no fridge; a space to crash in by the side of the road. His life as a budding deadhead had come to a screeching halt when the band decided to stop touring. Ready for a change himself, he took a leave from growing weed and headed for southern Mexico in search of Mayan ruins and magic mushrooms.

Jake had read a bit about the ruins of Palenque. The ancient city sat atop a high plateau. At its back were steep cliffs amidst a tall and tangled jungle. Impassable by all two-legged creatures, with the notable exception of howler monkeys, there was no possible threat from behind. Out front, it looked down over a wide flat plain. Potential enemies were visible for days in advance. So yes, like the book said, Palenque was an important Mayan spiritual center. Also an impressive fortress.

Jake spent the night at a run-down hotel in the town named after the famous ruins. Less than an hour from the archeological site, he arrived early the next morning. Was the first one in. Alone, and liking it, he came upon 'The Palace' and gazed at incomprehensible glyphs, limestone sculptures, and layered bas reliefs. It was a cool, overcast day. Lucky, because Orph had to wait in the van. Jake didn't mind that his dog would not be tagging along. He appreciated these moments to himself and tried not to waste them.

To *truly understand* where he was, he decided to go meditate at his primary destination, 'The Temple Of Inscriptions,' tallest of the Palenque pyramids. The hotel's owner, an old alcoholic Texan, had told Jake things he didn't know. "Has a secret passageway down into its center where they buried the head honcho. Yessirree, young fella, the whole damn deal is just one big grave!"

Jake started climbing. And *yessirree*, just like the Texan said, there were eighty-eight steps to the top, and they were steep, which left him winded and a bit off balance. Rather than meditate, maybe he'd get stoned. What better way to commune with the gods? But as he reached for the joint, a familiar sound echoed from behind the near wall--a loud voice with a strong mid-western accent. His high school biology teacher, Mr. Garth, used to make fun of their non-Kansan neighbors, could imitate them perfectly, and glowed when his students, most of whom were flunking, could mimic him. Curious whether he'd learned anything in that class, Jake leaned against the wall and listened. A Hoosier maybe? A cheese head? Oh no, much worse: a loud-mouthed Illinoiser! Somewhere in Jake's head, Mr. Garth and all the gods were cringing.

The guy suddenly emerged from around the corner, mid-monologue. He was a stout, aging lion, with a cropped silver mane and a matching majestic mustache. His muscular tanned arms were covered with thick white hair. He was busy explaining to a young blond woman how "spiritual power often becomes a weapon of oppression." Chicago, Jake guessed. South-side raised, north-side evolved. And, true to form, the guy kept right on talking, as if unaware of Jake's presence. Or perhaps he'd merely seen it as an irrelevant detail, accustomed to people gathering around, listening to him talk. "Take these temples," he said. "They may, indeed, be a testament to the gods, but were built by the forced labor of indoctrinated peasants."

Ah, of course, a professor. No wonder Jake had no interest in college. "Indoctrinated?" he said. "Couldn't it be a matter of belief?"

The lion professor glanced at him sideways. *"Belief by force.* That is what *indoctrinated* means."

"I understand," Jake said. "I'm just saying it might be possible, since no one knows for certain, that the peasants trusted their priests' visions and actually *wanted* to build the temples." Though not believing it himself, how could he resist hassling this chump?

"Well," the lion professor said, "call it what you want. The fact is, given what we *do actually know* of Mayan society, the options for a common man were to either kill himself lifting and lugging all day or be ostracized for betraying his religious duty."

The young woman nodded, seemed familiar with the lecture. Maybe she was his daughter. More likely a student he was having an affair with.

The lion professor continued, in his low bristly roar, to explain the 'hierarchy of oppression' in 'primitive societies'; the lack of any 'real choice' among its 'servant class'; and, of course, the 'stark injustice' of it all. Jake nodded for a couple of minutes--pretending to listen, choosing to be polite--and looked for the chance to offer an opinion. Finally realizing it was not going to happen, he turned and left. This day at least, in such a beautiful place, he would avoid a fight. Amazed by his self-control, Jake headed back down the steep uneven steps.

At last hitting bottom, he feels disillusioned--not with ruins but with their inevitable experts. He wanders off into the jungle and sits at the edge of a flowing creek. He lights the joint, takes a draw, and holds it in. At his feet, a line of leaves march by. Beneath them, Jake sees, are ants. *Wow, lots of weird bugs in Vietnam, but none of these little suckers.* He exhales a stream of smoke, watches it swirl up, dissipate and disappear, and for a few grueling seconds imagines himself *there*. His head, like an angry rattle, shakes away the thought. He takes several deep breaths, then another toke. Strange, in spite of the horror he experienced (things he hoped to never think about again) he's let himself wander into a jungle! And get stoned! And now, oh boy, here he is: *thinking!*

No, wait, don't worry, he thinks, because this is a different place. And he's a different person.

Knowing it, however, is not the same as feeling it.

A caramel-colored frog jumps onto his knee, its luminous green eyes half the size of its body. Everywhere, like in Nam, are vines and roots, thick and strong. Some twist upward, grabbing hold of anything they can. Others hang from hundreds of feet above. 'Sky Ladders' was the common name. He and his squad used to call them 'Ladders From Heaven.'

Oh, Christ, never mind, for Pete's sake! Never mind!

Jake looks around for something less likely to freak him out. He tries to calm his breathing and focus on the beauty. It rained hard last night, the big black spiders now working to repair their glistening webs. *And what else? What else?* Something to his right, probably a lizard, disappears into the shadows. Much of what is here cannot be seen. Fifty percent of the original city lies hidden, he read, covered by roots and vines and webs. These Mayans had carved a place for themselves out of a jungle that would not stop growing. Ever. Jake remembers, as a soldier, running through jungles just like this . . .running as fast and as far as he could. . .running until his breath gave out.

Sunlight breaks through the dense overhanging canopy. Insects go ballistic, whether in complaint or celebration Jake can't tell. The air has gotten warm and wet. He wants to go, go now, get out of there fast. Instead he strips naked, lays his clothes on a rock.

Time, he decides, to stop running.

He steps into the brown waist-high water and moves against the current up the creek. He's shivering, but keeps on going. Around one corner he sees a ten-foot totem of bright crimson flowers, like prehistoric birds, their beaks gaping open, their long sleek bodies diving out of spiky purple stems. Razor slim silver fish dart around his legs. White boulders hug the shore, backed by heart-shaped leaves the size of small children. In Nam he'd be holding an M16, on the lookout for any movement. A large bird squawks and takes off overhead. Jake looks up. Blinded by the sun, he sees only a silhouette of flapping wings. A monkey howls in the distance.

Nothing to be afraid of.

After a few minutes he comes to a wide pool beneath a short slender waterfall. An orange butterfly flexes its wings on a lime green leaf. Jake kneels in front of a boulder, water cascading over its face. There, in the dappled sunlight, eyes watch him through the rusty moss. Beneath their gaze is a high arching nose, and a mouth that does not need to speak.

Jake sees--in this face, these eyes--the spirit that guides shamanic vision. Here is where the Mayan Gods live, in the depths of a jungle that every day swallows itself alive.

Then, from the back of his mind, rushing to consciousness comes the sound of Orph whining.

Oh shit, oh no, how long have I been gone?

After a quick bow to the jungle deity, he splashes back down the creek to his clothes. Sweating and shirtless, he sprints through the ruins to his van, where Orph greets him with a slobbery kiss. He holds the dog close. The bowl of water is still half full. Yes, of course, Jake should have known, there really is nothing to be afraid of. That's how he needs to think. Good thoughts. Only good.

As Jake leaves the parking lot, the first tour bus pulls in. Soon the place will be crawling with experts. A good time to be gone.

Coming down the mountain, he sees the Palenque creek cascading to his right. For Jake it is a sign to stay by the water. In the flatlands below, it crosses under a bridge into the Otulúm river, and there, close to that juncture, he spots a narrow dirt road that enters a grove of large-leafed trees. He takes it, thinking there might be a place to camp. Other travelers have thought the same. Vans and mini-buses and trucks with camper shells are tucked into their own secluded spots along the river.

A guy walks over. He has long curly hair and a thick brownish beard. "Welcome," he says. "I'm Ben, your camp counselor."

"Cool," laughs Jake, and shakes his hand.

Ben explains the deal. Once farmland, he says, this will someday be a big resort. He was told by a former worker that until then--because the new owners are from Mexico City, and don't yet have the funds to build it--no one is around. Ben and his wife have been camping for days without a problem. "So park anywhere you want," he says.

"Cool," Jake says again, wishing he hadn't, then drives for ten minutes to the very end of the scant dirt track. There he finds a bald, bony, wasted-looking guy, in a saffron-colored loincloth, spread-eagled under a bamboo palapa. Jake turns his van around and heads back the other way.

Settling on a spot approximately equidistant between the palapa guy and his next visible neighbor, he parks the van, takes off his clothes, and dives into the river. Hundreds of those same silvery fish surround him, dodging his every stroke. The water is cold but the current gentle. He empties his lungs, lets himself sink to the bottom of smooth flat pastel stones. He doesn't come up until he absolutely has to, until his only need is air. Then he dives down again and plays with the fish. When the shivers get strong, he gets out of the water, lies on a big warm boulder, and looks up at a single white cloud in the deep blue sky.

Finally a thought slips into his mind: Ah yes. . .mushrooms.

Jake finds Ben in a hammock outside his fancy camper, and asks if he knows how to find them.

Ben laughs, then slumps his shoulders, squints his eyes, and rubs his hands together--a bad imitation of a mad scientist--and says, kind of spooky, "Yes. . .*in fact*. . .I do." He slaps Jake on the shoulder. "Uh, Boris Karloff."

"Got it. . .master."

"Good, very nice--a fresh, willing soul. You want to come with us tomorrow?"

"Can I bring my dog?"

"Sure, why not? Long as he doesn't chase other animals."

"Orph. . .*in fact*. . .doesn't chase anything. Bad case of hip dysplasia. Plus, he's a coward."

A woman comes out of the camper. Her long dark hair is tied in a ponytail. She is attractive in a simple, solid, no-nonsense way. She smiles and says, "Hi, I'm Kate."

"The better part of *us*," Ben says, hugging her to his side.

While the three of them are talking, a younger woman comes up from the river. Her hair is short, bleached silvery-blond, and glimmers in the sunlight. She introduces herself with a strong French accent. Jake, however, caught off-guard by the sparkling turquoise eyes, does not get the name. "I'm sorry," he says, "I didn't--"

"W-I-S," she spells, her petite hand shaking his. It comes from a long slender arm attached to a short curvy body. "It pronounces like geese, but wis a W."

201

"Weese," says Jake, imagining her naked. "Pretty name." He smiles, tells her his, then turns and shakes Ben's hand. "Thanks again, man. So, what time tomorrow?"

"At dawn," Ben says. "I'll wake you."

The call actually comes a bit before dawn. Dawn is the estimated time of arrival at the mushroom field Ben heard of, a twenty-minute drive uphill toward the ruins. They go in Ben's camper, also a Volkswagen, but this is a '74 *Westphalia*, one of the heavier pop-up types, with a propane stove, a fridge, a bunk above the foldout bed, and lots of other stuff. Jake learned, from Mickey's expertise, that these models lack a big enough engine to haul the extra weight, and tend to blow cylinders trying. Ben is doing his best to coax the beast up the mountain--patting the dashboard and whispering sweet nothings--as it growls through the dense wet fog.

Jake says, "What are we looking for?"

"An old wooden gate," Ben says. "The guy who--"

"You have by now passed sree," Wis says, in the midst of lighting her second cigarette. She's been pissy from the start, asking why it was "so importantly necessary" to "rush off in zih black of night wisout a cup of coffee." Wis is also miffed by the panting dog, and tosses Orph another disdainful glance. Apparently not offended, he shifts and re-settles beneath her feet. Jake sees her straining to keep quiet. Her unhappiness comes in the prettiest of packages. She is a delicate woman, her body white and smooth as a blanched almond.

Ben explains it is a 'double gate' they're trying to find.

"Oh yes," Wis says, "whatever zat is, I am convincing zair must be only one of zose."

"Well," Ben says, "in fact, that's true. It's a *two-sided* gate, to be more specific, and hanging from one of its posts is a broken metal sign that says PROHIBIDO PASAR."

"Huh?" Kate says. "NO TRESPASSING?"

"You cannot be serious," says Wis.

"It's a very old sign," says Ben. "The guy told me not to worry."

"Just maybe perhaps," Wis counters, "the landowners of zis place are not in agreeing."

Ben downshifts from second, hunting for first, metal teeth grinding in the darkness. Time pauses like a bird shot in flight until the motor once again whirs into action. "Look," he says, "the guy told me no one cares. That's the main reason we're going early."

"If no one is caring," Wis huffs, "*why* must it be a matter for us to go zair in zih dark?"

"*Why?*" Ben says. "Because it so happens that dawn is the best time to find mushrooms. *Why?* Because the guy told me it gets crowded later. *Why?* Because no one pays attention to the NO TRESPASSING sign. *Why?* Because, Wis, like I told you, the owners of the land don't give a crap."

"Ah," she sighs, grinning to herself, as if his ridiculous tautology requires no further comment. "Bingo!" says Jake, pointing to his right.

Ben sees it too. He pulls off the road, up to the long horizontal gate of cracked, sunbaked wood. The two sides are locked in the middle with a rusty chain. The metal sign, its once painted warning half-peeled away, droops from one of the rotting posts. Ben putters ahead, under the branch of a large oak tree. He turns off the engine.

"Wait," says Wis. "I am sinking your idea here is to be a bad one."

"We're going." It's Ben, staring back at her over his right shoulder. His voice is sharp and without a trace of doubt. "I mean I am. OK? Everyone else can do what they want. It's less than an hour's walk to camp." He gets out of the van and slams his door. Kate gets out too. Jake, from the bench-seat they've been sharing, slips past Wis with a tender bump, followed by Orph. Ben opens up the rear hatch to get their packs. "We're going," he announces to the back of Wis's head.

"I will wait until you are returning," she says. She sits stiff, not budging, as if the slightest hint of movement might suggest a change of mind.

"It could be awhile," says Kate.

"Fine," Wis says. "How long?"

"I don't know. Three hours, maybe more."

"Oh. . .well. . .what will you say if I drive myself to our camp? I can stay zair sree hours and--"

"No," Ben says.

"But why? Why is it? Why can you not?"

Because you're a selfish bitch, thinks Jake. *Because no one trusts you. Because you have no fucking clue that you're asking something crazy.* But he decides not to say it.

"Listen," Ben says. "I'm locking up and we're going. Whatever it is you decide to do, Wis, right now you need to get out."

With abrupt movements and a dramatic groan, she vacates the camper and stands there looking miserable. She glances at Kate, perhaps hoping the rude man's wife might defend her.

Kate starts following Ben. "C'mon Wis, grab your pack."

Getting past the gate is easy: dog under, humans over. Orph stays close to Jake's side. "Good pup," he says. They hike the eroded dirt road, up hills and down, crossing and re-crossing a shallow muddy stream while the sun rises slowly above the faraway mountains and lights the fields of scattered cows, goats, and sheep. It occurs to Jake that nothing much has changed since the ancient Mayans lived here. *Did they come looking for magic mushrooms too?* What a mysterious and beautiful place, a joy for everyone but Wis, who keeps stumbling along behind, her sighs morphing into moans as the heat begins to build.

Finally, no surprise to anyone, she stops. "Wait, wait, where is it we are going to? Because if you cannot say zis to me, I am ready to return."

Ben, sweating, drops his pack, grabs his bottle of water and takes a long deep drink. Then he eyes Wis. "The guy told me to look for Brahma bulls, all right? That's what he told me."

"Haven't seen a one," says Jake.

"Yeah," says Ben.

Wis steps forward and plants herself directly in front of him. "Tell me, Ben, for once and ever, how much longer we are bozzering to look?"

Kate puts a friendly hand on her shoulder. "Please, you need to think of it as an adventure."

"I am tired and hot and not in zis mood. I would like to choose what are my adventures, not have zem to be piling on my back, you know? You know what I mean?"

"There," Kate says, pointing beyond Wis's head.

The rest turn and see a Brahma bull grazing on top of a nearby hill.

"Well, hello," Jake says.

Ben slaps him on the back. "Cowabunga."

Wis follows as the others climb toward the bull. He moves on. As the humans arrive at where he was, he is cresting the next hill. When they get to the next hill he is still walking away, now joined by a few other bulls, perhaps heading for some distant cows.

"Hold it," Ben says. He sits down on the grass. "Something's wrong."

"Why?" says Jake. "Those are Brahmas, right?"

"It's not the bulls that matter, man. What matters is the shit."

"Shit?" says Wis.

"Cow patties," says Kate.

"Shit," says Ben. "*Shit* is what makes them grow. I'm seeing lots of that now, but not a single mushroom, which is weird because it rained a couple of days ago. The guy told me this should be the perfect time. Doesn't make sense."

"None of zis makes sense," Wis says, kicking a dried-up patty with her shoe.

"Whoa," Ben says. He crouches down, grabs a stick, and pokes at what is left of the pile. "Didn't expect them to be underneath." Jake then sees it, the small whitish dome. Ben gently uncovers the rest. He plucks the mushroom from the crumbled patty, takes his bottle of water and carefully washes it off.

"Wait," says Wis. "Really? You are sinking zis to be a magic one?"

"Don't know yet." Ben cracks open its stem. A few seconds later the insides begin to turn a grayish purple. "Yep, see, purple. That's the psilocybin being activated. All right, sports fans, here we go." He holds it out to Wis, who smirks and shakes her head. "Hey, girl, you're the one who found it."

"Truly, Ben? You would eat zat?"

"Oh yeah," he says, and pops it into his mouth.

Wis winces, squeals "oooh," and clenches her teeth.

Ben closes his eyes and chews. Everyone watches. Wis now shows an impish grin, maybe with the secret hope he might start puking. Or, better, turning purple. Ben smiles at her, swallows, then kicks at another pile. He spreads it out with his stick and finds another. "Boom," he says. "Guess I got the radar now." He cleans the mushroom well and gives it to Kate, who pops it in her mouth.

Wis just shakes her head and sits on the grass.

The others keep looking. Kate finds the next one and hands half of it to Jake. He gets the other half, too, after Wis waves it away. Soon they seeing mushrooms everywhere, sometimes two or three under the same patty. Jake has already filled a plastic bag. It feels more like they are finding him.

"What's a good dose?" he says. He's eaten the two halves, and two wholes, before the thought occurs to him.

Ben says, "Oh, yeah, sorry man. The guy told me no more than two. Says the fresh ones are really strong. We can save the rest for later."

Jake smiles and gobbles down another. Strong is what he wants. By the time they start back, around noon, he's stashed four big plastic bags in his pack. On the trip home, neon-lit Brahma bulls wander through his mind.

The next morning Jake cleans the mushrooms, all sixty-five of them, and then eats six. He spends the entire day lying on a big warm rock by the edge of the river, staring at its ripples. At some point, Wis wanders over in a black bikini. Wants to talk. She tells him about her ex-husband, Brad, an Englishman she met on a vacation to Indonesia, then married back in London, their marriage annulled after three months when "his addiction, you know, for zih beer and zih rugby, zih fish and chips and sex, was just too much." She wrinkles her nose at the awful memory and says how happy she is "to be free of a man who is not appreciating me." She asks where Jake is from, why he's in Mexico, and where he's going next. Like maybe, just maybe, she could be convinced to tag along. Naked under a towel, he just wants to be left alone. It is difficult to look at her because clothing of any sort (and especially her skimpy bikini) seems unnatural to him, a kind of armor, and he knows she's not about to take it off. Even if she would, he doesn't want her to. Not anymore. He doesn't think it in a mean way, or say a single critical word (is grinning like a fool) but every syllable he must utter is an effort. After a few minutes he lies back down--refocuses on the ripples--and she leaves.

Orph has also grown bored with him. Disappeared hours ago. When it starts to get dark, Jake goes looking. He finds his dog three camps away, playing with a red setter, and brings him home.

The following day Jake eats ten. Too bad for Orph, because the setter and his people have gone. From time to time the dog wanders back to see if his master might want to play, which he really doesn't. "C'mon, boy," Jake says, and Orph lies down beside him. Then Jake goes back to what he was doing, gazing up into a massive tree of wide green leaves and long red flowers puffed open like parachutes, their stamens like skinny bare legs dangling underneath. The fathomless blue sky peeks at him through tiny swaying windows in the foliage. *Exactly*, Jake realizes, *as it always is. Always.* Again he is mesmerized by the thick white trunk, here and there visible amongst its many branches, reminding him of Jack's beanstalk. He is full, completely full, of peace.

Is this what enlightenment feels like?

On the fourth day he decides to eat the rest. Forty-nine of them. How else will he know?

He starts at eight in the morning, right after a breakfast of two oranges and a cup of mint tea. He has plenty of purified water set aside, along with a bunch of bananas and a big bag of granola. He has filled Orph's bowl to the very brim. All is well. No, he thinks, it's perfect. Everything. Perfect. It's going to be another clear hot day. The river is right there whenever he or Orph needs it.

One after the other, Jake chews and swallows the first ten mushrooms. Follows them down with another cup of tea. He can sense the drug pulsing through him, adding to what is already there. Like clouds parting, the dense curtain of his protective mind dissolves into brilliant sunshine.

He takes out a brand new journal. At the top of page one he writes <u>MAGIC MUSHROOM TEST</u>, and below it the number ten.

Assuming his thoughts will evolve toward wisdom with each successive dose of psilocybin, he begins: *To begin with*, he writes, *I'm tired of the constant emotional ups and downs. How many times do I have to fool myself with some harebrained plan (or, worse, a sensible one that succeeds and always falls short of expectation) only to learn, again, I'm missing what really matters. Then, thinking I've learned what really matters, I come up with another plan!*

Does this shit ever end?

What's the use, he wonders, of trying so hard to figure things out? What does that even mean? Being constantly worried about 'what to do next', he worries, has a lot to do with fearing death and the petrifying prospect of everlasting nothingness. Better to distract himself, right, with some clever hare-brained plan. *The best plan of all*, he writes, *would be to stop planning altogether. Is that even possible?*

He was a freshman in high school during Kesey's infamous 'Acid Tests.' He'd not yet read any Sartre or Kafka or Castaneda--was totally clueless--every day wishing he could play sports with the other boys; every day confounded by pretty girls and wet dreams and the fear of rejection; every day angry at his parents' rules. . .at religion. . .at corn.

No wonder he knows so little about the sixties. Except for The Dead. He knows they took part in Kesey's tests. That, by itself, is good enough for him. *Jerry would not be Jerry*, he writes, *without doing psychedelics*.

Risks must be taken to free us from the prisons of our mind!

He can hear--of course he can--how simplistic that would sound to someone else. He doesn't care. At least it gets him thinking in the right direction. And just a few turns later, sometime during the next ten mushrooms, all judgmental voices disappear as his need to explain the wonder of life, even to himself, becomes less and less necessary.

Mushrooms twenty through thirty bounce him back and forth, up and down, between the multi-layered complexities of sex, birth, natural selection, human nature, chemistry, impressionist painting, dead sea scrolls, air, politics, religion, addiction, reincarnation, fast-food restaurants, traffic signals, international time zones, science, fate, the divine right of kings, death, decomposition, *and*--as Jake knows Vonnegut would say--*so it goes.*

At number thirty-five he details, in crisp illegible shorthand, exactly why the concept of God (which neither proves nor disproves the existence of God) had to be created (his analysis a sort of undercooked Kierkegaard with a side of stale Nietzsche).

He looks around--wants Orph's opinion--but the dog is gone. *No problem, we can talk about it later.*

By mushroom forty-two, down to isolated words and jagged lines squiggling between them, Jake feels certain, has no doubt, that all life forms--which includes stones, ideas, and every remembered dream--are intertwined by celestial threads invisible to the human eye, inconceivable by the modern mind. There's nothing much more to it than that, but that's a lot.

Across the way, on the other side of the river, a car pulls in, its Ranchero music blasting. He hears doors slam, the sound of screaming children. The trees block his sight of them.

A woman yells in a frantic voice, "Cuidado! Cuidado!"

Jake groans. Gets himself upright. He slides into flip-flops and wraps himself in a flowery white sarong--adequate coverage for a quick peek through the bushes.

Two small boys are on the opposite shore, throwing rocks into the water. The woman, must be the mother, is trying to keep an eye on them while spreading out a blanket near the car. A plastic cooler sits off to the side. Beside it is a cardboard box. The father walks off in the other direction, sipping from a bottle of Coke, gazing over the river as if it were his, a mighty king perusing his taken lands. The man's fat belly protrudes from his opened shirt like something trying to get away. Not once does he give a glance toward his wife or children. He stops and spits. Then, after downing the last of his Coke, the man flips the bottle in a high arc toward the water.

It shatters on the shallow rocks right beneath the surface.

Surprising himself, Jake lunges forward through the bushes and steps out onto a big flat rock. The man sees him. Their eyes lock. Though nothing can be done to change what happened, Jake feels like something must be said. He lifts his hands to demonstrate his dismay. "Por qué?"

The man gives Jake a quizzical look. "Por qué?" he says, questioning the question.

Having not spoken for two days, and a beginner at Spanish, Jake wonders how he might explain his complicated feelings. Yes, the loud music is a drag, and the screaming kids, but it's the danger of broken glass, the unconscionable disrespect and carelessness of this guy that he cannot understand. Jake takes a deep breath. Obviously the man doesn't know any better and must be forgiven his ignorance. Yeah, OK, Jake will try. . .if the guy will only make it a tiny bit easier. . .like losing the nasty sneer that makes Jake want to swim across the river and grab his greasy hair and stuff his head underwater until he finds every fucking shard and swears he'll never do it again! The guy is smiling at him now, like at a child for making a silly fuss. Though Jake would like to be tolerant, kind, compassionate, this asshole does not seem worth the effort.

"I don't understand *WHY!*" Jake yells in Spanish.

The man, solid on his wide flat feet, staring with bold defiance, lifts his arms and gives them a feeble little shake. Jake sees the guy is mocking him, laughing at his gringo distress.

Then the asshole says, "*PORQUE. . .PORQUE. . .PORQUE.*"

Ah, thinks Jake, so that's *WHY* he threw the bottle in the water: "*BECAUSE. . .BECAUSE. . . BECAUSE*" *he could.* *Because he felt like it, gringo! Comprende that?*

Jake retreats back through the bushes. He turns upriver along the path and walks away fast. His rage, his sense of powerlessness, follow close behind. He passes the palapa guy, who lies open to the universe in what seems a state of absolute surrender. Fuck him too. Jake follows the path through high willowy reeds, then up a gravelly hill. Several minutes later emerges onto an expansive tract of dirt. Though the path ends there, he cannot stop walking.

The fat Mexican is now just a bad memory, but impossible to forget. His spiteful voice rattles on inside Jake's head. It says, "This is my country, gringo." It says, "If you don't like how we live, go back to where you came from!"

Jake is panting. Exhausted. The air is hot. . .unusually dry. . .thick and resistant, as if trying to hold him back. Why, he wonders? *What's going on?*

Then he hears it, faintly at first, and hearing it makes him stop. He plops down onto the soft warm earth. Closes his eyes. After a few minutes his breathing slows. While the Mexican's insults continue to loop on, beneath them there is something else, a high melodic hum, like a breathless chant. He bends his ear toward the earth and listens, close. It sounds like tender voices, barely audible, are calling to him, trying to get his attention.

For whatever reason, Jake thinks of angels.

Yes, all right, sure. . .why not angels?

Thinking about angels, he thinks, might be a way to lighten things up.

So he does. . .and, thank God, things do lighten. . .because it's true, if angels did exist, this is exactly how they'd sound. He shakes his head at all he does not, will not ever, understand. Is it any harder to believe in angels than to believe in God? If one exists, why not the other?

Thus convinced, he feels grateful that angels are, this very instant, singing to him.

He opens his eyes and sees something, a strange sort of slithery movement, coming his way. It reminds him of a blip on a radar screen, a short wavy line shimmering vertical in the layered heat. He thinks of Tinker Bell. No, he tells himself, this is real. This is truly happening. He shields his eyes from the dazzling sun. The blip gets bigger, more solid, and the angels louder. Now he sees what looks like a body, with arms and legs floating below a faceless head. A ghost maybe? A spirit guide?

Oh, no. . . really?. . .was Castaneda telling the truth?

Whatever it is that's coming, Jake feels no fear. He wipes at the sweat dripping into his eyes. He squints, trying to clear his vision. His heart beats with peaked anticipation. His mouth is dry with awe. Then a short middle-aged man appears. *What a trip if. . .if this is my Don Juan.*

The thought makes his feet tingle. Or maybe they've just fallen asleep. He shifts position, calms himself, and waits to see what will happen next.

The man stops, a dirty white sombrero on his head. He is wearing dirty white pants and a dirty white shirt. Worn-out tire-tread sandals wrap around his dirty feet. He nods and steps closer, his body now blocking the sun to allow Jake a look at his face. It is a lined, sun-beaten, ancient face, as if carved by machete from a block of stone, its gaze full of sad, hard-earned truth.

Could this really be a messenger from another realm? Jake smiles up into those dark drooping eyes. "Hola," he says. "Buenos días."

"Hola," the man says. Then he says something Jake can't follow. Apparently confused by the gringo's confusion, the man points to where Jake is sitting.

"Qué?" says Jake, wondering what the man is pointing at.

"Señor," the man says, his eyes furrowed with concern, "*por favor.*" He makes a gentle motion with his hands, a sign for Jake to *please get up.*

Jake, intrigued by the urgency in the strange man's voice, lifts himself off the ground. Could it be, like Castaneda, he's wandered onto the dangerous power spot of some evil brujo? Could this spirit, disguised as a poor farmer, be warning him? Guiding him? Could Jake be on the verge of a lesson, or a way of living, never before imagined? Excited, he looks down to where the man is pointing and spots something small, hardly noticeable, flattened in the dirt. It's a. . .*a baby plant.*

Jake blinks, then looks around and sees the many baby plants everywhere around him. He's been sitting in a field of newly sprouted seedlings. Beans maybe? Zuchini? He doesn't know. He focuses on the tiny plant sprawled out at his feet. Sees that he has crushed it.

Jake drops to his knees and touches the severed stem. *Stupid fucking gringo.* He closes his eyes, listens for angels, but hears nothing.

He picks up the dead plant. Holds it in his open palm. Eyes spilling tears, he looks at the farmer, who seems embarrassed, looks away, clearly uncomfortable by his uncontrolled emotion. Jake can do nothing to change that either. He cannot remember how to say he's sorry. He cannot remember how to say anything.

The farmer looks back at him. The man's eyes are steady and insistent.

"Mira. . ." he says. "Está bien."

Jake knows *exactly* what he means: *Look, it's all right, because it has to be. Because there is no other choice. Because you are a foreigner,* the man is telling him, *because you understand nothing of a poor man's life, I forgive you for coming into my field and killing my plant. That is what you did, gringo. That is what happened. It happened, it is done, and there is nothing either of us can do about it. So why make things harder with your useless tears?*

Look, the man is saying, *the best you can do right now is go. . .just go away. And please, Señor, from now on, please. . .be more careful where you walk.*

Todos Santos

Jake finds his journal the next morning down by the river, soaked with dew. He can find no more mushrooms, so assumes he ate them all. The sadness he experienced with the farmer has softened his heart and focused his mind. He is grateful for the painful lesson. . .is watching every step. For several days he stays close to the water, or under his tree, either naked or partially covered by the flowery sarong. At night he sleeps as if wide-awake, as if aware of every sound, every movement, every unseen creature dancing out its life. Orph snores at his side while Jake follows lucid dreams streaming from his unconscious. There is no separation, everything overlaps, which gives him a sense of some grand design: a sense of himself, like the earth, as a heavenly body.

Then one morning he thinks, *Oh shit, is this what happened to that palapa guy?*

There is no chance to tell Ben and Kate goodbye. Not that it really matters; he knows they will understand. He drives south over rolling green hills, their pastures full of pitch-black cattle, toward the Guatemalan border. It feels like he's being guided. He skirts San Cristobal de las Casas, has no desire to stop. His mind is stuck on the concept of borders, *crossing borders*, the absurdity of trying to change a place by changing its name--keeping some people in, some people out-- trying to alter a natural fact with an arbitrary line. How weird is that? Familiar, which he now is, with the essential sameness of everything, will he see any real difference at a border?

Oh yes. Yes indeed. He arrives at ten in the morning, and, like a big nasty dose of reality, an armed soldier orders him out of the van, confiscates his passport, and leads him to a small dark room. There is a dirty window with a ragged curtain. A bare light bulb hangs from wires above his head. He sits on a metal folding chair in front of an old wooden desk.

A few minutes later a man comes in. He stands behind the desk, holding Jake's passport in his hand. CAPITÁN ROJAS is written on his name-tag, but he doesn't bother to introduce himself. In perfect English he says, "We need to know where you are coming from, where you are going, and what are your reasons for visiting Guatemala?"

Jake smiles. Same questions as Wis, only no bikini.

"Is something funny?" says the capitán.

"No."

"Then answer me."

"Sorry, sir, I can't. Where I've been, yeah. . .in Mexico. . .but the rest," he says, showing all ten fingers and both empty palms, *"quién sabe?"*

"Who do you work for?"

"Work for? No, I--look, really, I'm just a traveler. I've never been to Guatemala before, so I can't be sure where I'm going."

The capitán frowns, sits down, and keeps asking questions. Does Jake know anyone in Guatemala? Does he have photography equipment in the van? Does he mind if they check?

Jake figures it's his long hair being hassled, as yet unaware that five days earlier, the day he ate the forty-nine mushrooms, an article appeared in the *New York Times* alleging that human rights violations had been committed by the Guatemalan army.

"Journalists," the Capitán Rojas says, "are not permitted."

"I am not a journalist."

"I hope not. Because if you are lying we may have to shoot you."

"What?"

"If you lie about who you are," the capitán says, "who knows what else you lie about? There are enemy agents bringing trouble to Guatemala. We must be certain you are not one of them."

"I'm not."

"*Bueno*," says the capitán.

He hands Jake his passport, then advises him to stay away from the mountainous areas to the east. "It is dangerous there. You understand? Not a place you want to be."

On the road south, there are no obvious signs of danger. Only a couple of broken-down buses. It's not until he gets into Huehuetenango that Jake sees the first truckloads of soldiers. He goes into a Chinese restaurant on the main square. There he meets Stuart, a Peace Corp volunteer stationed in *Huehue*, who recommends the Guatemalan version of chow mein, which is bad enough, but then decides to be a tour guide.

"Sounds like you got some good advice," Stuart says. "Who knows what those fuckers are hiding up in the mountains. Best to stay away."

Jake just cannot deal with more directives on where not to go and what not to do. Perhaps reacting to his sense of helplessness at the border, he listens to Stuart's ambiguous alerts without much concern. He's been told to be afraid of something his entire life, and often believed it--often, except in Vietnam, without good reason. Sure, he needs to be careful, but rejects the idea of avoiding all possible danger. Leary once claimed that a proper dosage of LSD lasts from six to eight hours and has no discernable side effects. Magic mushrooms, Jake would have to conclude, are different. At least when taken to excess. It's now been five days since he ate the last of them, the only discernable effect being his total lack of fear.

Stuart pulls out a map of Guatemala. He spreads it over the table and points at the mountainous region above *Huehue*. "It's for sure they don't want anyone snooping around up there. Our supervisor told us to stay away."

"Why?"

"Who knows?" says Stuart. Then laughs. He looks a bit embarrassed by his lack of curiosity.

For Jake it seems imperative to go against Stuart's advice. And the capitán's, and his parents'. He examines the map and spots a town in the mountains called *Todos Santos*. *All Saints*. Hell yeah, he thinks, sounds good to him. "What about here?"

"Wish I knew, man. And probably glad I don't."

Stuart's doubt makes Jake certain he's chosen well. *Cool*, he almost says, but catches himself. What a stupid thing to say. Realizing how much he dislikes the word, he decides to never say it again. He wishes Stuart a nice life and heads for the van.

Orph licks his face, and looks happy that they're back in motion. Jake is happy too, for awhile. But the road to Todos Santos soon becomes a steep, curvy, perplexing mix of dirt--some packed hard as concrete, some loose as fairy dust--a great deal of it pot-holed, with two deep grooves formed by tires much larger than his. He stays far to the right, straddling the groove nearest the upper escarpment. Twice, however, forced to move inward by fallen rocks, he slips into the double rut, his under-carriage dropping, crashing, grinding against the dirt. Both times it is the softer kind. Both times, Jake leaves Orph whining in the van, and drops to his belly, and digs--a hammer's claw and bare hands his only tools. Both times, he feels lucky not to find any significant damage.

The dusty drive goes on and on. There are also streams to ford, the road in places close to gone because of all the water. So far he's escaped getting stuck, a possibility he refuses to worry about.

So OK, true, the ride to Todos Santos is a pain in the ass. Orph agrees, and keeps on whining, which makes the whole thing worse. Jake remembers Kate. "Please," he tells the dog, "you need to think of it as an adventure." But he keeps the truth to himself, that his confidence is fast eroding.

Jake tries to stay positive. North, south, east or west--the same. Clouds or potholes, dusty roads or waterfalls--the same. On the surface of things, of course, life's adventures are each a bit different. . .and some, without a doubt, more difficult than others. Some, like this nasty-ass road, are probably meant to agitate him--test him--gauge his equilibrium.

Right then, a big truck full of rifle-toting soldiers barrels around the corner. Jake swerves to avoid it, his left tires bouncing in and out of the high-side groove as he heads toward a protruding boulder. Panicked, too late for brakes, he swings the wheel back, the tires jerked down and up and down again into the waiting ruts, grinding him to another halt.

He turns off the engine, shakes his aching head, then squeezes and rattles the steering wheel as if to shake some sense into it. Orph barks. Jake throws open the door, climbs out, slams it behind him, and crawls under the van to dig and toss, dig and toss, until he can assess the damage.

The tail pipe is broken off, buried by thick red dust. The muffler is cracked.

"All right," he says, eyes closed, his inner therapist taking over. "All right." Head throbbing, nerves shot, he admits that he's had it, is sick of this, and tired of pretending otherwise. But, the thing is, he's now three hours in, over halfway there. . .and besides, what's more important, the road is far too steep and narrow for him to turn around.

That's when Jake surrenders; resigns himself to an adventure he does not want; accepts, as he knows he must, this long white-knuckled journey to who the fuck knows where?

Plain and simple, like it or not, this is what he's chosen.

It takes eight hours to reach Todos Santos. Three more than expected. Jake is beyond exhaustion, his body drained, his mind struggling to function. On the edge of town, barely visible through the thick dark fog, is a hotel--a small bluish concrete building called Tres Hermanas. Its owner, an Indian dressed in traje, rushes out to greet him, then opens a creaky metal gate for Jake to drive through, and locks it behind him. Jake grabs his pack--complete with water bottle, Orph's bowl, some dog food, a box of stale crackers, and his journal. He follows the owner back inside. There are three ugly bluish rooms, all on the second floor, each stinking of bleach. Jake sees no difference between them, so takes the last. He shuts the door. Locks it. Lies on the cold stiff bed, Orph cuddled up beside him.

He awakes to light flooding through his window, bright and warm and welcoming. The sky is a deep luxurious blue. Birds are singing. People are laughing down in the street, yacking at each other like a huge happy family. He checks his watch, sees it is already past noon. Orph's tail starts wagging hard. Jake hugs the beast, kisses his furry head, and gets him a bowl of food. At last free of yesterday's ordeal, back to his fearless self again, Jake can hardly wait to go see the village. And eat. Eat, yes, eat. He hasn't been so hungry since before the mushroom trip.

"My turn," he whispers in Orph's ear, and out they hurry into the new day.

Jake looks around at the Cuchumatanes mountains, engulfing Todos Santos like a crib around a baby. This is a magical place, he senses that right away. Other than Tres Hermanas, all of the buildings are whitewashed adobe structures with steep thatched-roofs. The road through town is narrow, filled with chickens, goats, dogs, and pigs. The women wear intricately woven tops, which Jake learned in Mexico are called *huipiles*. But it's the men who really surprise him--are even more colorful--dressed in red knee-high pants, red and white striped shirts with big embroidered collars, and short brownish hats that are too small for their heads. Most of the people gawk as he passes, as if wondering why he is there, but some show shy smiles, and a few of the men nod. One even shakes his hand as he passes. He's never felt this different, this alone. Now, he thinks, the true adventure begins. He would think he was dreaming except it's all too vivid. . .too strange. . .and here he is, greeting it face to face.

A small yellow dog, lean and scruffy, leaps from behind a group of men and snaps at Orph's snout. Orph somehow dodges the fierce jaws, snapping back in self-defense. Three other dogs charge his flank. Jake kicks back at the varied assaults. Owners shout, throw rocks, and tug at tails. Finally, the mongrels run off. A woman says something, some kind of apology, then scurries away.

Poor Orph. Whimpering, trembling, he cowers while Jake examines the wounds. A small girl comes over and pets the dog's head. Orph licks her face and she giggles.

"Gracias," says Jake.

Other small children begin to gather. At first they pet Orph. After a few minutes, though, they start stroking the curly blond hair on Jake's arms, smiling at him with huge brown eyes, and speaking softly in their native language. An older boy, missing an arm, stands across the way and watches. He seems to understand that Jake has no idea what the little ones are saying. With a determined look, he walks up and holds out his only hand. *Right*, thinks the gringo. *Should've known.*

Jake stands, reaches into his pocket, grabs all his coins, what amounts to less than a dollar, and distributes them among the children. Seeing that, others rush toward him. He uses a five-quetzal note to buy bananas and oranges. He gives most of those away too. And the change.

Keeping just a few pieces of fruit for himself, he heads for Tres Hermanas. The horde of children follow close behind. At the entry, a boy he had not yet seen, this one with severely sunken cheeks, blocks his way. The shamed look on the child's dirty face says he does it because he has to. Jake stares at the boy, who is staring at him--each of them, it seems to Jake, pleading with the other, and also apologizing--both trying to understand why life has brought them to this terrible moment.

The owner of Tres Hermanas watches from the door. Jake doesn't know how to ask for help. Overwhelmed, he drops the remaining fruit and squeezes past the boy. A barrage of tiny hands grab after him, tugging at his sweatshirt. The owner lets Jake and Orph in, then closes the door. Overjoyed the night before, when the gringo showed up to rent a room, the man now looks sad, perhaps feeling sorry for him, or the children, or both. He gives Jake a tender smile and pats him on the shoulder.

The gringo sighs and returns the pat, then goes to his room for what's left of the stale crackers. He locks himself in, lies on his bed, and opens his journal to a blank page.

TODOS SANTOS, he writes, but doesn't know what to say.

He sets the book down and closes his eyes. Time for some serious thinking. Why does he have this sense that something is missing? As if by instinct, he reaches into his pocket to make sure his wallet is still there, which it is. *Oh come on*, he thinks, ashamed at his distrust of those poor children. He tries, for hours, to understand his discordant feelings. How can this simple place, so plainly good and innocent, at the same time seem so dangerous? Still trying to make sense of it, he falls asleep.

Or half-asleep. He's aware of being in this room, lying in this bed, while dreaming of his high-school girlfriend, Gail. She stands at the counter in his parent's kitchen, mixing a batch of pancakes. Gail was the first girl to intentionally, hands-on, give him an erection. Then let him have sex with her. Or, rather, try. It happened on the floor of the old granary building. Not sure of what to do once she squeezed him in--and confused by the unknown voices in his head, one of which sounded like his mother, warning this would happen--he quickly went soft.

"Don't worry," Gail says in his dream. Same as she said back on the granary floor. The wooden spoon clatters round the clear glass bowl as she stirs and stirs. Smiling, she glances at him over her shoulder and promises, "We'll try again."

Gail stands there in her cheerleader's costume, Salina's green and gold, but in the fabric of Jake's dream it is transparent, her naked ass jostling back and forth as he watches from the kitchen table, as he lies there in his bed at Tres Hermanas--in both places, simultaneously--horny and anxious. He is certain this would be a most enjoyable dream if he did not already know that shortly after her actual promise, in spite of how often she said she wants to marry him. . .have children with him. . .and a yellow house with a white picket fence. . .she would say she's fallen in love with someone else.

Suddenly, as dreams often do, everything changes. It is now dark in the kitchen. Dark as his hotel room. A mosquito buzzes close to his right ear. He hears Gail outside and looks through the invisible wall at her riding a horse, a long-legged obsidian stallion. She is holding something in her right hand. A flag? Yes, a flag, a white and blue striped flag. She stops the horse, looks up at him and cries. He opens his eyes. His watch says 5 A.M. *What, so soon?* He goes to the window. Orph is with him, whimpering at his side. This is not a dream, it can't be Gail crying, so what's going on?

Down in the street, in the hazy light of dawn, people are passing by. Each holds a candle. Some are crying, others moaning. He opens the curtain further. There are many more people behind the ones in front, crammed together up the road as far as he can see. Some are grouped together, hands above their heads, carrying large cloth-draped bundles.

Bodies, Jake realizes, cued by the oblong shapes. Dead people.

Then comes a sound that makes him gasp: a sustained, high-pitched howl. It is a human voice, a wail, though more like that of a screeching animal, a creature in unbearable pain. Orph begins to growl. Jake muzzles him with one hand, closes the curtain with the other, and huddles down below the window. The dog stays quiet as Jake covers his ears to block the awful noise. But he can feel it searching for him. No, not searching, because it knows exactly where he's hiding.

A warning is what it is. Maybe a threat. *You should not be here!* it howls. *Not here! Not now!*

Floating Fish *April 30, 1976*

Jake left Todos Santos early the next morning. Late that afternoon, back in Huehuetenango, he found a mechanic to patch his muffler and reconnect his tailpipe, then slept on the outskirts of town in a cheap hotel. No, he realized, there could be no perpetual high in this world. . .no enlightenment that did not include the darkness.

Jerry said it right. When life looks like easy street, man, there's sure as hell danger at your door!

The following day he drove straight to Lake Atitlán. He'd heard about it, like so many others, not from the writings of Aldous Huxley but from someone who had heard about the writings of Aldous Huxley. The famously mystical Englishman put Atitlán on the map in 1934 when he agreed with Von Humboldt that it was 'the most beautiful lake in the world.'

Jake stopped at one of the lookouts, and looked for a long time at the glittering expanse of water beneath the massive volcanoes. The magnificence of it, maybe because of all he'd been through lately, felt overwhelming, almost frightening.

That night he stayed at the RivaBella--an arrangement of blocky little duplex cabañas on the edge of Panajachel. He slept most of the next day, only venturing out to let Orph do his business. Or for food. He could not resist the chicken grilled by a street vendor. That's what he was hungry for, so that's what he ate. Jake's vegetarian days were over. No more idealism. No more *creating his own reality*. No more pretending his fear was finally gone. He needed to sober up, get real, see things as they truly were.

He decided to travel on the mail boat to Santiago, the biggest village, and from there go the rest of the way around the lake by foot. He would stop in all the villages. He felt the need to know this place. The attendant at the RivaBella would watch over his van in exchange for the advanced payment of a two-night stay whenever he returned. The boat, he was told, left early the next morning, so he readied his backpack and went to bed as soon as it got dark.

Next thing he knew, Orph was whining loud, pawing at the bed. Jake grabbed his flashlight and looked at his watch. *Three in the morning? Really?* He aimed it at the dog's crazy eyes. "Give me a fucking break!"

Orph, now barking, jumped up on the mattress.

"Dammit!" said Jake, and slapped his nose hard. "No!" he shouted, "bad dog!"

Then he felt the shaking. At first he thought Orph was doing it and slapped at him again. The dog bee-lined for the door as a vase of flowers came crashing to the floor. One of the windows shattered.

"Oh shit," Jake said, scrambling from the bed and charging outside.

There were others in the central garden area. They, like the trees and buildings, were swaying back and forth. One woman was down on her knees, her tear-drenched face opened to the starry sky, praying for something Jake could not understand. *"Que mis ojos veian!"* she kept pleading.

The earthquake lasted only a couple of minutes, maybe less, though it seemed much longer. When it was over, everyone remained in the same positions. Stunned.

The praying woman saw Jake in front of her and slapped at the air. *"Ay, Dios!"* she screeched at his nakedness, and hid her face with both hands.

Jake covered his genitals and rushed back to the room. Eventually he fell asleep. Then Orph started barking like before. Jake bolted upright. What, was he dreaming? No, because it was now light outside. When the shaking came he jumped up, slipped on his underwear, and ran for the door. The same people were in the patio, the same woman on her knees praying.

"*Por favor, Señor,*" she screamed, "*perdónenos! Perdónenos por todo!*"

From then on, every two or three hours, the earth shook hard and everyone ran to the garden. The praying woman was always there, always on her knees.

Late that afternoon, needing to get away, Jake decided it safe enough for a walk around town. He saw only a few collapsed buildings, but was certain the damage had been much worse. He went down to the lake, and was surprised to find so many people there, standing along the shore. They gazed out at the water as if into a crystal ball. A few were talking, but sound seemed to stop just beyond their mouths, sucked into the deafening silence like gnats into a vacuum cleaner. Most, including Jake, could not manage to speak, mesmerized by what they saw: the lake covered with thousands and thousands of dead fish--silver bodies floating on the water, flashing in the sun like an armada of sinking ships.

The mail boat was cancelled. All roads were closed except for emergency vehicles. Aftershocks, too many to count, came intermittently over the next few weeks, some nearly equal to the primary quake of 7.5. Those were what caused most of the damage, the tectonic plate shifting in different directions, taking down the already weakened structures.

Jake learned these facts from the newspaper, *La Prensa*, delivered every day or two as part of the government's emergency response--a way to keep people, and especially the tourists, aware of what was going on.

It was translated by a middle-aged guy named Richard, a Canadian, who liked to hang out at the Bluebird Cafe, drink cup after cup of coffee, and analyze the news for anyone willing to listen. Adobe huts had crumbled. Lots of villages had been leveled. The death toll had reached 20,000, with 50,000 wounded. Hundreds of thousands of homes were destroyed and at least a million people displaced. The full breadth of the disaster would not be known for some time.

Soon after the initial earthquake, the newspaper said, President Laugerud García invited foreign ambassadors to tour the affected regions by helicopter. From those heights, Richard concluded, one could identify the ruined villages without seeing or speaking to any of the people, who might also have complained of other things. "Like," he said, "the long history of government abuse, of stealing indigenous land, of killing anyone who made a fuss." He talked about the United Fruit Company, Land Reform in the 1950's, the CIA coup in '54, and many other things Jake had never heard of.

There was something about Richard that rubbed Jake wrong. Maybe it was his bald head--or his too-white, too-wrinkled face--or the heavy dark pouches under his steely blue eyes--or the acid-burned certainty of his voice. Maybe it was the way he sat there making speeches, holding court, like it was his sworn duty to inform the ignorant masses of truths they would otherwise never know.

"Wait," Jake said. "Someone told me that things have gotten better with this president, that there's less violence."

"Less, maybe. Or maybe just less obvious. Or less investigated. People were beginning to notice all the dead bodies, so something had to change. Garcia is not really better than the rest," Richard said, "just smarter. More convincing. Since returning to their countries, the ambassadors have arranged for financial assistance. More important than the money, I'm sure, it must be a great relief for García and the ruling aristocracy to be out of the news as human rights violators. . .to be seen as victims. Finally, you know, they get a bit of sympathy. The foreign money will go to roads and bridges used by tourists and the army. Doubtful that any of it will reach a poor village."

"C'mon, Richard, how could you possibly know all that?"

"I couldn't. That's the point. That's how they get away with it."

"So it's just your opinion?"

"I've lived here for ten years, man. I've paid attention."

"But the United States is providing a lot of the relief, right? Wouldn't they be able to direct where it goes?"

"Oh c'mon, where the hell have you been? The U.S. government knows exactly what's happening here. And approves. They know what roads need to be fixed. They know which villages need to be ignored. The earthquake is a perfect opportunity to isolate and punish their enemies. The way your government sees it, Indian insurgents are nothing but communists. Period. For them it's a revolution against Guatemala's supposedly democratic government, which is much more catastrophic than a natural disaster."

Three days later, foreigners were publicly asked to leave. It was on the radio and in the papers. 'A chance for the country to heal itself,' government officials said.

"Like butchers," Richard said, "pretending to be surgeons. It's their way of getting what they've wanted for years, to rid themselves of nosy journalists and us pushy humanitarian types. Of course they'll keep the construction engineers and corporate reps--people who can help re-build Guatemala, re-make it into the kind of country fit for a ruling class."

Jake's initial skepticism, he realized, had been aimed at Richard.

He'd just wanted the arrogant prick to be wrong. What a drag when the guy kept proving he knew the relevant history, understood the politics, could analyze the connection and articulate it so well.

It was not, of course, any great surprise to Jake that The United States had once again bet on the wrong horse, and would kill to see it win. What was this, another Vietnam?

Again the rage rose up in him.

As the days wore on, however, his anger gave way to a deepening sadness, a widening despair. Ordered or not, it was time for him to get out of Guatemala. While knowing little of the actual facts, or if any of Richard's specific accusations were true, it was the sorrow of the people that moved him, their dirty bare feet scurrying for safety with each and every aftershock, their tender eyes traumatized with grief.

He would remember this as a beautiful place, a magical place, a place where he'd learned some important lessons. In spite of all that, he'd never have returned were it not for Luanne.

New Job *March, 1980*

Luanne dreamt in the same colors as Jaime. Many years earlier, in the pre-dawn darkness of her Grateful Dead acid trip, the dreams had begun: orange women balancing yellow baskets on their heads; purple volcanoes exploding green; red men reaching for a blue sky; objects and people mixing, threading together, like a shape-shifting lightshow.

Her parents knew nothing of these dreams. Not something she could share since they already thought her *flighty*, especially after discovering the thorough deception of that Winterland night. From then on, they'd carefully screened her friends; prohibited any sleepovers or late night parties; outlawed all rock concerts; insisted she attend the local junior college; made sure her time was accounted for and well spent. Even when she turned eighteen, though 'encouraged' by the excellent grades, they'd kept her on a tight leash. Their strict parental guidance, however, while halting any obvious types of trouble, had one huge unintended consequence: her dreams increased and became more luminous.

Luanne earned a bachelor's degree from San Jose State University, in Northern California, in May of 1978. She majored in art (specializing in fibers) and minored in Spanish. After graduating, she worked days at a bank, nights at a pizza parlor, and saved her money. She talked to lots of travelers--
gave it plenty of consideration--before buying a ticket to Guatemala.

"Where?" her mother said. "You're going where?"

"Isn't there a war," her father mumbled into his morning paper.

"Yes," her mother said. "And from what I've seen on the news, it's getting worse."

Luanne could not deny it. That, in a sense, though she could not say it, was her main reason for going. "It's not happening where the tourists go."

Her mother's right eyebrow arched. Not a good sign. "Oh?" she said. "Is that what the generals told you, dear? When did you receive your last report?"

The sarcasm was fair. Luanne knew next to nothing about the war. It only mattered that people were suffering there and she felt a connection to them. She felt responsible somehow, but had no idea why. So it would sound silly to say it. . .or that she'd been thinking of Guatemala ever since meeting the bracelet woman at the Dead concert five years earlier.

For Luanne, it had to do with doing something meaningful. How could she explain such a thing to her parents when she did not understand it herself? They would call it *impulsive, rash, self-indulgent*. Further proof of her *flightiness*. Ugh.

Then came the most wonderful idea. Yes, of course, she'd say it was a way to make money: a job that would also allow her to be socially responsible. They'd think her creative and ambitious.

In the closed circuit of her idealistic mind it seemed absolutely reasonable.

"I'm going to start a business," Luanne said. Soon as the words came out of her mouth she knew how impulsive and rash and self-indulgent they must sound to her parents. "I can buy beautiful macramé bracelets from the Indians there and--"

"Bracelets?" said her father. "Did she say bracelets?"

"Oh. . .please," her mother said. In spite of her slight frame and prematurely lined face, she was an imposing presence in Luanne's life, strong and silent except during times, like these, when anyone dared oppose her. Her words--when angry, like now--could stop the very earth from turning. "You're almost twenty-one, dear. Don't you think it's time to take life seriously?"

Luanne felt her heart shiver. There was no point trying to explain. But the voice of the bracelet woman soothed her mind and urged her on. *It's OK, hon. Really. It's OK.*

"Yes, Mom," she said. "That's what I'm trying to do."

It is late afternoon. The sun lights the swirling tops of puffy white clouds. Then, as they descend, a foggy gloom swallows the plane with one great gulp, hiding the tin rooftops of Guatemala City, the deep ravines carving them apart, and any sign of an airport. The plane seems to be falling. Luanne's stomach falls with it. Prayers can be heard throughout the cabin. Suddenly they're jerked back upward, as if God has reached down from the heavens to grab the plane by its scrawny neck. Then shake it. The man sitting next to Luanne mumbles to himself in Spanish. He kisses the cross that hangs around his neck.

Seconds later comes a rubbery bounce, then a series of thumps and skids before the tires finally grip the runway. People cheer at the mighty pull of hydraulic brakes. Some laugh out loud while others wipe away their tears. The man pats Luanne on the knee and says, "Milagro . . .milagro."

Outside the airport, four taxi-drivers rush toward her. She fends them off and walks to one on the outer fringe, a heavyset man with a gentle face, who smiles and puts her duffle in his trunk. He opens the back door and waits as she settles in.

"Gracias," she says.

"Me gude luke," he smiles.

Once he's behind the wheel she hands him a piece of paper. It's the name of the hotel where her friend Evelyn advised her to stay: El Placer

(The Pleasure). After seeing what she's written, he gives Luanne a strange look. His hesitation confuses her until she realizes that he's thinking of how to say something. His smile wobbles, turning to a frown.

"Gooing theece place?" he says. "To be shore?"

She takes it he does not approve. Also that he believes she speaks little or no Spanish. Her fault. In her nervousness, she forgot to say Buenos días, or Qué tal, or any of the other common salutations which might let him know she understands his language. She doesn't speak much, it's true, but enough to have been more polite. "Sí," she says, "una amiga me avisó."

"Ah," he says, driving off, "usted habla Español. Bueno. Me llamo Pedro."

"Hola Pedro. Me llamo Luanne."

"Mucho gusto."

"El gusto," she says (thrilled for the phrase that in Spanish class had seemed so stilted) "es mío."

Pedro, relieved by their switch to Spanish, now speaks faster than she can follow, repeating the word *cómodo* (*comfortable*) many times, then something about *another hotel, a better hotel* than El Placer.

"Good," he says, and this she gets exactly, "I will bring you to Las Palomas."

"No," she says. "I want to go to El Placer."

He slows his Spanish to guarantee she understands. "Please, Senorita...not El Placer. I know you will not like it."

"Why?"

"Very old. Very dirty."

"*Cheap*," says Luanne. The word is *Barato*. Evelyn's word. A word he definitely understands, so she decides to underline it. "Very *cheap*, Pedro. *Cheap* is what I want."

"As I said, Señorita, Las Palomas is my uncle's hotel. It is a clean place. Not expensive."

Yeah, right, got it. Evelyn warned her this would happen. Some hotels give taxi drivers a commission for bringing them tourists. But even if it really is his uncle's hotel, what guarantee is that? Why should she trust him instead of her own friend? The problem is, she has no idea how to express her thinking in proper Spanish. She would need a better command of the language for it to not sound insulting. The best she can do is say, "Sorry, Pedro, I do not know your uncle."

"Yes, yes, I will take you there to meet him. And my aunt and cousins! You will see what a--"

"No. . .thank you," Luanne says, her voice firm. "Please, Pedro, take me to El Placer."

"Si Señorita," Pedro says. He hesitates, then says in English, "me gude *play-shore*."

She sees him eyeing her from the rear-view mirror. He's smiling, making a joke, and it's clear he's taken no offense.

Nothing wrong with trying, that's what his smile is telling her.

Luanne is surprised by how long it takes to get there, and the shabbiness of Zone 1. Zone 1, she hoped, might have something to do with its relative charm. Uh. . .no. Evelyn made a big deal of the fact that El Placer is close to the main bus station, but said nothing about how crowded the area is, or how run down and dangerous it looks. Apparently more important to Evelyn (an 'extra bonus' she said), it's across the street from a fast-food chicken place, Pollo Campero, the Guatemalan equivalent of Colonel Sanders. "What more could you ask for?" she said. "Instant dinner!"

While the happy chicken of Pollo Campero gives Luanne a laugh, the sight of El Placer makes her shiver. A once yellow building, like a forgotten banana, it shows definite signs of rot. Pedro lifts his eyebrows as her disappointment meets his gaze. "Seguro?" he says.

"Sí," she says, lacking the confidence to go against her friend. "Seguro."

"Bueno," he says, getting her duffel from the trunk. He rings the bell. She pays the fare, and includes a good tip. Pedro shakes her hand, wishes her luck, hops in his taxi and pulls away.

The door opens. There stands a small middle-aged woman who reminds Luanne of her mother, though more purposefully proper, her hair pinned back in a tight little bun. "You want a room," she says in rapid Spanish. A statement of fact. Business, just business.

"Um, yes."

"Bathroom?"

"What?"

"Do. . .you. . .want. . .a. . .room" says the woman, careful to enunciate each syllable, "with. . . a. . .bathroom?"

"Oh," says Luanne. "Yes. Please."

"Two. . ." says the woman, showing with her fingers. . ."quetzales."

A room, with a private bath, for the equivalent of two dollars? Luanne's shoulders relax a bit. For that price, hey, how can she lose? "Yes, all right."

"Good. Come with me." She hurries Luanne through a cramped foyer that leads down a long dark stuffy hall. "The room is at the end." When they get there, the woman opens a door into moist dead air and flicks on a light. Luanne looks up at a bare bulb hanging from the ceiling by a pair of wires. She discerns the conflicting odors of chlorine and mold. The woman hands Luanne the key. "Our best," she says.

"Oh. . .thank you."

"Two quetzales," the woman says, holding out her hand.

Luanne sets her duffle on the yellowish linoleum floor and fumbles with the money pack hidden inside her skirt. She fingers through the violet five quetzal notes and red tens and blue twenties she got at the airport. Finally she finds the green ones. Two of them. The woman looked away while Luanne hunted for the money. Sensing she's found it, her attention returns. Luanne hands over the bills and the woman walks off.

Luanne closes the door, examines her room. Surrounding the yellowish linoleum floor is a square of bare pinkish walls, like mottled flesh. One of them has a tiny window that looks out at the tiny window of another building. It is getting dark outside. She pulls the curtain closed and sits on the rock-hard mattress. To the right is an old fruit crate. There is bible on it, but no lamp. Luanne lies down, closes her eyes, and tries to imagine sleeping. Seconds later she is staring at the glossy white water-stained ceiling.

She gets up and goes to the bathroom, its floor covered with the same yellowish linoleum. There is a grungy sink, a grungy toilet, and to her left, as if hidden away behind the mildewed curtain, a grungy shower stall of brownish tiles and grayish grout. Luanne forces herself not to care. *Yes, thank God, at least there's a shower!*

She makes sure that the room's door is locked before taking off her clothes. Her nakedness accentuates the cold floor, the cold room, the bone-chilling coldness she feels toward this terrible place. She runs, shivering, to the shower, and turns the rusty spigot to the left, the only direction it will go. But nothing happens. She looks up at the rusty headless pipe sprouting from the wall. Above it is a rusty metal box. Two wires--one white, one black--run from the box and are clamped around the pipe. *Huh?*

Luanne puts on her clothes. She finds the woman in the kitchen, washing dishes, listening to a loud man's lecture--or maybe it's a sermon--coming from the radio.

The gringa clears her throat. "Excuse me."

The woman twists her head around. "Yes?"

"There is no water."

The woman looks at her wet hands. "No?"

"In my shower," Luanne says.

The woman's apparent puzzlement turns to obvious irritation. "Berto!" she shouts.

"Yes?" comes a pathetic male voice from the adjoining room.

"You need to turn her water on!"

"Ay!" he yelps, as if being whipped. "Yes, yes, I forgot."

"One moment," the woman says, and goes back to her dishes.

"Um. . .also. . ." says Luanne.

The woman does not bother to turn around. "Yes?"

"I want hot water."

"Hot water, yes, of course."

Not knowing the word for wires, or switch (or if, perchance, there is a particular bible passage she must recite in order to avoid electrocution), Luanne says, "Can you show me?"

"Berto!" shouts the woman, and turns up the radio.

"Hay que hacerlo!" ("It must be done!") the loud man orders.

Luanne hears the Spanish words for 'communist' and 'insurgent' and realizes he's a politician of some sort. She hears 'in the mountains' and 'innocent victims' and 'What a shame! What a shame!'

The woman glances back at Luanne, apparently annoyed that she is still there.

"Berto!" she shouts again.

"Yes," says an old man, panting as he enters the kitchen.

Eyeglasses hang from the end of his nose. There is a newspaper in his hands. "Yes, I turned it on."

"Show her how to get hot water."

His eyes light up when he sees Luanne. "Oh, yes, all right." Berto re-aligns his glasses and sets the paper on the kitchen table. "Come," he says with a short wink, gesturing her to follow.

Back in her bathroom, as if performing a bit of magic, Berto smiles and turns on the spigot, which issues forth a sound of distant gurgling and several foul burps. A few seconds later comes a short brown spurt, then some semblance of clear, flowing, water. Not much, though perhaps enough to wash her hair.

"To make it hot," Berto says, "you turn the faucet to the right."

When he does, the flow returns to a dribble and a buzzing sound is heard. Electricity, Luanne presumes, coursing through those wires.

"You understand?" he says.

"I understand."

"Go on, go on, try it," Berto says. He seems surprised that she is not more impressed.

"Yes," Luanne says, nodding, and touches the water, agreeing that it is, indeed, "not so cold."

"If you want it hotter, just keep turning the pressure down."

"Gracias," she says, convinced there is no use complaining.

"De nada," he says (a phrase that has come to mean "You're welcome" though literally translates as "For nothing". . .which for Luanne, right then, feels closer to the truth).

She locks the door behind him, sits on the bed, and checks her watch. Eight o'clock. There's no point trying to sleep, taking a shower is out of the question, and it's far too dark to read. She'd love to go outside, but knows that nights are not safe in any city. Especially

Guatemala City. Can she bear the idea of going across the street for fast-food chicken? No. She lies back on the bed, and cries, and berates herself for never once questioning Evelyn's advice. Cheap is one thing, but this is ridiculous.

"Oh well," she whispers, which does not comfort her in the least. Still, she's aware that anger and disappointment will not make *The Pleasure* any nicer. *C'mon, c'mon, it's not Evelyn's fault. Not anyone's fault.* Luanne hates the saying 'shit happens,' but saying it somehow calms her down. She tucks in under the scratchy blanket and thinks about friendship bracelets. The bracelets are why she's here. That's what she needs to remember. With her eyes closed she can almost see them, thread after colorful thread, white arrows shooting across a deep blue lake, rising above green volcanoes into a crimson sky, like birds flapping toward the thin black line of horizon, the line thickening as they approach, absorbing them and turning lighter, a silvery gray, then violet, then glowing pink.

And, wonder of wonders, just like that it's morning! Shocked silly by the sunshine against her curtained window, she grabs her duffel and flees the room.

In the foyer, Luanne finds Berto. "Buenos días!" she beams.

"Buenos días!" he beams back.

The world is suddenly vibrant, everything seems possible, and, best of all, she's thinking in Spanish! Certain of the words, she lets them go tumbling from her mouth: "Can you tell me, please, where to find the bus to Lake Atitlán?"

He leads her out through the front door. "There," he says, pointing up the street. He looks at his watch. "But," he frowns, "there is only one and it's leaving soon."

"Thank you," Luanne says, and starts running.

"Faster!" he shouts.

A multi-colored bus goes zooming by. A boy hangs from its passenger door screaming, "Pana! Pana! Pana!" It screeches to a halt by a small building up ahead. The boy jumps out in front of the exiting passengers. He climbs the back ladder to the top of the bus, unties ropes, and starts lowering some of the cargo, mostly small crates, one of them full of what look to Luanne like live chickens. Now half a block away, she must stop and switch her duffle to the other hand. New people are piling into the bus. Another boy rushes from the building and tosses a few satchels to the one up top. Luanne is panting, not quite there, but the boy on the ground sees her. He runs to grab her bag, shouting, *"Apúrate! Apúrate!" Hurry! Hurry!* He charges ahead and throws the bag to the kid on the roof. Out of breath, she reaches the door, climbs the steps, and sees the bus is full, which stops her cold, but a tiny Indian woman nudges from behind, forcing her forward.

"Disculpe," says Luanne, squeezing past akimbo knees and feet and elbows, to the rear of the bus, where she stands in the narrow aisle with a line of others. The pushy woman backs up against her and the bus roars down the road.

Luanne cannot help smiling. "Riding a chicken bus," Evelyn told her, "is an experience you'll never forget! Best way to know the real Guatemala!"

"Aquí, Señorita." It is a young Indian man, offering her his seat. Or, rather, the outer edge of a seat already occupied by two large Indian women.

"Gracias," Luanne says, and sits. The Indian women look at her. "Buenos días," she says, and they turn away, giggling with each other, jabbering in a language she has never heard. From her studies she learned that there are twenty-two different Indian languages in Guatemala, and that a majority of Indians speak little or no Spanish.

No problema, she thinks, glad for the chance to be respectfully unsociable.

It is supposed to be four hours to the lake via the 'new' Pan American Highway, but lengths of it are still being fixed after the devastating earthquake of 1976--meaning regular delays. That, plus the random stops every time someone wants to get on or off, means the trip will take far longer. At some point the 'Pana! Pana! Pana!' boy decides to collect fares. To do so, he slithers through the people packed in the aisle, or climbs over those in the seats. No one seems to mind.

Four hours into the journey, in Chimaltenango, lots of people leave. Luanne sees a spot up front. She goes for it and slides in next to a disheveled old man. Though he smells, which may be why everyone else has avoided him, she feels grateful for the extra space.

Soon they are lumbering up a steep two-lane road. Directly ahead is another old multicolored chicken bus, this one spewing clouds of thick black smoke. Luanne tries to close the window. Can't. Everyone coughs and covers their faces. No way around it. No safe way, that is, a fact which deters their driver for only a few brief moments, until the first possible opportunity--a short level straightaway before another uphill curve--when he veers into the other lane to try and pass his stinking twin.

Luanne screams, "Oh my God!"

The smelly man looks at her and laughs. Halfway into the blind curve, their driver cuts the other bus off, somehow missing a large dump truck barreling down the hill.

Luanne is shocked that no one seems upset.

For the next four hours there are many such moments. The *gringa* learns to tame her terror by pretending she is already dead. She looks around and smiles at all the blank Indian faces.

Maybe that's their secret too?

At some point, a heavyset woman, along with two small children and a dog, pile in beside her and the smelly man. The bus continues to careen around blind corners like a chicken with its head cut off. The kid next to the woman vomits on the floor and the dog licks it up. Luanne covers her nose. An old guy from across the aisle kicks the dog, and, to Luanne's amazement, screams "Slow down!" Which seems to really piss the driver off. As he squeals around the following turn, Luanne focuses on the large decal displayed above his head: GOD IS MY GUIDE, HEAVEN MY DESTINATION.

She can only hope he hasn't yet given up on this difficult world.

At Los Encuentros, lucky for her, he stops for other passengers. Before they can get on, she gets off. The 'Pana! Pana! Pana!' boy gives her a strange look, then tries to explain that this is not Pana, that she needs to get back on the bus.

"No," she says. "I'm staying here."

The boy looks embarrassed for the stupid gringa, but hurries to untie her bag and lower it down.

For more than an hour she just sits on side of the road, thankful to be alive.

Los Encuentros is a busy place, full of buses coming and going, people scurrying from one to the next. Though she'd rather stay right where she is, Luanne sees that the sun is beginning to set.

"Which bus goes to Panajachel?" she asks a woman selling melons.

"No other bus until tomorrow," the woman says. Then, seeing the gringa's obvious worry, she points toward a line of pickup trucks. "Now you have to go in one of those."

Luanne thanks the woman, secretly thrilled at the chance to avoid a bus. She climbs into the back of the first pickup. Her timing seems perfect. She settles onto the right bench seat, its final open slot, and feels happy, breathing normally again. She looks forward to the ride, but the driver seems in no great hurry. People keep piling in, filling the space between the benches, until there is no possible way to fit anyone else. Then two men stand on the back bumper and hold on to the tailgate.

The truck lurches forward, is soon at full throttle, charging like an angry bull down the mountain. In the village of Sololá, there is a quick re-shuffling of bodies. Three off, three more on. The tailgate men have disappeared, replaced by two others and a small boy. As they pull away, someone up front shifts position, the movement rippling back, a sack of what smells like onions swinging in front of Luanne's face. She stands in search of air and her seat disappears. The woman who took it now maneuvers for a bit more room, poking her knees into Luanne's calf. The man with the burlap sack turns and their noses almost touch. He smiles. . .a nice smile. . .but not right then a welcome one. *Calm*, Luanne tells herself. *Easy*. She reaches over and clenches the wooden railing.

The road keeps getting worse, now ridiculously steep and narrow, with nothing but tight curves. Her stomach churns. Her heart groans. Her head drowns in worthless thoughts. All these different buses and trucks, all these different drivers, every one of them the same--like lemmings on speed--as if manufactured in some demonic underworld factory to produce a constant state of danger for these poor unfortunate people who have no other means of transportation.

At last the lake appears, down below, like heaven. She steers her skidding mind out into the sparkling water and lets it sink.

Twenty minutes later the truck stops.

"Panajachel!" someone shouts from the cab.

Luanne climbs out and finds the twenty-centavos to pay the driver. Stunned and nauseous, she waits for the earth to stop swaying, then waddles down the street with her duffle, directed by locals to the Cacique Inn--what someone, somewhere, said was the nicest place in town.

Thirteen quetzales a night, who cares? It's a bright, clean room . . .with a soft bed for later. . .a warm shower for now.

Having not eaten since early the previous day, she throws on her clothes and hurries for the restaurant. And a stiff drink. A white-shirted, black-tied waiter, with a pretty face, shows her a menu. Yes, she can get a steak and a Jack Daniels on the rocks. Good enough. Luanne has never had hard liquor, and believes the time has come. Sipping it, she considers her next move.

Evelyn suggested she see the lake first, then go to the more interesting village of Chichicastenango (Chichi) where the better crafts are found. The problem is, that would mean more pickup trucks and chicken buses. She orders another drink.

"You're new here," says a guy with a Hawaiian shirt and a clipped blond beard. He sounds English, or maybe Australian. She nods and smiles and looks away.

"My name's Phil," he says. "I'm the village idiot."

"Really?"

"Well, no, but that's what all the idiots think."

She laughs. He's older, maybe late thirties. . .tall, good looking, and indeed an Australian. The best part is his sense of humor, which is great for Luanne because, she knows, before anything else can get figured out, she needs to laugh, loosen up, get out of her traffic-jammed head.

To that end, once she's finished her steak, she lets him buy her a third drink, then agrees to go to his room (no funny stuff, he promises) and smoke a joint. After the first toke, Phil tries to kiss her. Luanne pulls away. She considers leaving, but decides against it. She does not want him to think she's afraid.

"What," she asks, "do the Guatemalans call you?"

"Used to be *Feel*. A tad creepy, don't you think? I mean who wants to be known as *Señor Feel?*"

Funny guy, no doubt about that. "But the name Phillip, I think, would be--"

"*FAY-LEAP-AY*," he says. Yes, that's right. SEÑOR FAY-LEAP-AY to you."

"Bueno, SEÑOR FAY-LEAP-AY."

"Well, you know, you'll have a problem too. Señorita Luanne simply won't cut it." He leans in to steal a kiss and she pushes him away.

"Listen," she says, "just to be clear, OK, I am not remotely interested in having sex with you."

Mere seconds later they're swapping spit and feeling each other up. The passion lasts for several minutes, until Luanne needs to come up for air. She flops her legs over the side of the bed and takes several deep breaths.

"I was thinking of a new name for you," Phil says. "How about Lucrecia?"

"Sounds like a witch."

"Yeah," he says, "that's what I mean. You sure put a spell on me, darlin'."

"I think I'm going to puke."

"No," he laughs, reaching out and pulling her on top of him, "I mean it."

"So do I," she says, her stomach heaving.

"Oh Christ," says Phil, pushing her off.

He guides her to the bathroom and stays by her side while she gets sick. He runs a hot bath and gives her a clean towel. And plenty of time alone. During her bath he goes to buy antacid, a hard thing to find in

Guatemala at eight o'clock at night. She appreciates his effort, agrees to stay the night, and is grateful when he lets her sleep.

Luanne tells him she is in Guatemala to look for pulseras, and Phil says he wants to help. He has no idea where these bracelets might be found, but that won't stop him. "I'm unstoppable," he says, kissing her cheek, "if there's something I really want." Chichi, Phil agrees, is a good place to look, and he knows someone with a car, someone who will take them.

"OK," Luanne says, "great."

While waiting for that to happen, they take a boat across the lake to Santiago--her idea--to look for pulseras there. No luck, but they end up staying a week--her treat--and have lots of great sex. After that they go to San Pedro for a few days, also her treat, and by then it's only about the sex.

Luanne, a twenty-one-year-old with a penchant for idealism, keeps thinking, or perhaps just hoping, it must be more. . .that they might actually be in love. She starts imagining herself with Phil, off on adventures all over the world. The thoughts come more and more frequently as she waits for him to come back from some trip he had to make to the city.

Then some woman named Frankie, one of Phil's former girlfriends, stops her on the Santander. There is no context for this meeting, they've never met before, but this Frankie seems on a mission, like passing a secret message intended to save Luanne's life. Her eyes are kind, her voice gentle. "You don't know me," she says, "but you need to know you're not the only one." Then she explains that Phil, as he did with her and others, has good reason to keep Luanne hoping. "He knows," Frankie says, "that by keeping you hopeful he'll get what he really wants: your money."

Oh shit, oh no. Though trying not to believe the woman, deep down

Luanne knows it's true. And feels so, so stupid. She should have known. The loan of a hundred and fifty *Q's*, he said, was to pay off an 'urgent debt.' He promised, of course, to pay it back the following week when the check arrived from his editor in London. That week passed, and another, and now he is nowhere to be found.

With a bit more research, which is free and plentiful, she discovers that 'Free-lance' Phil (what they call him around town) is one of those world-hopping 'independent journalists' whose check from some editor is always due. OK, OK, she blew it. *Dumb.*

Luanne is now down to her last hundred dollars and has to start skimping. She does anything that does not cost much money, which includes pickup truck rides to Santa Catarina, to San Antonio, even to San Andrés. She also hangs out at the lake and does a lot of swimming. Tries to stay positive. In spite of indisputable evidence, she holds on to the irresistible hope that Frankie is just jealous, a liar, and that Phil will soon come back, will pay what he owes, will somehow prove he loves her.

He never does.

In a way it is a blessing, forcing Luanne to re-focus on why she came to Guatemala in the first place. Her flight back to California is in five days. She will use what money is left to do her buying. But no one has any idea where to find the pulseras.

"Go to Chichicastenango," they keep telling her. "Chichi is where the good stuff is."

So yes, *OK*, she'll make herself go.

She gets up early to catch the first pickup truck to Sololá. Like awaiting certain death, she stands shivering on the street. And here it comes, rumbling toward her, screeching to a brake-challenged halt while her shivers turn to shakes.

Eyes glossing over, a solitary *NO* in her mind, she scurries away like an escaped chicken. At least she finds some humor in that, laughing at her cowardice while fighting back the tears. *Silly gringa, what a joke!* How will she be a buyer in Guatemala when she can't even handle curvy roads and crazy drivers? Maybe she should give up now, admit it was all a bad idea.

Luanne wanders off, lost and disappointed--has no clue where she's going or what she's going to do--and a few minutes later finds herself outside the local Pana market. The street is full of vendors selling fruit and vegetables, baskets and pottery, flowers and coconuts. Then she sees them.

A middle-aged Indian woman, holding a bouquet of roses, calls out, "Mire, amiga, mire mire!"

Luanne moves past the flowers and drops to her knees by the tightly bound bundles of pulseras. She looks into the equally surprised eyes of the young woman selling them. It feels to her like the end of a long pilgrimage. "Cuanto?"

Pulseras *Portland Memorial Coliseum, June 12th, 1980*

Luanne digs into her satchel and pulls out another six-dozen. She expected to sell the bracelets a few at a time, from concert to concert, but that is not going to happen. Within an hour of setting up they are almost gone. *Qué frigging milagro!*

"Hi," says some guy, "do you remember me?"

"No," she says, making change for a young girl's five.

"It was at a Dead concert in San Francisco."

She ignores him and re-arranges the scattered pulseras. Little does this poor guy know that the last thing she needs right now is a lame pickup line. After *FAY-LEAP-AY*, she's had her fill of men, even handsome ones. Cannot be bothered.

"It's been awhile," he says. "Winterland. Five or six years ago."

"How much," a girl asks, "if I buy twenty or thirty?"

"They're two for a dollar."

"Yeah, yeah, cool," the girl says, "but if I buy lots of them, I mean, don't you--"

"No," Luanne tells her, remembering Consuelo. "I don't bargain."

"I said you looked like an Indian princess."

"What?"

"An Indian princess," the guy says. "That was my line."

"Oh God." Luanne laughs. "That's pitiful."

"I'll take these," says a Chinese girl who has been waiting patiently. She hands her some bills and a bunch of quarters and disappears into the crowd. Luanne has no idea what she took.

"Anyhow," the guy says, "my name is Jake."

"Listen, I'm busy here, OK?"

"Oh," he says. "Yeah, sorry."

She reaches into her satchel, grabs hold of what is left, and tosses the final four-dozen down on the blanket. Hands collide trying to get at them. People hand her money and rush off. The guy has not moved. Planted front and center, he picks from the dwindling pile.

"Doors are open, girl!" It's her friend, Becky, running by.

"OK!" Luanne shouts. "Yeah, I'm coming!"

Having also heard the news, the crowd disperses. Poof.

The handsome guy is the only one left.

"I've got seven," he says, and hands her a ten.

"It's two for a dollar," she says. "I'd have to charge you for eight."

"No."

"No?" *Really?* Why is 'two for a dollar' so hard to understand? If this is some weird kind of flirting, she doesn't want it. Her single focus is to finish the sale, finish with him, and get to the concert. "The thing is, see, these are *friendship bracelets*. You wear one yourself and give one to a friend. It's to show support for the indigenous people of Guatemala." She offers him another, which would make it four dollars, but he does not seem to understand the math, just keeps looking at her with the same idiotic smile. An acid-head maybe? Or, maybe, mentally ill--she should be nice. Best to get it over with, give the guy his change and move on, but as she reaches into her money bag he leans out and touches her hand.

"No," he says, "I don't need anything back."

"What?" Her first instinct is defensive. "Why?"

"Consider it a small donation to the cause. I've been there. I know."

Looking at him now, with no one else around and nothing to distract her, she does remember. "Oh yeah. . .yeah. . .you're the, the bald guy's friend."

"Not exactly, but my name's Jake. And you are. . .Luanne?"

"You remember my name?"

"I wasn't sure."

"Well," she says, suddenly bashful, scooping up the remaining pulseras and tossing them into her satchel, "thanks for the donation, Jake. Very nice of you. But I need to pack up and--"

"Wait," he says, holding out his right wrist, "can you help me with this?"

"Uh. . .sure, OK. Which one?"

"You pick."

She looks at what he's bought and quickly chooses the yellow and red arrows, one of her favorites. She ties it loosely on his wrist. "There."

"Thanks," he says, holding out the others. "Now you."

"Me?"

He's smiling again. She blushes. The guy isn't giving up and there is no use pretending she doesn't like it. His greenish eyes hold on to her, make her feel, in some strange way, that this is meant to happen. She points at the matching pattern in blue and green.

He gently, respectfully, ties it on her wrist.

"There," he says. "Friends."

Jake waits as she rolls up her blanket. Waits as she puts it in the car and hides the money.

She's made a hundred and forty dollars, and the pulseras cost her less than ten. Yes, all right, she's promised to pay Consuelo more, and there is airfare to consider, and other costs of traveling. Still, if she can find other vendors, can buy a lot, this could be a successful business. Of course her parents won't agree. It doesn't matter.

If not for her mother's cancer, she'd have returned to Guatemala early the following winter. As things go, however, she will not return for another three years, long after Consuelo gives up waiting.

Los Tres Amigos

At the end of his sustained magic-mushroom high, Jake had crashed hard and returned to Northern California severely depressed. He was hanging around Garberville, camping and drinking down by the river--alone except for Orph--when Mickey convinced him to help out with another crop. He trusted Jake, and would allow him to grow plants of his own in exchange for helping manage the rest. And "Yeah, absolutely," Mickey said, Orph was welcome too.

It ended up a good arrangement. Both man and dog were happy, with plenty of room to roam. Jake read all of Kesey, Hesse, Dostoevsky. Then, even better, he met Luanne.

Out on Mickey's land one night, she brought up the Grateful Dead concert where they'd first met. That ended by telling Jake about her strange reaction to the pulsera woman; about her years of pulsera-colored dreams; about the studying, the planning, the working to save money; and finally about her trip to Guatemala.

"There," she said, "they call me Luna."

This happened during the only acid trip that either of them had had in years. They sat in an open meadow, with a view of fading ridges and a big, clear, black as coal sky. It was a warm summer night. The moon was full. "You have to change your name," Jake said.

"Yeah, right."

"I mean it," he said. "Sometimes, who knows why, other people see who we really are."

"Oh Jake."

"What?"

"You're so damn cute, and sweet, and delusional."

That got them laughing, and kissing for a long time. Jake felt completely, and forever, overwhelmed by this girl. Her smile lit him up. "Look," he said, pointing at the moon. "Look at that big goofy mug."

"Yeah?"

"That's you, sweetheart. That's you exactly."

She laughed until she cried, and by dawn, probably because he would not let up, agreed with him. It was one of those *very stony things* that usually seem stupid the next day. Not this time.

"Morning, Luna," he said when she opened her eyes.

"Morning," she said, and that was that.

Luna would visit Jake in the small cabin he'd built on Mickey's land. She didn't stay often at first, but after her mother died she rarely left.

Two years went by. Everything seemed perfect. Mickey called the three of them *Los Tres Amigos*.

Whatever, thought Jake. He knew Luna was happy with their relationship, but he'd begun to worry. How did a guy like him end of up with such a wonderful woman? Never mind that, he decided. More important, how did he never lose her? One morning in August, while finishing their coffee, he made the mistake of mentioning marriage.

She squinted at him. "Why go and mess things up?"

"I was just thinking, Luna, what if I buy land?" They'd already gone to check out a few pieces and the plan was to start a scene of their own the following year.

"Yeah?"

"I mean, we'll be doing a crop together, right, and later, I guess, building a house, and--"

"The land would be yours," Luna said. "The crop we could share. No need to rush anything else, honey, OK?"

She left her coffee, and the cabin, and went outside.

Jake decided not to push it. There were other, more urgent things to think about, like the forty acres they would be looking at today. The owner, an old curmudgeon named Wiley, had known Jake from the Branding Iron days, and liked him. They saw each other in town yesterday and were shooting the shit. Then they got to talking about land.

"So happens," Wiley said, "I'm sellin' mine."

"What?"

"Yeah," Wiley said, and made sure to mention its year-round creek, its views, its great southern exposure. He'd already sold the main homestead and was in a hurry to sell the connected acreage. He just wanted to live near his grandchildren in Sacramento.

The land sounded amazing. And affordable.

"I'd love to see it," Jake said.

"Come tomorrow morning," Wiley said. Then he took a look at Orph, panting in the van, and told Jake not to bring his dog.

"Oh, he's OK," said Jake. "He'll just stay inside the van, maybe whine a bit."

"Nope." Wiley was frowning and scratching his bald head. "Who knows what he'll do. He's a dog, ain't he? Deer don't trust 'em and neither do I. Wish to God they'd never been created!"

All right, so, Jake had a problem. He couldn't bring Orph along today, as usual, and he couldn't tie him up because. . .well. . .he just couldn't. No, no way. But the dog would not put up with being left behind. . .would never *sit* and *stay* like he was supposed to. Luna, trying to help, had offered to stay behind with Orph. Jake had said no. She needed to see the land too. He didn't say it, but was thinking, hoping, this might one day be their homestead.

He found Luna and explained the plan. She looked at him like maybe he'd gone crazy, then said, "Sure, whatever you want."

Before closing Orph inside the cabin, while she distracted him in the driveway with a game of fetch the stick, Jake cracked open the back door, separated it from the jamb with a pen, then blocked the exit with a chair. By the time Orph could get past the chair and sneak out--or so the theory went--they would be gone.

And, *shazaam*, it worked! The dog kept whining, focused on the front door, while they escaped down the long dirt road.

When they returned, three hours later, Orph was not around. Jake thought that strange, used to the dog staying close, and went out looking for him. Couldn't find him anywhere.

Orph came limping back at dusk.

"Where you been," Jake said, shaking his old friend's snout, "off hunting deer again?"

A few minutes later, Orph started puking.

It was a bloody mix of grass and the grainy little pellets that Jake knew was rat poison. He'd spilled it outside one of the plant enclosures a couple of days ago. Orph had been with him. Thinking it a treat, he'd wanted that poison. Wanted it bad. Jake had pushed him away, forcing the dog to sit and stare while he cleaned what he could from the tall grass. Jake thought he'd done a good job. He'd picked up every damn pellet he could see.

"But I'm not a dog!" he shouted, petting Orph's head as he lay there, half-conscious on the floor, unable to move. "I should've fucking known better!"

Luna tried to comfort him, but Jake was inconsolable.

"Stupid!" he yelled at himself, slamming his head with a clenched fist. *How could I be so stupid?* He'd let himself pretend it wasn't a problem, let himself be rushed, distracted by dreams of marrying Luna and buying land and building a home and having a family--stupid pie in the sky shit in his head--trying to do too many things at once!

Orph puked the whole night, and the next morning, on their way to find a vet, he died in the van.

Jake buried his dog outside the cabin, in a place he saw every day. Though Luna tried to get him talking, he couldn't. There was nothing to say. He worked hard on the crop. Took long walks in the woods. Other than that he slept, or drank, a lot.

He managed to stay through harvest, then had to get away. When Luna asked if he wanted her to come, Jake smiled, picked her up in his arms, and carried her to the bed.

On a windy morning in November, 1981--in Jake's same '67 Volkswagen bus, now with a make-shift bed and a Coleman stove and a portable cooler--they headed south to Mexico, camped for weeks along the pacific coast, then went inland through Oaxaca and San Cristobal to their main destination, Luna's choice, Guatemala.

Mothers

November, 1981

Aura was angry at her mother. She blamed Dolores for the sadness in their house ever since Consuelo came to visit. What horrible things had they said to each other? Why did her mother let the strange woman cry and make everything so hard?

Until then, Aura could imagine Raul in El Norte. That was the main thing she shared with her father, though they never discussed it. She knew he saw Raul's leaving as a betrayal. "A betrayal to both of us," she'd heard him say to her mother. The two of them would argue about it when Aura was not around. . .would suddenly turn quiet, and stop talking, when she showed up. But the day after Consuelo's visit she hid beneath the kitchen window, in the afternoon shadows.

Her mother said that Raul's being gone might have something to do with the army. "Maybe he was mistaken for a *guerillero*," she said. "Maybe he's in a jail somewhere."

"*Por favor,*" her father said. "I'm tired of your constant excuses." He insisted that Raul had taken his government payment, his money, and run off to El Norte.

"My son does not steal," her mother said.

Salvador laughed. "Did I say steal? Oh no, your son would never *steal*. The boy was always complaining about how poorly he and the other workers were paid. To him it was what he'd already earned, his way of getting even."

"Raul would never do that."

"Don't be a fool, woman. He's off someplace making fun of me with his new friends, thinking I was stupid to trust him."

"You don't know."

"I know you worry yourself sick for no reason. Fine, he's gone to El Norte. Why worry over something you wanted?"

"What?"

"It was you who encouraged him to go."

"No, I never--"

"You told him he should *believe in his dreams!* Well, woman, where do you think his dreams of leaving here came from? Soon we'll get a big fat letter saying he is rich. . .saying he wants you and Aura to come join him."

"I wish it were true."

"Yes," her father said, "I know."

"But it isn't. I know it isn't."

"Do you? Really? Then what hope is there?" Salvador said, slamming out the door.

Yes, thought Aura, he's right. Hope was what they needed, not this constant worry. Her father did not trust Raul. If he was right, if Raul had stolen the money, that was bad enough, but why, like her mother, think the worst? Someone once told Aura how thinking bad thoughts made bad things happen. She didn't believe it, but why take the chance?

She decided not to think like either of her parents. She would have her own thoughts. What she needed, more than anything else, was to believe in Raul's dreams of El Norte, to make them hers. It seemed the best way to keep him safe. So she imagined his promised house in her mind, complete with a white picket fence out front, and lots of bougainvillea. Every day she looked for his letter. He would be sending money, too, proving her father wrong. . .telling them all to come.

Two weeks after Consuelo's visit came another *Banking Day.* Dolores could see, as usual, from Salvador's silence and cold stares, how much he resented her going. This time she left Aura behind with him. Both of them seemed pleased by that.

First, Dolores went to Pana's Sunday market. She did not find Consuelo, but managed to locate the spot where her friend sold onions. "Oh yes," the flower woman said, pointing to the narrow space between her and the coconut man, "Consuelo is usually here with me."

The next morning, Dolores was first in line at the bank. After cashing the check, instead of heading home, she caught a bus to Sololá. She'd heard of the army base, and it was easy to find--the large black concrete boot, topped by a concrete army helmet, visible from the road. The guard at the gate told her to go away. "Véte!" he said, like ordering a dog, and she scurried off, intimidated by his harsh face, his rifle, her own feeling of powerlessness. *What did I expect, to just march in and take Raul? How do I even know he's there?*

She went to the market and roamed the food stalls, full of locals sharing gossip. Hearing her story, everyone agreed that the army had taken her son. Many of them told her to go see a certain man in the government building. Señor Peralta would help her, they said. He would know.

Dolores found him in a tiny windowless room. She was surprised when he invited her to sit down. He was an old ladino man in a silver suit, with slack freckled skin, a tiny gray mustache, and thick glasses that made his eyes look huge. Yes, Señor Peralta agreed, Indian boys had been *stolen* (his word) from every area, including the lake, but he doubted her son was in Sololá. For almost a year it had been a permanent base, the newer soldiers taken somewhere else.

"Where?"

"I'm not sure," he said, his big eyes reaching out, kind and gentle, as if wishing they could wipe away her fear. "Probably to the new base in

Chimaltenango, what used to be the Alameda school."

She got on the next bus. It was a three-hour ride. From the main road she walked twenty minutes to the base, then past another big concrete boot and helmet.

Two soldiers, young ladino boys, stood guard at the gate. Though one was taller than the other, to Dolores they looked like twins. Both had handsome faces. Neither responded when she said hello, but at least they were not mean. She began asking questions and the taller twin cut her off. "I'm sorry," he said, "you need to leave." The shorter twin pointed to his right, to the high barbed-wire fence that began not far from the gate. "You can stand with the others if you want."

Far down the line, she could see people gathered.

Dolores followed along the fence until she reached them, a few dozen Indian women, most wearing huipiles she did not recognize. Everyone was quiet, gazing through the metal grid. In the distance, amongst the scattered buildings, were groups of soldiers: some marching; some firing rifles; some crawling on their stomachs or climbing over barricades. Dolores watched too, looking for Raul. One of the women, from Sololá, came down the fence to greet her.

"Your son is missing?" she said, speaking Kaqchikel.

"Yes," said Dolores.

"How long?"

"Almost six months."

"Then he is gone," the woman said. "These boys haven't been here long. The ones before them left a couple of weeks ago."

"Where?"

"Somewhere to the north, up in the mountains."

"They must know inside."

"No," the woman said, "you can't find any answers here. Only trouble. If you ask, amiga, they will beat you. We can stand and look, that's all. Those are our boys out there now. We can see them. But when the trucks come to take them away, they won't say where. Not a word. Then we will be like you. Best you go home and pray for Jesus to keep your son safe."

Though the woman was trying to help, Dolores saw it as giving up, something she would not do. Determined, she went back to the gate and tried to get by the soldiers.

The taller twin grabbed her by the neck. "Try again and I will shoot you!"

"Go," said the shorter one. "Please, just go."

Dolores rejoined the women by the fence. She stayed three more days, rationing herself the tortillas she'd brought from home, looking and looking until absolutely convinced Raul was not there. By then, at least, she was certain the army had taken him.

Other mothers told how their boys were taken too.

Taken from every village.

Taken right out of their fields. They'd seen it themselves.

One mother told how soldiers had chased her son into their hut--how she'd tried to hold onto the boy, fifteen years old--how they'd beaten her and pulled him away and thrown him in the back of a truck. "It is against the new law," she said. "It says a soldier must be seventeen."

"They do what they want," said another.

"We are not the first," said the woman from Sololá. "Others told us the same. No one knows where they're taken, only that they don't come back."

"You should go home," said a young girl holding a baby. Saying that, her eyes welling with tears, she looked away from Dolores, out toward the soldiers. "There is nothing you can do."

All of them agreed with the girl.

Dolores woke up Friday morning knowing they were right. Several of them touched her shoulder and said goodbye. They wished her well, some in dialects she could not understand.

She stayed in Pana with her aunt, and on Sunday went looking for Consuelo. The flower woman saw her coming and pulled Consuelo to her feet, holding her by the elbow, as if otherwise she might go running off.

"Here she is, amiga. I knew you'd be coming."

"Thank you," Dolores said.

The flower woman stood tall, like she expected a reward.

Surprising her, Dolores took Consuelo by the hand and walked down the nearest callejón. She knew it emptied out on the south side of the Catholic Church. A quiet place. A place where they could talk in private. Until then, because of all the voices haggling, she didn't say a word.

They settled on the cold stone steps in the early morning sunshine.

"It is bad," said Consuelo.

"No," Dolores said, "not bad. Not good either." She explained what had happened at the base, what she'd learned. "The boys might be anywhere. There is nothing we can do."

Consuelo said she understood. She closed her eyes and crossed herself and prayed at length for God's infinite mercy. "May Raul and Jaime be spared, dear God, and come home soon."

Though not a religious woman, Dolores knelt along with her, crying and silently praying that all her life she'd been wrong, that there truly was a God.

She was trying to believe, trying hard, but her heart knew she would never see Raul again.

Back home, after Salvador berated her, he ignored her. For him, his wife's deception was unforgivable; an affront to his authority; a thorough, and final, embarrassment. Were it not for Aura, he said, he would never speak to her again. For the sake of appearances he let Dolores stay in the house; let her sleep in their bedroom; let her have the bed. He slept in the far corner on a foam pad. He did not miss the occasional sex, which had never satisfied him, which had only made him weak and needy, dependent on her, trapped by desires he did not want. At last he could rise above all that.

His harshness toward Dolores was shared by Aura. The girl could tell her mother had gone to see the strange woman; that she believed something bad had happened to Raul. Aura now desperately needed her father, his hugs and silly jokes, his lively spirit, the order he created wherever he went. Every day after school, Aura found him waiting. She held his hand as he walked around checking on the workers. She helped with whatever had to be done. It made her feel safe.

The New Year came. More months passed. Aura and Salvador grew closer as all got worse for Dolores. Except for meals she was left alone, abandoned, a mother who had now lost both her children.

Gracias A Dios

The Guatemalan border, as expected, is a hassle. But that's just the beginning. There are lots of military checkpoints further south. The gringos are stopped often, asked lots of questions, forced to wait for whatever time it takes to search the van. Jake says, "I think we should turn around." Luna, feeling pulled to find Consuelo, talks him out of it.

It is early January, 1982, when they reach the central highlands of Guatemala, famous for the craft markets of San Francisco El Alto and Chichicastenango--places Luna missed on her first trip. Once again she chooses to pass them by, in a hurry to reach Lake Atitlán. And a few hours later, at first sight of it, her mind begins to calm. It's like breathing for the first time in months. She marvels at the wide blue expanse; the steep, forested perimeter; the three volcanoes jutting from the lake's distant shore, peaks washed purple by the setting sun.

They cross the river on the far side of Pana and sleep in their van, close to the water, backed by someone's milpa. The next day, Sunday, they go to the market, but can't find Consuelo.

Jake says, "That's OK, sweety, we can hang around until next weekend."

"No," Luna tells him, "let's do what we planned." She might have stayed, but has spotted Phil. Luckily, he's walking the other direction.

They drive to San Lucas, beneath the sibling volcanoes of Tolimán and Atitlán. Monday morning they pay a man to store the camper behind his locked gate. They ready their backpacks, will take the next week and hike around the lake. Jake's idea.

The path winds through oak and eucalyptus, corn and bean and onion fields. The sky is clear, the air warm and dry, the Xocomil a cooling whisper.

As they walk, with each and every step, Luna feels more certain that something incredible is happening, something they share but cannot yet understand, or begin to verbalize. It is a sense--strong and vibrant--of belonging. It's as if everything has happened in order to get them to Lake Atitlán, get them here *together*. The feeling is so mystical that she dares not mention it. Best to be cautious with what might be wishful thinking.

They stop to rest on a small sandy beach. An lone egret, conscious of their presence, flies away. Luna strips and dives into the cold clear water. Jake, surprised, watches until she comes up, then takes off his clothes and dives in too. He remembers sitting with Fish in the farm pond's mud, its brackish slime coating his legs, its grainy residue filling his bellybutton-- what once seemed such a wondrous thing--*But hey Ma, look at me now, swimming beneath a volcano!* A velvet chill rattles his teeth. *Oh my God, is this actually happening? Can this beautiful place, this gorgeous woman, this bliss I'm feeling possibly be true?* He takes a deep breath and plunges straight down, surprised to find no bottom. He struggles to the surface and gulps for air.

Luna swims to him. "You OK?"

He's blinking, trying to clear his vision. He's only thirty feet from shore. "Wow," he says.

"What?"

"Really. . .really. . .deep."

"Yeah," she says, squinting her eyes at him. "*Duh.*"

He pushes her head underwater. She pulls him down. They wrestle for a minute, then she frees herself, swims out further with a long line of silky, measured strokes, water sparkling in her wake. He wants to follow, but having grown up on a farm in Kansas he's never learned to swim like that. He's happy she can, and maybe someday he will too. Here, in Lago Atitlán, with Luna.

They stay the night in Santiago at a small Indian hotel called Xajulcoxa. The room is dingy, its single tiny window looking out on a matrix of dilapidated buildings. No sight of the lake. The bed is hard, and creaky, and they don't care. Luna wonders out loud if their potent orgasms might be a gift from some Mayan God. "No," says Jake, who credits the nearby evangelical church, its tumultuous roars and disharmonic moans propelling him into yet another apocalyptic trance.

Anyway, for whatever reason, they've never had such great sex.

Long after they've finished, the church service keeps grinding on. Eventually it ends, bringing a few moments of quiet, before another service starts up. Jake remembers back to his trip in 1976, to the sight of that woman on her hands and knees all day, pleading with God. He remembers Richard complaining about the evangelicals. "In the last year or so," he said, "with unsolicited help from North American Pentecostals, this shit has spread to every village on the lake."

Luna also remembers the noisy churches from her first visit. She and Jake laugh, and cringe, at the cacophonous onslaught--"like a choral death squad"--but agree that it will not affect their dream, suddenly hatched, of living close to the water, far from any village.

Then, after making love again, they talk for hours about this incredible chance to share their lives with farmers and fisherman, the simple people of this beautiful land.

The perpetual corn, of course, does present a problem. Jake is amazed by his visceral discomfort. Luna gets him to acknowledge that living with it in a different place--a wonderful, magical place--might be the way to reconcile his past. Besides, she makes him see, it isn't just corn, there are onions and beans and tomatoes too. . .mangos and papayas. . .a volcanic lake a thousand feet deep, and the friendliest people they've ever met! Yeah, OK, their knowledge of Spanish is not good enough for a genuine conversation. "But that will come," she says. "That will be our future."

In the present, asked if he speaks Spanish, Jake says, "Sufficiente para communicar"--a phrase learned in Arizona where he picked up enough words to at least, as he says, communicate. Luna, though understanding a lot more than Jake, tells the locals, "With us you have to speak *very slow*."

On their fourth day of traveling around the lake, attracted to dozens of places yet attached to none, they cross over a boulder-strewn hillside beyond the village of San Juan. . .and there. . .like a vision. . .there it is! The water below is translucent turquoise, its sandy bottom glowing white.

"Wow," says Jake, baffled by his instant certainty. "That's, um, Spanish for--"

"Wow," says Luna.

"Exactly," he says.

It is evident that no foreigners live anywhere close. There are no roads. No houses. Aside from lots of corn and a few large trees, they see only one small hut. And a gorgeous beach. Unfortunately, upon reaching it, Jake has to once again face the fact that nothing is as it first appears. What a perfect place this would be if not for the mess of plastic bags and pop bottles, tin cans and shards of glass. A mine-field of garbage, he thinks, afraid to scratch beneath the ugly surface.

"Fucking unbelievable," he says. "How can people trash such a beautiful place?"

Luna says, "We could pick it up."

"Yeah, and if you lived here you'd probably have to. Every day."

"I wouldn't mind. I honestly wouldn't. Maybe by doing it, if we showed people we care, they would too."

Jake smiles at her optimism. A wishful dream, yes, but not completely unreasonable. Luna always hopes for the best. Her big shining eyes make him happy. More important, hers is not an idle sort of optimism. She loves nature with a passion equal to his.

"I wish we could live right here," she says.

"Yeah? You wouldn't miss your friends? Your dad?"

"Well, of course. I know it wouldn't be easy. When are big changes ever easy? The good news is, during rainy seasons in Guatemala it's dry in California. We could help out on Mickey's land in the spring and summer if we want to. I can buy pulseras--other things too--and sell them at concerts. Why not split our time between here and there?"

"Yeah, sure," says Jake. "Why not?"

Uh huh, he's thinking, *right*, because he knows exactly why not. . .a crucial bit of truth she's choosing to ignore: that to leave a house in Guatemala they would need to hire someone to watch it. "That's part of the deal," a German guy from San Pedro said. "To live in Guatemala you have to build a second house for a *guardián* and his family. Someone needs to always be around," the guy said, "to stop thieves from breaking in, taking every damn thing that's not nailed down."

Jake knows they can afford to buy land and pay for a basic home. *But hire caretakers? Really?*

They sit on a large rock on the nicest stretch of beach. Jake wants to stop thinking, wants to give his brain a rest. Behind them, he spots a path through the corn. "C'mon," he says, grabbing Luna's hand, and up they go into the field.

The land is steep. After a few minutes they stop, winded, at a wide flat landing surrounded by tall dry stalks, terraces of the same climbing higher. Up against the southern sloping hill is a huge avocado tree loaded with fruit. To its side is a group of papaya starts. "Here's where we'll put the house," he says, surprised at the words tumbling from his mouth. He cannot help imagining himself on a second floor balcony with an incredible view of lake, volcanoes, and endless sky. Damn it though, he knows better! Knows, doesn't he, that dreams like this never come true? But it's a knowledge he'd rather not have, at least not now, and he's trying to ignore it when distracted by something moving through the milpa.

Out comes a small Guatemalan man, dressed in soiled white pants and shirt.

Pascual Rosario holds two dead chickens by their scrawny red legs. Seeing the foreigners, he says a silent *Gracias a Dios*--his own private dream now close enough to touch.

The chickens are meant for Pascual's closest neighbor, Señor Pérez. No, he thinks, not something these strangers need to know. Nor that he owes the man a great deal of money, borrowed to pay for his wife's complicated pregnancy, her hospitalization in the city.

Yes, praise the Lord, she and the baby were spared, at great cost. An amount he knows impossible to repay. And Señor Pérez, a doctor from Guate, he knows it too. Is counting on it. Pascual is sure the man envisions a vacation chalet beneath his beloved avocado tree, overlooking his sandy shore. A week ago, having thus far received nothing but an occasional dead chicken, the doctor came with a local policeman and forced Pascual to sign a paper. It stated that if he didn't pay the loan, plus interest, in less than four months, Pérez could take the property.

Since then, Pascual has prayed every day to be rescued from ruin. Between prayers he imagines various possible ways that it might happen, all of which include the sudden death of his neighbor. While his heart hopes for a better alternative, his mind thirsts for vengeance. Many of the scenarios are quite violent, quite bloody and gruesome. The poor man does his best to push them from his mind, pray them away, but without much success. What he needs is a miracle. . .a gift from God.

That is why (because Pascual fully expects his heart-felt prayers to be answered) the abrupt arrival of Jake and Luna is no surprise. Nonetheless overwhelmed by the efficiency of providence, the grateful man's first impulse is to get on his hands and knees and kiss their sandaled feet. If only he could unload, could explain the numerous sad details of his desperate situation!

But a voice in his mind, at the periphery of his consciousness--in that open space Pascual has come to trust--tells him no. It is a clear message from Jesús, a stern warning, advising him to wait, to hold his tongue, that speaking too soon might put him at a disadvantage. Though Pascual feels certain that they are here to buy his land, Jesús repeats the fault of wishful thinking and reminds him, once again, that this is not a perfect world. "You have lived long enough," He says, "to know that believing in what *should happen* does not necessarily mean it will."

The humble man nods his understanding. Christ, in His infinite wisdom, has gifted these strangers at precisely the right moment, which does not guarantee anything.

It is Pascual's job to make the dream come true.

Lucky for him, he already knows what a foreigner might pay. Others have sold their land too. For outrageous prices! It has been hard for poor Pascual to understand. What before seemed to him a sinful deception, however, at this very instant appears to be God's will. Why else would people so willingly part with their money? Why but for the sake of redemption? *Yes, that must be it!*

Trusting in the All Mighty's devine sense of fairness, he quickly settles on the high number that has popped into his head, a sum adequate to cover his debt to Señor Pérez, with plenty left over to buy and build on a lesser piece of land. Poised to complete the deal, he is in no hurry. The Lord advises patience. First, he must let his guests know they are welcome. At home. With that in mind, he smiles and waves and says hello.

"Hello," says the tall stranger, meeting Pascual's smile. Not a native Spanish speaker, the gringo hesitates at what to say next. "Good day to you, Mister."

"I am blessed to have found you," Pascual says.

"Us too," says the gringo, which makes no sense whatsoever unless he means, as Pascual assumes, that they also feel blessed to have found him. "The place we are," the gringo says, "you?" "He means," says the pretty gringa, "you are the owner of this land?"

"By the grace of God I am," Pascual says to her beaming smile. "The Great Shepherd has brought us together, as is meant to be, and wherever He leads us we shall go."

"What?" says the gringo.

The gringa then shakes Pascual's hand and soon they have learned each other's names.

Vicente emerges from the milpa and grabs hold of his leg. "My son," Pascual says.

"Hello," says Luna.

The small boy gazes at her, transfixed, clearly spellbound by those long ebony locks. Pascual laughs. He pats Vicente on the head, hands him the dead chickens, and tells him where to take them. The boy runs off.

"Come," Pascual says, and leads them up the hill to his house.

He wants to impress them with his hospitality. It does not help that Concepción, his wife, seems ashamed of their dirt floor, and to have only straw mats to sit on. As if failing some important test, she hurriedly stirs the embers of the afternoon fire to re-heat the cold tortillas. The gringos glance around the room. They smile a lot while waiting, but look a bit nervous. His mother is in one corner, lying on a mat, softly moaning. His two sisters, one with a newborn baby, come inside and sit directly across from the strangers, and giggle. Vicente rushes in. Freezes. Out of breath, he stands by the door, fidgets with his hair, and stares at Luna. Pascual clears his throat. He apologizes for his simple home, and the *too-smoky* fire, then hands each of the visitors a small pile of slightly burnt tortillas.

Time, now, to get serious.

Jake feels odd and out of place. He is introduced by Pascual as Jacobo ("Like the famous President!" his host says. "Also the Saint of Ladders!"). And no one seems surprised by Luna's name. "Of course," Concepcion says. "You look like the moon." The gringos both smile a lot and keep eating tortillas. Lucky their water bottles have a few swallows left from the last batch they disinfected.

As they eat, Pascual asks the expected questions: Where are they from? Do they like Guatemala? How long will they stay?

Jake sees a strange look come into Pascual's eyes when Luna hesitates at the last question. She raises her hands in a gesture of doubt and says she doesn't know.

Pascual reaches out to touch her hand. "I believe," he says, and then makes a little speech, something Jake can't follow, something about God and responsibility and sacrifice.

Concepción looks baffled. She frowns at Pascual and speaks to him in their Indian language. His sharp response to whatever she's said causes her to eyes to flutter.

"I don't understand," Jake says.

Pascual now touches the gringo's hand and repeats what he said, slowly, word by word, but Jake still doesn't understand.

"I think," Luna says, "he's saying we can stay."

"Oh," Jake says, relieved that he'd gotten it so wrong. "Gracias," he says to Pascual, assuming they've been offered a place to sleep that night. He wants to say more but doesn't know how.

"Si," Pascual says, looking pleased, "Gracias a Dios." He signals the couple to follow him outside, then leads them around the property. He points out its various assets, including the vertical pathway he's building to what will soon be a dirt road between San Juan and San Pablo. He shows them his onions and tomatoes and chickens. The jocote trees too. He shows them the pit where he mines the adobe clay, and the stands of tall thick bamboo. He takes them to the far border, to the long line of pine trees that he's planted, Jake thinks he says, *to separate him* from his neighbor. At last he brings them to the beach, to the large rock they'd sat on before. "Everything you see," Pascual says, waving his hands around and above his head, "is yours."

"What?" Jake says in English. "What did he say?"

Luna looks puzzled too. "I think he. . .he's saying we can. . ." Then Luna turns to Pascual. "Do you mean," she says in Spanish, "you are selling this land?"

"Yes," Pascual says. Then he makes a longer speech. God is mentioned several times.

"He thinks God wants us to buy his land," she says. Her eyes fill with tears.

Jake almost laughs. Instead, he holds her hand and smiles at her glowing childlike smile. *I mean c'mon, darlin', we just met this guy! Can't you see it's too good to be true?* He looks at the strange little Indian man, whose eyes are also glossing over. *Huh? What the hell?* OK, Jake thinks, enough's enough. Anxious to clear away all false hopes, he forms the necessary Spanish words in his mind and says, "Please, Pascual, tell me how much?"

Pascual nods, now flush with confidence, and states his price. Once converted from quetzales to dollars, however, it causes the gringos to talk amongst themselves, and sigh, and the light to diminish from their faces. He thinks perhaps they do not understand. He explains, slowly, that his land is four hectares in size, including thirty meters of beachfront. He emphasizes that lakeside property is in high demand, with lots of rich people from Guate, and foreigners also, looking for such a place, wanting to build themselves expensive vacation chalets.

Once he seems to understand, the gringo tells him that they are not rich, and not looking for a vacation chalet. . .that all they want is "a simple life."

The ensuing negotiation, stalled by frequent translation and constant confusion, continues for an hour. Pascual believes that he must stick to God's price. Luna still looks hopeful. Jacobo, however, keeps sighing and shaking his head. Then, with the sun sinking beyond San Pedro on the opposite shore, everything changes. Jacobo's eyes light up and he digs a piece of paper from his pack. His obvious excitement makes Pascual excited too. *Thank God*, he thinks, *the gringo finally sees.*

Jacobo writes a number on the paper, with the word FINAL above it, underlined twice. It is exactly Pascual's price, cut in half.

The poor man looks at the number and wags his head in disbelief. *No, it is not possible, no.* He is shocked that a wealthy gringo, who seemed an intelligent person, a kind person, would bargain so recklessly with his soul! *Does he not realize it is his destiny too? Can he not sense the hand of God upon him?*

Pascual closes his eyes, awaiting clarity. It comes fast. The price this gringo has offered would pay off his debt to Pérez, but not come close to buying another property and building another hut. His eyes shoot open. Stare at Jake. What could the strange man be thinking? What is it he's telling his wife to make her look of concern turn to one of relief? And why on earth are they smiling? Why?

Dear God, he thinks, *I beg you, let me understand the mystery of your ways!*

And thus it comes to pass, as if heavenly divined, that Luna turns her loving eyes upon him and explains. Jake's reason for half the price is simple: they just want half the land. The part down by the lake. Pascual can keep the upper terraces, she says, can grow his corn and other vegetables there. They will share the avocados, the papayas, the jocotes. "Also," she says, "we will pay for the pathway to the road."

"What?" says Jake, as if he must have misunderstood.

"Yes," Luna says to him, still speaking Spanish. "It's only fair. And a new house too." She turns to Pascual. "I mean, of course, a house for you."

Jake gulps. Knowing her well, he is sure she's been thinking of Pascual's dingy little hut and feels a desperate need to help. *Oh boy*, he thinks, *here we go.*

Pascual says something about a 'gran casa' and points upward.

"Did you hear that?" Jake says to her, readying himself to intervene, if necessary, before she gives away the whole damn farm.

"He wants to build his house up by the road."

"Yeah. A big one."

"Well," Luna says, "compared to what they've got now, Jake, I guess anything would--"

"Right," he says, and holds his tongue, because when she gets her heart thumping like this there's no sense trying to stop it. Best to keep her happy.

Besides, he thinks, paying for them to live at the top of the land could turn out to be a good thing. An Indian house couldn't be too expensive, right, and having them live up there would, if nothing else, give him his needed privacy.

Suddenly in total agreement, he takes the paper and adds a thousand dollars to the price. "For the house," he has her explain. In exchange, Jake asks that his and Luna's house be watched over while they're away during the rainy season. A built-in guardián, he's decided, is a win-win situation.

Pascual wipes away his tears. "Gracias a Dios," he says, kissing their hands. Then he looks up to the sky and says, *"Que puedo merecer sus regalos, Señor."* Whatever that means.

During the next couple of days the details are worked out. Jake and Luna's building site is officially chosen. The great avocado tree will shade their imagined rear terrace. That tier and those below, including the beach, belong to them.

The tiers above are Pascual's, though the gringos will pay for a watering system that everyone can share. It will include a pump, pipes, and at the top of the land a couple of holding tanks.

The properties will be separated by a thick hedge of izote mixed with bougainvillea. For now, they mark their border with a long line of rocks. At a designated place, not far from Jake and Luna's future home, a break is created for what will someday be the cobblestone path from road to shore.

Completing the deal will take several weeks. During the first week of waiting, Jake and Luna swim in the lake and clean their beach. On Sunday everyone leaves the land, the Indians for their evangélical church in San Pablo, the gringos for Panajachel, to get supplies and look for Consuelo.

They find her in the market, crouched between the flower woman and the coconut man. Luna understands--clear as day--that Consuelo is not happy to see her, and the woman will not even look at Jake. He excuses himself and takes a walk.

Luna says she's sorry for not coming back when she promised.

Consuelo gently cuts her off. She seems embarrassed that a gringa is apologizing to her, and knows enough Spanish now to speak. "Please, Señora Luna, not your fault."

"Why should it be her fault?" says the flower woman. "The poor girl's mother was dying, amiga. How could she leave?"

"Yes," says Consuelo, "I understand."

"She understands," the flower woman says.

But Luna does not hear. A strange buzzing has started in her head, and her sight goes foggy. Then, strong as the sun itself, Consuelo's eyes burn through. . .finding her. . .telling her. . .something is wrong. . .terribly wrong. There are no words, but a definite image, like a shape cut out of paper. The shape of a person. Consuelo is trying to hide a secret, but Luna somehow sees it. "It's your boy," she says. "What happened to your boy?"

The two Indian women look at each other. Consuelo begins to sob.

"The army has him," says the flower woman.

"What?"

"Yes, it's true," she says, "they took him and made him a soldier."

Instinctively Luna reaches out and holds Consuelo's hand. It is warm and soft. She feels good, as if this woman she barely knows were an old friend. "Where is he now?"

"No one tells," says Consuelo, wiping at her eyes. "In mountains. Fighting. I don't know." Again she starts sobbing.

"Poor thing," the flower woman says, patting Consuelo's leg, "she is afraid he might be--"

"No," Luna says. "He is all right. I am sure. Please, Consuelo, please do not worry. I can feel your boy's life. He is going to be fine."

"I do not understand, Señora Luna."

"I know," says Luna. "Neither do I."

On the fourth of April, contract signed, the purchase sum arrives from Jake's bank in Garberville. Three days later, a mere two ahead of the deadline, Pascual marches into Señor Pérez's office in Guatemala City, accompanied by the same policeman from San Pablo: a witness to the fact that he pays his debt in full. . .plus interest. The doctor, shocked, can do nothing to stop it. "Gracias a Dios," Pascual tells him, a young pretty nurse standing by his side, looking every bit as guilty as her boss, "your many sins shall soon be addressed." He leaves them alone to ponder that.

Jake helps Pascual with the stone steps, the conduit between their separate lives. It is Jake's idea. With the rainy season less than a month away there are too few days remaining to start his own house. First, he decides, we should finish the path from shore to road, then level the site for our guardián to build on.

Pascual thanks him for the gesture. . .says he now thinks of him as a brother.

Each and every day thereafter, he says to Jake, "Hola mano, como estás?" And Jake, knowing better than to treat Pascual as less than an equal, says, "Bién, mano, y tú?"

Late one afternoon, tired from carrying stones, the two men take a break and sit looking out at the perfect lake. It truly is, as Pascual says, a glorious day. There is no Xocomil, and nothing much resembling a cloud. Only a thin band of mist atop the Atitlán volcano.

"Like a halo," Jake says.

"See, Jacobo, you are a believer!"

Having long recognized Pascual's religious leanings, Jake is determined not to react. He looks around and lifts his arms to include the limitless entirety of nature. "I believe in this," he says.

"Gracias a Dios."

"Sí," Jake says, whose rejection of religion has never included a disbelief in God.

By the first of May the stone path is finished and the house site cleared. Jake and Luna have already over-stayed their visa by a month, and will surely face a heavy fine at the border. Any longer, though, might mean real trouble.

Pascual accompanies them along the path to San Pedro. From there they will catch a boat to Santiago, then a truck to San Lucas to retrieve their camper. At the dock--the boat's captain glaring, revving his engine--it is a tender goodbye between friends.

Surprising Pascual with a quick hug and correct Spanish, Jake says, "Goodbye, brother. Take care of yourself and your family. We will see you in November."

"May God be your guide," says Pascual.

"And yours too," says Jake.

Judas

Sacapulas, April 10, 1982

An effigy of Judas hangs above the high arched wooden doors of the Catholic Church. He was chosen the patron saint of this town sometime after Spain, and Catholicism, took control of Guatemala. It is generally agreed that he represents the perennial injustice of their rule. As in other Mayan communities of the mountainous northwest, where no true conquest was possible, such sacrilege is tolerated. Local ladinos tend to regard the provocative elevation of Judas, betrayor of Jesús, as a harmless expression of Indian primitivism: a false bravado; a minor aggravation.

Then, each year, comes Easter week, when their extreme patience is tested. On *Sábado de Gloria*, the day before Jesús rises, Judas is lowered from his post and made to gallop through town on the back of a bull. It is a purposefully wild ride. People say it symbolizes his power over nature, religion, and politics. Indeed, over power itself. Jaime has heard that no one is safe from the tainted saint's harsh judgment. Beyond the accepted logic of this world, his chaotic romp is meant to root out hidden sinners--especially ladinos--so that God might forgive them; or, should they choose to keep hiding, damn them for all eternity. Judas, the greatest sinner of all, sure as hell knows evil when he sees it!

"Bueno," Raul says, and slaps Jaime on the back. "Let's go, *Manito!*"

That's how Raul treats him, more as a *little brother* than a friend. He likes to take Jaime under his wing, pretend he knows what's best, and Jaime knows why. Soon after they became friends, he mentioned to Raul that he'd been captured while trying to reach a finca called La Gloria. Raul laughed, explained why, and then said, "You see, I knew it was my fault!" He promised Jaime a good job once they returned. The guy was always joking.

"You and I don't belong in this stupid army," Raul said. "Before we go home, Manito, we'll find some pretty girls and a fancy place to dance."

He'd said that eight months ago, back in Chimaltenango, the day they left for Santa Cruz del Quiché. From there they came to Sacapulus, to help build this military base. All the time, every day, Raul just kept on joking. "La Gloria could use something like this," he said, "only bigger, of course--much bigger, and better--and my father would have to be the boss."

Finally, the base is finished. Now, before going somewhere else, they get a break to celebrate Easter. Time again for Jesús to rise. But here in Sacapulas, first comes Judas. All the soldiers are talking about it. The townsfolk, they say, worry who he will accuse this year. Even the ladino officers are excited, looking forward to the only part they care to see, when Judas rides a bull through the streets and maybe, if they're lucky, skewers someone.

By the time Raul and Jaime reach the plaza, the effigy has been lowered and mounted on the bull. It is dressed in camouflage gear, its head topped by a New York Yankee's baseball cap, its eyes covered by sunglasses. The bull's neck is wrapped in flowers, its tail in firecrackers.

Then the crowd blocks their view. The town square is packed and buzzing. Raul hoists Jaime to his shoulders for a better look. "What's happening, Manito?"

"There is a man dancing," Jaime says. "He's dressed in a shiny golden suit, with a mask."

"What kind of mask?"

"I don't know. A big pink face with long curly white hair, and a beard, and a golden hat with lots of points."

"A king," Raul says.

"Yes," says Jaime, as if the name has slipped his mind. "He's dancing around the bull, and poking it with a stick. Ay, Dios mío!"

"What?"

"He's lighting its tail on fire!"

"He's really doing it?"

"Yes," Jaime says, "and the tail is, it's. . .exploding! The bull is going crazy! Kicking its legs and twisting its head. People are, are running, they're. . .oh no it's. . .it's. . .coming!"

The crowd in front of them jumps backward. Raul and Jaime go crashing to the ground. Jaime lies there, trapped by the scrambling feet, people tripping over his body in their frantic escape. Raul grabs hold of his leg and drags him off the street, safe underneath an abandoned fruit cart.

"You all right, *vos?*"

"Yes," says Jaime, ashamed to look so foolish. He slaps away the dust.

They stay still until the bull charges past. People flee in front of it, or chase behind it, screaming Spanish obscenities that both the boys know well. The ground is strewn with sheets of white paper. People are picking them up.

"What is it?" says Jaime.

"Ay Manito," Raul says. He picks up one of the papers and shakes it in his friend's face. "You never pay attention."

"To what?"

"This is the testimonial of Judas. This is what matters, not a stupid bull!"

"All right. . .so. . .what does it say?"

"It says," says Raul, giving full concentration to the hand-scribbled text. He laughs.

"What?"

"Well, I don't know, I'm not sure, *vos*. You may be too young."

"Kiss my ass," Jaime says, a Spanish phrase he's learned well since becoming a soldier.

"Bueno," Raul says, "but I hope dear Jesús forgives us both." Then, one word at a time, with his usual dramatic flair, he translates to Kaqchikel. It's not easy, the scribbled Spanish not that of a native speaker:

> *Dear Children it is beyond evil the way you cannot stop these things you insult me with. You butchers son Rogelio who should keep your cock up the chicken's ass and out of carpenter Guillermo's wife. And sister Anna even if he is your brother let horse-faced Carlos go licking somewhere else like in his cow of a wife who never gives a fair bushel of beans! But I do not forget you Juanito keeper of the robber's store where you charge too much for your pigshit slop instead of looking to your wife and how she bends over for the teacher. Repent you sinners all of you or know my wrath! Sincerely Judas.*

Raul drops the paper to the ground. A gust of wind sweeps it away. Jaime stands there spellbound, shocked. Why is his friend making fun of him? Usually it's no big deal, but now, right now, he feels demeaned by it. Raul picks up another piece of paper and reads:

> *Dear Children of mine who fornicate with anyone you can like a secret. Not from me you know who sees your dirty cocks and cunts dripping with sin. You mangy Esteban mounting anything that moves including your dog I hear and for certain your oldest daughter who is more afraid of your fist than the truth of all the people knowing. The easy fuck you get will haunt you son and make you pray I spank your gangly ass! Best you suck yourself boy! Either that or cut it off before I--*

"Stop!" yells Jaime.

"What?" says Raul. "What's wrong?"

"I thought you were my friend."

"I am."

"Then why say these things to me? You think I'm an idiot, Raul? You think I've never heard these words before?"

"What, am I making it up?" He hands the paper to Jaime. "Look, *vos*, you don't need to know much Spanish to see for yourself!"

Jaime examines the paper carefully, line by line.

"You see!"

"Yes, all right, I see," Jaime says. "But I don't understand what it means."

"Me either. I heard it happens this way every year, Judas saying whatever he wants."

"Yes," says Jaime, who heard the same, "but not like. . .I mean, how can he just say these things? It's all against ladinos, right? Why do they put up with it?"

"Who ever understands," Raul says with his clever smile, "why *pinche ladinos* do what they do?"

Jaime laughs. A good joke because it's true: *pinche ladinos* are a mystery he long ago learned to accept. "Yes," he says, feeling better, slapping Raul's back, "who knows?"

Patrulleros

On the 20th of April, 1982, while Raul and Jaime are still in Sacapulas, an army truck rumbles up La Gloria's road. It parks in front of the dueño's house and twelve soldiers empty out. Salvador, who heard them coming, waits. He asks the officer in charge how he can be of service.

"Is Señor Alvarez at home?"

"No," Salvador says, "not until next week sometime. I am his crew chief."

"We are looking for three men," the officer says, and hands him a piece of paper.

"Yes, these men work on the finca. I can bring them to you."

"Best if you bring us to them."

"Of course, sir. Come with me."

Within an hour, the men are found, arrested at gunpoint, and thrown into the back of the truck. The other workers stand around watching, whispering amongst themselves.

Fredo, one of the older ones, steps forward. "Excuse me," he says to Salvador, "we are wondering what they did?"

"They have been accused of conspiring with the enemy," the officer says, facing Fredo. "That is all you need to know."

"Yes, sir."

"What is your name?"

"Fredo Cuz, sir."

"Fredo Cuz," the officer says, jotting it down in his notebook.

Salvador, sensing the workers' eyes on him, knows he needs to do something. Fredo is one of his only friends on the finca. Well, not a friend, exactly, but not in any way hostile to his authority. Fredo is a calm, sensible, generous man. A good influence on the others. Salvador cannot afford to lose him too. "Good," he says, "we're finished here. Let's get back to work."

At his word, the men disperse.

The officer seems impressed. "Well done," he says. "You are a man who demands respect."

"That is my job, sir."

"Exactly," the officer says. "Now I need to talk with you in private."

They walk the short distance to Salvador's house and sit down for a cup of coffee. Dolores also serves them tortillas, fried plantains, and a large square of goat cheese. Aura, trying to help, keeps the officer's plate full while he asks lots of questions about the finca and the workers. Then he asks if Salvador feels a sense of duty to Guatemala. The officer watches him closely. Salvador says what he knows he must, speaking of his loyalty to their new leader, General Ríos Montt.

"You realize," the officer says, "that there are people, all around, being influenced by outside troublemakers?"

"I have heard that, yes."

"So you agree that these people must be stopped from threatening the government."

"Oh yes, sir. That cannot be allowed."

The officer waves off Dolores's offer of more tortillas. Suddenly finished, he stands. He thanks her for the hospitality and motions Salvador to follow him outside.

Back at the truck, the officer rummages through a storage compartment in the cab and hands down five rifles. Salvador, confused, sets them on the ground. He also gives him camouflage pants, shirts, hats, and, finally, a big black book, then pats him on the back and says, "Congratulations, you are now the chief of La Gloria's Civil Patrol."

"I'm afraid I can't, sir. There is a great deal of work to be done around here and I--"

"The army cannot be everywhere," the officer says. "Your country needs men like you, Salvador, to keep order in places out of our way."

"I am honored by your confidence."

The officer explains the necessity of weekly patrols, then opens the black book of empty pages. "This is your journal, where you will record anything suspicious, or anyone you think might cause a problem. We will come to check it once a month."

"Yes, sir," says Salvador. "Thank you, sir."

The next day, Salvador gathers his workers together and explains that they represent a nation-wide defense force, established by Guatemala's new leader, Ríos Montt. "The General will not listen to excuses," he says, as instructed by the officer. He hopes they understand he has no choice. "Either you help the army fight its enemies," he says, "or you are one."

Every Saturday thereafter he leads his troop of 'volunteers' on 'reconnaissance patrols' around La Gloria's vast property, primarily along its outer ridges where coffee bushes meet the steeper forest. Soon the patrols seem a common thing, as if it has always been this way.

Salvador knows that Aura hates the days he goes off. . .that she feels stuck, which she is, with her sad-faced mother. One Saturday morning the girl comes running after him, crying. "What, princess, what is it?"

"Can I go with you, Papa, please?"

He smiles, glad to see his hold on her has not weakened. "It is too dangerous," he says. "You must stay home, with your mother."

"I'm afraid to be here without you."

"There is nothing to be afraid of. I have many people guarding the finca. They will not let anything happen."

"Then why do you have to go?"

"Because the army needs my help, sweetheart. I am doing it to keep you safe. Our job is to patrol. . .look around the mountains, that's all. . .make sure no one is out there causing problems."

"Do you have to kill people, Papa?"

He sits down on the ground and holds her on his lap.

"I hope not," he says. And so far it's been true. Though, as expected, he's written a few names in his journal--people who have not willingly answered his questions--he's seen no actual guerillas, or anything out of the ordinary. "But in war we have to always be prepared."

"Who are we *in war* with?"

"Well," Salvador says, "it is difficult to explain."

"Why?"

"Because the troublemakers don't show themselves. They hide and plot against us. Such people are hard to understand, Aura. People get very selfish sometimes and try to take things from others. They cheat and steal and do not respect authority. Do not want to follow rules. Some of them make a lot of problems and have to be punished. Does that make sense?"

"No," she says, as if not understanding might keep him from leaving.

Salvador sees she is embarrassed by her childish behavior. Avoiding his eyes, Aura hugs him hard around the neck.

"You are a good girl," he says. Then, like he used to do when she was small, he carries her back to the house. He sets Aura down by the front door stoop and kisses her forehead, well aware of Dolores listening from the kitchen. "One day," he says, looking into his daughter's big wet eyes, "you will be a wonderful wife. A wonderful mother. We have to keep you safe for that."

The Colonel

On the evening after Judas had charged through Sacapulas, Colonel Blanco introduced himself. As the new commander of their regiment, he started off by speaking of his pride to be a soldier, and to be wearing the same camouflage uniform as his men. The colonel was an impressive man with piercing amber eyes, like birds of prey, perched above a slender curving nose. His thick black beard surrounded soft pink lips. His voice was deep, sure of itself, and demanded attention.

"You have seen," he said, "the strange custom of this town. They keep a box outside the Judas church to find out who are sinners. Ladinos who do not give enough money to the coffers, it seems, tend to get picked!" He laughed, and they all laughed with him. "The priest tells me it is how the poorest of parishioners get revenge. Says he can do nothing to stop it. He thought, being a Catholic myself, I might not approve, but I assured him I do. Because we are also here to confront sin, our base now has its own information box. We need to learn about the sinners who come from Mexico and Cuba, backed by Russian money and arms, to incite those here who hate Guatemala. They come to villages like this and threaten to kill anyone who does not join them. It is our duty, men, to defend these poor frightened people, to gain their confidence, to let them know we are on their side. We start tomorrow, on the day our Lord rose from the dead. . .*to save mankind.*"

He paused then, and Jaime saw his face change, become softer.

"These are the holiest of days for us Catholics," he said. His voice had softened too. "I understand that Easter may not matter to some of you. Perhaps, like General Montt, you have different beliefs. Nevertheless, he demands that ours be respected. Let us not disappoint our leader, men, or the good people of Sacapulas."

The next morning, Easter Sunday, Colonel Blanco personally distributed bags of beans and rice. He ordered that the food be given away to whoever needed it. The soldiers set up a booth in the main square. The townspeople shook their hands. Some of the Indians kissed their feet and prayed for their salvation. Even Jaime and Raul felt proud to be in the army.

A few days later a huge flatbed arrived with more supplies, which meant more kisses and prayers. People came from miles around. They arrived suspicious, and left grateful.

It was a good time, a happy time, a time full of hope that did not last long. Two weeks after Easter a man was shot for concealing weapons in his hut. They strung him up in the main square by his ankles and left him hanging for days, right above the place where food had been handed out. *NO MORE BEANS AND RICE*, said a sign attached to the man's chest, *UNTIL EVERY TRAITOR IS FOUND!*

With the next several days came more arrests. People had learned that information meant food. It would also help them avoid suspicion, so they lined up outside the army base to tell what they knew. During that same time, many villagers fled for the nearby mountains.

On Sunday, May 1st, right after dinner, Colonel Blanco called a special meeting ahead of General Montt's weekly 'discurso' with the nation. Though all soldiers were required to view the broadcast, Jaime noticed that Blanco never stayed. As the TV set was wheeled into the hall, the colonel hurried to his business: "I congratulate you, men, on the work you've done. The good people of this town have learned to trust us, and given crucial information. Tomorrow at dawn we go to where the traitors are hiding. Be ready," he said with a quick salute, and abruptly left the room.

Tables were cleared, carried away, and benches relocated in front of the screen. Though Jaime liked to stand toward the back, with Raul, tonight it was not possible. Tonight he somehow got trapped by the shuffling crowd and had to sit. It happened fast. The lights were dimmed and there he was, front and center, with General Montt looking straight at him.

"This is for you," the great man said. "You, brave soldier, who risks your life every day for the sake of our country. As you know, we have been accused of horrible things by those who want us defeated. . .those who work, either by intention or folly, for the forces of evil. The sins of these people must be exposed, and the best way, I believe, is to clarify the sanctity of our mission. I therefore state my promise to the nation, dear soldier, which must also be yours."

He held up a piece of paper, which listed his 'PROMISES,' and spoke each of them out loud. While the list was long, these were the ones Jaime remembered:

> -During battle, in spite of the danger, we shall never abuse an innocent person.
>
> -We shall protect the villages and crops against those who would do them harm.
>
> -We shall be courteous to elders and children, even in the villages of our enemy, even though they may be the father or mother, sister or brother of a traitor.

"These are our promises to those who love Guatemala," Ríos Montt said. "Promises for the people we honor, the patriotic citizens who make our country great."

The caravan of eight trucks was off by sunrise, slowly curving up the steep rocky grade on the northern side of Sacapulas. At last cresting the ridge, they dropped toward the verdant valley of Nebaj. Farmers were already out in their fields along the road. The village itself was nearly empty, a few dogs basking in the early sunshine, a little girl running across the street after a chicken.

Colonel Blanco pulled up to an open *comedor* on the town plaza, across from the church. He got out and signaled his officers to join him. They sat at a table, drank coffee and ate tortillas, talking in whispers while the regular soldiers stood by the trucks.

When they were finished, Jaime saw that Colonel Blanco tried to pay. Though the owner would not accept his money, at least he'd tried. To the waiting soldiers he turned and said, "Most of you will stay with me. For the rest, Sergeant Ortiz is in charge."

Jaime and Raul and a handful of others were directed to a single truck, now under the orders of Óscar Ortiz, the failed Kaibil, who Raul liked to call 'the eater of pet puppies.'

It was another hour and a half to the smaller village of Chajul. Like Nebaj, the place looked empty. The doors of the white Catholic Church were locked with a chain.

"Break it," the sergeant ordered. A soldier with an axe charged up the steps to do what he was told. "Listen up," Ortiz shouted to the rest. "First we need to find the priest. Go get people out of their houses. Bring them here. Shoot anyone who refuses!"

The soldiers spread out in teams of two. Raul and Jaime stayed together. They saw one man, trying to run away, get shot in the back. The vast majority of villagers, however, did not resist, and came to the church as ordered. They lined up on the lower steps. There were about eighty of them: old men and women, small children, teenage girls and a few young boys.

Ortiz did not hide his irritation. "Who of you speaks Spanish?"

A man raised his hand. He was not old, but crippled, the toes of his left foot aimed toward the heel of his right as he hobbled forward. "I do," he said.

"Good," Ortiz said, and made it clear his words must be translated exactly. He did not want any possibility of misinterpretation.

"I will do my best," said the crippled man.

"I am sure you will," Ortiz said. "Where is the priest?" was his next question to the crowd, which was exactly translated and perfectly understood.

"We do not know," said a middle-aged woman in the front row.

"Liar," Ortiz said. He turned to Elicio, standing at his side. "Shoot her."

Elicio raised his rifle and aimed it between the woman's ample breasts. At first Jaime thought it was meant to frighten her, get her talking. Then he looked at Raul, whose stiff blanched face told him the sergeant was serious.

"You heard me, soldier! *Ahorita!*" shouted Ortiz, and Elicio pulled the trigger. The woman buckled and fell backward into the arms of those behind her.

The bullet had passed through her chest and lodged in the leg of a small boy, who burst into tears and was squirming around in pain.

"Shoot him too!" Ortiz said, but two old women covered him with their bodies, crying and pleading for mercy. "Very well," Ortiz said, "then tell me the truth. The priest is off with the young men of the village, am I right?"

The crippled man translated and everyone began nodding. Jaime saw they would agree with whatever this soldier wanted to believe.

"I knew it," Ortiz said. "Ask them *where?*"

The crippled man said a single word and the crowd all began shouting at once.

"In the mountains," said the crippled man.

"No," Ortiz said, "that's not good enough! Tell them we need someone to take us!"

The crippled man translated. No one offered. They looked at the ground or glanced at each other, as if not knowing what to say.

"I will speak to each of you in the church," Ortiz said, waiting for the translation before he continued, "where God Himself has forbidden you to lie!"

The villagers seemed to understand, their eyes huge with fear.

"You come with me," Ortiz said, and the crippled man limped behind him up the steps, carving a wide pathway through the distraught crowd, past the dead woman and the whimpering boy. At the door of the church, Ortiz ordered a few soldiers to come inside, including Elicio and sharpshooter Miguel. The rest were told to keep their rifles pointed at the prisoners. And they did. . .for many hours. . .long silent hours occasionally broken by groans or screams coming from within the church, as one by one the villagers went to be questioned. Some of them came out bent over with pain. Some were bleeding. Some, like the injured boy, were allowed to return to their houses, while others (Jaime counted eleven--two women, a few old men, and every teenage boy) were left to the side, on the bottom church step, and made to sit--warned that anyone who tried to leave would be shot.

Soldiers not on guard set up camp in the small schoolhouse. Village women came to bring them food. A few older girls were taken to the church, where Ortiz and Elicio and Miguel were staying.

Jaime saw one of the girls, when returning from the church, stop every few feet--in spite of her hurry--overwhelmed by great gasping sobs . . .sobs like those his mother sometimes made when returning from Manuel's hut.

The next day was the same, villagers brought in one at a time to be interrogated, or raped, or worse. By the time Ortiz was done with everyone, around 3pm, there were seventeen people bunched together on the street. "So," he said, "what should we do with traitors?"

Just then, a jeep showed up. The driver told Ortiz that Colonel Blanco needed them in Nebaj.

The sergeant's eyes burned with rage, like a child robbed of his favorite toy. "Soon," he said to the messenger, "once I've finished my business here."

The soldier looked confused, but turned the jeep around and drove away.

Once he was out of sight, Ortiz ordered that all the villagers come to the church. He smoked cigarettes while people slowly gathered. He told them to sit on the steps. "For a show," Ortiz said, "a great fiesta, in honor of those who love our country."

Why would he say such an evil lie, Jaime wondered, when he knew no one believed him?

Elicio reported that many of the villagers had disappeared. Jaime counted sixty-two in the crowd--including the seventeen sitting down--at least twenty less than the day before.

"It is plain," Ortiz said, lighting another cigarette, "that some people did not tell me the truth." He took a long casual puff and blew out the smoke. "Why else would they run and hide like frightened dogs? Why leave everyone else to blame? When the cowards come crawling back, *you can tell them* it is their fault what happened. And you must tell them it will happen again if they continue to lie and support the traitors. This is your warning," he said, nodding at Miguel and Elicio, a signal that it was time to do whatever had been planned.

They each grabbed a can of kerosene and doused the group of seventeen. Two of them were shot trying to get away. The others stayed put, on their knees praying, or laying on their stomachs, covering their faces, crying for mercy as Ortiz threw his cigarette at them, then jumped back to avoid the bursting flame.

Back in Nebaj, close to sunset, they found the caravan of trucks at the western edge of town, parked on a wide flat below a small hill. Ortiz and the other officers met with Colonel Blanco in his tent. The regular soldiers ate their rationed tortillas, then slept on the ground. Each had just a single blanket. Some crawled beneath the trucks, and slept close together--little protection from the chilling mist.

In the morning they were roused and ordered to the top of the hill, where Colonel Blanco waited. From there they could see the nearby plots of onions and beans. Beyond that, past the patchwork tracts of upturned soil awaiting its maize, stood a stack of high peaks, thick with evergreens. A violet sky made the forest look darker than it was, a dense tangle of things unknown.

Colonel Blanco gazed in that direction. "The enemy," he pointed, "is hiding out there. Not in places where decent people live and tend their milpas and raise their families, no, but where criminals go to escape the law and make trouble for others." He turned to a large piece of butcher's paper mounted on a wooden easel. Drawn on the paper was a simple map. It showed the towns of Nebaj and Chajul, and engulfing them, stretching west, the rest of the Cuchumatanes mountains. "We know where they are," he said, pointing at the X's on the map, "from helicopter surveillance provided by the North Americans. They support our war against the communists. They give us whatever we need to destroy these festering sores. But it won't be easy, men. First, we must abandon the trucks here in Nebaj and--"

Suddenly, coming toward him past the sitting soldiers, were a few old men, dressed in Nebaj traje. They apologized for interrupting and were promptly forgiven by Colonel Blanco.

The younger of them said, "We are the village leaders."

"Oh?" said the colonel. "And how did you become leaders?"

"Only by learning Spanish."

Colonel Blanco laughed. "Aha," he said, looking the man over, apparently humored by his honesty. Though in fact no longer young, maybe in his early sixties, the man seemed full of life, stout and solid, with strong tight calves showing beneath his white knee-length pants. "Well," Colonel Blanco said, "you have a beautiful village."

"Thank you, sir. I am sorry we have not come earlier. My mistake, because we should have asked if there is anything you might need, or--"

"No," Colonel Blanco said, slapping him on the shoulder, "we're fine. And we know that Nebaj is a peaceful village. Your young men work hard in their fields. They do not make trouble."

"No," the man said, then looked confused, perhaps wondering if he'd said the right thing. He laughed and slapped his head. "I mean yes, of course, it's true. None of us mean you any harm."

"Don't worry, friend, we're just passing through. But might I ask a favor?"

"Yes, oh yes, anything."

"Is it possible to get some food before we leave?"

"Certainly," the man said, full of smiles. "We can grill some chickens."

"No, that's not necessary, don't bother yourselves with--"

"Please, sir, it would be our pleasure," the man said, and the three elders went running off to make it happen.

Two hours later, around nine o'clock, after a feast of grilled chickens, tortillas and beans, Colonel Blanco shook the man's hand, thanked him for the hospitality, then told his soldiers to gather their things. "Oh," he said, "I almost forgot."

The elder, walking away, looked over his shoulder at the colonel. "Are you talking to me, sir?"

"Yes, yes, I forgot to ask your name."

"My name," said the man, smiling, as if receiving a great honor, "is Toribio."

"Well, Toribio, what we really need is for you to guide us through these mountains."

Toribio tried to keep his smile, but couldn't. "Sir, please, I have my milpa to plant and--"

"A milpa is important, I understand. So the faster you get us to a safe place, Toribio, the better it is for you. And we need to leave now. Are you ready?"

"Yes. . .of course."

"Good," the colonel said. His subordinate officers were smiling. So were some of the regular soldiers. Jaime and Raul looked at each other, knowing to keep their mouths shut and get in line. "Drivers will return to Sacapulas for supplies, then meet us," Colonel Blanco said, touching his finger to the map, "here, in Capellañia, on the road to Todos Santos. Is that clear?"

"Yes, sir." the drivers said.

"Good," Colonel Blanco said, and told Toribio to take the lead.

They climb to the ridge west of Nebaj, then down the other side. The few farmers they see are trenching their milpas, trying to look busy, pretending not to notice the patrol passing by. If caught peeking, they give uncertain waves. They would hide, thinks Raul, if there were any maize to hide behind. Better to drop their hoes and run. Especially the boys.

After Chajul, his thoughts are like bullets without a gun: thoughts of killing that bastard Ortiz if he ever gets the chance. He is relieved when Colonel Blanco keeps his soldiers marching, does not bother the farmers. Maybe he is wrong about the man. Maybe, with him in charge, there is hope.

Below the milpas, they enter what Raul sees used to be a village. There is almost nothing now, just a handful of lean-to shacks made of old bent corrugated tin, hardly distinguishable from the collapsed houses. They reach a small Catholic Church and stop to rest under the large pine tree out front. Gathered off to the side are a few of the town's old women, some of them holding babies in their arms. On the surrounding hillsides, Raul sees the familiar checkerboard of bean, onion, and cabbage fields.

"This is Acul," Colonel Blanco says. "A very sad story explains the destruction. About a year ago, because villagers would not cooperate with the guerillas, the traitors burned their town."

Raul glances at Toribio. It is the slightest movement of the old man's head, and his dull sad eyes, that tell the truth. The colonel is lying.

"The devils come to places like this and spread their evil," Blanco says. "They steal the food, and threaten everyone with death if they do not take up arms against us. They force the poor villagers to sabotage roads and bridges. If they refuse, this is what happens. At least in Acul they had decency enough to leave the church unharmed. Or maybe it's a fear of what will happen if they dare burn God's house too. Anyway, I am here to say that we, the Guatemalan army, are determined to help these people." He turns to Toribio. "Tell them that General Ríos Montt himself has promised to rebuild the village, even better than before, and to protect it from ever being harmed again. Carpenters and supplies are on their way. Go ahead, tell them."

Toribio speaks to the old women, but their faces remain blank, unaffected by the news.

After a few minutes, and some needed water, the soldiers again start walking. Toribio looks miserable. Head down, he leads them further west, out of the valley, toward the next of many looming ridges. It is a quiet, somber march.

In the late afternoon, they set up camp along a fast-flowing creek just below the tiny *canton* of Xexocom. Blanco sends someone after fresh tortillas. Everyone drinks from the stream and fills their bottles. Surrounding them are the baked grasses and thirsty trees of summer's final days. Today, though, it is cloudy. Cool.

One of the ladino officers says he thinks it's going to rain. Though it is May, and he should be right, the Indian boys smile at each other, knowing better.

Straight above is a massive, nearly vertical mountain.

Toribio explains that the great central plain of the *Altiplano* lies above, but it is a long way up. The colonel seems to understand the old man's hint and decides to spend the night in Xexocom. They eat leftover chicken and tortillas and go to sleep as soon as the light is gone.

The morning is full of birdsong, the misty fog already burning off as they begin to climb. Within an hour the heat returns like a punishment. Jaime remembers, as a boy, the steep mountain passes to their milpa, how he'd hated those long sweltering days, how he'd tricked himself into making it bearable--*breathe and step, breathe and step.* Now he does the same, one steep gravelly switchback, then another, ticked off in his mind like a game. Thirty-two, he counts. Thirty-three.

Just keep going, that's the way, no matter what.

At one rest spot, Toribio says to the colonel, "The rest of the path, I promise you, is obvious."

Maybe, thinks Jaime. But that is not why the elder is here. That much is clear to everyone.

"I'd prefer," Colonel Blanco says, "that you take us to the top."

"Si, Señor," says Toribio, and on they go.

For the ladino officers, especially, the going is tough. Their breathing is heavy, their faces soaked with sweat. Jaime remembers the terrible *monstro* hill of his childhood. This is not as hard, and he says so to Raul, who is in front of him. He says it in Kakchiquel. And too loud. One of the officers up front stops to remind him--"a warning," he says-- that they only speak Spanish.

That's when the first shot comes, ripping through the officer's neck. His head snaps to the side, then collapses to his chest as he falls.

"Get down!" shouts Colonel Blanco from above.

Shots ricochet against the rocks as they lie there, helpless to fight back. Jaime hears the colonel barking out orders. On the switchback above, number forty-nine, he sees Toribio stand and hold up his hands.

303

"I am Toribio from Nebaj," the old man shouts, and the firing stops. It is not Jaime's language, but the words are close enough that he mostly understands. Or thinks he does. "These soldiers," Toribio seems to be saying, "are friends of the village. Don't shoot! Let them pass!"

A few quiet moments go by before Colonel Blanco, sounding confident, orders that they get up and continue climbing. Jaime counts two officers and six soldiers dead. He returns his focus to the trail. Fifty, fifty-one, fifty-two. . .breathe and step. . .one at a time. . .same as ever.

At around noon, after eighty-seven switchbacks, they reach the high, flat plain. It looks to Jaime like they're entering another world. The sunlight here is different, stark and unforgiving. Atop the browning grass are piles of ancient, oddly shaped boulders, baked a deep dark gray. There seems nowhere to hide from the pounding heat.

Then, as if by magic, a tiny hut appears, standing by itself.

Colonel Blanco tells Toribio to stop. "You can go now," he says. An obvious dismissal. "I only wish your help might have better protected us."

The colonel walks past the old man. Toribio turns and heads toward Acul. Jaime sees Ortiz walking behind him. Everyone sees.

Colonel Blanco and the remaining officer go inside the hut. The regular soldiers sit outside, lined against the northern wall, away from the sun, and drink their rations of water. A single shot shatters the silence. No one says a word. Jaime lies on his back and pulls his cap down over his face.

Of course, he thinks, *Blanco is the same. They're all the same.*

Ortiz returns and enters the hut. Jaime can smell smoke, and tortillas cooking, and his mouth begins to water. At some point a woman runs outside to bring in more firewood. Finally, Blanco and his officers emerge. "You see," the colonel says, "how hard it is to know the truth?"

He makes no attempt to explain what he means, just hands each soldier a small stack of tortillas.

They walk through the long dry valley that runs from east to west. In some places it is wide, scattered here and there with those same strange boulders, the trail infested with tufts of spikey grass and juniper bushes, at times so thick they must machete their way through. Jaime has never seen any path so straight. No twists, no turns. It just goes on and on. At the valley's rims, north and south, is a continuing forest of pine trees. In between, only them. Goats cry somewhere in the distance, following their invisible herder away from the soldiers. The only water is at the bottom of a well outside the vacated canton of Chotzul. The huts are searched, but have no food. "By tomorrow night," Blanco tells them, aware that their rations are getting low, "we'll be in Capellañia."

But he's wrong.

Toward the end of the day they are ambushed again, this time from the northern ridge, and forced back into the southern trees. Crawling through the dense underbrush, they manage less than a mile by nightfall. In the morning it's worse. Bullets ring out whenever they dare to move. On the third day, making it to the plain's western edge, again they're met with heavy gunfire and forced to stop. Another two days pass. The food runs out. Still trapped, it begins to pour. By the time they break free, nine more are dead, and, for all their effort, not a single enemy. At least none that they know of. Not once have they even seen their attackers.

No one is waiting in Capellañia--perhaps having given them up for dead. The fact does not seem to faze the colonel, who locates a comedor and orders piles of tortillas and beans, which are gobbled down by the soldiers. The owner, at gunpoint, then agrees to take them to Todos Santos in his flatbed truck. Jaime, his hands shaking, stomach still growling, mind numb and spinning, feels grateful for the colonel's power.

He's glad the Indian man does what Blanco says. He doesn't care what happens to this person, this stranger, this man he will never know. He just doesn't care.

Three or four hours later, the stranger lets them off at the Tres Hermanas hotel. Along with the others, Jaime climbs down from the flatbed and goes behind the building, past the chain-linked fence, to where the army trucks are parked. As if alone, as if no one, not even Raul, exists, he huddles by himself under the eaves, soaked by the endless rain, and is handed more tortillas. He can hardly believe he's alive. Can hardly remember what that means. It's like the break he used to get at El Mirador--*chew and swallow. . .chew and swallow.* That's all life is anymore. But it's not his father now, it's this bearded man, Blanco, giving the orders--a man stronger, and much scarier, than Manuel.

Soon the man will tell him what to do. And, whatever it is, Jaime is ashamed to know he'll do it. Raul tries to get him talking, but there is nothing to say. He doesn't want to be told how to feel. He doesn't want to feel anything.

The injured are taken to Huehuetenango. The remaining twelve, all Indian soldiers, sleep in shifts, six at a time, in one of the hotel's tiny rooms. The second room holds Sergeant Ortiz and Sergeant Ramirez. The third is for Colonel Blanco.

For weeks, through the end of June, during General Montt's proclaimed 'amnesty', the soldiers sit around, hoping to themselves that the war is really over, while Blanco and other regiment leaders meet in the one-room schoolhouse.

School, they decide, is 'suspended.'

Every able-bodied villager is required to report for 'community service' each morning.

Supplies from the various little stores are 'donated' to the army.

Beans and tortillas, meats and vegetables, arrive fresh from the market.

Cooks are provided and water canisters kept full.

No one anywhere is ever heard complaining.

Raul cannot get Jaime to talk. A few words, here and there, is all the kid can seem to manage. And not about anything that matters. Raul, of course, is not much better off. He knows they both need time to start feeling better. While he waits, all he can think of is finding some way out.

Then, on the sunny morning of July 7th, after a night of torrential rain, Blanco jumps to the steamy hood of a truck where everyone can see him. "The amnesty," he says, "has failed. Once again, we must defend our country from those who would destroy it. And I promise you, we will succeed! We will! We must have courage, men, and protect each other, and see things through. It is our sworn duty! Our fellow soldiers need help up in the mountains. I'm on my way tomorrow. Are you with me?"

"Yes!" shout most of the soldiers. Enough of them, thinks Raul, to cover his silence.

When the colonel asks again, Jaime shouts out too, lifting his rifle with the rest. The boy looks stunned. Close to tears. Raul puts a hand on his friend's shoulder and slowly, gently, lowers his arm.

Demons

San Pablo, May 29, 1982

Pascual Rosario peruses the flattened site where his new house will be built. Then, dropping to the ground, with his wife and son looking on, he begs God's forgiveness for not seeing earlier the error of his ways, for not walking the true pathway of salvation. As he kneels there crying, repentant for his many sins, he also wonders how, in God's name, his father had been so blind?

Pascual's father was a righteous man, full of religious fervor. Also named Pascual, he came from a long line of Rosario men to join the *Cofradía*--the *Brotherhood* set up by early Spanish missionaries to help spread Christianity among the new world natives. By the late 1500's, however, Guatemalan Cofradías had taken on a distinctive Mayan flavor, and in many ways were at odds with Catholicism. They became powerful organizations in and of themselves. Often led by shamanic vision, they 'Mayanized' certain Christian saints, created others, and performed ceremonies unsanctioned by the church. Perhaps their most egregious affront to the mother faith was a ritualistic use of the fermented alcohol called *aguardiente (firewater)*.

In short, Pascual's father--like so many *Cofrades* before him--became a drunk for God. His greatest revelations, in fact, happened when he was most intoxicated, his fervor so profound that he could barely walk. The morning after one such night, as he lay facedown, snoring on the floor, a bit of hell broke loose inside their little hut. It started with young Pascual giving his father a gentle shake.

"Please," the boy said, and rolled him to his back. His father responded with angry moans, a milky foam dribbling from his dry cracked lips. After being up all night in ceremony, the elder expected to be left alone. But the son could not let it happen. Though still only

April, it was time, *now*, to plant the corn. The rains had come early. Another storm was brewing. The boy awoke that morning to birds singing, sunshine, steaming terraces, and he knew the reprieve would not last long. There was no time to waste, yet here they were, wasting it! He gave his father's shoulder another shake. Then another.

Desperate, young Pascual raised his hand and slapped that drunken face. The elder's eyes shot open, stared at nothing, and closed. It was no use.

Young Pascual left him on the floor and went to work. He had to get at least some of the seed planted. To his surprise, the weather held, allowing him to work the entire day. . .the entire day without rest, without food, without water. . .and the job less than half finished.

In the evening, when it became too dark to see, he trudged toward the hut. Heavy dark clouds covered the moon and rain began to fall. By the time he made it back, his clothes were soaked. His father was sitting, dry as an old bone, heating himself by the fire. His mother, coughing, cooked their tortillas. No one said a word while they ate.

Once full, old Pascual got up, put on his poncho, and started for the door.

"You're going out?" young Pascual said.

"There is another week of ceremony."

"And a milpa to be planted. Which cannot wait."

His mother looked at him, a warning.

At the door of the hut his father paused. "Yes, son, I know." His voice sounded strange, lacking its normal tone of authority. "I am sorry," he said. "It would please me to work the field with you, but God needs me with Him."

His eyes were full of sorrow when he said it. It was his duty to suffer--that's what young Pascual heard those eyes saying. Spiritual devotion, they said, was the heaviest of all burdens, and needed to be acknowledged. It was his father's destiny to suffer because he'd been chosen as one of God's sacrificial lambs. That's what they were supposed to believe.

Later, in the middle of the night, as usual, he stumbled back home blubbering God's praises, and puking, pissing his pants and apologizing. He thanked young Pascual for cleaning up the mess, for getting him to his mat, for taking care of daily responsibilities and all the other things he was no longer able to do. "I must accept my fate," he cried. "Please, son, you must understand."

A son, by tradition the family's servant, was expected to honor his father's authority. Moreover, as the son of a sacrificial lamb, young Pascual must later become a lamb himself, must never complain, must do what was expected. It was a mandate he refused to accept. He would be the first Rosario to not join, or by any means support, the Cofradía. He would, indeed, actively reject it.

From that day on, he never spoke of faith with his father. Only with God.

Still on his hands and knees, Pascual whispers, "Gracias a Dios." He prays that in death, at least, his father found the truth. He kisses the ground, thankful for his blessings and determined to show his gratitude. Because the original site for their house would have been too small, he's expanded it out into the upper milpa. A sack or two of corn is well worth the sacrifice!

It is far past the date he should have planted.

"Nothing matters," he tells an anxious Concepción, "except finishing this house."

It does not occur to him how much he sounds like his father.

Six weeks later, on the 8th of July, he's down on his knees again, kissing the newly poured slab of concrete. "This," he cries, "is my gift to you!"

That same day, Colonel Blanco leads his troops into the Sierra Madre mountains. On July 12th they arrive in Jacaltenango, a place known for guerilla activity. It is a shabby little town made worse by the steady rains, the muddy streets, the ceaseless mold.

They are met by Juan Cuitúm. Juan is the leader of the local *patrulleros*. In distant localities, like that of Jacaltenango, every man is responsible to leave his milpa one day a week and *patrol* the surrounding hills. Citizens are to inform on anyone in any way sympathetic to the rebels. . .and everyone is suspect. Juan's reports, unfortunately, sometimes lead to arrests, but it seems there is no other choice. Refusing to do his duty would mean certain death for him and his family. Patrulleros are encouraged to make the arrests themselves, and occasionally that means killing someone. They drag the body back to town, take pictures, record the person's name in Juan's government-supplied ledger, and bury the remains. He knows that many of the men regret betraying fellow Indians, and suffer lasting pangs of guilt. Not Juan. For him, leading the patrulleros is a chance to keep his family safe. Also a means of escaping his Indian heritage. . . of becoming someone who matters.

The man reminds Raul of his father. He is about the same size and build, but that isn't it. It's the look of self-importance in his step, of ambition in his eyes.

"My name is Juan Cuitúm," he says to Colonel Blanco with a grand salute. "At your service." They meet outside the Catholic sacristy, which

311

the colonel has commandeered as a makeshift headquarters. Juan and his four men wear government-issued camouflage shirts above their traditional knee-length pants. "This," he tells the colonel, "is our Tuesday patrol." Each is barefoot, armed with a machete, standing at stiff attention. Only Juan has a gun, an Israeli Galil rifle. He reports that his patrols have flushed the guerillas from town, out into the mountains.

"Good," Blanco says. "Where?"

"North, toward the village of San Francisco Nentón. People from there cannot be trusted. We in Jacaltenango do not tolerate traitors, Colonel, but those people are not the same. Until now, there have not been enough guns, or men, to attack the devils."

"Well, since you know the territory, you may lead us."

"It will be my honor," Juan says with another proud salute.

The road to Nentón is a mess--impassable by truck--just one long muddy rut. An undergrowth of spiny reddish bushes cover the hills on both sides, with oak and pine and juniper trees looming overhead. It is a dark, narrow passage, the sky above thick with black clouds, thunder clapping in the distance. Juan has collected all of his men, a group of twenty-three.

Colonel Blanco makes sure that the patrulleros go first.

They look back to see if Juan might be joining them. He shakes his head. No.

Forty minutes later comes the first ambush. Seven patrulleros fall in the mud and everyone else rushes for the spiny bushes. From there, fighting thorns and drizzling rain, the troops inch forward, or side-ways, or sometimes cannot move at all. Hours crawl by like snails. At last comes the blackness of night, though little sleep comes with it.

Raul keeps himself and Jaime quiet and still. For three soaked days the guerillas hold control, but on the morning of the fourth the sun shines bright. The storm is gone, the air dry and getting hot. Before long, Raul expects to see trucks full of soldiers.

Blanco and Juan retreat from the rear, promising to make it happen soon. The colonel again leaves Sergeant Ortiz in charge. Raul sighs, certain that something bad will happen.

It doesn't take long. Ortiz orders the patrulleros back onto the main road. One of them, bolder than the rest, refuses to go, and Ortiz shoots him. Another runs for a break in the bushes. Ortiz is taking aim when a bullet hits him in the chest and he falls. The devil lies there in the mud. Dead. Just like Raul has hoped for. Dead.

He feels stunned, as if the bullet had hit him. Strange to have no sense of relief. He doesn't care anymore who deserves what. Hungry and exhausted and scared, Raul just wants to go home.

The next afternoon, out of nowhere, a U.S. helicopter whirs over their heads. The soldiers cheer until its machine-gun turns on them. They dive behind trees and cover their heads. When it finally goes, everyone somehow realizes that the guerillas are also gone, retreating deeper into the mountains, leaving the road clear.

Within an hour, Raul sees the outskirts of Nentón. As with Acul, the village sits in its own private valley, surrounded by crops, the forested mountains rising on all sides.

Trucks come lumbering up from the rear. Blanco is in the lead, along with Juan Cuitúm. The colonel leans out the window and orders them to pair up, to get everyone out of their huts.

"Bring them to the church," he says. "Shoot anyone who refuses."

The exact words Ortiz used in Chajul. One devil after another, thinks Raul. And it will only get worse. They have to get away. He grabs hold of Jaime's arm and heads for the most distant hut he can see, beneath a steeply terraced milpa, the forest right behind.

They will go and ask for help. No one will miss them, of that he's sure. But sharp-shooter Miguel and another soldier are walking close by. Raul hurries to establish his direction.

Miguel spots him, hesitates, then aims for a closer hut. He and his partner enter it and start shooting. Jaime stops and turns toward the sound.

"Come on," Raul says, "there's nothing we can do."

Jaime goes along, one step after the other. He remembers his father saying the same thing about the dead man from San Antonio. "Nothing we can do." It seemed wrong before, but now he understands. No, it's true, there really is nothing. . .nothing to be done.

They walk up to a hut and Raul pushes open the door. It is black inside, like a hungry mouth.

"Perfect," Raul says. "I'll get us clothes."

Jaime stops at the door, shivering in the sun. He is confused. His mind isn't working right. Though he wants to be with his friend, there is a voice in his head, whispering, cautioning him not to go inside. He's been taught to never enter anyone's house uninvited. Never! *Doesn't Raul know that? Why is he in there? Clothes, is that what he said? What clothes? What is going on?*

Then he hears it, the dull whack of a machete.

He rushes into the hut and sees Raul on his hands and knees. An old man stands above him, dealing a second blow. Jaime sends his bayonet through the old man's back. His body falls on top of Raul. His friend's neck is cut open, gushing blood, his head twisted off to the side. A woman comes screaming into the hut and Jaime slams her in the face with the butt of his rifle. Then he shoots her. Then shoots her twice more. He turns around and yanks the old man off Raul's back.

He wants to bring his friend into the sunlight, but the lifeless head screams at him, "NO, *VOS*, LEAVE ME BE! GET OUT OF HERE! NOW!"

Jaime crawls from the hut and vomits on the ground outside. A small boy, the boy of his dreams, watches from the edge of the milpa, staring at him through the cornstalks.

Jaime remembers running away from the small boy's piercing eyes. He remembers an Indian man sitting by the road. The man is begging mercy, and is shot in the face. He remembers other things too, but it's someone else seeing it, doing it, pretending to be him. Like a bad dream, something he can't wake up from. It isn't him locking men in the courthouse. Or him, outside, standing guard. The sky is a weave of tight blue thread. The mountain is green, the huts brown, the hands dripping red. Women and children are ordered to stay inside. They are crying. Screaming. A naked girl runs into the road. A laughing soldier chases, catches her, and slices her belly open with his knife. Another soldier is after a small boy. With one mighty swing he cuts off the boy's head with a machete. It bounces to the ground and rolls away from the body.

The soldier kicks it and yells, "Goal! Goal!"

In the middle of the road a bull roasts over an open fire. Soldiers rip at its burnt flesh. He does too--yes, that's Jaime--lying on his back, gobbling the bloody meat like he's starving. He remembers the sleek white birds flying overhead, calling to him, flapping their way to heaven. He laughs and looks down for the water beneath his cayuco, finding only dirt.

He grabs for another piece of meat. Someone slaps his face and hands him a gun and points where to go.

A group of men are lined up against a building.

They will not look at him. Not a glance.

He does not know these people.

Does not care if they look or not. They mean nothing. Nothing.

Rifles are ordered to aim and fire.

Then go to another line and fire again.

Lots of bullets. Lots of bodies falling to the ground.

But it isn't Jaime.

It isn't him.

Angels

November 27th, 1982

"I know, Luna, you can pull out the *New York Times*, or whatever, and point at the pink highlighted parts to prove how informed you are, how knowledgeable, and make it plain that you forgive the little boys their ignorance and will teach them, for their own good, how to treat their fellow man. Then you can cry and kick your feet while they confiscate our van and shoot us in the head and dump our bodies in the nearest ditch. How about that?"

It had been difficult for them since returning to Guatemala. There was an extra-long interrogation at the border, and lots of army checkpoints to get through, with soldiers more suspicious, more aggressive than before. Passports to show again and again, and the same questions to answer (Why are you here? Where are you going? How long will you stay?) while the van was getting searched from top to bottom.

"We need to be sure," the boy soldiers would say. Or sometimes just, "Don't move."

"No problem," Jake would answer. Every time. He'd been on the questioning side of checkpoints like this in Vietnam. He knew what young frightened soldiers were capable of. The anxious faces of these Guatemalan boys freaked him out. He tried not looking too close, like he'd learned as a child to behave around unknown dogs. He tried not to see what lurked, fanged and vicious, behind those distrustful eyes. Tried not to care. It was their war, not his. His, thank God, was over. Let these people do whatever the hell they had to do and please, *por favor*, leave him the fuck out of it.

Was that so hard for Luna to understand? OK, OK, she'd signed letters to protest against the military here--*check*--was opposed to anything having to do with war--*double check*. *Got it.* Yeah, uh-huh, OK, but she needed to keep those feelings to herself, be more careful with her mouth.

"A bunch of little boys killing all those people?" she mumbled at the last checkpoint, far too loud, a sour look on her face as two of them rifled through their van.

One had turned and looked at her, wondering what she'd said. The kid had no idea she'd read all those articles about Indians being displaced from their land; people shot for no reason; crops and villages burned, that sort of thing. He had no clue how hard it was for Luna to imagine *little boys* like him pulling those triggers and lighting those matches.

Well, yeah, so did Jake. But he had no doubt it was true. And, more important, knew he could do nothing to stop it. Nothing. He and she were different that way. For him, war was inevitable--as natural as gravity--the dark side of human nature. Life, for him, was a paradox of opposites. Yes, human beings were capable of climbing to great heights (could build those heights themselves, way up into the clouds) and were equally prone to falling, like from the top of the Empire State building to the concrete street below. Sometimes they were a damned ugly mess, human beings, unfortunately and unavoidably irrational. In Nam he'd seen, and done, such ugly things. Things impossible to justify. He remembered the day he and his unit set fire to a mountain village where they knew, or thought they knew, the Vietcong were hiding. He'd had to shoot a small boy running out of a burning hut. Why? Because he could not see what the boy was holding, which turned out to be a cat. Because it might have been a bomb and he could not take the chance.

"Sometimes," he told Luna, "fighting for your life means doing horrible things."

She listened, then shook her head.

Jake knew she was not doubting what he'd said, or judging it--just trying to understand. She'd been too young to remember Vietnam. Had never given it much thought. *Any?* No, probably not. This was the first war she'd truly paid attention to. Because of Consuelo. Because of Jaime. And though she'd read those articles, was certain of the horror, she had a hell of a time pinning her outrage on these rifle-toting children.

Jake worried she might say the wrong thing to the wrong children. Luckily, thus far, she hadn't, but with every new checkpoint he held his breath.

They arrived at their land on the first of December via the recently cut dirt road. During their months away, they'd cashed in on another pot harvest and Jake had drawn up a basic house plan. It would be two-story, framed with the large bamboo they could harvest from the land. Between the posts they wanted adobe bricks, also from the land. The floor would be covered with adobe tiles. There would be a simple kitchen and shower system, the biodegradable waste-water filtered through a gravel leach field before it was used to irrigate the lower gardens. Water would be pumped from the lake to a holding tank up by the road, thus providing maximum pressure down below. For cooking and drinking they'd brought a reverse osmosis water purifier. They also had a large jar of chlorophyll tablets, three bottles of Pepto-Bismol, and, just in case, a week's dose of penicillin. They both looked forward to shitting in an out-house. . .or pissing on the ground whenever nature called.

Pascual directed them to park in the bamboo-enclosed slot he had created at the top of the land. While they were gone, he'd also been busy. To Jake's surprise, he'd built his house of concrete block--not adobe, as originally planned. There was a large metal door in front, and a blood-red carpet over the slab. "Well, brother," Pascual said, "what do you think?"

"Wow," Jake said. "Big!"

"Yes!" Pascual said, "isn't it magnificent?"

"You are happy," Luna said, looking happy for his happiness.

"God forever blesses and guides me," he said, beaming.

The gringos smiled and nodded. They understood his words, but not much else. Later, between themselves, they tried to make sense of it. Maybe, because Pascual had grown up in such extreme poverty, he'd never learned to manage money. Otherwise why the carpet? Why the extra-wide front door? Oh well, they thought, why not? Who cares? Maybe a big house was needed because he and Conseulo wanted more children. Many more children. But why, then, not build many small rooms? Why just one? It was hilarious for Jake, trying to imagine a bunch of people actually wanting to live in the same room. Privacy? Who needs privacy? Or maybe, due to inescapable custom, Pascual could think of nothing else?

His problem, thought Jake. Let Pascual use his money however he pleased.

Besides, Jake had problems of his own.

With Luna helping when she could, he cleared a pad by the road, poured concrete, and set the two tanks, one for Pascual and one for them. In the middle of the land they placed the new gas pump. They buried a run of flexible plastic pipe down to the lake, and another from the pump up to the tanks. Jake did most of the work. And all of the plumbing. Anxious to give it a go, he pushed the magic button on the pump. The engine whirred into action. Pleased with himself, he scrambled up the stone pathway.

"Qué milagro!" he shouted, as water poured into the tank. He climbed up top and watched it fill with bulging pride. Luna handed him a beer and called him Robinson Crusoe. He hugged her, and laughed, because he'd never felt so inventive, so capable, so in-control. . .his self-satisfaction bubbling over. When the tank was full he turned the lever and sent the water downhill.

The two of them ran to the site of their future home.

"It feels like Christmas morning!" giggled Luna.

"Well," Jake said, "I guess that makes me Santa!"

He solemnly crossed himself, then cracked open the large brass gate valve he'd installed in front of the purifier. He watched Luna jump with joy as the thousand-dollar high-tech gadget produced their first purified gallon before its main seal ruptured, water squirting in her face.

Huh? What?

Jake shut off the valve and stormed away. Not being an actual plumber, he hadn't known of any special fittings. . .pressure reducers or . . .or what. . .some sort of regulator? Who knows? *Who the hell could possibly think of every damn thing?* He came back and examined the purifier. Useless. *Oh, hell, forget it!* A temporary set-back, that's all it was. At least there were plenty of sanitation pills, which would have to do because he needed to get going on the house.

That's when the bigger problems came.

Pascual, trying to help, sent down a few workers. Jake, in no mood for compromise, also judged them useless. After the plumbing fiasco he had to be more focused, more serious. Things had to be done right the first time. No cutting corners! No mistakes!

The workers did not understand. They thought that getting the work done fast was what he expected. Told to slow down, they looked lost, not knowing what to do.

"Well, no, how could they," Luna said, "without reading your mind?" She wondered out loud if he'd inherited the perfectionism from his father. She'd never seen him, she said, so 'obsessive.'

"I have to be," he yelled at her. "Details are what make the difference!"

Luna tried to stay patient as the work went on, and on, ever-so-slowly . . .and the slower it went the more frustrated Jake got, and critical, until at last he fired them all. She tried to reason with him, but he was adamant. Said he preferred to do it alone. He only seemed really bothered when having to lift a too-heavy piece of bamboo, meaning he had to ask her for help. She was willing, she wanted to do her part, but had not been well, occasionally suffering intense migraine headaches.

Stress, Luna thought, feeling often overwhelmed by Jake's increasing stress.

"I need a break," she told him one Saturday night. "Concepción invited me to go with her to the market in Pana. We're getting a ride in her friend's boat." From the look on his face and how he turned away, she knew she'd said it wrong. "I'm going to stay and see a doctor on Monday."

"Good."

"Which means probably coming back on the Tuesday boat."

"OK. Whatever you want. Do what you need to do."

The next morning, he saw them off from their own beach. Juan Carlos, the friend, came puttering up in his small skiff. Its motor sounded like an un-tuned lawn mower. He cut it to a sputtering idle and glided the boat into the shallows. Jumping out, he anchored himself in knee-high water while helping the pregnant Concepción climb aboard.

Luna hugged Jake hard. "See you in a few days," she said.

"Bye," he said, letting go.

"C'mon Jake, sure you're OK?"

"I'm fine," he said, stroking her hair. "You go take care of yourself."

In Pana, first thing, Luna went to see Consuelo, who said she was planning to make more friendship bracelets, that she needed money to go find Jaime.

"You will buy them, Luna?"

"I could use twelve dozen," Luna said. A lie. Yes, all right, she wanted to help, but this would not do any good, and Luna knew it. Though certain that Jaime was alive, she couldn't imagine Consuelo being able to find him. Going to look for him might even make things worse, might put Consuelo herself in danger.

Consuelo asked if it was possible to get the money in advance.

There, thought Luna, *serves me right. Because now I'll have to lie again.* "I can't right now because I have to pay the doctor and buy medicine," she said.

"What's wrong?"

"I don't know. The doctor says it's nothing serious. I'll be better once I take the medicine."

"Please, Señora Luna, I am sorry to be bothering you. Do not worry about me."

On Monday, Luna went to the clinic. The doctor, a ladino from the city, had no idea what was causing her headaches and the occasional buzzing in her ears. Yes, perhaps it was stress. Or, perhaps, some kind of parasite. He took a blood test and a stool sample.

"Probably," he said, "it's the normal discomfort most travelers experience adjusting to a foreign country. I wouldn't worry. Come back in a week and we'll know."

She decided to stay until Thursday. The truth was, she did need time away from Jake. Away from the whole scene. She visited the shops along the Santander and had a nice conversation with one of the vendors. Sorry, Luna told him, she was not there to buy anything--which to a poor man who rarely made a sale was impossible to believe. To him it seemed an opening gambit, a bargaining strategy. He kept asking for her best offer.

She spent the weekend with Jake, then returned to Pana the following Monday on a private boat. The test results were negative. "It does not mean there is nothing wrong," the doctor said. "I would suggest other tests at our hospital in Guatemala City. An MRI. Perhaps a CT scan and--"

"No," Luna said. She hated the thought of telling Jake he'd have to leave his work on the house and travel several hours over winding mountain roads to stay in a dank hotel, spending money they could not afford on who knows how many tests. "I think it's getting better."

For the next few weeks she did a Sunday-Tuesday run to Pana. It gave her a chance to visit with Consuelo, and bring back groceries, and beer for Jake. He was drinking a lot these days, and talking less. She was glad to be gone.

While she didn't feel any better, the headaches still coming and going, she enjoyed the many distractions of Pana. She spent her nights in town at a small *hospedaje* called Rooms Santander. There, and at the restaurants, she met and talked and laughed with foreigners from around the world. She missed people. Missed California. Even missed her father. Luckily, she thought, she also completely missed that asshole

Phil, who had apparently left town.

It got harder for her to be on the land. The headaches were most intense when she was around Jake. Not a good sign, but she didn't talk to him about it, certain he would get defensive.

She stayed down by the water during the day, by herself, and walked along the shore, cleaning up whatever had come across during the previous day's Xocomil. She could hear Jake pounding up above. Sometimes cursing. It was sad to separate herself, stay clear of him, but she had to have her time alone. She couldn't explain it, and refused to discuss what could not be explained: her strong intuition that everything was about to change. Change forever. To Jake it would sound crazy, and maybe it was. Best, for now, to keep quiet. . .keep it to herself.

Jake knew that Luna loved him, but was not sure anymore what that meant. Their sex had lost its feeling. . .like something she felt obliged to do. . .like tiny bits of charity. What, he thought, sensing her distance, another mercy fuck? He didn't understand what the hell had happened? Would she rather be in town, with her friends, than here on their land with him? Was she having an affair? Really? Because that's what it felt like and he hated thinking it, fucking hated it, and could not, *just could not* bear the thought of asking her.

Instead, he worked harder. Kept to himself. The rainy season was coming and he had to finish the building.

At night, after dinner, he usually fell asleep--could sometimes hear himself snoring--a great gaping beast who gobbled at the air and pawed for Luna in the middle of the night, wanting it then, in the darkness, when he was too tired to think, unable to see her face as he panted and held her close, making her his.

It came to a head one late afternoon at the end of February. Jake was on his fourth beer, staring down at the mess of nails he'd spilled in the powdery dirt. Many were hidden beneath the surface, some with their points sticking up like tiny bayonets. He could not get himself to bend over and pick them up. The Xocomil had been blowing hard, making it impossible for him to concentrate. Like a demon, it pushed his mind to places he did not want to go. Missing Luna's smile, her general happiness, her hope, he felt isolated, abandoned, incapable of blocking memories of Vietnam. He heard Lieutenant Sanders whispering as he and the other men hid one night in a swampy jungle. "It's the things you can't see that you have to watch out for." *Yeah, no shit.* And the very next day, Sanders got blown up by a land mine. Jake remembered looking down at the dead man's bloody face in the mud, hearing what he'd said--the undeniable truth of it.

He heard it now, too. . .the words clear as day. . .invisible threats blowing through the cornstalks like a hot whisper.

Jake turned and walked away. Just tired, he figured--he hoped--from the long weeks of hard work. He'd managed, by himself, to finish the rough framing of their lower-story walls, the bamboo posts braced and ready for adobe bricks to bind the structure together. Yes, God knows, he'd done a lot. Deserved a rest. He stopped and sat and gazed at the lake--his slight dizziness, he assumed, from dehydration. Or because he hadn't eaten since early in the morning. A cold sweat covered his face. He should go eat a banana or a few tortillas, but didn't want to. Didn't want to be like a damned machine in constant need of re-fueling. Didn't want to need anything!

Whoa, he thought, *calm down there, boy. Stay positive.* He swiveled his head around to look at the skeletal structure of their home. *See, see, things are coming together, things are going well.* He should be pleased. But wasn't.

None of it mattered, he knew, not without Luna, and knowing that none of it mattered--knowing it in his bones--left him feeling alone. Alone and afraid. The truth, like a poisonous snake, slithered down his spine. He shivered. Refused to cry. "Please," he said, staring at the sky, "I'm doing my best. What else can I do?"

I don't know was his only answer. *I don't know* he kept thinking, *I don't know*. . .like a mantra, a prayer. . .and after a few minutes he suddenly got how obvious and reasonable and wise it was to know he didn't know.

His neck relaxed a few notches at the thought, so he purposefully thought it again.

"Oh, yeah, thanks," he said, laughing, grateful for God's excellent sense of humor.

Jake slowed his breath, in--out, and for one abiding moment life looked deep as the lake, high as the towering volcanoes. The sky opened up above. The earth below. Wind blew, cicadas buzzed, birds called back and forth. The sounds of nature were, for him, the voice of divinity. Exactly what he needed to hear. Amazed and grateful, he closed his eyes. Listened. The mighty Xocomil rattled through the corn. . .whistled through pines. And there was another sound too. What was it? Voices? Singing? With the wind so strong he couldn't be sure.

He remembered many years earlier, in Palenque, while tripping on mushrooms, he'd heard what seemed a choir of angels. *Yes, remember, angels!* At the time he felt certain they were real, and singing to him . . .warning him not to crush that baby plant. But how could he be so certain about such a strange thing? How, when there was no possible way to know? He had no doubt, of course, what others would believe-- that he'd been hallucinating--which was why he'd always kept it to himself, the sweetest of his inner secrets.

Suddenly, as if attacking his slight semblance of peace, a cacophonous squeal stunned Jake's senses. He winced and opened his eyes. The screeching increased, joined by an oscillating drone of what might be human voices, loud and dissonant, like the overlapped flapping of a thousand angry wings. He half expected flying monkeys.

Luna came running from the lake. "Oh my god, what is it?"

"Definitely not angels," Jake said. One voice in particular, a man's, boomed down from above. "Oh hell," Jake said, head in his hands . . ."oh, hell, no."

Pascual had named his church LA ESPERANZA. He'd painted it in bold red letters across the entry. With what was left of the land payment, along with contributions from his flock, he'd gone to Guatemala City and bought a small generator, an amplifier, a microphone, and a set of jumbo speakers. He had the speakers aimed directly at Señor Perez's land. The doctor was now obliged, along with Jake and Luna, to hear the tone-deaf psalms and bombastic sermons. And, worst, long public confessions of sin followed by longer prayers for redemption. Each bi-weekly gathering brought the same basic assault, only louder.

Jake decided it was time for a visa-run to Mexico, a chance to get away for a while. He hoped Luna might start feeling better. She didn't. On their way back, he promised he would take things easier. That didn't happen either. He tried, but Pascual's evangelical noise continued to overwhelm him. Jake's rattled mind could not block the growing aggravation. He lacked the words, in either language, to express his jagged, disconnected emotions. His only escape was to drink and stay busy. Always busy. He avoided Pascual, who kept inviting him to the services. Since Jake would not answer, would not look him in the eye,

Pascual finally stopped asking.

March turned to April, and the two grew further apart, Jake stuffing his anger, his disappointment, sublimating his violent temptations into harder days of work. He had the adobe walls up, and the main bamboo timbers of a roof. Still no doors or windows. Things were happening slower than ever because Luna was no help, her condition worsening every day. She'd already taken most of the penicillin. She spent the majority of her days in a hammock beneath the avocado tree, with a wet compress over her face. "Don't mind me," she'd tell Jake, "I promise, honey, I'll be fine." And he tried to believe it.

One evening, though, her hands shaking and her eyes swimming, she refused to eat. When he insisted she try, she pushed the plate away. "Just leave me alone!" she yelled.

"Yeah, OK," said Jake. He walked out the door-less entry and hurried toward the stone steps.

Concepción was alone in the adobe hut. The family continued to live there in spite of the new concrete house, which they had dedicated solely to the word of God. She was heading up for the evening service as he came rushing in.

"Luna," he gasped, trying to catch his breath. "Sick," he said.

"I understand," Concepción said, and started down the hill.

Though meaning to follow, Jake turned the other direction and bolted upward. Moments later, from the door of Pascual's church, he saw the bulk of believers settled in their seats, singing the first song--about how the blood of Christ has nothing to do with wine.

Pascual stood off to one side. He was listening closely, adjusting the amplifier dials toward maximum volume.

"No!" yelled Jake, waving his arms.

The guitarist stopped playing, stunned by the intruder.

"Please," Jake begged, and then, because he had no idea how else to say it, screamed the rest in English: "GOD DOES NOT HAVE TO BE SO FUCKING LOUD!"

Surprising himself, he charged toward Pascual, who tried to keep him from the sound equipment--his hands stretched out in an urgent appeal for reason. Both were knocked off balance by the main singer, a burly man who twisted Jake away from the pastor and tackled him to the ground. With the help of four others, they dragged him outside.

The singer cursed Jake and insisted that the drunken gringo be taken to jail! Ignoring Pascual's objections, he went for the police.

Luckily, Concepción arrived first. She'd found Luna shivering, soaked with perspiration, her eyes, she said, *too clear (demasiado claro)*, as if looking for some way out of her head.

"Jacobo, please," she pleaded, "Luna needs you!"

Hearing that, and seeing the urgency in Concepción's face, the men released him.

Luna's weakness and disorientation had carried her to the point where she no longer resisted it. Convinced she was dying, why let these walls hold her in, these rafters keep her from the sky? *Why bother with any of that if there is no separation. . .no alone. . .no longer any difference?* Though death was close, and Luna knew it, she felt no fear. She was moving on, that's all. Moving in a whole different direction. *Because I am ready now. Because I need to know.*

Gathering her strength, on hands and knees, she got outside. Her headache was gone, replaced by a warm emptiness that expanded out, beyond her body, deep into the night. Blessed with animal wisdom now, she followed her senses. She would find the place she needed to be, and was not surprised to see it everywhere around her, everywhere she looked, as if she were the one creating it just by looking. She sat on one of the stone steps and faced the lake, took all of it in. A crescent moon floated through the ebony sky, among the stars, like a cayuco without its fisherman. There was no need to go any further.

Then Luna let Jake find her, let him hug and kiss her.

"I'm glad you're here," she said.

"Are you OK?"

She looked into his eyes. Touched his face. Smiled. "I am."

That was when Jake broke. She saw what he could only feel, what he might never understand, the rage he was holding, the sense of betrayal, the stifling fear gushing from him in a great flood of tears. He buried his head into her shoulder and let the whole world go. She held him like a baby in her arms. "It's all right," she whispered, rubbing his back. "Everything will be all right."

Hearing voices, she looked up.

There was a long string of lights descending from above. It was Pascual and Concepción and a dozen men and women coming down the hill. Each of them held a candle. It was her neighbors, her friends, coming to help, but that's not what Luna saw.

She saw them clearly, and knew they were angels.

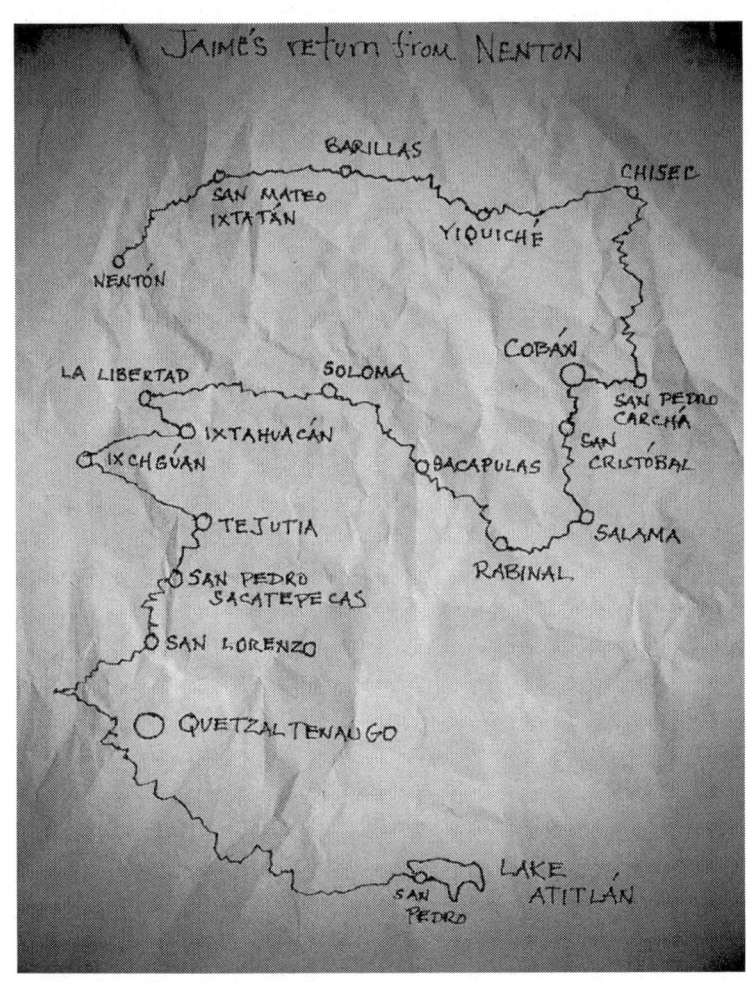

JAIME'S SIX-YEAR RETURN FROM NENTÓN

BOOK THREE

Todo Mundo

Do not forget us
Conjure up our faces and our words.
Our image will be as dew in the hearts
Of those who remember.

(Popul Vuh)

Handles
Panajachel, December, 1988

At some unspecified date in the early 1800's, Alexander von Humboldt, the great Prussian explorer, called Atitlán "the most beautiful lake in the world." His detractors, primarily wealthy ladino landowners and army generals, called him a blatant exaggerator, since he also wrote about the "disgusting mistreatment" of their Indian slaves. Had the concept of *handles* existed back then, von Humboldt might have been known as *Loose-lipped Al*.

Aldous Huxley later called Atitlán not just "the most beautiful lake in the world" but "perhaps too much of a good thing." This quirky compliment appears prophetic. . .*perhaps* a glance at the area's inevitable future of excessive tourism.

In general, the more adventurous first-world tourists began noticing Guatemala during the late 1960's. A civil war did not deter them. By 1983, in spite of Ríos Montt's counter-insurgency policies, they were coming from all over the world. Often hippie backpacker-types, they came to the lake because it was a known destination along the gringo trail. Also, and primarily, because the Guatemalan Indians were known for their colorful dress, their glowing smiles, their playful good will. This was the land of *Buenos Días, Buenas Tardes*, and *Buenas Noches*--everywhere a friendly greeting--an ancient culture alive with cheer. What a change from the cool indifference back home. In general a pleasant bunch, the foreigners were always kind toward the natives: politely fending off unwanted solicitation; feigning deafness whenever convenient; waving away the more persistent vendors with a friendly smile.

A vast majority of these travelers were merely passing through, ticking Guatemala off their 'to do' list. But there were those who fell in love with the lake--its beauty, its people, its growing first-world subcultural charm--and found ways to return each year. They rented simple houses from indigenous landlords, or small rooms at inexpensive *hospedajes*. Some supported themselves as *artisanos*, selling their handmade jewelry or flutes or drums on the street. Some eked out a living as musicians. Some became therapists of one stripe or another, either counseling the richer expats, massaging them, or supplying whatever new-age craze had made it to the lake.

The more entrepreneurial types started their own businesses. The place was just beginning to take off, and there was money to be made. The lion's share of it, of course, went to the stream of *típico (indigenous handicrafts)* dealers, who bought up loads and loads of dirt-cheap weavings, huipiles, purses, hacky sacks, pulseras, and so on, to feed the frenzy back home for ethnic goods. They sold the stuff for huge--what critics called *ungodly*--profits. . .then came back for more. And when they did, again and again, the indigenous dealers were overjoyed, as were the craftspeople whose products they sold. Everyone's life had been improved, and promised to get better.

Foreigners living around the lake remained exempt from danger so long as they stuck to their own private business. While seeing plenty of things that disturbed them, they knew to keep their mouths shut, at least in public.

Rich ladinos from Guatemala City had already managed to buy, for next to nothing, most of the fertile shoreline from the impoverished Indians. They'd built majestic *chalets*: their grounds adorned with sunny decks and shady patios; huge manicured lawns and colorful gardens and swimming pools. These, their weekend retreats, had to be maintained-- kept pristine and guarded--the work often given to the same indigenous families they'd displaced, who were now their servants.

Foreign *expats* would eventually buy up the remaining steep slopes, or distant shorelines--buy them cheap--and build their houses. They did not appreciate the term *chaleteros*, yet that was what the Indians called them. To the poor, marginalized Indians, these were also people they thought rich. People who might give them work. People, also, for all they knew, to be feared.

Many of the foreigners did--eventually--become trusted. Or, at least, actively sought out for whatever mercy, or bit of help, they might provide. They showed respect for the indigenous community, were known to treat workers well, and paid higher wages than ladinos. They started an 'alternative school' in Panajachel for their own children, and provided scholarships for a few select Indian kids as well. They funded various 'foundations' in support of indigenous culture and local handicrafts.

By 1989, expats were an essential element of the lake community, living out their simple dreams and trying to avoid Guatemala's always looming nightmares. Thus the famous saying: *Todo es posible aquí, y nada seguro (All is possible here, and nothing certain)*.

Panajachel was the first town on the lake after the dangerously steep curvy bus ride down the mountain from Sololá. Its long narrow valley had once been full of *ajachel* trees (their fruit like a small tough-skinned papaya, only not as tasty). Thus its name: *Pan* (in Kaqchikel meaning *The way through*) the *ajachel*.

It was now famous simply as *Pana*. A mecca for adventuresome souls. Huxley, who on the day of his death injected himself with LSD, might have wished he were doing it here. Thanks in part to his famous quote, Pana began re-shaping itself to welcome the increasing crowds. Just around the corner from its Catholic Church, on Calle de los Árboles

(Street of Trees), the ajachels were all chopped down, replaced by restaurants and discotheques...an art gallery...a health food store. Calle Santander, once a dirt road leading through onion fields to the lake, was widened, and eventually cobble-stoned. It would slowly fill with more restaurants, more cheap hotels, bars blaring rock and roll until the wee hours of the morning. There would be boutiques, massage parlors, travel and real estate agencies--all of it threaded together by colorful *típico* stalls and constant, relentless, street vendors.

From early on (who knows when it actually started?) the expats began to take on *handles*. This happened in various ways and for various reasons, not all of them good.

'Born again' Len was a handsome man with long brown hair and a long brown beard. He lived in San Marcos, but frequented Pana to party, shop (and once a month cash the 'crazy money' check he got from the U.S. government, which would buy enough cocaine from 'Acapulco Bob' to get him through). Once a year, or so, he'd have to go back to California and re-convince psychiatrists that *God*, indeed, *had chosen him* as the new prince of peace.

'Watch out' Walt was more infamous than Len, because Walt, all agreed, truly was nuts. A paranoiac extraordinaire, he believed the world would soon be ending. Each Sunday he came from San Pedro and, from the goodness of his heart, gave loud warning to his friends in Pana.

People hid when they saw him coming...which was strange, since most expats enjoyed each other's company and looked forward to their meetings.

Aside from Len and Walt, handles were not usually given to demean. Rather to define. To distinguish one foreigner from the rest. If you were born with a unique name (Ling, Duncan, Anastasia, Eirto), no handle was required. Or if there was only one of you, like Ray. Until a second Ray showed up, people knew who was being talked about. But if you happened to be yet another Larry, David, Jennifer, or Karen (or, especially, Bob), something had to be done.

Handles were almost always assigned for obvious reasons: Gallery Tomás, for example, as distinguished from Swedish Tomás; 'Gypsy' Jen from 'Massage' Jen; 'Carpenter' Karen from 'Camera' Karen; 'Old English' David from 'Young English' David.

The Bobs ended up a class of their own. Among the many, some stood out: 'Chocolate' Bob, who made chocolate; 'Donut' Bob, who made pastries; 'Acapulco' Bob, who still went back twice a year to keep up his cocaine connection; 'Mango' Bob, who loved mangos. . .proof being the dried amber residue imprinted on his chin; and 'Chile' Bob, who was not from Chile, nor did he eat them, but felt pleased--in his characteristically cantankerous way--that having this handle meant he would never be confused with any of the other Bobs.

Beyond the Bobs were the Larrys. There was 'Barbecue' Larry (a connoisseur of fine meats) and 'Aces' Larry (who'd never learned better than to play poker with people who constantly called his bluff) and 'Mercenary' Larry (an exorbitantly tall, handsome, charming sociopath, named for reasons no one ever really wanted to know). He and 'Acapulco' Bob, among the more infamous expats, were in Pana to escape troubles they'd encountered, or created, elsewhere. But most were just there, well, because they loved it, even the weirdness of it, no matter what.

While handles were usually self-explanatory (as with the Bobs and Larrys), some, like Marco Solo or Walk-On-Water David, came with a story.

Mark, a musician from the United States, could play numerous instruments--a kind of one-man band. He got his name when Rene, one of the Circus Bar owners, made it clear that Mark's wife, a *sanyasan* named Elena, was no longer invited to sing there. Rene, after too many complaints about her bad voice, fired her, and hired Mark separately, and changed the sign out front from "Marco y Elena' to 'Marco Solo.' Though Elena was not pleased, most of the customers were.

Rarely were handles used in a person's presence. They only made sense if he or she was not around, and needed to be identified. At times, even then, people had to be on guard, their voices reduced to a low whisper. Mercenary Larry sneered his charming sneer and pretended he'd kill anyone who called him that. In truth, however, he loved how his handle titillated the women and got him laid more than any other guy.

On the opposite end of the spectrum was Walk-On-Water David (a scraggly ex-truck driver from New York who 'couldn't give a shit' what other people thought or said). His handle had come about for three main reasons. *First*, because he'd started a food kitchen for the Indian street kids in Pana. . .a rather saintly act. *Second*, because he had long white hair and long white beard. *Third*, because (while well respected for his genuine goodness and selfless deeds) he could sometimes get a bit self-righteous--reacting, as he put it, to "the do-nothing sponges who cared only about themselves."

Foreigners, being foreigners, did, in general, lean toward the core of that description. They kept a low profile and continually avoided any glimmer of trouble. Walk-On-Water David, by contrast, was a lightning-rod. At times quite boisterous. In spite of his slight build, he said whatever he thought, and 'Freelance' Phil was a perfect target for David's wrath. Phil dodged him whenever possible. The easy-going Australian did not want any hassles. Or responsibility. Or anything that came anywhere close. An unfortunate representative of the expat crowd, his lone duty was to himself--for him a fairly easy task. He stayed in Pana because he was handsome and witty. . .because the plentiful tourist girls liked him. . .because they could often be persuaded to support him. If any problem developed, he'd slip away for months on end.

Fellow expats knew his game. With the exception of W-O-W David, though, they tended to cut him slack--the men in particular, who shook their heads and laughed at all the chaos he created. Phil was somewhat awed himself, a self-confession that smacked of bragging.

So no, the guy was not well-liked. . .was usually shirked or shaken off. . .but there was a collective agreement among most expats. . .an unspoken deal. . .a rigorous attempt to just 'let people be who they are.' This loosely-knit group, from various villages around the lake, continually rose above whatever bad blood had passed between them. They appreciated the difficulty of putting down roots in a foreign place. They laughed at each other's differences, defects, goofs, and downright fuckups, and accepted as normal every type of eccentricity. There was a clear sense of community, and in many cases genuine love. These were strong, independent, creative types--people who more than anything else excelled in the ability to put up with, and magnanimously relish, whatever came their way. Even Freelance Phil.

Phil had been gone for a couple of years, back in Australia to visit his dying mother. He'd needed to avoid a few debts in Guatemala. Also to make amends with his *Mum* for being such a difficult, wayward son. Luckily, for him, she could no longer remember much. Or talk.

Once she passed on, while settling the will took far longer than expected, Phil knew it was worth the wait. The five thousand Australian dollars he inherited meant a lack of money woes for the foreseeable future. Now back in Pana, he was already on the prowl, strolling down the Santander with his fellow countryman, and horn-dog, Barbecue Larry. He spotted a long-legged brunette dart into a little restaurant called El Patio.

"Who the fuck is that?" he said.

"Not your type," said Larry.

"What, those weren't real legs?"

"She's way too weird, mate."

"Hey, c'mon, I like weird. With those legs, what the hell's wrong with weird?"

"She's been in Pana for about a year. Used to live with a guy named Jake. You know Jake?

"Nope."

"Loner type," said Larry. "Big drinker, pretty good poker player. Has some land over by, uh . . .I don't know. . .somewhere by San Pedro. Word is, she gave him up. Wasn't *evolved enough* for her. A very, you know, *spiritual* chick. Reads auras or whatever."

"What's her name?"

"*Luna*, or maybe it's *Loo-nee*, I don't know. Good looker, yeah, but definitely not to touch. Nope, no way. We call her *Woo-woo Lu*."

"Later," Phil said, taking a sharp right and stepping onto the patio of El Patio.

At first he can't see her, hidden off in the darkest corner. But she sees him. She watches closely as his stalker instincts lead him to a nearby table. Then, who knows why, she thinks of Consuelo's boy, Jaime. His smiling little-boy face just pops into her mind. Maybe because Consuelo keeps asking her if he's all right. *Yes*, Luna says, *don't worry, he's fine*-- though in truth she hasn't sensed his spirit for a long time.

Phil sits and examines the menu with pretend concentration, then glances her direction.

"Oh my God," he says, 'it's you!"

Luna relies on her intuition for each and every move. Today, obviously, the radar has malfunctioned. She collects herself and forces a smile. "How's it going?"

"Fine," Phil says. "Top notch."

"I'm not surprised."

"So, wow, you look great," he says, eyes full of lust, as if she might have forgotten, or dismissed, among other things, the two hundred Q's he still owes her. "Is it true you live in Pana now and read auras or something?"

"Or something."

Luna has learned not to go into it. People rarely understand, and think her weird. Thus the 'Woo Woo' handle, which, *oh yes*, she's heard. And doesn't care. Let the idiots think what they want. The people she's helping, they know better--do not call her names behind her back.

"Listen," she says, "I gotta go."

"Why such a hurry?"

Luna moves around and past him

"What," he says, "you don't want to talk to me, is that it?"

Her smile now turns real. "Well. . .yes. . .that's it exactly."

"Wait," he says, following her to the street. "Yeah, OK, I know I owe you an apology, I--"

"Look," Luna says, answering his stare with soft, apathetic eyes, "You don't owe me anything, Phil. I'm not angry, and I don't expect you to pay me back. I don't want anything from you. Got it? Nothing at all. It's simple, really. . .I just don't want to know you anymore."

The Prisoner *Unknown Aldea, department of San Marcos, January, 1988*

The girl looks at him with large brown eyes. She is maybe twelve years old, her strange beauty accentuated by a cluster of tiny moles, like petrified tears, on her left cheek.

"You can have me," she says.

An older woman cowers in the corner, hands over her face, whimpering. He's seen this often over the years, like he's some kind of monster. He's used to their fear, and today he's also afraid, shocked by the suddenness of his decision. As always, he entered the house ready to shoot. You never know what might happen. "No," he says, lowering his rifle, "I'm not here for that."

The woman and girl glance at each other. He sees they don't believe him. Why should they? He's barged into so many huts, has done unmentionable things. Killing, yes, and worse than that. Making people suffer first. He's stood by and watched, has done nothing to stop it, so is as guilty as the rest, and knows it, and hates himself for it. Angry that they're making him remember, he battles back the rage. It is not their fault.

"Where is your husband?" he says to the older woman.

Again she covers her face.

"Dead," the girl says. There is a challenge in her stare. "We're alone now. My mother doesn't think right anymore."

"Where did you learn Spanish?"

"My father was a teacher."

"Look, I don't want to hurt you."

The girl is intelligent, her eyes searching his. "That is what the others said too."

He blinks, remembering his first time, saying it to a girl no older than her before the others took their turns, then pushed him on top, laughing and cajoling and shaming him into it.

"Please," the girl says, "leave my mother alone. Take me instead."

Surprising them both, a rifle pushes through the door, followed by Elicio. Jaime almost shoots him. Wishes he could. Both lower their guns.

For a few seconds, Elicio looks like that same young frightened boy he used to be. "I thought it was you," he says. His eyes now harden and find the woman sobbing in the corner. "The colonel says we have to go. There isn't time for this. You could get in trouble."

"I won't be long."

Elicio spots the pretty girl standing in the shadows. "Well, well," he says, "hola, *mija*. Looks like I might get in trouble too."

"Leave her alone," Jaime says. "The mother isn't worth a shit. The girl is mine."

"Relax *vos*. I'm only saying, you better hurry. We're the last ones. You don't want to be in this piss-stinking village by yourself."

"Don't worry about me."

"Bueno," says Elicio, and spits on the ground, perhaps injured that Jaime does not appreciate his warning. He turns and goes, leaving the door open behind him.

Jaime closes it and looks back at the girl. "Please," she says, "get it over with and let us be."

"I need your help," he whispers.

"What?"

"I need you to get me clothes."

"Clothes? What clothes?"

"Whatever will fit," he says, pointing his rifle at the old woman.

"Get them or I will kill her."

The girl runs into a second room and quickly returns with a pair of frayed, white and red striped pants, and a dirty white shirt. "We buried my father in his good ones."

Jaime keeps his gun on the mother, who has flipped to her stomach and is face down on the ground, praying to Jesus, begging that she and Adelina be taken to heaven soon.

"You are Adelina?"

"Yes."

"Turn around," Jaime orders, and when she does he sets down the rifle, and sits, and unties his big black boots. Pulling them off, he remembers his mother and Felipe, the three of them working together late at night by the flickering glow of a prayer candle, hoping it was not too bright, afraid of Manuel bursting in at any moment. And for what, Jaime thinks...for these? Shoes? Disgusted with himself, he tosses the damn things off to the side. Felipe must be sixteen. Maybe in the army too. Or dead. And his mother?

Mayazak Pabey, she'd said. But he cannot let himself think about the sadness in her face.

Relieved to feel his bare feet on the dirt floor, he peels off the army pants and shirt and shivers in his nakedness--not from the cold but from what he plans to do.

The mother peeks at him between her fingers. She cries out, *"Por favor Jesús!"* and turns away. Jaime pulls on the father's clothes, which fit well enough. He goes to the girl and turns her around to face him. Her eyes are wet with tears, certain of what is going to happen.

"Please, Adelina, listen to me. Burn my clothes when I'm gone. You don't want the guerillas to find them. But sell the boots."

"What?"

"The boots," he says. "The boots are worth something."

She looks at the boots, then at him. . .looking at him differently now, at last realizing he's not going to rape her, not going to hurt them. "No," she says, "I can't."

"Why?"

"People would think I'm a whore."

"Look, you could say you killed a soldier and--"

"No. No one would ever believe that, they--"

"Yes, you're right, you. . .look, just keep them hidden. Someday you may need the money and will have to take the chance. I'm leaving my rifle, too. The next time a soldier comes through your door, shoot him."

She wipes at her eyes, but the tears stay. "I don't understand."

"If I have a rifle I'll be seen as either an army deserter or a guerilla. Either way, it gets me killed. Better I leave it here. Is there any food I can take with me?"

"Tortillas. A few bananas."

"Please," he says, which seems a small request. Then he's struck by the strangeness of it, of asking this girl for anything. Why should she help him escape? Would she help if he did not have a rifle by his side? "I'm sorry. I don't mean to--"

"Why?"

"What?"

"Why are you doing it?" says the girl. She glances down at his bare feet as if shocked that they look so comfortable outside those boots. Her eyes return to his, lost.

"Leaving the army?" he says. "Is that what you mean?"

"Yes." Her look, though still unsettled, is softer now.

"Because I. . .I have to go home. I never wanted to be a soldier," he says, and tears fill his eyes too. "I swear to you, Adelina, I never wanted any of it."

"Where is your home?"

"Santa Catarina Palopó, by Lake Atitlán."

"That is far away. Many days. Do you know how to get there?"

"I've seen maps. I know it is to the south."

"My father sometimes went to the lake. There are many mountains. Probably soldiers and guerillas too. It will be hard."

"Yes."

"It's best you wait until dark. I'll see if there are any eggs," she says, walking toward the back door of the hut.

"Stop," Jaime says, lifting his rifle.

"Our chickens are out there. Really, I'm only going to get some eggs."

He again points the rifle at her mother. "Any trouble and she is dead, you understand?"

"Yes," says the girl, who does not look the least bit frightened, "I understand."

An hour later they are sitting together on the dirt floor, like any normal family might, eating eggs and beans and tortillas. The fire in the corner of the hut has finally stopped smoking, though the sting of it, sharp and acrid, keeps them blinking. It is past dusk, the last fading light of day. The mother has stopped praying. She eats fast, her head down. Then, whispering to herself of God and salvation, she returns to her place and lies there, facing the wall.

Her mother's name, the girl tells him, is Rosa María. "She used to be a lively woman, with the most beautiful voice in the village. She sang at all the evangélical services. At funerals too."

Jaime nods, assuming she no longer does. He hopes the girl won't tell him why she stopped.

"And you?" asks Adelina? "Who are you?"

"Me. Yes. My name is Jaime," he says, "and I sing like a toad. I am a gardener, not a soldier. I used to be a good son to my mother. A long time ago." It's been years now, how many he can't remember. Does not want to remember. Or to know why he stayed a soldier all this time, why he let himself hurt people, why he never before considered running away. "Thank you for the help, Adelina. For the clothes and food. I should be going."

"No, it's too early. You can't be seen leaving the hut."

"I'm sorry," he says, "you're right."

"You look tired."

"I'm fine."

"You can sleep if you want."

"I'll wait until later."

"Please, Jaime, I promise you can sleep. I will wake you in an hour."

For what he's done he deserves to be dead. If this innocent girl thinks the same, let her be the one to kill him. He reaches over, picks up the rifle, and hands it to Adelina. Then lies on the floor and closes his eyes.

Sometime later she shakes him awake. He looks up, baffled by her stark, rigid face, lit by the prayer candle in her right hand. For a second, like when he was a small boy, he doesn't know where he is, or what he's doing here, but the girl he remembers clearly, as if he's known her all his life. "It's time," she says.

Jaime gets to his feet. Adelina hands him a bag. He can smell the fresh-cooked tortillas. The girl walks in front of him to the door, moving with such purpose that he feels like a child following his mother. He waits for her to tell him what to do.

"Come," she says, "I'll show you the path."

"I should go alone."

"You don't know the way."

"I'm afraid you might be seen with me."

"I won't," she says. "It's cold. People stay in their huts at night, close to their fires. Come, the path isn't far."

She blows out the candle and opens the door. He follows her outside. Hearing something, she blocks him with her arm. Listens. A couple of dogs barking. Apparently not a problem as she steps ahead, moving to her left, her shape visible in the moonlight.

They pass several huts, take another left, an immediate right, go down a small hill, through a muddy creek bed, and up the other side.

She stops. "This is the main path. You will pass through a few milpas, and two more creeks. After the second one, which has lots of water, there will be a larger path going uphill to the right. Follow it until you get to the main road. To the left is San Pedro Sacatepecas. I once went there with my father. That is where I think you want to go."

"Thank you, Adelina. I will never forget your kindness."

"You are a good man," she says. "You remind me of Alonzo, my brother. Three years ago I was with him, right here, saying goodbye. It was the last time we saw each other. He is a guerilla now. I don't know where."

"Somewhere safe, I hope."

"Yes. I hope."

Then she laughs.

Jaime says, "What's funny?"

"No," she says, suddenly serious. "Nothing. If Alonzo were here, he'd kill you. Or you him. That is the world we live in. Not funny at all."

349

Aprovechar: *to take advantage*

Jaime stayed off the main roads. When he got to a new village he asked for the safest path to whatever village came next. He wanted to avoid soldiers, he'd say, which everyone understood, including those afraid of the guerillas. He claimed to be returning from the Mexican border, where he had been turned back from a quest for El Norte. People had no problem understanding that either. Many of them knew the same disappointment and were sympathetic, quick to share their own sad stories in great detail. They would let him stay the night in their huts, and the next day provide a stack of tortillas for his journey back home. In some of the smaller aldeas, no one had heard of Lake Atitlán. Or perhaps had heard of it but did not know where it was. Xela, the old capital of Guatemala, became his initial destination. From there, Jaime could figure out the rest.

Four days after saying goodbye to Adelina, he was getting close. Thus far, no problem. Always a hut to sleep in at night. Always fresh tortillas. Then, as he came over the top of a ridge, a group of guerillas stood across the path, their guns ready. They sat him down and one of the older men asked questions. Few of them spoke Spanish, the man explained, so he translated everything into Mam, a language Jaime didn't know.

The *commandante*, as the older man identified himself, had a black stubbly beard full of stiff white whiskers. He had grown up, and was educated--taught Spanish among other things--on a large coffee finca. He was an illegitimate son of the dueño. Had become a guerrilla, he said, "by necessity," though he did not bother to explain. And did not like Jaime's story of leaving for El Norte. None of the others liked it either.

"Why not join the guerillas and fight for your country?" said one of the Spanish speakers.

"Why go when your people need you?" said another.

Yes, Jaime lied, he regretted the mistake, but it was done, it was over, and he had to get back to his wife, his infant son.

Some of them were nodding. Beneath their disapproval, Jaime could sense their empathy.

The commandante said, "Many of us have been forced to leave wives and children behind, to live like animals, to fight for our lives. Why should you be any different?"

"I'm not," Jaime said. "But I have no gun." *Ay*, he thought, the moment it came out of his mouth, *what a stupid thing to say*.

The commandante translated and everyone laughed.

"A gun is not what matters," he said to Jaime. "We had no guns either. Not to begin with."

"If I could just go home first."

"Look," the commandante said. "Look at who you're talking to. You've been gone a few months. For some of us it's been years."

For me too, thought Jaime, but could not say it. "I understand. If you want, I'll stay."

"Yes, that's what we want. Because it's the right thing to do. Also because the army will kill anyone coming out of these mountains. Soldiers are in every village leading to Xela. Not a safe way to go. It is best--for your sake--to stay with us. We can show you a way around them, if escape is what *you want*. Or, who knows," he said, slapping Jaime on the back, "maybe we'll find you a gun!"

With their leader smiling, the others smiled too, and shook the newcomer's hand, and said their names. Jaime made sure to remember the commandante's: Román.

They walked back toward the town of San Lorenzo, where Jaime had spent the previous night. Before reaching it, they swerved to the west onto a smaller path that traversed the ridge. During the next three days they passed by various small aldeas. Esteban, a boy of fourteen, knew the area well, had lived here his whole life, and could say which villages would help, give food and information, and those they must avoid.

They dropped down out of the mountains and marched into a larger village whose name Jaime never learned. It was around noon. People peeked from inside their huts. The guerillas went directly to the one concrete building in town and barged through the door. The man inside, behind a big brown desk, said there must be some mistake. Said he was a doctor. "Yes. . .doctor," Román said, "we've heard of you. A Naturale, like us, who sells medicine to other Naturales for far too much. The deception has made you a very rich man. A very important person. Almost a ladino!"

The commandante ordered him to open the small metal box hidden beneath his desk. Inside were stacks of quetzal bills, mostly fives and tens. Román gave the money to Gaspár, his right-hand man, who led a few of the others to go buy needed supplies: food, matches, coca cola. Those who remained, including Jaime, picked through the various drawers--taking syringes, bandages, bottles of disinfectant--while Román tied the man to a chair and cut off his mustache with a pair of scissors and swore he'd cut out his tongue and make him swallow it if he ever cheated people again. Then, as if unable to resist, he slammed the man's face with the butt of his rifle.

It was three nights later, high on a westbound ridge, that Jaime felt most frightened. He knew he had to get away, soon, and his sparking sense of urgency, he worried, was visible to anyone paying attention. The thought made him even more nervous. He was angry at himself, at his timidity, because he'd already missed a few opportunities to get away. He couldn't let another go by. Must be ready. Always ready. He remembered his father telling him the same thing. He shivered, remembering that frigid stream beside their onion field.

But this is not the time for thinking such silly things!

For now, he decided, trying to calm himself, it was best to act normal, act like one of them, listen to their stories and laugh at their jokes. It was a cold clear night. All but the two men standing guard sat huddled around a fire. After walking the whole day, everyone was exhausted. And hungry. For now there was no talk whatsoever. The deadening silence made Jaime's anxiety grow. He was on the verge of saying goodnight when someone asked about his trip to the border.

"Oh, no," he said. "No, please, I'm embarrassed to talk about it."

"Go ahead, talk," Gaspár said. "Better a good story than listen to my angry stomach."

"You made a big mistake," said Renaldo, the jokester, looking very serious. "Now you have to suffer, *vos*, and tell us the whole thing."

Román translated and the rest of them laughed, urging Jaime on.

He was trapped. Pushed for details, he included some interesting facts he'd collected during his travels. . .from people who had actually made the trip to Mexico. He mentioned the parrots and iguanas for sale in the border town of Tecún Umán.

"Big ones?" someone wanted to know.

"What did they cost?" asked another.

"Let him finish," Román said, and instantly it got quiet.

Jaime saw he was gaining their trust, an opportunity he had to take advantage of, so he went all out, remembering one man's story of the endless fruit stands close to the green-trimmed Catholic Church. He mentioned the *licuado* venders with their bright new silver and glass machines. He avoided the whorehouses, he said, because he could not afford them, which was easy to translate and got a good laugh. Last, for a suitable finish, he described the huge inner-tube rafts, covered with plywood, that were used to ferry illegals across the Suchiate river. Because he had no money for that either, he waited until the middle of the night, a night with clouds covering the moon, to wade across. He told them how warm and muddy the river was. . .and, in the middle, deep.

"Lucky," he said, "being from the lake, I learned to swim." Another necessary lie. He told how the Mexican police caught him on the other side, in Ciudad Hidalgo, where they beat him, put him in jail, and the next day drove him to the border town of Talismán. He described the bridge there, and the pig-faced guards on both sides of the river. "I hadn't eaten for three days," he said. "I didn't care. All I wanted was to get back to my family."

Most of the men were nodding, and he began to feel truly accepted. The story had worked its magic. They were impressed he'd been so brave. Some shook their heads, but in a sympathetic way, sad for his ultimate failure.

"Wait," said Timiteo, "when did you say this happened?"

Timiteo was the one man among them who had never been friendly. As if he were holding a grudge. A grudge toward everyone, not just Jaime. He kept to himself and rarely said a thing. Who knew he could speak such good Spanish?

"Last month," Jaime said.

"But the new bridge has been there for six months."

Román looked back and forth between two.

"What?" said Jaime.

"The Mexicans," Timiteo said, "built a big concrete bridge just upriver from Ciudad Hidalgo." His eyes were flashing, a slight smile playing on his lips.

It seemed some kind of test. Or maybe a joke, though he'd never seen the man joke before. Still, no matter what, it was best not to change his story. "No," he said, "there is no bridge."

"I was there five months ago," Timiteo said. "I saw it plain as day."

Román said, "What were *you* doing there?"

Gaspár poked at Timiteo's shoulder. "Because *you* had the same idea, *vos*. Admit it!"

"Ooooh," said Renaldo, pretending to squeeze his own neck, always looking for a laugh. "Truth, like they say, is a hard thing to strangle."

Timiteo was now the one on the spot, everyone staring at him, waiting to see why he'd kept his story secret. The distraction gave Jaime a few seconds to calm himself.

"I didn't say anything," Timiteo said, "because. . .unlike him. . .I changed my mind."

"Why?" Román said. "Because you don't know how to swim?"

"Once I got there I realized my mistake," Timiteo said. "I knew I had to stay. To fight." He turned and looked Jaime in the eye. "You're the one who needs to explain," he said. "How could you not see the new bridge?"

"I guess I came into town another way."

"That's not what I mean. I mean after the Mexicans caught you. The new bridge is just a few kilometers from Ciudad Hidalgo. Why would they waste all those hours driving you to Talismán? It makes no sense."

Everyone now watched Jaime. His heart was pounding and there was no time left to think. Then, as if Raul were with him, inside his head, whispering in his mind, he remembered what his friend once said about ladinos. Thinking no further, he blurted out, "You're right, it doesn't."

"No," said Timiteo.

Román was staring at Jaime, confused.

Jaime laughed. "But come on, *vos*. . .who can ever make sense of what a *pinche Mexican* does?"

There was a long second of absolute silence.

"Hah!" shouted Renaldo, slapping Jaime on the back.

And the rest started laughing along with them. Román too. Even Timiteo could not help grinning. The fact was: ladinos were always a target for insults, regardless of nationality--like a gaping hole inviting the foulest garbage. Jaime's joke had distracted further suspicion. At least for now.

Besides, it was late. . .cold. . .and everyone wanted to be finished with the day. The men headed for their mats, their waiting blankets.

The next morning, to improve his position, Jaime said he would be honored if they allowed him to stay. Román shook his hand, and one by one the others followed, welcoming him to the fight.

Timiteo made sure to be the last, waiting until the others had gone about their business. "I still don't trust you," he said.

But their commandante, apparently, had no doubts. That same night, as a show of confidence, he handed Jaime a rifle and ordered him to stand guard alongside the boy, Esteban.

By the time the big fat moon began its descent, everyone was fast asleep. Timiteo lay flat on his back, his mouth wide open, snoring, gone to the world. Jaime considered running, but Esteban was too close. Then he got lucky. The boy came over, eyelids heavy, and communicated, with hand gestures and minimal Spanish, that they take turns, each giving the other an hour to sleep. Though it was against the rules, and both knew it, Esteban did not seem concerned.

Jaime guessed it a rule often broken. "Good idea," he said.

"You first," said Esteban.

Jaime shook his head and pointed at him. "No *vos*, you." He felt sure, because of his youth, that the boy was not accustomed to any kind of preferential treatment.

"Gracias," said Esteban, noticeably pleased.

The boy lay beneath a nearby tree, one hand on his rifle. Soon he was asleep. Or seemed to be. Jaime, fearing it might be a trick, waited several more minutes, until the full moon's frowning face slipped from behind a cloud and urged him on. Or was it Raul? *Go, vos. . .GO!*

So he set his rifle on the ground and padded off down the trail, retracing the steps they'd taken during the day. The brilliant night sky let him move at a steady pace. It also meant that they would have no trouble following him. Maybe, because he'd left the gun, they would see he was no threat? Yes, maybe. Or maybe not. At first, every few minutes, he stopped to listen.

Soon, though, he was running down the trail.

He found a smaller path that dropped off steeply to his right. By sunrise he reached the valley below, was wandering through the milpas on any trail aiming east.

He skirted the western edge of Zunil and again started climbing.

He slept that night in the foggy mountains above.

Early the next morning he headed south toward the lake, his home, his family.

Something Else

Luna sensed Jaime getting closer. Well, not him specifically, but something. Something coming her way. She felt its presence, misting in her mind like a distant memory, frail but insistent, trying to take form. She'd first become aware of it on the night he escaped the guerillas. She'd awoken in a panic, as if also running for her life.

Sitting in the dark, Luna lit a candle and focused on the flame. She knew this was important. If able to sit still enough, long enough, the calm might dissolve the clatter of her mind and allow an image to show through. So far there was only this amorphous shadow-like blur, moving with great purpose. Searching for its essence, she balanced on a familiar vibration, something she could feel outside herself, like millions of pulsing fingertips holding her in their tender grasp.

The trances, once they came, usually lasted about an hour. This time it took the full glow of morning to shake her back to into the world.

Luna's eyes popped open. Whatever it was had not come clear. The shape of it, though, reminded her of something else. It was like a reflection of the movement she'd felt years earlier on her night so close to death. Then, it had been Luna who was moving. Moving away. Aware of Jake being there, of holding him while he cried, she was already gone, alone and floating above, free of his endless pain. She no longer wanted a piece of land, or a child, or a partner. . .could no longer be stifled by any of it.

Jake stayed on their land in San Pablo. Rumor was, he also caroused a lot in San Pedro. She didn't care. Their separation, while not official, seemed to her permanent.

She rarely gave him any thought these days, was still adjusting to her new life in Pana. It had been three years since that fateful night by the lake. . .and it hadn't been easy. . .and she couldn't help that he was suffering too.

On the verge of tears, she closed her eyes. She felt the need to once more think it through. Was it his fault? No. It was no one's fault. It happened, that's all. There was no denying it. Her life had changed, and kept on changing. She was now a different person in a place she knew little about. No wonder it was hard. But it had gotten easier since she'd stopped resisting, stopped thinking about Jake. There was no way to help him. Let him do whatever he had to. *Buena suerte.* It was his responsibility. His life. This, however, was hers--all hers--and exactly as it should be.

"Righto." She smiled kindly at her heart's pain. Rising above it, she stretched toward the clear blue sky, trusting in the new day, curious to see what would happen next.

Two hours later, Luna sits at The Patio restaurant and orders manzanilla tea. She feels it again, something moving, like the first breath of a Xocomil. Or a boat on its way to shore. Whatever it is, she wants to go find it. But can't. She's promised to meet Mary for breakfast. Her friend is leaving town, and told her she needs to talk. So Luna waits. Watches the street. She waves to some of the Indian ladies, who this morning seem to know not to try and sell her a scarf, or a blouse, or whatever they might be carrying on their heads.

She closes her eyes and thinks of the dock at San Juyú.

There are two boats on either side. The engines sputter and smoke while people crowd onto the narrow benches. She walks down the dirt path. A boy runs up, wants to know where she's going. "Santa Cruz?" he says. "¿Quiere usted un privado?" No, she thinks, shaking her head, scanning the lake for something else--another boat perhaps, waiting for the others to leave, give it space to come ashore.

"Hey there, girlfriend."

It's Mary, bounding up in front of her, vibrating with her normal high-pitched energy, looking around for the waitress. She's in a hurry, wanting to order before she even sits down. Mary is in her late thirties, a thin, long-legged brunette from New York. Everyone says she and Luna look alike, often mistaking one for the other.

"Sorry," says Mary, "I can't--" then catches the waitress girl's glance and signals for her to come over. "My bus leaves in forty minutes," she says to Luna, "and I still have to buy a--wait," she says, seeing that the waitress is distracted by something in the street. *"Por favor, amiga, tengo prisa!"*

The girl comes rushing to the table. Mary smiles, pats her arm, and orders coffee.

The girl rushes off.

"Bueno," Mary says. "Let's talk."

"Bueno," Luna says. "What's up?"

"I've been thinking over what you said at our last session. You know, about me leaving the lake without ever really leaving. . .how I do it all the time. . .and yeah, yeah, it's true, I go back to New York but I'm never completely there, I'm hating it, always wishing I was in Pana, you know, and I'm thinking I should just tell Bill we're finished. . .make the move. . .admit I'm not happy with him anymore. Like you told Jake. Kind of the same thing, right?"

"Well, I don't know, I--"

"Yeah yeah, exactly. You can never actually know. Not for sure I mean. I mean yeah, OK, it's this incredibly strong feeling I have, but God knows I've been fooled by that before. That's how I ended up with Bill in the first place, because of feelings I couldn't resist."

"His dick you mean."

Mary laughs. "Hey, I was young."

"Horny."

"Fucking starving, yeah. But not anymore. Swear to god, sister, what's happening now is way stronger, like I truly belong here by the lake. Like I've finally found my home."

"Uh huh, well, maybe you should--"

"The thing is, I can't do it, not yet. I have to go back and...wait--" she says, and raises her cup to the waitress. "Por favor," she says, and is certain to be extra nice when the girl comes hurrying to fill it. Mary is a client--wants a psychic reading every once in awhile--but first and foremost they are friends. "I have to give it another chance," her friend says. "I owe Bill that. Also, if totally honest, I suspect I'm way too romantic about this place, these people.

"Romantic?"

"OK...fuckin' duped."

"By who?"

"Never mind," says Mary, and sips her coffee. "Same old story. I don't want to talk about it."

Ah, thinks Luna, familiar with the 'same old story.'

Mary is a jewelry designer. She designs it herself, back in New York, then brings down the samples and tools and accessories necessary for that year's line of ankle bracelets, necklesses, and earrings. The different items are assembled by an Indian family from San Jorge, the Tzaabnals. Mary teaches the patterns to the mother, Sandra, and the two older boys. Pays a high wage for their work. Pays more, she's determined, than a public school teacher makes, and for much less time. She also pays for five of the seven children to go to school. She'd send them all, but can't afford it, which bothers Mary, hating to leave anyone out. The thing is, in addition to the good stuff between her and the family, it seems there are always problems. "What happened?"

"No, really, forget it," Mary says, pushing away her coffee. "I gotta go."

"Wait," says Luna, and takes hold of Mary's hand. No psychic awareness necessary to feel her friend's pain. She's aware of Mary's recent disappointment with her namesake, María. The Tzaabnals had named the baby, their first girl, after her, and for many years Mary felt honored by it. She, a woman who'd never had children, with a cute little Indian girl who depended on her. María was the first to go to school, and always showed gratitude. Got good grades too. She wanted to be a nurse, and Mary encouraged her, was willing to pay whatever it took. But lately things had gotten difficult. The girl turned fourteen and suddenly became secretive. Mary, reading the signs, insisted that they talk about it. A lot. Becoming a nurse would first mean dealing with her attraction to boys. The crucial thing, Mary told her, over and over, was *don't get pregnant!* The girl had promised so many times that it became a joke between them. "It's María," Luna says, certain that no one else could drag her friend so low.

"She's lying to me."

"About what?"

"For months I keep asking to see her grades, but it never happens. Always some lame excuse. Yesterday we were supposed to meet and she didn't show up."

"She knows you're leaving today?"

"She knows."

"What does her mother say?"

"Sandra's the one who makes excuses. Then asks for more tuition money. I couldn't even sleep last night wondering how I'd--I swear, Luna, they think I'm stupid. They're using me."

"You don't know that."

"I'll bet my ass she's quit school. I'll bet a baby's already coming."

"C'mon sister, what's the use of--"

Mary jumps up. "Oh, shit," she says, pointing at her watch, "I'm gonna miss the bus!"

Luna stands and holds her close. Mary kisses Luna's cheek, then pushes away, eyes wet with unwanted tears. Grabbing her bag, she rushes down the street, forgetting to pay her bill, and suddenly stops cold. Spins around.

"Christ on a stick!" she says, and digs the money out of her purse. She runs back, hands the waitress far more than necessary, and gives Luna a wave goodbye.

Jaime arrived in San Pedro two days earlier. One of the new public boats would get him to Pana in an hour, someone said, but he had no money. Instead, he walked along the shore. He passed below the villages of San Juan, San Pablo, San Marcos, Tzununá, and Jaibalito. Reaching Santa Cruz at dusk, he eyed the steep slope ahead. He could see no path, perhaps because of the fading light. He lay down and fell asleep.

The next morning, Jaime tried his best to traverse the sheer incline, holding tight to whatever bush might support him as the loose gravel kept giving way beneath his feet.

A man fishing from a cayuco watched him struggle. Finally, after Jaime slipped several feet, clinging to the branch of a half-dead *jiote*, the man paddled over. "You might as well stay put, there is no path." His name, the fisherman said, was Kique. He was from Panajachel. He'd spent a few days fishing on this part of the lake without any luck. Then Kique asked about him.

Jaime said he was trying to get home, that he'd been gone for many years. He confessed, without any sense of shame, to having deserted the army, and why.

Kique listened closely. When Jaime finished, the fisherman said, "I'd have done the same." He maneuvered the boat parallel to the hillside. "Come on, friend, let's go. I miss my family too."

"I have no money."

"I didn't ask for any. I see you are a good man. Who knows, you might bring me luck. Or maybe one day you'll build me a chalet!" They laughed and shook hands on it. Kique made room in the cayuco, helped Jaime climb inside, and handed him a bucket. "You're going to need it."

He was right. Jaime bailed while Kique rowed for Pana.

"I never tried it before," Kique said, "straight ahead like this, but today we're in a hurry."

They joked that neither of them could swim. As they went further out into the lake, however, and the water became more turbulent, the idea of drowning was much less funny. Kique said, "No use being stupid, right?" and retreated back to hug the shore.

One of them rowed while the other bailed.

They arrived at San Jujú four hours later, at half past eleven, crawling along like a pincher-less crab. Kique left Jaime at the dock. "Mayazak Pabej," he said. They shook hands, then the fisherman rowed toward his house at the far edge of town.

Though it would be faster walking straight up to the main street, Jaime went along the shore to the bottom of Calle Santander. There, on a grassy knoll, were a few gringos lying on towels, their white skin burning in the sun. Coming up to them was a young *indígena* from Santa Catarina. When she removed from her head a heavily packed tzute, all but one of the foreigners went running toward the water. Left behind was a tall skinny boy with long blond hair. He stood up, ready to follow his friends, but the girl handed him a pair of pants from Santa Catarina, exactly like the ones Jaime used to wear. The boy laughed. The girl was laughing too, flirting with him, asking over and over, in Kaqchikel, how much was he willing to pay? When the boy showed how short the pants were, she dug out others, piling them on the ground, as he kept laughing and shaking his head.

Jaime made his way up the Santander. There were houses now among the onion fields, and a new dirt road going to the right. Almost all the trees were gone. About halfway up the street was a vendor, an Indian from Sololá, who had set up a rickety wooden stall. There were tote bags and change purses; carved wooden masks and flutes; ceramic bowls and plates and candleholders.

There were pulseras, too, dozens of them in a straw basket. Jaime moved in to take a closer look. Not as good as the ones he used to make. His mother would have taken them apart, told him to start over.

Then he saw the stacks of huipiles. Huipiles from villages around the lake. He knelt, fingered through the first pile, and found many from Santa Catarina. But the vendor's helper, or mother, an old woman without teeth, came shooing him away. No, her sour look said, he could not afford any of this. This was not a place for him.

At once sunken, numbed with fear, he wandered off, glancing down at what he was wearing. His torn and dirty clothes were not from here. They did not belong. And what about him? Was this still his home?

He thought of the women in Chajul, remembering their beautiful huipiles of horses and birds. *Are all those women dead now? Is some vendor somewhere selling their clothes too?*

He'd never considered it until now, never given it a single thought, but maybe Santa Catarina was gone. . .burned to the ground like the many villages he'd helped destroy in the northern mountains. He was shuffling like an old man, ogling the típica stalls, their vendors calling out to the foreign faces, tourists side-stepping skeletal dogs and piles of shit and children hawking chiclets. Indian women trudged past him toward the lake, their eyes down, heads piled with baskets of bananas or oranges or avocados.

A man in a big white hat scooted from one foreigner to another, very serious, shoving a large plastic bag of nuts in their face. *"Cah-chews!"* he said. *"Cah-chews! Cah-chews!"*

The tourists smiled and shook their heads and waved the man away.

A pickup truck came roaring down the road, bringing a cloud of dust.

Jaime stopped, closed his eyes and covered his face. When he looked again he saw her. The tall narrow frame, the glowing smile. She looked different, her hair short now, but yes, yes, it was the moon lady, Luna, coming straight at him, seeing him too.

"Jaime," she said, holding out her arms.

How was it she knew his name? It didn't matter. His mind went blank as he stood on his tiptoes, forehead against her shoulder, and held on tight, letting her long thin arms engulf him.

La Bella

San Pedro la Laguna, January, 1989

As Jaime and Luna hug on the street, Jake crawls from the rock-hard bed of a cheap San Pedro hospedaje, his sight cloudy, skull pounding, stomach churning with the promise of yet more diarrhea. This has been going on since dawn. He stumbles outside to the shared toilet. Its door clangs shut behind him. The filthy green stall stinks of stale urine, a perfect place to own his shame. He closes his eyes and bows his head, as if preparing to meditate. Deep within, his cramped bowels rumble, flush, are squeezed to a pitiful dribble. . .then fill again like an evil spell. A mosquito lands on his forehead. He slaps at it and misses. He's breathing hard. Sweating. The poison in whatever he ate last night continues to boil inside him and must be gotten rid of.

An hour or so later, hopeful as a repentant monk, he rises from the toilet seat and wipes his tender ass. At last emptied out, his mind opens, his heart beats fast, gratitude drips from his eyes.

"I'm fucking alive," he whispers. No monastic retreat could have yielded greater results. He is alive, still breathing, still able to feel, to think, to do what needs to be done. It is the same stark message that saved him in Vietnam. How could he forget? How could he let things slide so far, and for so damn long? How could he blame Luna for leaving him? Hell, were it possible, he'd have left himself! And since those crazy days--the selfish, idiotic stuff he'd done to drive her off--he's made it worse, *on purpose*, going out of his way to mess things up, turn himself into a genuine no-holds-barred asshole, until she won't even speak to him. Neither do his former pals in Pana, or San Pedro, or anywhere around the lake. People avoid him like the plague, like the toxic lump of shit that he's become.

Suddenly dizzy, he sits back down. Again *OH GOD NO* his stomach twists and knots. *Not done yet.* He bows his head and prays for release, pressing into his mind a little Sufi chant he learned from Luna. "May all be well," he pleads. "May all be happy. May all be free from suffering."

He is ready to chant it out loud, scream it to the heavens, do whatever his demons demand, when a flow of gut-scalding liquid sweeps away the torment.

"Praise the frigging Lord!" he shouts. Then thinks better of it. Why go asking for trouble? "No, not your fault," he tells God. "No one to blame but myself." And the best he can do right now is stay put. As if on a crowded chicken bus, he needs to be patient, calm, thankful for the empty seat.

He hears a gentle knocking as his stomach again begins to rumble. The two sounds blend together, becoming one. Jake realizes it's someone wanting to use the toilet, but he says nothing. Let 'em wait. The whole damn world is just gonna have to wait.

Pushing back against the agony, he remembers, weeks after Lieutenant Sanders was killed, how he and his remaining squad, five lost boys without a leader, were pinned to the ground by enemy fire. By then they'd torched several villages and killed who knows how many innocent people. But were they innocent, really? By then no one cared. By then it was only about surviving, destroying anything that might in any way threaten one's life. That was all the lost boys fought for. To stay alive. None of them knew where they were or where they were going. In each village they took what was needed. Usually food. Sometimes sex. They killed only what had to be killed. If there was no resistance to their needs they moved on, stole away, back into the jungle.

Now they were here. . .wherever they were. . .and unaware that the present attack resulted from an army battalion moving up the valley to rescue them. Firing at Jake and his squad was a small group of Vietcong who'd been surprised by these stray Americans. In their confusion, the Vietnamese soldiers mistook them for a wing of the larger advance, and were busy over-reacting.

Jake lay sprawled in a two inch puddle, the mucky slush covering the entire left side of his face, up to his lower nostril. . .his left eye shut, submerged. . .his right staring off at the slate-gray sky above a nearby tangle of trees and vines. The sheer amount of gunfire had him convinced it was a large troop of Vietcong. He lay there certain his death was close, and felt no fear. The inevitable truth of it, after all he'd been through, was a comfort, a soft place of welcomed rest until the bullets found him. Each second seemed an eternity; each breath a revelation. *Because*, he thought, for at least this one last instant, *I truly understand!* For this final lingering tick of time--as blood pumped through his heart, beating in his chest--he saw it clearly. "I am alive," he told himself, and a peace he'd never known took hold of his entire being. The simplicity was overwhelming. He smiled, and in through the slightly cracked opening of his lips the muddy puddle seeped. His mouth filled with the taste of liquid earth. He swallowed it down, grit and all, and felt fulfilled. Yes, that was enough. To be totally alive, for just another second, was enough.

At some point he realized that the shooting had stopped. He lifted his head. Got to his feet. Only he and Little Billy were left, and Billy was gushing blood. A bullet had torn through the boy's right bicep. Strands of flesh, like stringy red papaya, hung from its exit. Jake tucked in what he could. He cut off the rest and bandaged the wound with his bandana.

Jake rolled to his back. It got dark, like night. Or maybe he was sleeping.

When it got light again he examined Billy's arm. The skin was puffy and discolored, a purplish tinge circling the lesion. After cleaning it in the creek, Jake re-tied the bandana.

He could hear Billy crying. Then nothing.

The next thing he remembered, some guy was trying to make him eat. The guy said Jake could trust him, he was an officer. "Don't worry," the officer said, "we're going to get you out of here."

"No," Jake kept saying, fighting him off, "we're alive, see. We're alive."

He and Billy must have been a problem because the officer called on his walkie-talkie for a helicopter. They were taken to a military base west of Vinh Moc. Within a month (of which he slept a lot) they were back stateside, someplace in Virginia, at a hospital. Billy had lost his arm and was not talking to anyone. Jake asked the doctor's permission to go home.

The doctor, Captain Reynolds, said that it was standard procedure to keep him awhile longer, that they needed to "clear things up." Jake had been talking to one of the nurses about what he claimed to be war crimes. The doctor wanted details. Dates and locations. He began nodding his head and blinking when Jake could not specify when and where these "alleged crimes" had occurred.

"The charges seem," said the doctor, "vague."

Not the least bit vague, however, was Jake's description of the mud puddle seeping ("like truth," he said) into his mouth. . .and how he'd willingly gulped it down. Definitely the wrong thing to say. Over the next several weeks came a long chain of psychiatrists to question him further, to help him "sort things out. . .come to terms with his experience." In their report, some four months later, they cited "extreme combat trauma" and "perhaps shell shock" to explain his "outrageous accusations." They suggested he receive "a continued regimen of therapy" to address his "unstable condition" in order that he might someday "take responsibility for what he, himself, had done."

After tearing their report to shreds, Jake started asking for a lawyer, which quickly brought Captain Reynolds, who sat him down and said, "Remember, son, you are a mental patient." He pointed at Jake's file and concluded he had "a persecution complex." His "allegations of wrongdoing," the doctor said, was a classic example of "projection," and it was in his best interest to stop talking about war crimes. "You need to concentrate on positive things. . .things that will get you back on track . . .make you feel better about your life. Are you able to do that?" Captain Reynolds asked.

"Fuck you," Jake said, and was immediately put in solitary confinement.

During the next five months the whole process kept repeating itself. Lots of psychiatrists, lots of "Fuck you's", and every few weeks a session with Captain Reynolds, who guaranteed more of the same.

"This is getting you nowhere," Reynolds said. "Do you understand, Jake? Do you?"

Finally, Jake told the captain he did. That seemed the only way out, so he took it. Seventeen days later, after many subtle warnings, and papers to sign, he was cleared for release. He went back to Kansas, to the quiet of his own room. Yes, he was still alive, but there was no peace--just the memory of it. Just one more thing he did not trust. The puddle was all dried up.

Pot helped calm him for a while. Then psychedelics. Then Luna. After she left, drinking was of some relief. Then cocaine. In San Pedro he tried heroin, which was by far his favorite drug until one rainy morning he saw his supplier--an old hippie known as *Bones*--dead from an overdose. The week before, Bones had showed Jake how to stick a needle in his vein. It might have been him lying dead on the street. He remembered Palenque and the lesson of all those mushrooms: *Be careful of the plants, man. Watch your step.* Since then, it's only been the booze.

The knocking returns with a vengeance. "Por favor!" cries a plaintive female voice with a strong German accent, like a ruffled feather slicing through his brain.

Jesus Christ, he thinks, flushing down another load. *"Espérame!"* he hollers.

He hears himself, his selfishness, and groans. Gets to his feet. After wiping, he leaves his new roll of paper behind. A token of peace. Maybe this small generosity will be a first step toward salvation. He zips up and goes outside.

"Sorry," he says to the red-faced woman.

She pushes past, into the stall, and slams the door.

Yeah, OK, he deserves that. Instant karma. Exactly right.

Jake clears out of the dollar-a-night room and heads straight for Pana. First he will apologize to Luna. Beg her forgiveness. Then he'll do whatever comes next.

But he can't find her anywhere. He goes to the room she's rented at Hospedaje Garcia, looks up and down the Santander, and wanders through the market. Someone saw her that morning at The Patio with Lilly. Someone saw her later, walking with an Indian kid. No one knows where she is.

Oh well, life is long. No rush.

The logical next step is to check his resolve, prove to himself he's changed. He goes to his favorite hangout, El Jardín, a flower-filled restaurant overlooking the lake. He heads straight for the bar, where he's been hopelessly drunk or stoned on numerous occasions.

El Jardín is owned by a young ladina woman, the gift of her rich father. The woman's name is Sofía--though many, amongst themselves, refer to her as *La Bella*, her beauty having reached near iconic notoriety. She is, without question, the most ogled woman on the lake. Men's necks turn to rubber when she passes. Jaws drop and knees buckle. Women tend to avoid Sofía because their husbands or boyfriends turn into blithering idiots whenever she's around. Even confirmed women-haters drool at the sight of her. That she is untouchable, beyond approach, dangerous as a thousand foot sheer granite cliff, has increased her allure and made her infamous. There is a well-known joke around town. A person referring to something impossible will say 'it's like a smile from La Bella.' Men suffering from chronic sexual deprivation have their own private version of the saying. As paupers might dream of being rich, or confessed sinners of someday reaching heaven, horny men, akin to heroin addicts, pray for just a few short minutes of abandon. 'Like a fuck from La Bella,' they whisper, rolling their bloodshot eyes and shaking their empty heads, a fantasy so incredible it almost hurts. Most do not dare look at her. Some, however, cannot resist the temptation, especially after too many drinks. If they're OK with being ignored, no problem. Overt advances, on the other hand, are met with her haughty scowl. End of conversation! Occasionally, should that warning not be honored, the restaurant staff (led by a thick hairy brute named Raimundo, known as *The Dragon*) is quick to collar the hopeful suitor and toss him into the street. Indeed, over the years, the legend of her guarded virginity has penetrated all of Pana, making every man leery of excessive drooling.

Jake sits at the bar. Sofía is not normally here this time of day, but the regular bartender is sick. She's learned the mixes and waits for Jake to order. He tends to be a beer guy. Lots of it. She's watched him closely over the years, has recognized a certain pattern. Beer means he's feeling mellow. If he's doing cocaine (she can tell by how talkative he gets with the other gringos) he switches to mixed drinks. Usually rum and coke. Usually not a problem either. But when he starts ordering whisky shots, she knows that trouble is coming. He always looks sad on those nights . . .and must hate looking sad. The whisky, she's noticed, resuscitates his rage. First come the pointed insults, aimed at some Hawaiian-shirted tourist who is trying to drink a piña colada and enjoy the sunset. Once the taunting starts, Sofía calls Raimundo. It's been three months since the dragon had to throw him out.

"Lemonade," Jake says.

"What?"

"Lemonade."

"Yes," she says, "I heard. I'm wondering what you want in it?"

"Nothing, Sofía. Just lemons, water, and a bit of sugar, thanks."

Oh? Really? She looks at him closer, at the smile curling his lips, at his big greenish eyes. He's having a bit of fun, no problem with that. Jake is the one man in town who has never shown the faintest trace of interest. Not a single line of drool. He is also the best looking, tall and lean and self-contained--reluctant as her to show emotion--until he smashes some tourist in the face. She notices his ponytail is gone. With a crew cut now, his tanned head shines through. She puts the lemonade in front of him. Her eyes graze the blondish hair on his arms, hoping he won't notice.

Sofía is, in fact, no virgin. She's no lesbian either, and unconcerned with what the asshole men say behind her back. She doesn't care what anyone thinks. She knows how men *take the slightest smile to be a tease, a promise of something more.* Those were her mother's words, also a beauty, a woman who well understood the perils her daughter would face. Sofía was warned plenty of times. Pursued, since she was twelve, by men twice her age, she learned to ignore them, to *in no way encourage their attention*. The one time she did, at sixteen, with a boy a few years older, it soon became clear (as her mother had said) what it was he wanted. He got it too, in an alley not far from their house. And the next night, again, in the exact same place. It was not until the third night that she stopped him. She wanted to know, "What, is this it for you? Just this, in a dirty alley?" When the question seemed to puzzle the boy, Sofía marched off, angry and disillusioned, and in that dark moment of weakness confided to her best friend, Iris (a cute, somewhat pudgy girl), who secretly hated her. Within a few days (because the boy was also talking) the news reached Sofía's parents.

"We are very disappointed in you," her mother said.

Her father was more direct. "People say you are a whore."

"It's a lie," Sofía told them, and explained the whole ugly experience. She made them see she'd learned her lesson. She was determined they would never doubt her again.

Later that year, Uncle Mario forced himself on top of her. Everyone else was outside, watching a troop of soldiers march by. She'd had no interest and gone upstairs. How could she know he would come into her room? How could she know what he'd planned to do? Mario was her father's favorite brother, and assured Sofía that no one would believe a whore.

She kept quiet. Kept it to herself. And never had another boyfriend. Never allowed the chance of being alone with any man. Her parents noticed, but were still not convinced she could be trusted. When she decided, at twenty-three, to get out of the city and move to the lake, they were, of course, concerned. Sofía counted on that, knowing they would find a way to keep her off the streets. Why not make use of their unjust self-righteousness? Why not get something for what she'd been through?

Her father, a rich executive with Coca-Cola, bought the El Jardín restaurant--a minimal investment, he must have decided, to protect his daughter's reputation. He was right that it would take most of her time, and she had no objections. She only wanted control over her life. It was also her father's idea to use Raimundo, once his trusted bodyguard, as a protector of his precious Sofía. . .to watch out for horny men, yes. . .and also keep an eye on her.

Raimundo walks up and stands next to Sofía. "You want the gringo out?"

"No, he's alright," she says, and moves away. She hates the big sweaty man getting too close. Like it's part of his job. Like he's entitled.

"I'll have another," Jake says.

"Yes?" she says. "The same?"

"Exactly," he says, and for the first time ever she sees his eyes meet hers.

La Gloria

Luna went with Jaime to Santa Catarina. His choice. In spite of how much he wanted to see his mother, he was afraid he'd changed to the point where she might not feel comfortable with him. Having Luna there would make it easier, he thought. She'd been going to the market every Sunday, telling his mother she knew he'd be coming back.

Luna sat next to him in the back of the crowded pickup. Neither of them spoke, it was not a time for words. Jaime just stared at his dirty bare feet. Time vanished, like when he was dreaming. Unbelievable, less than an hour after meeting on the street, that he and this strange woman, who he thought must be an angel, were already climbing toward his house. He looked around at the same decaying adobe walls, at what seemed to be the same dogs lying in the shadows. Nothing had changed, but everything was different. No one in the village recognized him. Everyone stared, like at a stranger. Or maybe a ghost. And what, they must have wondered, was the tall beautiful white woman doing here, winding her way up the steep callejones with him, an Indian man?

Almost at the house, a young woman came walking down the path. At first struck by the sight of Luna, she stopped. Then she saw him. "Jaime?"

He knew it must be Flor. "Yes."

All three of them started crying, and they held each other close, which brought the neighbors out of their huts to see what was happening. "Hijo!" said his mother, head in her hands, calling from their front stoop. Her tears made him a boy again, a small tender child who knew nothing of the world, nothing of sin.

Manuel and Felipe were off harvesting the milpa, would be gone until the following day. Consuelo took advantage of that fact and ignored her chores. She let her daughters ignore theirs too. The girls kept asking questions about the army. Where did he go? What did he do? Cora, six years old, born after Jaime had been taken, said, "Tell us, Jaime. Tell us everything."

He did not know what to say. If only Luna had stayed to distract them. Finally, overwhelmed, he said he was tired and needed to sleep.

"Of course," his mother said, and chased the girls out of the hut.

When he woke, he noticed a large pot cooking on the fire. The girls were back, surrounding him. They giggled and held on tighter whenever he tried to stand. "No," Flor said, "you're not going anywhere."

"Not unless we say," said Adriana.

"Leave him alone," his mother said.

"I don't mind," he told her.

Cora combed her fingers through his hair and twisted small handfuls of it into dense little curls.

His mother leaned down to him. "Close your eyes," she said.

He did. From behind, Cora snuggled her head next to his.

Flor said, "Don't let him go, Cora!"

"You can't go," the small girl whispered in his ear. "You have to sit and do nothing."

"Nothing?"

"Yes, because you're going to be surprised when you see what--"

"Cora!" Adriana yelled. "It's a secret, remember?"

"Oh yes," she said, covering his closed eyes with her tiny hands, "I forgot, no peeking. It's a secret," she whispered, her soft cool lips tickling his ear, making him squirm with joy.

From between Cora's fingers he watched, taking all of it in, and savored it: the wood smoke filling his nostrils; the warm sweet moisture of Cora's hands; the wooden spoon stirring round the thick earthen pot.

Then came his mother's gentle voice. "All right, Cora."

"Can I let go, Mama?"

"Yes, yes, let him see."

Cora wrapped her arms over his shoulders and plopped her head on top of his.

"A special meal," his mother said. "To celebrate you coming home."

Though Jaime doesn't want to leave, he starts off early the next day, first an hour's walk over the ridge to San Andrés. From there, he remembers exactly what Raul said. It's as if his friend were with him again, telling him where to find a pickup for Las Cruces, then a bus toward Godínez. "Tell the driver to drop you at La Gloria," Raul says, "he'll know the spot." And he's right about everything: the big arched sign, the steep windy road, the tall trees with long rows of coffee underneath. Jaime keeps walking and Raul keeps talking in his head. Never shuts up. "I'll make sure you get a good job, Manito."

"No, Raul, that's not why I'm--"

"I promised," says his friend. "And you'll get your own hut, too."

"I thought your father doesn't trust you."

"Yeah, well, you're not me!" Raul says. "Besides, it won't look right to deny a soldier."

"I deserted."

"No one needs to know that, *vos!* And the less you talk, the more respect you'll get."

"Maybe you're a bit too sure," says Jaime.

"No, I swear, they're all going to love you. Especially Aura."

Jaime remembers how Raul described his darling little sister: her dimples, how quick she was to smile, to laugh. Also the other side of her, the way she cried at any cruelty. "Once," Raul said, "she went hysterical when my mother started killing ants. I had to get her out of the house, distract her with something while the evil deed was done."

Raul had told him many such stories.

"She'll be sad I'm not with you," he says. "Don't worry, Manito, it will pass. Just joke with her, make her laugh, that's what you have to do with Aura." Raul keeps talking but Jaime stops listening. He's prepared himself, as best he can, to tell what happened, and is certain no one will be laughing. "Oye, *vos*, did you hear what I said?"

"Leave me be," Jaime tells him. "I have to think."

He will not say it all, he reminds himself. Only that Raul was killed. Where and when, not how. Never how. He knows it's going to be hard. He hopes he'll be able to say it, straight out, and leave. Just get it over with.

A man with a rifle steps out of the woods. Not a soldier, though he does wear a uniform. Maybe a policeman. "You have business here?"

"I am looking for the crew manager, Señor Salvador."

"I'm sorry," the man says. "Salvador is dead."

"What?"

"It happened last year. The guerillas murdered him. Others too. They did terrible things. Everything has changed."

"Where is his wife?"

"In the dueño's house," he says, "but no visitors are allowed."

"I have to see her," Jaime says.

"Why?"

"It has to do with Raul, her son. We were in the army together. He was killed."

"Oh no," says the man, lowering his gun. He takes a deep breath. "I'm sorry," he says. "I know you must have come a long way but--"

"She has to know," Jaime says. "I was ordered to tell her."

"Well. . .I. . .I. . .uh-huh, yes, I suppose it's best to get the bad news over with." The man pulls out a walkie-talkie and tells someone he needs help. He hangs up, then starts talking about himself. He was in the army too, in the Petén, which led to this job as a private bodyguard. He says many former soldiers are hired to protect the landowners. "The army, as you know, is needed elsewhere."

Jaime nods.

"I should warn you," says the man, "things are bad with Señora Dolores."

"Who?"

"Salvador's wife. She never comes outside. No one knows what happened to her. Some say she was raped by the guerillas after they killed him. A terrible thing. And now her son?" He groans and shakes his head.

"What about their daughter?"

"She works in the dueño's house."

"No, I mean did they, did they also. . .?"

"I don't think so. I hope not." He goes silent and the two of them breathe together like brothers at arms. The bodyguard pats Jaime on the shoulder. "We must keep doing our best," he says. "We must."

Two men, with rifles, come running down the road.

The bodyguard tells them, "Take this soldier to Señora Alvarez." Then he turns to Jaime. "Good luck," he says.

At the dueño's house, Jaime is handed off to another man, who walks him up the front stairway to a wide wooden porch and a tall front door. A young boy opens it before they can knock. He stands several inches taller than Jaime, and does not seem to like the look of him.

"Who is he," the boy says to the guard.

"We were told to bring him here. He needs to talk with--"

"She is busy," the boy says.

"Who's there, Esteban?"

"I don't know, mother. A very short man."

A middle-aged ladina woman appears at the boy's side.

"Yes?" she says to Jaime.

"Please," he says, "I need to speak with Señora Dolores."

"Why?"

"I was a friend of her son, Raul. I was in the army with him. I came to--"

"Oh," she says, "yes. Yes, certainly. Come in."

"Mother?"

"It's all right, Esteban. Why don't you go outside for awhile."

The woman says it in passing, apparently not concerned whether or not the boy does what she says. She brings Jaime into a large living room. He has never stepped foot inside such a beautiful house. There is a stone fireplace; hand-woven carpets adorn the polished wooden floor; paintings of people, lots of people, hang on walls covered with flowery paper. It's not as fancy as the castle chalet, but there he'd only had a chance to peek through the windows when the owners were gone.

The woman points at a long chair with thick cushions. He sits down on its very edge. The woman sits next to him as though it were perfectly normal.

"I am Juana Alvarez," she says.

"Hello, Señora Alvarez. My name is Jaime."

"Glad to meet you, Jaime. You must forgive my son. He is twelve, a horrible age, and bored with school vacation. Misses his father, his friends in the city. I am afraid I can do nothing to please him." She smiles. "Oh well," she says.

"Yes, Ma'am."

Then her face turns serious again. "Raul has died, am I right?"

The stark clarity of her words rattle in Jaime's mind. But at least it's been said. "Yes."

"Dear God," says Señora Alvarez, instantly crying, wiping at her eyes. "Dolores and Aura have been through so much. I suppose you heard what happened to Salvador?"

"He was killed."

"Oh, no. Far worse."

Jaime looks away, stares straight ahead at the wall, at the ornate vines connecting one group of flowers with another. She seems to be waiting for him to look at her again. He does.

"You should know what happened," she says.

"Please, Señora, I--"

"No, son, you need to understand. And you must promise to treat her gently. Very gently."

"I promise."

"The guerillas came after Salvador. I was here too, you would think they'd be after me, but no, it was him they wanted. Him and his family. He had gotten lots of people arrested for who knows what? I suppose many of them were tortured. Some of them murdered. There is no good side to this. Both sides are guilty."

"Yes."

"They cut the man up with a machete in front of his wife. Can you imagine? How could anyone do such a thing? I don't know what happened to her. She won't talk about it."

"And Aura?"

"You know Aura?"

"I know her from Raul, things he told me."

"Poor girl. She was away for the week with her aunt in Panajachel. Thank God, they were gone when she returned."

"She is here, with her mother?"

"No," says Señora Alvarez. "I mean not with her mother. The girl is a dear, she really is, so I do not understand why she. . .well, never mind . . .it is something between them. Aura works in the kitchen, is learning to be a cook. She sleeps downstairs with the other workers. She also needs to know about Raul, but you should talk to Dolores first. Are you ready?"

No, he's not. He drops his eyes, stares at his feet. They look so out of place on the finely woven carpet. "I'm not sure," he says, "I don't see what, what I can--"

Señora Alvarez reaches out and puts her hand on his. "Listen," she says, "Dolores has told me, more than once. She already knows. Has known for a long time." She takes his hand and helps lift him to his feet. They stand facing each other. "Your friend would want you to tell her, to help her if you can."

"All right," says Jaime.

He follows Señora Alvarez down a long dark hallway to the back of the house. She knocks on the final door. "Dolores?"

"Come in."

She opens it into a small sunlit room. There, in a chair by the window, is a gray-haired woman, her small sad face turned toward them.

"Someone has come to see you, Dolores."

The woman says nothing, looks back out the window.

"This is Jaime. He has come to talk to you about Raul."

Dolores begins to cry. Though her face is turned away, the tears are evident from the dropping of her head and the tremor in her shoulders.

"Go ahead," Señora Alvarez whispers to Jaime, steering him

384

forward by his elbow. "Sit down, son. Say what you need to say."

She turns and leaves, closing the door behind her. Jaime goes to the only other place to sit, on the edge of the bed. It seems wrong somehow, its softness, him sitting in this bright pleasant room with such bad news to tell.

Then, like the dueña, Dolores saves him. "Raul is gone."

"Yes, Señora."

"You are his friend."

"Yes."

"Were you with him, when he died?"

"I. . .I was, I. . ."

"I'm glad," she says. "Raul was a good boy. He will always be a good boy."

"Yes, Señora."

Her shoulders heave, her eyes well with tears. She wipes them away and blows her nose on the handkerchief in her lap. It's been there, waiting, all along.

"Thank you," she says. "Now, please, go tell Aura. She also knows, but will need to be told."

Jaime feels stunned. No, he thinks, it's not his place. Hasn't he done what was necessary? Shouldn't the mother be the one to tell her daughter? How could she ask him?

"I think, Señora, it would be better if--"

"No," she says. He eyes are muted, covered by a light gauzy film. "Aura will not hear it from me. You must do it. Go," she says, and turns away.

He gets up from the bed and leaves. Señora Alvarez is standing at the far end of the hall. Signaling him to follow, she leads Jaime back into the main room, back to where he was sitting before, and says to wait.

A few minutes later a girl appears. She wears a stained white apron--has been busy, Jaime guesses, preparing the mid-day meal. She is smiling, eyes sparkling, tiny dimples beneath each of her puckered cheeks. Aura, Jaime knows, is in her late teens, but she looks much younger. She is a beauty, as he'd imagined, with long dark hair and Raul's handsome face--only softer, sweeter--the prettiest face he's ever seen. And how familiar she seems. Like he's seen her many times before. Had Raul described his sister so well that Jaime would think he knew her? His mind might have puzzled it out, that he saw her in the market nine years earlier. . that he felt the same then, too. . .but her face suddenly changes, becomes cold and stiff. His eyes must have given him away, the sadness in his heart, the words he cannot find to express it.

"What is it?" she says.

"I'm sorry to disturb you, Aura, I--"

"What? What do you want?"

"It's about Raul."

"Where is he?"

"I am sorry," says Jaime, "I. . .I came to--"

"No!" she says, with such inner force that her body shakes. "You're wrong," she says. "You don't know."

"I was with him," says Jaime. "I was his friend."

"No! No! Stop!" she shouts, running from the room and down a nearby set of stairs.

Señora Alvarez must have been nearby, because she comes in right away and again sits next to him. "You did your best," she says. "These things take time."

"Yes, Ma'am. Thank you. I think it's best I leave."

Jaime stands and walks toward the door. As he does, something tries to stop him--an intense urge to go after Aura. To comfort her.

Though he knows she would reject it, he sees himself running down those stairs, to the depths of wherever she's gone, and holding her in his arms, letting her cry. It feels wrong to be leaving, but what can he do?

At the door he says goodbye to Señora Alvarez. Esteban is outside, sitting on the porch, sulking. Jaime descends the stairs to the stone pathway and walks toward the guard.

"Jaime, wait."

It is Señora Alvarez, coming down the stairs behind him.

"Yes, Ma'am?"

"Where are you going now?"

"Back to Santa Catarina."

"To your wife, your children?"

"No, Señora, I am not married."

"You have a job?"

"No, I...not yet, I just got back, I--"

"I'm sorry, maybe it's too soon, but I was wondering if you might want to work here?"

"Here?"

"If there is nothing else you need to do."

"Well I...no," says Jaime. "I mean yes, Señora, yes I would. I only need to go tell my mother."

"Good," she says, "you do that. Then come stay with us. I've lost a lot of good workers lately, including my gardener. Do you have any experience with taking care of plants?"

New Castles   *1989*

In 1983, General José Efraín Ríos Montt (instigator of a coup fourteen months earlier) was himself deposed by another general. Montt had taken his vicious anti-insurgency policies further than the rest of the world could tolerate. Even the United States stopped defending him, cut off military support, and *wham*, he was gone. It was time for a true democracy, said the new general, and called for public elections. The ladino aristocracy hoped that might end the long war. The repressive policies continued, however, because the guerillas did not trust the government and refused to believe that a new president would make any real difference. They kept fighting throughout the 1986 elections. Later, as President-elect Cerezo spoke eloquently of a *peaceful reconciliation*, atrocities were being reported in the mountains of Ixil and the jungles of Petén. True, the reports had diminished. No wonder. Few journalists dared poke their noses where they might literally get cut off.

Expats on the lake did their best to stay safe. Voluntary exiles from around the world, they discussed the violence amongst themselves, whispering their disgust to the privacy of trusted ears. Neither stupid nor naïve, by 1989 they all knew of the massacres, assassinations, and *desaparecidos*. Some of the more cynical were relieved that the hopeless situation (which they could do nothing to stop) relieved them of responsibility. It was not their country, after all, so they kept a low profile and did not cause the slightest stir. Same as they'd been doing for years. Why get killed in someone else's war?

Thinking back to his first trip, in 1976, Jake remembered know-it-all (and now long-gone) Richard. He wondered what might happen to a guy like him, a guy with plenty to say, and no fear of saying it. Oh yes, things had changed a lot. Though he wished he could do something that mattered, Jake knew the deal and dealt with it.

He decided to stay in Pana. He rented a room at the Rooms Santander, and ate his meals either in the market or at a funky little restaurant called El Ultimo Refugio, run by a former cocaine buddy named Acapulco Bob. He also kept drinking lemonade each night at El Jardín. The sweet stuff was growing on him, for obvious reasons.

A few days after settling in, he found Luna and made his apologies.

"No need," she said. They hadn't seen each other for a long time. She kissed his cheek and wished him a happy life. Because they'd never been legally married, she said, there was nothing to resolve. The land in San Pablo was his. So yeah, sure, why couldn't they be friends?

That settled, Jake went back for more lemonade. Soon he and Sofía were sharing a pitcher, with plenty of ice. . .and having regular talks . . .then early morning walks along the lake shore, across the river to Jucanyá. At the very end of the trail, on a narrow strip of beach known by some of the foreigners as *Malibú*, Jake would strip to his underwear and dive in.

Sofía always had a towel ready to rub him dry. She could feel it, of course, how much he wanted her, but was not going to let it happen. At least not yet. And she would not say when, if ever, that might change.

Jake was in no hurry. Patience had gotten him close--which for him, for now, was plenty close enough. They drank lots of lemonade and were sometimes seen on the Calle Santander, strolling hand in hand. They kept to themselves because others, Jake could tell, were talking shit behind their backs. The men, his old drinking pals, just smiled and winked. *Assholes.* They'd caroused through plenty of fucked-up nights together and thought they knew him. All they knew was how crazy he could be, an easy-going guy until one too many drinks turned him sour and mean. *Yeah,* they were thinking, *sober now. . .right. . .as if that will last!* He knew how these assholes thought. If he seemed a friendlier, happier guy, well, why not, right. . .what man wouldn't look happy with Sofia rubbing up against him? Tits and ass was all they saw of her, the pigs. Barbeque Larry came close to saying it one day, losing his cool as Sofia slipped away in her skimpy tight shorts.

"Damn!" he said, his eyes feeling her up as she moved down the street. "Tell me, please, how is it that a loser like you gets such beautiful fucking women?"

"Hell if I know, man. Maybe they feel sorry for me."

"Must be it," Larry said, and ordered another beer.

Jake got similar responses from other men. Lots of drool and disbelief. Far more bothersome was that Luna's women friends seemed to go out of their way to avoid him.

"What's up with them?"

Luna laughed. "Oh, don't sweat it, Jake, it'll pass. It's their mothering instinct," she said. "They think you left me for her."

"And you tell them it's not true?"

"If they ask. Usually they don't. People believe what they want to believe."

"Yeah, uh-huh, whatever. A damn shame. She's nice you know, there's no reason to--"

"See what I mean?"

"What?"

"She's not *nice*, Jake. Let's get real. Something terrible happened to Sofia, that much I see. I don't hold it against her, OK, but you can't honestly believe she'll ever be *nice*."

"She was raped by her uncle."

"Oh. . .I'm sorry."

"Understandable, don't you think, if she's a bit hard?"

"Understandable, yes. Changeable, I doubt it. Not with her."

"You don't know everything, Luna. Sometimes you--"

"OK, OK, maybe I'm wrong. Yeah, I could be wrong. I hope I am."

Proving she meant it, Luna tried to make friends with Sofía. Whenever seeing them in the street she went out of her way to say hello. But Sofía didn't want anything to do with her. Told Jake she thought Luna was trying to win him back. She even accused him once, because he'd laughed at one of Luna's jokes, of still being in love with her. That same night, Sofía showed up at his room and wanted to have sex. When he resisted, she started unbuttoning her blouse.

"No," he said, "not like this."

"You want to be with *her*, is that it?"

"I want to be with you, Sofía, but not yet. Not until you're ready."

She cried, deep and long. He held her close. Would not let go. Outside, a heavy rain began to fall. They lay on the bed and listened to it pound the roof.

It was the first time they slept together, and just after dawn Sofía's hand found his erection. She fondled it. Squeezed it. He pulled her on top. She sat upright on his hips, and smiled, her ass in his hands. She bent over to kiss him--a long, sloppy kiss--and then he lowered his head and licked cautiously at one of her hardened nipples. . .was trying to be gentle. . .but when she pulled his head closer, and started moaning, he practically lost his mind. Rolling Sofía onto her back, he held her wrists above her head and went for her neck. She let out a cry as he massaged its muscled flesh with his teeth. She moaned again, louder now, freeing her hands and pushing his head back toward her breasts, but he passed them by and slipped down to her vagina.

"Please," Sofía said, "please," which he took as encouragement, nosing through the bush and parting her labia with his tongue. "I said no!" she screamed, batting at his head.

He looked up at her tear-drenched face. "What?"

"I don't want that!"

"Oh. OK."

"It makes me feel like a whore, or, or like, anybody, like I could be anybody and--"

"No, honey, no, it's--"

"Like it's not really me you love, that all you want is--"

"OK," he whispered. "Shhh, OK." He scooted up and held her as she cried. "Please, honey, I do love you. "Only you, Sofía. . .I promise."

Jaime, as Raul had promised, got his own hut at La Gloria. It was dark and dingy. He didn't care. Since becoming the gardener his mind had cleared--like the air after a Xocomil--and he knew, for certain, what he wanted: to marry Aura. She was the first girl he'd ever thought of in this way. In other words, constantly. Thoughts of her filled his days and kept him awake at night. For many months, throughout the rainy season, he peeked for a glimpse of her in the kitchen window. He imagined it to be the window of their future home, with her inside, preparing a meal while he worked in the garden. She would see him through the glass and hold up their baby and wave its tiny hand. When finished with work, he would change to clean clothes and they would eat tortillas by the fire, then lay down in a real bed. He would feel her there, warm by his side.

A family with Aura was what he wanted. Only that. And he did once see her standing in that window. But Aura, when she saw him watching, turned and disappeared.

Out of respect, and fear, he never looked again. It had to be enough for her to be near, just the other side of those walls.

The rainy season ended late, the garden not dry enough for planting until mid November. A huge pile of bedding soil, dark and rich, sat at the top of the road, covered with a blue tarp. It was for Jaime to use however he saw fit. The very sight of it made him happy.

Señora Alvarez came to the garden often, and always had something to say, usually about the flowers, pointing at the blossoms beginning to show. Whenever he asked for a certain additive or insecticide, she had it delivered. With the passing months he kept gaining her praise, continually doing more than she expected. He calibrated sprinklers, added faucets, and repaired whole sections of pipe--things he'd learned while working at the chalet. Though not his job, and not asked to do it, he climbed the roof to clean the chimney and unplug the gutters. He painted the picket fence and put new hinges on the gate. When the big brass handle on the front door kept sticking, he fixed it like new. . .then replaced a broken window. . .then the kitchen sink.

By late April, with the coffee harvested and rain coming soon, most of the workers were gone, back to their villages until the following November. Only the bodyguards were certain to stay. The prior year, Jaime had gone to spend time with his mother in Santa Catarina. This year he planned to do the same. He'd asked the dueña when it would be best for him to leave. Now she was coming to give him an answer. "Good afternoon," she said. "I came to ask a favor."

"Yes, Señora?"

"Two favors really. First, please call me by my first name. Juana."

She was smiling, thinking it would please him. For Jaime, though, it was a strange thing to ask. Unnatural. He hesitated, not sure what to say.

"I know it is a big change," she said. "I like big changes. Can you do that for me?"

"Of course, *Seño* Juana, whatever you--"

"Juana. Please. . .just Juana."

"Juana."

"Thank you, Jaime. And before you leave to visit your mother, I need something else."

"Yes, anything."

"I want you to go with Aura to Sololá."

"Sololá? Why?"

"I have been teaching her how to cook. Marta is getting on, she won't be here forever. I want Aura to take her place, and I prefer to have official contracts with my regular workers, their monthly salaries legally recorded."

"But, Juana, you have been paying me for two years and I--"

"Yes, yes, I know. That is the other reason I need you to go. It is usually my husband who takes care of these things, but since Salvador's death he has been gone a lot, and left it up to me. Obviously I am not so good at it. *Two years, Jaime? Really?* You could get us into trouble if you want."

Jaime smiled. "Well. . .good thing I don't."

She laughed, and he laughed with her. "Oh," she said, "*good.*" He could see what a beauty she once was. Even now, when happy, Juana looked like a young girl. Then her face turned serious. "Most employers do not bother with a written contract, and workers never ask. Still, it is best, for everyone's sake, we make it legal. Both of you will want other jobs some day and it will help if you can prove you worked here."

"Yes, all right."

"Here is the document you will need. See, my husband has already signed it. The *Ministerio* in Sololá knows him and is used to this. The official there will date it after you sign, and give you a copy. Tino will drive you tomorrow morning. On the way back, he can take you to Santa Catarina."

"Thank you, Juana."

"No, thank you, Jaime." She started toward the house, then stopped and turned around. "Oh," she said, "if you decide to come back early--which means any time you want--I will need someone to work inside the house."

She pretended it an afterthought, but Jaime wasn't fooled. "Really? Doing what?"

"As you know," she smiled, "there are always things needing to be fixed."

On the drive to Sololá, Aura stayed silent. At the *Ministerio Del Trabajo*, Jaime held the door open for her. He then let her get ahead of him in line. She nodded both times without saying a word.

The young man at the counter asked Aura a lot of questions. Jaime saw that she had no problem speaking with him. And laughing. Maybe even flirting. After he handed Aura a copy of her signed document, she passed by Jaime and gave a tiny grin. But when he got his, and smiled at her, she turned away. . .and didn't make a single sound throughout the drive to Santa Catarina.

Jaime got out of the car. "Thank you for the ride, Tino."

"Hasta pronto," said the driver, a saying which assumed that Jaime would not be back at the finca for several months.

"Good bye," said Aura, probably thinking the same.

"See you in a week," Jaime said, closing the door.

"What?"

Her eyes widened as he turned away. She could not see him smile. Some things, he knew, took lots of time to fix.

A year had passed since Jake and Sofía became a couple. He would stay the week in Pana, at her place, and go to San Pablo on weekends. He liked puttering around on his land, pruning trees and putting in new plants, checking water lines to make sure the drip system worked.

He slept on a thin foam mattress under the avocado tree. Never went into the house, he supposed, because it reminded him of Luna. He had installed windows, and a front door with no lock, but had not finished the kitchen, nor put in any furniture. Had no interest in any of that. Nonetheless, while he was gone, Pascual made certain it was never disturbed. He also took it upon himself to give Jake's garden the extra care it needed. Jake was aware of the unsolicited help, and thanked Pascual on every visit. Soon they were friends again.

Sofía had no interest in what she called "your property." She'd visited once and said almost nothing. "Yes," she'd agreed, "the beach is very nice...but I want something that is ours, Jake. Just the two of us."

One day in early April, coming to the land by himself, Jake insisted that Pascual put his milpa, like before, down by the lake. Pascual was not easily convinced. He finally gave in when Jake made clear he'd made up his mind, that it was his way of apologizing for all the trouble he had caused.

"Only until you come back," Pascual said. "I know that someday you and Luna will live here."

Jake smiled at Pascual's prophecy and they shook hands. He felt happy to return what was never really his to take. Then, though it had not been his plan, he stayed. For the next two weeks, he and his friend worked hard to re-build the terraces. The beds had to be ready before the first rains came. Soon, thought Jake, the milpa would be as it should be, as it had always been. He let the corn grow tall and green in his mind, his once virulent hatred of it gone.

When he returned to Pana, Sofía was cold and distant. Finally she said, as if it had been well-rehearsed, "Look, I understand. You have your own life. I have mine."

He apologized again. He'd had no idea, until it happened, that he would give away his land, or would stay, for weeks, to help Pascual with the terraces. Yes, he should have made the extra trip to tell her, or found a phone, or something.

"You should have realized how much I miss you!" she screamed.

Jake decided not to tell the truth, how he'd completely lost track of time. All that had mattered was fixing the terraces and preparing the beds. He'd never been so busy, so focused, so happy. He and Pascual became like brothers, digging and raking from dawn till dusk, eating tortillas together, both asleep short after nightfall. There was no *time* to think of time. They were men working, as men were meant to work. Nothing more, nothing less. Hour after hour, day after day, the gringo-- the *extranjero*--no longer existed. Did not need to exist. Not for Jake, not for anyone. So yeah, sure, no wonder Sofía missed him, and was angry, and thought him selfish. "Please," he said, "forgive me."

"Never mind, Jake, I'm just being stupid. I don't own you. I have no right to tell you what to do. You can do whatever you want."

"OK," he said, sipping his lemonade.

"Yeah, yeah, OK," she said, getting up from the table, ready to move on.

He stood and held her sad little face in his hands. "Then let's get married."

"What?"

"I am done with the land. Done forever. I've told you before, Sofía, only want you."

At first she looked confused by the certainty in his eyes. Then she surrounded him with those strong arms of hers. "We can build something amazing together," she said, crying into his shoulder.

"Yes," he said, "whatever you want."

"A castle."

Jake kissed the top of her head, convinced she was exaggerating on purpose, making a silly joke.

"A castle," she said, "all our own."

The Whole World   *1992*

Soon as their elaborate wedding was over, Sofía began hunting for where the castle would be built. For seven months she was very annoyed. Nothing pleased her. "All of it is so plain, so common."

Then her father mentioned "a magnificent property" owned by a family friend, which he thought might be for sale. Desperate, she decided to have a look. It was halfway between Santa Catarina and San Antonio. As directed, she and Jake parked his Volkswagen camper on the road, across from a series of three painted boulders, one word on each, together reading CARPIO POR PRESIDENTE!

They found the narrow dirt trail and followed it along a descending ridge, through scrub pine and overgrown brush. The slender peninsula jutted westward, aimed at the volcanoes of Tolimán and Atitlán. At the tip was a single, massive, multi-level rock, folding out into the lake like a medieval fortress. From the upper southern edge it towered a hundred feet over a tiny oval bay. From the northern cliff it dropped in leaps and bounds toward a small open valley and the remnants of a milpa, then flattened onto a stretch of pristine beach.

"Oh yes," Sofía said, "this is perfect."

Not so much the land, she told Jake, as the rock itself. She loved how alone it stood, how noble, gazing over the water like a sentry on guard: tall and proud and indestructible.

Sofía's father, Paulo Hernández, had never seen the property. All he knew of it came from his best friend, Fernando Perez, who had purchased the small valley, once covered with corn, in the late sixties. Fernando was an executive with Banco Communidad: a large man known for large ideas.

Paulo had heard the fantasy many times. His friend would transform the milpa into a paradise, complete with a huge chalet above that gorgeous stretch of beach on what he agreed was *the most beautiful lake in the world*. There would be a tall wrought-iron gate on the main road, with a uniformed guard stationed there, around the clock, to keep out unwanted visitors. The footpath would be widened, big enough for his Mercedes. Paved with concrete, lined on both sides with lemon trees and streams of bougainvillea, it would wind like a well-trained vine to his mansion on the shore.

At first anxious to get started, he'd been counseled to review his vision. Paulo remembered his friend's extreme frustration. Any sort of road, claimed three different engineers, would be a waste of money. For various geological reasons, it would simply slide away with the next bad storm. Fernando refused to believe them. After other engineers confirmed the prediction, they were fired too. Specialists were necessary, Fernando decided--perhaps from The United States--which would no doubt be very expensive, so he went back to work with a vengeance. He opened three new banks and nearly got indicted for various legal infractions impossible to prove. He got divorced, re-married, and re-divorced. Fourteen years passed since Fernando had bought the land. He was now old and fat and lazy as a drunken afternoon. Still, he held fast to his dream. . .seemed to have no doubt of someday seeing it to fruition. . .was merely too involved, he said, with other things.

True, thought Paulo Hernandez. Such as drinking. A lot.

This afternoon, like every other afternoon, they sat on the patio of their favorite bar, La Perla, sipping away the hours while smoking Cuban cigars and discussing contemporary politics.

"Our army," Paulo said, "has gotten soft. It is a big mistake to placate those crazy damned Indians and their constant demands."

Fernando sighed. "If they want the war to end, why keep making trouble?"

"Ríos Montt was the only one they listened to," Paulo said. Fernando nodded and Paulo filled their half-empty glasses with Napoleon Brandy. Today he'd bought an entire bottle. His treat. He needed to get Fernando in the proper mood: which meant first discussing the exact same things they always discussed: things Paulo knew they would agree on: the war, the stupid politicians, the genetic inferiority of Indians. "Because Montt was the only one they feared!"

"Exactly," said Fernando.

Paulo tonged a fresh cube of ice into each glass. He hesitated to interrupt their serious conversation with his daughter's dreamy request, but guessed his friend was drunk enough to go along. Besides, he thought, dreams were Fernando's favorite thing to talk about. How many times had the man described his imagined chalet, right down to its walnut door and solid brass toilet? Bringing up the land might lead to a repetition of all that, but Paulo had to take the chance. "Oh," he said, "I almost forgot, Sofía has a proposition for you."

Fernando's eyes lit up. "For me? Yes, yes, what?"

"I don't know why, but she is fascinated by that big rock of yours on the edge of the lake. She wonders if you might sell it."

"Really?" Fernando said. "Sofía wants to buy my land?"

"Well, no. . .not exactly." Paulo sighed and rolled his eyes. He was willing to suffer this chance of humiliation because he could not bear to see Sofía sad. Also, he reminded himself, for the sake of his friend. He had watched Fernando weaken over the years, his muscle turn to flab, his pride lose its luster. Paulo knew very well why he had done nothing with the property: to avoid being proven wrong about the road. Pitiful. It was Paulo's hope that he might save his friend from further self-inflicted injury. Fernando was a businessman, after all--that was his truest passion--so to make a bit of money off an otherwise wasted dream could only do him good. "She just wants that rock," he said.

"I don't understand."

"No, neither do I." Paulo laughed. The trick was, how to get Sofía what she wanted while convincing Fernando that his dream was still alive and well. "What can I say, she's in love with it!"

"Why?"

"Who knows? Like you, I am far too practical a thinker to understand. Sofía acts on intuition, Fernando, as if dreaming were enough to make something happen. She does not have your vision. I told her so, I tried to reason with her. The other side of the property, I explained, with the flatter land and sandy beach, is the only suitable place for a chalet. I assured her you would never sell that."

"Oh no, never."

"Yes, yes, exactly what I told her. She was disappointed, of course, but understood. 'That's all right,' she said. 'Tell him I just want the rock.' Which, I admit, baffled me, so I went to take a look." He laughed again, and shuddered. "I did my best to change her mind, Fernando. A waste of breath. You know my daughter once she wants something."

"Yes," Fernando said, nodding sympathetically.

Paulo saw his friend weakening. Ever since she was a small girl, Fernando, too, had tried to please the beautiful Sofía, as if withholding any kindness were an unpardonable sin. "I told her it was impossible. A road would have to go along the northern side of the ridge," he said, "through the grounds of your chalet. I explained you would never allow it."

"Well, you know, a woman's feelings often confound her ability to think."

"Well said!" said Paulo. "She talks as if a road were unnecessary!"

"Poor dear girl."

"There is no talking her out of it," Paulo said, filling Fernando's glass. "What can a father do?"

Fernando patted Paulo's hand. "Naturally, because Sofía is like a daughter to me, I would hate to deny her wishes." He took a sip. "On the other hand, she is asking a great deal. *A great deal indeed.*" He downed his brandy and poured himself another and took a lot of thoughtful breaths before finally agreeing. Well, all right. . .if she insisted. . .he would sell her the rock (at a price higher than what he'd paid for the entire property) under certain conditions: There would be no access deeded along the ridge, and the eventual road would be his alone.

Seeing that Fernando would not budge, Paulo sighed, as if reason itself had been defeated, and ordered them each a lobster dinner. Ah, the endless cost of pleasing his difficult daughter.

Sofía grinned when she saw the contract. There was no need, she told her father, for Fernando's fantasized road. She would build a five-star hotel on that rock, and had already envisioned the entrance she wanted: a large wooden dock of thick dark cypress. "Part of our hotel's mystique," she explained, "will be its relative inaccessibility. People will have to arrive by boat. By reservation. They will pass beneath our magnificent stone head, awed and humbled by its fabled gaze."

She had learned, and made clear to Don Paulo, that this was not just any rock. It was, in fact, well known around the lake: a perfect resemblance, people said, of a Mayan face. She and Jake had rented a boat to look for themselves, and it was true. Coming from the north, one could see the great arched nose hanging over the water. An eye was easily imagined beneath a furrowed brow. "That nostril is actually a cave," said the shaman they'd brought with them, "where shards of ancient clay pots can still be found. It used to be a sacred place, a place of ceremony and sacrifice, until 1976, when the gods blocked our way."

Sofía assumed he was referring to the infamous earthquake.

"There was a tunnel that went back and back," the shaman said, "like a blood vessel into the rock's brain, deep into its primordial memory, to the long-forgotten secrets of the world. Only the bravest of young Kaqchikel boys had the courage, and size, to test themselves. Stripping naked, they crawled on their bellies through the breathless stone. Legend told them that the slick narrow passage would lead to a mysterious, solitary place. Few ever made it. Those who did stayed three full days--with no food, the only water dripping from a fissure overhead-- and prayed for a holy vision. When they returned, it was to another reality, their souls transported beyond the land of men, beyond the lake and its surrounding villages, beyond the volcanoes and even the endless sky. The *Whole World* was now their home, which was why they'd named the rock *Nojer Wuchulef*."

Thoroughly inspired, as if she herself had made the grueling quest, Sofía said she would name her hotel NOJER WUCHULEF. Her father, who had not seemed the least bit impressed by the Mayan lore, said it was a silly idea. He laughed, kissed her forehead, and left, shaking his head.

Sofía told Jake she didn't care. She would build her castle on the southern side of the rock in order to preserve the Mayan face. There would be a pathway down the backside of the head into the nostril cave, with daily excursions, led by this same Indian shaman, who would light copal, chant and pray, and tell the ancient story.

Jake didn't care about the name. Let her have whatever name she wanted. Let her dream. What excited him was the challenge of somehow creating a castle on that rock, a project that would demand every ounce of his attention, imagination, and skill.

His mind had been idle far too long. He needed something to do.

There was, however, a problem. A big one. Though he still had cash saved from his dope-growing days, it would not begin to pay for a frigging castle. Most of the money would have to come from Sofía through the controlling hands of her persnickety old man.

Jake disliked Paulo Hernández with a passion equal to the overbearing patriarch's adoration of his daughter. He remembered back to wedding week, which had been a nightmare. The man was a master at showing disapproval without uttering a single harsh word. His occasional 'Dear Jake' always had a condescending ring to it, a way of keeping the proper distance, as if from something dirty. Otherwise, it was a steady dose of 'Darling Sofía' getting whatever the hell she wanted--even this scruffy, worthless gringo. It seemed that the father's earlier distrust of his daughter had been replaced by an endless pandering for her love. For Sofía he was simply *Papa*. For Jake, on the other hand, in deference to tradition, the man insisted on being called *Don Paulo*. What a jerk! No problem, thought Jake, had he lived long enough to deserve the traditional respect, but he was forty-nine, for christsakes, only eight years older than his son in law!

So fuck him, right? No. No way. Being married to Sofía meant putting up with her asshole father. At least while he was paying the bills.

Don Paulo scoffed at the idea of Jake designing the hotel. His distrust came in the form of a repetitious sniff, as if his nose were itching, or perhaps needed extra air to process the pollution sneaking uninvited through his ears.

"Really?" he said. "And where is the last hotel you designed?"

Bueno, thought Jake, trying to calm himself, *maybe the asshole's right*.

Yeah, OK, sure, he was willing to get some help.

The next day, an 'assistant architect' was provided, who brought with him an engineer from the city, and within a week the two of them, accompanied by Don Paulo, were visiting the land by themselves, "calculating" the possibilities, "adjusting" and "improving" Jake's roughed-out plans until they were unrecognizable.

Finally, encouraged by Sofía, Jake stood his ground. To hell with practicality! To hell with standard practices! They would mold every visible trace of concrete to look and feel like actual stone. . .like a castle that had created itself. It was Jake's signature idea, and he refused to budge.

Paulo claimed to not understand. "Why the extra fuss, the extra time?"

"Who cares if it costs a little extra?" Sofía said. "I promise, Papa, you are going to be proud of what we build! Everyone will know it. Everyone will come." She kissed his cheek. "Besides," she challenged, "it is up to me. My choice, right?"

Well, no, actually not, Jake might have pointed out, since her old man was putting up the money, but he knew that Paulo would not oppose her. His sole defense was a lingering silence.

"We will pay you back," Sofía said. Jake could see she was angered by her father's lack of confidence, and determined to prove him wrong. "You can count on it! With interest, too!"

She cried for hours that night, but the next day was full of smiles. "I had a dream," she told Jake. "There was a small Kaqchikel boy selling chiclets on the Santander, and he smiled at me." It was *a premonition*, she explained: Wuchulef must reflect its indigenous roots. . .must be built by local Indians. Besides saving a fortune on labor costs, it would renew the Mayan spirit of their holy place. "By supporting the Kaqchikel community," she said, "we will encourage their good will. And, who knows, maybe win us favor with the gods!"

Doubtful, thought Jake, though it might keep down the thievery.

"The truth is," Sofía told him, "no matter what my father thinks, we don't need some expensive contractor from the city. You have those skills, Jake. You can manage the construction, right?"

"Well. . .yeah," he said, then looked away. Though he'd always assumed he could, Don Paulo's constant pessimism had had its desired effect. "I don't know, let me think about it."

But Sofía took his honest concern as unnecessary modesty, the following week surprising him with two rented boats. One was full of tools, the other of Indians from Pana who needed work. Twenty of them awaited his instruction. What could Jake do but appreciate her faith?

He and the men motored from Jucanyá to the land's southern bay. They moored the boats next to the mighty rock's thick limestone edge. Just above was a large, slightly sloped shelf. . .a mixture of typical limestone with strains of greenish travertine. While tools were unloaded, Jake studied the recent plans. They made no sense. The structure, as drawn on paper, could not possibly fit within the available space. He got out his tape and measured its perimeter. From side to side there was plenty of room, but from front to back the foundation would need another thirty feet. *Huh?* Then, staring at the engineer's notations, it came to him. The cliff behind would have to be chipped back. Out front, a retaining wall could be built up from the lower edge. That's what the broken blue line was meant to indicate. The wall would allow huge concrete girders to cantilever out over the water. Thirty feet easy! Oh yes, Jake could see it, and frigging *Don Paulo* was about to be impressed.

From that first day, and every day after, the project progressed. Slowly. Ever so slowly, true, though Jake didn't mind, pleased by his surprising reserve of patience. He'd learned from the failures on his first piece of land. He went to work with the men every morning at dawn. He sweat alongside them, pounding at the stone with sledgehammers and picks, until everyone's hands were blistered. They took breaks together and ate together and went home together late each afternoon. Jake could afford to go slow (be sure of his calculations, his execution) because the Indians were happy for a dollar a day. And they worked damn hard for such a pittance!

"Don't hurry," he told them. "Be certain."

He wanted to avoid any major mistake. What mattered was that no one get hurt and nothing be wasted. Sand and water were free and plentiful, but the rest came at a high price. Steady streams of crucial supplies were piled into rented boats. For many weeks, it was cement and rebar; then piles of dimensioned stone. Once the foundation was finished, and the lower concrete pillars shaped, boats came full of copper pipe and fittings and faucets. Jake did the preliminary plumbing. His workers were busy stringing electrical lines out to the road. All of it took longer than expected. He'd hoped the hotel's basic structure would be finished by the time his workers went off to plant their milpas.

Not even close.

The following November, once the rains ended, the work resumed. Boat after boat arrived, full of yet more stone. Then milled and sanded timber: cypress and mahogany, mora and walnut, tahuari and rosewood. Huge teak beams arrived from the Petén; Spanish tiles from Mexico. Unfortunately, there were a number of people injured while maneuvering the heavy loads. One worker tumbled from a ladder and his head was crushed against the rock. Another fell into the lake and drowned.

Jake insisted that everyone slow down even more. Then came April, the rainy season near, and again the workers had to go plant their milpas.

Again construction ended. The expensive wood was stickered and covered by tarps. Men were hired to guard it day and night.

Don Paulo called for a meeting. It was time, he wrote in the letter, for a 'serious conversation.' They met in Guatemala City at the family home. "Something," he said, "needs to change."

Sofía nodded, sharing her father's worry, but insisted that Jake had done his best. She admired his perfectionist approach. As evidence, she mentioned the mortar-less limestone façade he'd overseen, the carved pillars, the serpentine sills.

Jake said nothing, certain what was coming.

"Well," Don Paulo said--no doubt aware that to gain his daughter's support he must give some acceptable amount of credit to her husband-- "yes, he has done an admirable job." Of much greater importance, Jake knew, was to admit he'd been wrong to ever doubt her vision. "And yes," the Don continued, "you were right, my dear, it is certain to be a wonderful place. I only wonder. . .when?"

"What's your point?" Jake said.

"My point is, unless I am allowed to take control of this project, I must withdraw my support."

Sofía ran crying from the room.

"I am sorry," the patriarch said, "but this hotel of hers needs to be finished."

By the time the rains ended, Jake stopped fuming. He was allowed to manage the final stages of construction while aided by an abundance of Don Paulo's control. Along with his ongoing advice, he sent a variety of specialists. Masons tiled the many floors and set the marble countertops. Carpenters installed antique doors and windows. Cabinetmakers built tables and chairs, beds and armoires. Licensed plumbers arrived with porcelain bathtubs, sinks, fountains and fixtures; electricians with a stainless steel stove and refrigerator, solid brass receptacles and switches, and, for above the main dining room table, a twelve-tiered crystal chandelier.

Still, in spite of all the extra hands, the hotel took another year to *nearly complete* at a cost of twelve million quetzales.

Sofía was thrilled. Wuchulef, precisely because of its lengthy construction time and exorbitant cost, had everyone talking. Its Grand Opening--April 12th, 1994--felt like a coronation. The guests followed her around like loyal subjects, quiet as mice, hanging onto her every word. She pointed to the first floor, explaining it would eventually include a steam bath, sauna, library, juice bar, and a state of the art 'movie room.' The rest lay open to the southern sky, soon to be the home of shade umbrellas and rattan furniture. Above, over the covered part of the deck, was the linen-lain restaurant. Against its far wall stretched a thirty-foot bar, the top and base carved from the trunk of a single ceiba.

The 'cabañas', as Sofía called them, six in all, occupied the third and fourth levels. Each of the six were different, each with its own name: La Princessa, El Guapo, La Valle, La Vista, El Favor and La Excepción.

On the fifth and final level was a single V.I.P. suite, to be furnished with the best of everything. Outside, on its granite, palm-lined deck, stood a hot/cold ivy-covered waterfall. On a second, even more secluded deck, was a serpentine wading pool next to a marble hot-tub. She had named the suite *La Bella*, and fantasized it costing a hundred dollars a night. Someday it, too, would be finished, but for the time being still lacked several final touches. Windows, for instance. And doors.

"Details," joked Sofía, "details."

It was her eleventh, and final, tour of the day. Hundreds of people had come to see the hotel, flabbergasted to learn it would soon be even more impressive. Many hoped for a gourmet meal. Or at least some kind of food. Sofía apologized, over and over, that she had not yet found a proper cook. All the guests could do right now, she said, was drink-- "on the house"--which made the vast majority of them quite happy.

The guests had no problem finding the free booze. Most of them were fairly lit up. The remaining group included Luna, *sober as a nun*. While pleased by her tardy arrival, Sofía felt impinged upon. Nevertheless, she went out of her way to be *oh so nice*. . .to make Luna feel comfortable. . .to show her what a gem she'd lost in Jake, and what a beautiful place he and Sofía had built together. *Thank God*, she thought, *the bitch will soon be gone*. The group had made it down to the lower patio, just above the dock, and were watching the sun set beyond San Pedro.

A couple from the city asked if they might stay the night.

Sofía pouted. "Sorry, we're not ready yet."

The hotel, in addition to numerous essentials, lacked a staff to run it. Sofía saw herself as the visionary hostess, the spiritual deva of Wuchulef, and had no intention of getting her hands dirty. Jake would be the overall manager, but they still needed a cook, a bartender, a boatman, a gardener.

"What we need most," Jake said, "is a guardián." He stepped to the edge of the lower deck and pointed up to his left. Around the corner from the bar, past the kitchen and the laundry facility, was a place where the hillside had been carved back above the furthermost slab of limestone. Part of a trail was visible, leading to an unfinished concrete building. "That will be the Guardianía," he said. "We want a man with experience and integrity. A man we can trust. We'll spend this whole rainy season looking."

"Maybe," Sofía said, "if we're lucky, he'll have a wife and children."

"To play with yours?" someone said.

"Oh, I hope so." Sofía beamed. "Wouldn't it be wonderful, Jake?"

Jake glanced at Luna, perhaps wondering if the talk of children might bother her.

Luna smiled and said, "I know the perfect person."

"Really?" said Jake.

"Believe me," she said. "Absolutely perfect."

"Yeah. . .OK. . .tell me."

Sofía, while also curious who it might be, and why so *absolutely perfect*, felt the familiar sting of jealousy. Ridiculous, she told herself. She had to forgive his past mistakes. Why not just smile it away, have mercy on the vanquished? On the other hand, where was the law? Where was it written that she had to be continually and unreasonably nice? Forced niceness was to her a sign of weakness. Besides, why bore everyone with business talk?

Determined to be a good hostess, considerate of the other guests, she cut off Luna's answer with a sharp clap of the hands and a playful giggle. All eyes shifted to her. Casually then, she gave her wrist a little outward snap, like flicking Luna, and whoever she might think to recommend, off the deck and into the bottomless lake.

"Details," she said, as if repeating the earlier joke might make it twice as funny. It didn't, but her message, she could tell, was loud and clear: Hearing an outsider's suggestion for their guardián was a waste of time. Choosing the right person was a problem only she and Jake were capable of solving.

Cabal! she was saying to him and Luna both. *Finished!*

The Guardián

While Jake had been busy courting Sofía, then marrying her, then building a hotel...Jaime came to work each morning, worked all day, and returned to his hut each evening. He knew of no other way to win Aura's trust. This went on for three long years. When, by chance, they met in the house, he was always friendly, respectful, and brief.

That, Aura saw, was his way with everyone. Juana often encouraged him to take time off, go see his mother in Santa Catarina, but he rarely did, as if something might go wrong should he ever leave La Gloria. And maybe it was true. Jaime fixed whatever broke, was quick to help whenever needed. Juana thought him indispensible. Others too. Even Aura, though she made certain not to show it, began to like having him around.

Thanks to Juana, Aura was now officially an *apprentice* to Marta, who had been the Alvarez family cook for over forty years. Marta made clear she didn't like it. Or, perhaps, merely disliked Aura. "Why you?" she said one day. "Because the Señora feels sorry for your mother, that's why. All the more reason not to take advantage, girl. A dueña should never allow a servant to use her first name. It can only lead to trouble."

But what else could Aura do when the dueña insisted on it?

It was Marta who told her that Jaime had quit. The old woman somehow managed to know everything. Often without any proof. "You're sure?" Aura said.

Marta looked away, snorted, and went on plucking her chicken.

"But...why?"

"Who knows?" Marta said, tossing aside the irrelevant feathers. "These things happen, girl."

"I don't believe you."

"Believe what you want. You, of all people, should know not to depend on anything."

Aura stopped peeling potatoes for the au gratin she was making, set her knife on the table, and went looking for Juana to find out what had happened. She'd been sure that Jaime was happy here. Others may not see it, but she did. It was in his eyes, it was obvious, like a child hiding in plain sight. She went into the living room, and from the window saw him walking by out front, carrying a satchel. With no chance to think it through, she ran to the porch, stood leaning over the rail. "What, you're not going to say good bye?"

Jaime stopped and looked up at her. "Sorry, I didn't want to bother anyone with--"

"Well," Aura said, knowing that Juana must be very disappointed with his lack of loyalty, "you have."

"There is no choice."

"Why? Where are you going?"

"My father had an accident and can't work. My grandfather needs help."

"What about your brother?" *Oh no, it sounds like I know something I shouldn't, like I've been collecting information on him.* "I heard Juana telling Señor Alvarez. About your brother, I mean. Isn't he there? Couldn't he help?"

"My brother went to El Norte. He sends money to my mother, but it's my grandfather who needs me."

"Isn't he the guardián of a big chalet? There must be lots of people looking for work."

"The dueño doesn't want just anyone. They trust my grandfather, so want someone from our family. For now, at least, it has to be me."

"Well, all right then," Aura said, "go if you need to."

"I'm hoping my father will get better and I can--"

"Good luck," Aura interrupted. "Good bye."

She hated being abrupt, but her heart was pounding and refused to let her say another word. Instead, she stayed there facing him, embarrassed, certain that her feelings showed.

"Good bye," Jaime said.

He continued down the road, not once looking back. As he finally disappeared, maybe forever, she could not block the tears.

The pharmacist had written Jaime a letter, on his grandfather's behalf, explaining what happened. Manuel had fallen off a ladder and broken his back. Senor Castilán, dueño of the chalet, wanted to send him to a hospital in Guatemala City. When Manuel refused, Héctor called in a *huesero*. The man was famous for his magical mending of broken bones, though his grandfather thought it hopeless.

Manuel lay on the floor of his tiny hut, unable to move. He did not want to see his son.

Fine with Jaime, who preferred not to see him either.

Still, the rejection hurt. Why? Would it always hurt, no matter what?

With his mother and three sisters it was the opposite. They hugged him, sat him down, and asked how long he'd be staying. Cora wanted to know why he didn't visit more often. It was almost a year since he'd last come home.

His mother asked about Dolores, who she knew must be suffering from Raul's death.

Jaime said nothing had changed, he hadn't seen her since that first day. He chose not to tell the rest. How could he mention the gruesome murder of her husband, or the horrible things they might have done to her? No, he would not tell any of that. For his own sake as well as hers. It would make him think of things he'd done, would ruin everything.

To change the subject, escape the demons, he gave his stomach a rub and widened his eyes, opening and closing his mouth like a baby bird.

"I'm sorry," Consuelo said. "What a good family we are, starving you to death!"

They ate in silence. For his sisters, he could tell, he'd just become another man, stuck in his own world, unconcerned with theirs. Even Cora was old enough to see it. And she wasn't wrong.

Early the next morning, Jaime went to the chalet.

Héctor was down on his knees, weeding the dueña's kitchen garden, and saw him coming. The old man stood up, perhaps too quickly, and lost balance. Jaime grabbed his grandfather's shoulder and pulled him close. He felt welcomed in the old man's arms. Neither was in a hurry to end the embrace, each patting the other's back.

"Thank you for coming," Héctor said.

"I'll do what I can, Grandfather."

"Please," he said, holding Jaime at arm's length. "Call me Héctor if you want. You are a man now, you have the right."

"You are my grandfather. For me, that will always be your name."

"Fine," said Héctor. "Whatever you want."

Suddenly, rounding a corner of the castle, there were the dueños, Señor and Señora Castilán. Jaime was surprised when they smiled and shook his hand, knowing his name and asking him questions.

Was it true he'd been a soldier?

Did he really work in the house at La Gloria?

"Congratulations," said the much younger dueña. "Our soldiers should be treated with utmost respect. You deserve every opportunity to succeed."

The dueño said, "I've heard from my friend, Señor Alvarez, that you are an outstanding gardener, a very hard worker."

"Like your father and grandfather," the dueña said.

They were looking him straight in the eyes. Then, apparently out of things to say, the Señor looked at his watch. "We're late for breakfast," he said to his wife.

After they left, Jaime said, "Strange that they should care so much about me."

"They wanted to meet you," Héctor said. "They didn't remember you as a boy."

"They saw me plenty of times. And never said a word."

"Yes, well. . .now they have a reason."

Jaime assumed the reason to be clear, that he'd come to fill in for his father and needed to prove himself a *very hard worker*. He waited to be given a shovel or a rake. Instead, for the next two hours, he and his grandfather walked around the grounds.

Yes, Jaime saw, a few things had changed. Like the swimming pool. Now twice the size, and fancier, his grandfather said it "automatically" cleaned itself. "Not such a big help," Héctor said, "because the pump and filter need a lot of maintenance. The water too. It requires special chemicals at special times, and the proportions change every day depending on what is called *The PH*, which depends on the number of people who swim each week, the kind of lotion they put on, and how often they piss."

Jaime showed a tired face and wiped his brow.

Héctor laughed. "Yes, yes, very complicated. And the whole watering system is on sprinklers. That means more work because I alone am responsible for controlling them. Also, they gave me a gas-powered mower to cut the grass, which takes most of a day and must be done every week. A bit faster than the old days, when there were three of us doing it with hand mowers, but still, now it's just me. You can see there is plenty to do."

"I see."

"Maybe less to do, overall, than when things were less fancy," Héctor said. "Maybe. But I'm sure it's not any cheaper. Expensive equipment is fragile and things go wrong. Then it takes an expensive expert to fix it."

"The señor doesn't know?"

"Oh, he knows. It's not the money that matters. Better to pay less of us and have fewer possible thieves to keep an eye on. One of the workers got caught taking a broken ladder. The señora suspected such things were going on and had a security expert install a fancy surveillance system. Rich people spend a lot of extra money protecting their things."

After they ate some tortillas, Héctor showed Jaime the new boat he washed every day. The shiny engine had lots of gears and pulleys, valves and things, which Héctor was never supposed to touch.

On their way from the boathouse to the children's castle, Héctor had to stop and rest, leaning on Jaime's shoulder for support. He was breathing hard. He said the dizziness happened sometimes and not to worry.

Looking up, they saw the dueños standing on their bedroom balcony. They were talking, pretending to gaze out at the lake.

The miniature castle had been turned into a guesthouse. The children were grown, and on visits home they wanted to sleep there, away from the parents, and be comfortable, drinking and partying with friends they brought from the city. Though it might sit empty for months on end, Héctor had to have it ready, same as everything else, at a moment's notice.

The last thing he showed Jaime was the new concrete-block house by the entrance to the road, what he said would be the new Guardiania. Jaime took a close look. It was three times larger than the tiny place his grandfather now lived in. It had a kitchen, an actual bedroom, and a bathroom with hot water. "Good for you."

"The idea," Héctor said, "was for me and Manuel to live in this house. Now they say I'll need to leave. They're right, I am too old to do the work alone."

"But I'm here."

"The problem is, they want someone permanent. If they could, they'd steal you away from their friends."

"To be the guardián?"

"Yes," Héctor said. "That's why they came today--to meet you, talk to you, see if they might want you to stay."

"What about my father?"

"They know he won't be back any time soon. Maybe never. Anyway, they've made up their minds. They're not going to wait. I told Señor Castilán you would help until he can find someone to take my place."

"He's already looking?"

"Yes."

"It isn't fair. Couldn't he let you--"

"Jaime, Jaime, look. The dueños have been good to me for many years. I'm nearly seventy. They don't want a sick old man to worry about. They've done enough."

"Where will you go?"

"Back to the family house," said Héctor. "I won't be any bother. When my day comes, I can go on the same mat as my father did."

Jaime hated the thought of it. "Let's go tell them," he said. "Between the two of us, Abuelo, we'll be a great guardián!"

A full year passed, the Castiláns 'extremely happy' with Jaime's work. On a whim, they decided to skip the coming rainy season and spend six months in Spain. The Señor was excited to go look for the original family castle, and perhaps find some relatives. They left in mid-May, a week after the first storm. Once they were gone, Jaime asked his grandfather for a couple of days off.

Héctor knew why he was going.

"Take whatever time you need, son."

Jaime had written several letters to Juana during the previous year, and she'd written back. Hearing that the Castiláns were leaving, she insisted he visit.

He arrived at La Gloria in the late afternoon, the sky not finished drizzling after a torrential downpour. The road was thick with mud. Still without shoes, Jaime sloshed through it with bare feet, his brand new blue jeans rolled up to his knees.

Juana opened the door and laughed.

"Wait," she said. She disappeared inside, a minute later coming out to the porch with a bucket of water, a sponge, and a big thick towel.

Though they cleaned him up as best they could, the new shirt was soaked. And the Señor's shirts, she said, or even Esteban's, would be far too large.

"Never mind," Juana said, and brought him into the living room. She went to a nearby drawer, pulled out a bunch of flowers wrapped in newspaper, and put them in his hand.

"Thank you, Juana."

"My pleasure, Jaime." She stood him in front of the sofa and combed through his hair with her fingers. "Yes, you look perfect. I'll go get her."

Jaime knew he looked nothing close to perfect. But when Aura found him standing there, drenched and shivering, holding out the flowers, she assured him it didn't matter.

The three of them fit well inside the new guardianía. Héctor did everything he could to please Aura. "Such a beautiful girl," he kept saying, hugging Jaime, then her, and laughing for no reason. Their months together were full of joy. One day, Jaime realized he'd stopped thinking of his life in the army. His dreams had turned colorful again, reminding him of the friendship bracelets he used to make. He could only think how happy he was with Aura in his life. Maybe, he hoped, as some were saying, the war was truly over.

The Castiláns returned from Spain. They'd been gone for nine months and were busy planning another trip. "But how can we leave," the señor said, "with this going on?" For them, he said, it was a disgrace for Jaime to go behind their backs and bring a complete stranger onto their property. "We expected more from you."

"I am sorry," Jaime said. "Really, I meant no harm. I realized, after you left, I could not stay here without Aura."

"You should have waited for us to come back."

"Yes, sir. If you want us to leave, Señor, I--"

"No. We are reasonable people, Jaime. We will find a way to make it work."

"Thank you, sir."

"But you need to know that we do not appreciate the additional responsibility. We have done what we can for your father and grandfather. We do not take these things lightly, you understand?"

"Yes, sir."

"For us it means another mouth to feed, another person to worry over."

"I understand."

"If you want this job, Jaime, you must never betray our trust again."

"No, Señor Castilán, I would never--"

"The señora wants to have a talk with. . .with your wife. What is her name?"

"Aura."

"Aura, yes. She wants Aura to know there are things she can do."

"Do? Work you mean?"

"No, Jaime, we already have a maid. I mean medical things. Simple procedures, and totally safe. To make sure there are no children. You understand?"

Oh yes, he understood. Later, at home, the three of them packed their things to leave. Aura was already pregnant. She had not yet begun to show, but could feel the baby moving inside her.

Héctor said he would go back to the Santa Catarina house. Then he asked if they would still have their jobs at La Gloria.

"No," Jaime said. "Juana would take us in a minute, but Señor Alvarez is angry. He did not agree to my leaving. Or my bringing Aura here." He laughed. "Turns out he and Señor Castilán are not such good friends. Juana warned there would be no coming back."

The next day he told the dueño, promising to stay and work until he could be replaced. Few words were exchanged between them. For both, lots of nods and sighs.

"No," said the Señor, "it's best you just go."

So they took their things and walked the thirty minutes back to Santa Catarina. Like entering another world. When Héctor led them into the house, Manuel bolted upright and waved his cane as if to defend himself from hungry wolves.

"No, father," he said, "they are not welcome."

Consuelo stood by the stove, looking stunned. Cora came in with her arms full of sticks. She dropped them and hugged Jaime's waist.

Manuel shouted, "Get out!"

"Come," whispered Aura, taking hold of Jaime's arm.

"This is my house," Héctor said.

"Not anymore," said his son.

"Please, Manuel." It was Consuelo, walking toward him. "Please."

He lifted his cane, eyes crazy, close enough to hit her. When Jaime moved to defend his mother, Manuel shifted toward him. "I'm warning you," he hissed. "I'm warning you all!"

Aura grabbed Jaime's hand and led him out of the house.

For the next several days they stayed with Rosa, sleeping in the yard under her lemon tree. On Sunday they went to the market with Consuelo to sell onions, same as when Jaime was a boy. "Fresca!" he called out, holding them up by their long green stems. He laughed, remembering his father's first instructions, and called out louder, *"LO MAS FRESCA POR LO MEJOR PRECIO!"*

Aura gave him a curious look.

"Wow!" said Luna, coming down the street, "my favorite people!" She reached into her pocket, pulled out some quetzal notes, and bought a bouquet from the flower woman, who glowed like the sun itself and slid a few extra blossoms into the mix. Jaime loved seeing her again. He knew that Luna had kept up with his job at the finca, then at the chalet. "And now," she said, turning to Aura, "finally, I get to meet you." She handed Aura the flowers. "Congratulations, *Mamita*, when's the baby coming?"

Aura looked stunned. "How did you know?"

"Oh," said Consuelo, "she just knows things, you'll get used to that."

"It is a hard thing to be celebrating," Jaime said. He explained what had happened at the chalet, that he'd lost his job, and the trouble at home.

Luna listened, not missing a word. Once Jaime finished, she reached out and held his hands in hers. "Don't worry," she said with her familiar smile. "Everything is going to be fine."

One week later, a few days after Wuchulef's Grand Opening, Jake and Luna were sitting at El Ultimo Refugio, drinking wine and discussing Jaime. "He's one in a million," she said, and Jake believed her. He'd learned to trust her intuitions. It was time to stand his ground with Sofía. Like father like daughter, though, it would not be easy.

He drove out to La Gloria and spoke with Juana. She gave him a copy of Jaime's work permit and wrote a long letter of recommendation. Señor Castilán wrote one, too, which included the dueño's regret at losing him.

"I admit he sounds good," Sofía said, "but there is probably someone better."

"If I am to manage things," Jake said, "I have to pick the workers."

"What do you know about picking a guardián?"

"Nothing, sweetheart. Neither do you. Look, it's my decision. I'll take full responsibility."

"Yes," said Sofía, turning away, "you will."

New Cook *1994*

Pressured by the United Nations, the first peace accords were drawn up in 1994 and the process would come to its legal conclusion sometime the following year. After 34 years of civil war, two hundred thousand civilians had been killed, with another fifty thousand 'disappeared.' Now began the long public discussion of who was to blame--a bubbling cauldron of toxic stew.

Similarly, at Wuchulef, discord was the daily fare. Jaime had been offered significantly more than what he was getting. Jake felt embarrassed, and assured him that the agreed-upon salary would begin once the rainy season ended. But Sofía objected. "Until we finish the hotel," she said, "he is just another laborer and should receive no more than anyone else." With Jake at her side, she sat Jaime down and explained the vagaries of a construction budget, how difficult it was to estimate actual costs. In order for him to keep his job, she said, they must first pay their debts to the bank. The excuse seemed to make sense to Jaime, who said he was willing to wait.

Another year passed. Sofía would not change her mind. Encouraged by her father to be *practical*, she told Jaime he must wait. Don Paulo had never let go of the purse strings, the fucker, and now cinched them tighter at the idea of a guardián who he did not believe necessary. Jake just closed his eyes as Sofía explained, wishing he could disappear. She lamented the hotel's meager profits, which did not yet cover its expenditures. "Don't worry," she told Jaime, "once the rooms are occupied on a regular basis, everything will be settled."

Jake sensed the extreme depth of Jaime's distrust. Trying to undo the damage, he drove to Guate and met with Don Paulo at his favorite watering hole. It was a short meeting.

"We have to keep our word," Jake said.

"It was your word, given without my consent. Where, might I ask, are all the tourists you expected? Until you have a thriving hotel," Don Paulo argued, "which may never happen, you're better off hiring a night watchman with a gun." Those were his more positive remarks. "You two live in a fantasy," Don Paulo said after a third glass of rum. "You would have a better chance of praying heaven into existence. Hah! Big useless dreams," he said. "Nothing but dreams."

Jake left before doing something he'd regret. His father-in-law was certain of the hotel's failure, and continued to say so, and could not have been more wrong. With the final peace accords, signed in 1996, came the first wave big tourism, and a year later the place was packed.

Jaime, though aware of the hotel's success, felt little hope. It was time to discuss his past-due wages, but he hated the idea of confronting Señora Sofía. Knowing he must, for the sake of his family, day after day he looked for the right moment to approach her. Talking to Señor Jake would be a waste of breath. The dueño had no power. He took whatever was given by his wife and ran the place as best he could. Which meant, it seemed to Jaime, keeping his guardián far too busy for any kind of complaining. Jaime's duties included weeding, pruning, and watering plants; cleaning roofs and gutters; sanding and re-varnishing woodwork; washing walls and windows; fixing whatever was broken (every day something different) and replacing whatever could not be fixed. Should a potential guest pull up at the dock, he was expected to be there waiting, pleased to carry any amount of luggage up (and, at some point, down) the many sets of stairs. That alone kept him running, often into the evening, and sometimes even dragged him out of sleep as a stray tourist arrived on a private boat in the middle of the night. Nevertheless, whenever the dueños needed extra help (every day something different) he was counted on to promptly, and happily, comply.

Aura had her own, also unspoken, complaints. Being Jaime's wife--and thus regarded as a part of the guardián deal with him--the dueña expected her to keep the place perpetually clean. True, there was some help from the two young girls who showed up every morning for eight hours of work. Without them, Aura could never have gotten all the sheets changed, the floors mopped, the sinks and showers and toilets scrubbed. But after they left there was always more to do. Like the linens, and Señora Sofía's silky clothes, all of which must be washed by hand. Raul, their three-year-old boy, was permitted to tag along with her, but not allowed to make a peep. Aura saw he was afraid of the dueña. Every day, Sofía gave him the evil eye and said, "Remember, now, do not to disturb the guests." Having learned the lesson well, he clung to Aura's skirt as she worked, or sat petrified in a corner.

The only work area out of Jaime and Aura's realm, the place they must never set foot, was the kitchen. This rule applied to everyone, including Jake and Sofía: Orders from Señora Baldón, the cook, who allowed no one except her two handpicked assistants into the inner sanctum.

Jake detests the woman. It was Sofía who hired the insufferable bitch, based on her father's recommendation. Don Paulo, who used to frequent the restaurant she cooked at in Antigua, praised her pasta primavera, her lasagna, her garlic bruschetta.

Jake just shakes his head. Will he ever understand these people?

True, as Sofía says, Señora Baldón is a 'unique' person. Sofía calls her *flamboyant*. Jake would say *outrageous*. Though reasonably attractive, the cook dresses her fifty-year-old body as if she were a sexy teenager. Sofía likes the way "she tries her best to look good." What can he say to that? While Sofía's svelte frame slips around nicely in her slinky tight clothes, Señora Baldón looks hopelessly trapped--an animal too big for its cage--her meaty flesh bulging in all the wrong places. Fat, in itself, is not a problem for Jake. But with Señora Baldón (no one knows her first name) it is a defining characteristic. Her inability to analyze a mirror's reflection is emblematic of much greater flaws: corpulent egotism and obese self-righteousness. Other workers have titled her *The Countess*, and make jokes behind her back. Rumors abound because she reveals nothing to anyone.

Sometimes Jake tries to read her mind, and this is what it says: *Go on, you parrots, squawk! Why should I care? Your awe of me is no surprise, I'm used to it. Go ahead, try to figure me out, let yourselves wonder!*

Though he has no idea how she turned into such a peacock, The Countess has qualities he recognized immediately. Her ingrained obstinance reminds him of Sofía on a bad day. Which explains why his wife is enamored by what she calls the cook's "strong personality." She defends Señora Baldón's "right to run the kitchen however she pleases." *Fine*, thinks Jake. *Let it be*. He sees, in ways his wife cannot, that these two hard-headed iron-willed women are speeding, full throttle, toward an inevitable collision, both without brakes, both without helmets.

It happens more or less as he expects. At breakfast one morning--a spectacular day on the lake, sunlight sparkling like a billion stars on the water, the three volcanoes standing at full attention--Sofía calls Señora Baldón to their table and says, "I think it might be good to cook the bacon a bit longer."

The Countess has heard the same complaint, Sofía told Jake as they sat down, from various patrons at the hotel.

Now she gives her fixed reply: "What, you want me to burn a perfectly good piece of meat?"

"No," Sofía says. "I did not say *burn*. I said *cook*. Some people do not want it fatty."

"My bacon, fatty?"

The Countess looks personally offended. She seems in no mood to consider humanity's varied desires, beliefs, or false interpretations of reality. (Jake knows--since she went out of her way to tell him--that the previous evening was a total nightmare. "I caught Angelina outside the kitchen with that, that . . .horny little urchin named Renaldo. They were kissing and giggling when the girl should have been doing dishes. Naturally, I blamed Renaldo for the scandalous incident and said I would have him fired, thus protecting Angelina's reputation. Hah!" she said, her face quivering anew from the remembered shock, "the ingrate showed no appreciation whatsoever. In fact, she did not talk to me the rest of the night. Obviously, it was not their first kiss. Nor the extent of their entanglement. Who knows," the Countess huffed, "what else they might be doing?" She then informed Jake, as she would soon inform Sofía, that since the girl did not understand the meaning of respect, she would also have to go. "Dear me," she said, blowing her nose, "what an unpleasant mess to deal with!")

Oh yes, a mess indeed. Jake sees that the run-in with Angela has taken its toll, with Señora Baldón now close to exploding. She must be appalled, after suffering the underling's ingratitude, at such a ridiculous command from this know-nothing bitch of a boss--a disgusting show of ignorance and lack of trust.

"*Some people*," The Countess says, "should know better than to think for themselves. *Some people* would eat cardboard if I covered it with ketchup." She picks up Sofía's plate and storms to the kitchen.

A bitter silence blares from her exit, reverberating like a slammed door back into the dining room. The guests begin talking less and eating faster. Jake watches his wife, her authority shaken, as she struggles to recover. Soon her eyes are burning, her fingertips pounding the table like a charge of mounted steeds.

The Countess comes marching back.

Here we go, thinks Jake, sitting back in his chair, poised to relish whatever happens. But Señora Baldón cuts the drama short. She will take no prisoners, and is not about to become one. Setting the plate in front of Sofía, eggs and toast cold as dead fish, bacon charred a dark volcanic brown, she says, "There. Exactly what you want. I quit."

Within an hour, The Countess is puttering off in a private boat.

"I am glad," Sofía says, "to be finished with that detestable woman." She laughs and waves her hand. "Good riddance!" she yells at the diminishing wake, but mere seconds later must realize what it means. "Oh. . .oh dear, this is impossible! We cannot run a hotel without a cook!"

Jake lets Sofía think it over. He lets her suffer through the afternoon, until true panic sets in: until she considers an emergency run to the city with little chance of finding a replacement; until she comes to understand how stupid that would be, how pitiful she must seem; until she calls her father and leaves a long rambling message that further embarrasses her, confuses her, forces her to hang up without saying goodbye; until the burden of self-doubt and certain doom become so overwhelming that she crumbles to their bed and bursts into tears.

"Oh Jake," she cries into his shoulder, "what can we do?"

"It's all right," Jake says, rubbing her back, "I have an idea." And he tells her, as if just remembering, of the conversation he had months ago with Señora Alvarez, who mentioned that Aura is well-trained cook.

"What? Why not tell me this before?"

"We didn't need a cook before. Now we do." Jake hands Sofía the phone, and a number, and urges her to call. "Can't hurt," he says.

The two women talk for almost an hour. "Really," Sofía keeps saying. "Paris, really? Quiche Lorraine, really?" And by the end of their talk she is smiling. "Oh, Juana, thank you so much, and please come stay with us--*yes, really*--I know Aura would love to see you!"

She hangs up, her smile vanishing, and stares at Jake. "Did you know that Juana Alvarez used to live in Paris?"

"She did tell me that, yes."

"And learned to cook from her aunt, who owned a French restaurant?"

"Yes."

"And that she trained Aura to make all sorts of famous dishes?"

"Uh huh."

"Uh huh?" says Sofía. "Really? And you didn't have sense enough to tell me?"

"You wouldn't have listened."

"How do you know, *my love*, unless you--"

"Truth is, *my love*, you were totally enchanted with Señora Baldón."

"Oh, God, stop it," she says, her face flushing with rage as she rushes out of the room, "please stop saying that horrible woman's name!"

Aura is in the laundry room, halfway through folding the latest pile of bath towels. The replacement sets of lavender-scented sheets are ready for tomorrow; Sofía's clothes hang on the line, flushed with the pinkish glow of sunset.

As the Señora bursts in, Aura stops and stiffens. She's heard what went on at breakfast from Angelina, who is celebrating with anyone to be found. Like everyone else, Aura has tried to stay out of the dueña's way.

"My dear," says Sofía, "if only I had known!"

Expecting a reprimand, Aura is confused by Sofía's gleaming smile. "What Señora, what did I--"

"No, you don't understand. I mean, how could you? I just found out myself."

Aura senses a trap. Sometimes Sofía puts on a smile while saying the meanest things.

"I have been talking with Señora Alvarez."

"Oh. . .yes?"

"Yes, yes, and she tells me what an accomplished cook you are."

"She is a very kind woman."

"I am sure she is. She also knows a great deal about gourmet food. I told her I fired our cook and she convinced me to hire you."

"What?"

"Yes, yes, isn't it wonderful? You will receive an additional wage, of course, and--"

"But Señora, who will do the--"

"Don't you worry, nothing else matters. Forget those towels, dear, come along, come. I want you to get acquainted with the kitchen."

An hour later, Sofía gathers the other workers and introduces the new cook. Angelina and Felipa bounce to attention, and that very night, given what she's been left to work with, Aura serves a spectacular *Raclette*. The guests are full of compliments. Sofía looks ecstatic, runs into the kitchen and trots back out to introduce an embarrassed Aura. The new cook gets a round of applause. She bows, then hurries back into the kitchen.

After plates are cleared, Sofía brings her to the office to complete the deal. The proposed salary is a lot less than what Señora Baldón was making. Sofía admits it, but says that once Aura has "proven herself" the salary will increase. When or how the proof might come is never made clear. For the time being, it is explained, her earnings will "compensate" for the money they still owe Jaime. Their combined salary, says Sofía, will "far exceed" what he was originally offered.

Aura chews on her lower lip, not knowing what to say.

Sofía, perhaps sensing the distrust, says, "You know, Aura, this is not what I'd hoped for either. You have no idea what it costs to run a hotel. Things you can hardly imagine, things you could never predict. It is a huge risk for me, every day, and I need a team I can count on. I want us to prosper together, like a family, and we cannot succeed unless each of us is willing to make sacrifices. Can I count on you, dear? Can I?"

"Señora," Aura says, thinking it best to change the subject, "you know I am pregnant."

Sofía blinks. "Yes, I. . .I've already, um, thought that through. When is the baby coming?"

"Sometime in May."

"Perfect. Lucky for us, there are not many tourists in the rainy season. I can take over the kitchen during the birth and your recovery. Everyone will understand. After you are up and around, you can bring the baby to work with you."

"What about Raul?"

"Raul?"

"My son. I mean, he's just a small boy, he--"

"Well, yes, of course he can be with you, it's what I have always wanted. One big family, helping each other, each of us doing our part. It's so, *so* wonderful!"

Sofía reaches out and pulls Aura into a short, awkward embrace.

For Aura it feels far too tight: a definite warning.

New Rules

The rains began in late April. The baby, named Erica, came on May 19th, 1997, after twenty-three hours of labor, leaving Aura bedridden for several days.

Sofía took over the kitchen. Aura worried about that, but according to Angelina, who guided her through the simpler recipes, none of the remaining tourists complained. By the end of the month, however, the dueña was frazzled by the stress of actual work. She came to their hut and told Aura it was time for her return.

Aura agreed. What else could she do? Ashamed to confide that a bleeding hemorrhoid had come with the birth, causing constant discomfort, the next day at dawn she bundled the baby in her tzute and slogged through puddles to the main building. It was a miserably cold, wet morning. Aura ducked into the laundry room and lay baby Erica in the small wicker basket normally used to hold folded napkins. She removed her own muddy boots, then took the basket and followed the narrow passageway to the kitchen. Angelina, who was supposed to be there, had not yet arrived. Aura sighed, set the basket on the floor, and started slicing onions.

Half an hour later, Jaime arrived with Raul. The breakfast prep was done. Still no Angelina. Aura was resting on a chair in the dining room, nursing Erica.

Jaime looked tired too. Nothing new or strange in that. He left the boy with her and hurried off to inspect the main hot water heater, which the night before had stopped working.

By evening, Aura was exhausted. In spite of the pouring rain, the door of the hut stood open, allowing her much needed fresh air. She was at the stove, cooking their tortillas, when Jaime came trudging up the path in his yellow rain jacket. He hung it on a hook outside the entry and slumped onto the bench underneath the overhang. He washed the mud from his feet. Aura handed him a towel. Their eyes met.

"Ay," he said, forcing a smile, repeating his grandfather's famous line, "Dios mio!" Aura knew it was his way of saying they must not complain. Better to have a sense of humor and keep each other going. He followed her inside the hut and set up some blocks of wood for Raul to play with. Then he bent over little Erica. "Tell me, *hija*, did you have lots of fun today?"

"Yes, Papa," Aura answered for the baby, "the señora was very happy to sit on her ass and watch Mama work. And the coffee, she said, was perfect."

Jaime's face turned gloomy. He looked at Aura. "Oh no, I'm afraid to ask."

"What, Jaime, what?"

"Did she. . .eat your bacon?"

Aura slapped his shoulder. Raul, who had been watching and listening, laughed at that unexpected slap, then came over to slap his father's other shoulder. Jaime chased the small boy around the room-- caught him, tickled him--and the rest of the night was full of jokes and smiles.

Every night they tried to keep the humor going. Every night it got harder.

By November, the long rainy season officially at an end, a new wave of tourists began to arrive.

No time for joking around. Only for the things that must be done.

One morning, the dining room full of hungry visitors, Erica started crying. Aura put a pacifier (given to her by the dueña) into the baby's mouth. She spit it out. She needed to be changed. The señora came into the kitchen, her face turning sour at the obvious smell. She ordered Angelina to stop doing dishes and take over cooking. "Deal with your child," she hissed at Aura.

Raul, in the corner, also started crying. Sofía gave him a look--which turned his cries to whimpers--then turned away, put on her smile, and returned to play the happy hostess.

After breakfast, she came back into the kitchen. "New rules," the señora announced. "The baby can no longer be in here. Or the boy either. Both of them need to stay at home."

"But Señora, you promised."

"I meant until now," she said. "Now, obviously, we are too busy." Her suggestion was that Raul, almost five, take care of Erica in their house. After meals, while Aura's helpers were cleaning up, she could go check on them. "Won't that be better?"

"No," said Aura.

"No?" the señora said with that *Oh, now what?* look on her face. "Why not?"

"Jaime won't do it."

"Do what? I am not asking him to--"

"Please," Aura pleaded, "you don't understand." She explained Jaime's terrible experience as a young boy, how he lost his baby sister. Also named Erica. "He named our baby after her. For him it is another chance, and I know he will not want Raul responsible for keeping her safe."

The señora listened to the entire story with what seemed to Aura irritated sympathy--both understanding the problem and bothered by its existence. "Oh, very well," she said, walking off, "I'll hire a babysitter."

From then on, as if cheated by having to pay a few extra quetzales each week, her voice grew sharp with Aura, and life at Wuchulef got even harder.

Though Juana never came to visit, she had written to congratulate Aura on her job as the new cook. Aura, proud of her ability to read and write, had kept the correspondence going. Letters passed back and forth between them once every few months. Aura shared that Erica had begun to crawl. . .then walk. . .then speak her first actual words; Juana gave news of Dolores's continuing depression.

Aura felt sorry for her mother. She had forgiven her, yet there was no chance to visit. "I'm sorry," she wrote in one letter, "but Wuchulef takes too much time."

She never once complained of mistreatment, but Juana must have guessed it, recently asking specific questions about her pay, her allotted time off, and so on. Having gotten her the job, Juana wrote, she felt responsible.

Aura answered honestly. Answering direct questions was not the same as complaining.

She kept Juana's letters in the cardboard box she'd made to hold nothing else. This letter stayed on top:

> You need to know, dear Aura, I am trying to get you and Jaime back to La Gloria. We miss you. Señor Alvarez can be stubborn. In his heart I am sure he regrets the two of you being gone. Sooner or later his mind will come around. Because, well, I can be stubborn too! May God bless and keep you safe. Let us think of better days ahead. To the future, my dear! Let it come!
> With much love, Juana.

Yes, Aura prayed, let it come soon. She was worried about Jaime, now more than ever because of his mother's death. His Grampa Hector had passed in his sleep last year. That was hard on Jaime, but nothing like this. The letter came a month ago from Flor, saying Consuelo died of a stomach ulcer. It had been there, the doctor said, for many years. Jaime should not worry about his sisters, Flor wrote, because she and Adriana were married, away from Manuel, and she had taken Cora to live with her.

Jaime, who did not know how to write, asked Aura to tell Flor that he'd received the letter. That was all. Aura added that he loved them, and that he would visit soon, but she could never convince him to go. When he did take time to rest, it was to walk down by the lake and sit. She once watched him from the cliffs. He just sat there on the sand, staring at the water.

Sofía's new rules included Jake. She did not like his "too-casual" way of dressing. She kept at him to wear the "nice shirts and pants" that she brought from the city. "The construction work is over," she once said. "You have no reason to walk around dressed like a peon."

When he laughed and wore what he wanted, she avoided him all day. That happened often.

The real problem, Jake knew, was their failure to get pregnant. After trying for two years, Sofía wanted the problem solved. More new rules. She had them on a strict schedule, their sex determined by a monthly calendar of her highlighted *Most Fertile Days*. Because of the hotel, she insisted, there was no time for romance, or foreplay, and usually no need to take off their clothes. Getting Jake hard was easy. She'd undo his zipper, pull down her skirt, and bring him in. Always in a hurry, she was nonetheless determined to get every last squirt. Another jiffy lube job, Jake thought to himself, feeling like an underpaid mechanic--then unemployed until the next service date. They never missed a single one. Still, nothing happened.

Finally, she went to see a doctor in the city, who was certain it had nothing to do with her.

"Your turn," she said to Jake.

Being forty-eight, her doctor told him, was not the problem. It was some kind of blockage in his plumbing. "Your sperm is not getting through."

The news did not come as a surprise. No wonder Luna had never gotten pregnant! Often, too horny for reason, they'd gone without condoms, were later amazed at their luck, never guessing he might be shooting blanks. Wow, was this about Vietnam. . .about the agent-orange? No point in asking this guy, right? "Any chance it can be fixed?"

"No," the doctor said. "I'm very sorry."

Well, OK, so what were they going to do? Jake knew Sofía would be miserable with a man who could not give her children. Though she never said it, and right away began considering adoption, someone else's baby was not what she wanted.

Before long, she lost interest in sex. At least with him. Was she flirting with the male guests, or did he just imagine it? The hints were subtle enough that he did not dare accuse her. In fact, they rarely spoke of anything personal. It was just about appearances now, like whether they should buy fancier dinner plates, or whether the door frames and windows needed a new coat of varnish, or why on earth couldn't he tuck in his shirt!

Jake escaped to Pana whenever possible. It was the 1st of December, 1999, and the very busy tourist season made it hard to get away. But there were things to take care of in town--preparations for the 'New Millennium Celebration' Sofía was planning. At first she'd wanted a huge party with hundreds of people. Having heard from her father, however, that he'd invited a very special guest, she changed her mind. It was a National Senator, a rising political star named Hugo Vasquez. Sofía had met the man before. She told Jake he was cultured, connected, and that soon, according to the rumor mill, he would be running for president. They should feel honored, she said, that he wanted to come celebrate at Wuchulef. "But you understand what that means."

"No. What?"

"Obviously, Jake, the senator's political clout has made him a lot of enemies. He must always concern himself with security."

"Which means?"

"Well, I don't know, exactly. That's what we have to figure out."

As Jake might have expected, her father had already figured it out for them.

"He looks forward to your beautiful hotel," Don Paulo said, "and is thankful for its isolation. He realizes other guests will be here, which is no problem. He only expects a reasonable degree of control. And a phone, he will need a phone. The senator is willing to pay five times the going rate if he can be promised the V.I.P. suite, and a room nearby for his bodyguard."

Sofía agreed and cancelled the party. She assigned *La Excepción* to the bodyguard. Six other guests, she informed Jake (those who had reserved the remaining cabanas), would be a good number: enough to make for a lively night without any chance of it getting out of hand. With a call to Señor Portillo, a wealthy chicken farmer from Quetzaltenango, she undid his reservation for *La Bella*, explaining that a government dignitary like Senator Vasquez must be granted priority.

"I bet he was thrilled," Jake said.

"He hung up on me," she said. "As if I care. That is the cost of doing what must be done."

Sofía went into full-on preparation mode. She made sure to tell Jake, every day, how much still needed to be done. His primary duty, other than running a phone line to the master suite, was to get their ugly old boat refurbished. "It must be magnificent," she commanded, "from top to bottom." She wanted brand new blue upholstered seats, with a blue and white striped canopy--a reflection of the Guatemalan flag. The boat itself must be painted glossy white, with the emblem of Wuchulef, the great Mayan head, embossed on both sides out of carved mahogany.

New Rules: Jake did as he was told, or else.

And he didn't mind. . .was actually relieved to have the time-consuming task.

He motored their boat straight to Eduardo, who owned the boatyard in Jucanyá, and helped him get it out of the water. Then Eduardo took over. An excellent craftsman, he promised to do the work himself. The job would take a couple of weeks. Eduardo was the one ladino who used to play poker with Jake and his buddies. An honest man; a good loser. Jake trusted him completely. On the phone, he lied to Sofía, saying he had to stick around and oversee the project.

She told him, "Do whatever it takes."

Jake rented a room at Mario's. In the evenings, he hung out at bars with his old friends. He and Luna saw each other every morning--before he started drinking, before she started predicting futures. One day he asked her to tell him his.

Looking at his palm, she said, "You're going straight to hell."

Luna didn't need much psychic skill to intuit his unhappiness because he'd already explained the salary problems with Jaime and Aura, and his shame at how poorly he'd handled both situations. Now, after downing his second cup of coffee, he told her more. He'd been writing Juana in the hope she might offer them another chance at La Gloria. "Sure," he said, "that would cause other problems. Better, though, than me always feeling like an asshole." Besides, he was used to problems. He told her about the father-in-law problem, the no baby problem, the obvious drinking problem, and his ongoing problem of avoiding it all, which just made everything worse. "I've really been fucking up," he said.

She tossed him a forgiving smile. "What else is new?"

"No, I mean it."

"Yes Jake, I see."

"Yeah, well, it's not like I. . .like I'm not. . .oh, hell, you know me."

"I do."

"So go ahead, Merlin, how do I fix this shit?"

"I'm supposed to tell you?"

"C'mon, c'mon, I need advice. It's getting pretty ugly over there."

"Then do something different."

"Right, Luna. Thanks. Why didn't I think of that?"

He closed his eyes. She reached out and put her hand on his. Squeezed it.

"Sometimes," she said, "the best thing is to leave. To start over. That much we know."

"Yeah," he said, smiling, looking away. "That we do."

The boat was finished on December 20th. When Jake brought it home, Sofia squealed with joy. That night, she made love to him like she meant it, was so excited she couldn't help herself.

They began to make final plans for the celebration. Senator Vasquez would be arriving four days early. Sofía, excited at the very thought of his presence, inspected *La Bella*. Its woodwork had been re-varnished, its mattress replaced, its tile polished, and every line of grout scrubbed clean. Also, the workers were given new uniforms. She considered ordering Jaime to wear shoes, then changed her mind, seeing that bare feet made him look poorer, more indigenous. A *nice touch*.

She was relatively encouraged by the final list of guests. Senator Vasquez should be entertained. There would be a young woman, a graduate student from UCLA. Also a mysterious French man, or possibly a woman--impossible to tell from the name, Rene, or the husky effeminate voice. Far less interesting was William Gast, the old bookish director of Pana's *alternative school*, OBRA. Sofía hoped his obvious intellect might impress the senator. Making sure the aged scholar arrived would be his middle-aged wife, Marianne, known for her cleverness, yet still, for Sofía, a lump of mud. Thank god for Barbeque Larry. Sofía had recruited him after a late cancellation, promising a hundred dollars, plus expenses, in addition to a free cabaña, because she'd heard from her father how Senator Vasquez loved a good rack of lamb. Larry would be cooking it himself, and bringing the best cuts of beef from his private frozen stash. Aside from knowing his meat, and loving to grill, he was a buff Australian with long blond hair and a handlebar mustache, large biceps and a weak sense of scruples. Sofía was certain, should she feel the need, that it wouldn't take much to get the brute drooling.

Last on the list was her father. A necessary evil. Though he no longer controlled the finances of Wuchulef, his endless advice remained a constant irritation. Sofía resented his patronizing ways, his presumptuous belief that the hotel's success had depended on him.

What an ass!

Still, she supposed he must be given credit for arranging the arrival of a famous senator.

Jake looked at the list. "An interesting mix."

"I think so," Sofía said. She smiled. "Something for everyone."

"Yes. Exactly. Which is why I invited Luna."

"Oh. . .did you?"

"I did."

What, are you trying to make me jealous? Determined not to take the bait, she said, "I'm sorry, dear, but there is no place left to put her."

"I thought she could stay in our extra room." He was referring, Sofía knew, to the room next to theirs, once meant for the baby. It sat empty except for boxes of odds and ends. "It won't take long to clean it out. I'll throw down some foam for a temporary bed."

Sofía kissed his cheek. "Of course," she said, "what a good idea." Yes, she thought, he may do whatever he pleases, thus freeing her to do the same.

Demons

December 22, 1999

Aura thought a lot about returning to La Gloria. Raul was now seven, Erica almost three. A good time to move. And Juana had sounded hopeful in the last letter. "It is my 50th birthday next week," she'd written. "Guess what present I'll be asking for?" Aura giggled when she read it. And re-read it every day. She could hardly wait to quit this job. She would say it straight to the dueña's face, then turn and walk away. Oh yes, soon the señora would understand how valuable they were!

Yesterday another letter arrived. She rushed to open it.

> My dear Aura, I am sorry to bring bad news in such a distant way. Especially at Christmas. I begged Señor Alvarez to let you and Jaime come back. He refused. I had no idea how personally he'd taken your leaving. For him it was a great betrayal, and he swears he will not change his mind. Like I said, he can be stubborn. It's really just a little boy's pout, but he pretends it a man's self-respect. What a shame. I'm not giving up, my dear, but it must be said, our chance seems small and shrinking. I do hope things are better for you there. Write when you are able. Your friend, Juana

Aura tore up the letter before Jaime could see it. As much as she wanted to get away from Wuchulef, his need was greater. His unhappiness had grown into something she could not soothe.

Jaime did not know what he needed. He'd stopped thinking about it. Always exhausted, he barely managed to eat dinner each night before collapsing on the bed, snoring within minutes like a man who hadn't slept for days, then suddenly jerking upright, awakened by the slightest sound, or maybe some scary dream. . .his body tensed, eyes wild. . .the real world once again on top of him, squeezing his throat.

He rarely slept through the night.

Even when he did, he woke up tired, his back aching. It ached all day long, and worse now because he drank so much coffee. Without it, though, he could not seem to stay alert. And he must always stay alert, always ready. Making a mistake, that was a constant fear, but not the worst. It felt like there was something out to get him, every hour of every day--something beyond the problems of his daily work--beyond the whims of his dueños--beyond whatever he might expect or be able to stop. The warnings came from deep inside his head. It was something he could sense but not quite see. . .a shadowy figure running in the distance. . .a face half-buried in the mud. At times he could hear voices mumbling, would look around and find no one there. Other times he thought it must be goats braying further up the mountain, their horrible sound like the cries of people in pain. If he took a chance to rest, he might doze off, might hear the voice of Renaldo Bej screaming in his ear: "GOD PROTECTS THE RIGHTEOUS!" That would jolt him awake, a stark reminder to never close his eyes.

But his eyes would not listen, sometimes closing against his will, and there was Señora Cocolajay pulling her pig down the callejón, or the fat Mexican, Mendoza, pushing her aside, or the earth shaking, or dead fish floating on the lake, or the small dirty feet of his childhood running from a burning hut.

Once he saw a little girl's head rolling along the ground. Then saw it was he who had cut it off. Sometimes, when he fell asleep, the small boy of his dreams appeared, staring at him, saying nothing. No, he realized, this boy had never been his friend. He was there to torment him, and only more coffee kept the boy hidden behind the cornstalks.

At night there was no escaping the boy, his whispers finally chasing Jaime awake, following him throughout the day like an evil wind. And Jaime knew why. Because he'd done unforgivable things, things that would not stop haunting him. Ever. A letter from Juana, no matter what she said, could make no difference. Jaime knew there was no way out.

He managed to do his many jobs, and, when necessary, he smiled at the dueños. On his own, however, he could not block the misery. Hopelessness consumed him. Each evening, after work, he hobbled home like an old broken toy.

The one person able to shake away his darkness, if just for a few minutes, was baby Erica. Jaime depended on her. Tonight, as had become their custom, he entered the hut with a low growl. The little girl froze solid. He stiffened his body, rolled his eyes back into his head and jutted out his lower teeth until they overlapped his upper lip. By then she was squealing. He tightened his fingers into twisted claws, sucked a chest-full of air through his nose. . .and ROARED!

Erica screamed bloody murder, slapped at the space between them, and raced for her sleeping mat--the place that put monsters to sleep if they even got near it. Jaime could not quite grab her leg in time. She sat up straight and waved him off, giggling as he crawled away, defeated, his growls turned to gasps as he keeled over in a mighty snoring heap.

Sometimes he had to snore for two or three minutes before she'd leave her sanctuary. Eventually, cautiously, she'd sneak up and pull his nose, then run howling to the mat. He'd look at her and growl, but it didn't matter. She'd aim her bright red tongue at him, knowing she was safe.

Tonight, though, as always when his sadness was overwhelming, she knelt down and pet his head. "Nice monster," she said. "Nice monster. . . .nice monster."

On Christmas day, as the dueño's and their guests drank special cocktails out on the deck, Aura was cooking a turkey, then serving it, while Jaime stayed busy with several odd jobs. At night, they were invited to bring their kids into the lounge. . .to sit by the big fire, drink hot chocolate, and eat cookies with the strangers. Politely they said no, choosing instead to stay home. . .to sit by their own small fire. . .to drink the atole and eat the tamales which Aura had begun preparing two days before.

Two days later, on the morning Senator Vasquez was to arrive, Sofía gathered her workers. "Everything must appear extremely normal," she ordered. "We do not want the senator to think we're fawning over him."

That said, she made the rounds from cabaña to cabaña, reminding her guests that they must soon be on their way. Most were busy packing, and none seemed to appreciate the reminder. Oh well, she thought, better safe than sorry.

By noon, every last one of them was gone.

Sofía sat on the balcony of *La Bella* and enjoyed the warming air. Soon, perhaps, she and the senator would be sitting here together, sipping lemonade. The Xocomil had started early today and it promised to be a bumpy boat ride. Good, she thought. Very good. It would make him grateful for the comfort and hospitality of Wuchulef.

The call came at three in the afternoon.

She hurried the boatman off.

One hour remained for final preparations. Sofía put on her make-up, slipped into a particularly revealing sun-dress, swallowed down a percocet, then sent Jaime scurrying from post to post, ordered to warn everyone that everything must be perfect.

Jaime was assigned to help Senator Vasquez off the boat. He stood and waited while the great man swiped a spray of unruly locks from his eyes. The hair, though turning white, was full, wavy, and the wind would not allow him to control it. He laughed and swiped again. He was clean-shaven, with the lips of an effeminate boy, full and pink. His thick arched nose carved in half a handsome sun-tanned face. He looked up and smiled. The amber eyes, clear and piercing, did not seem aware of Jaime's confusion. Perhaps the man was accustomed to Indian servants feeling nervous around him. He grabbed hold of Jaime's outstretched hand and was pulled to safety.

"Gracias," said the senator. He turned and was embraced by the beaming dueña.

Jaime then offered his hand to the other man in the boat, a young baldheaded ladino with a crisp black mustache, who frowned and waved him away. A bodyguard, Jaime realized, must never need help. Or at least never show it. With two quick steps he was on the dock, following behind Señora Sofía and the senator as they walked toward the first stone stairway.

Jaime retrieved their suitcases. It was a four-story climb to *La Bella*, which gave him time to think. But not enough. It took another two days to be certain, seeing Senator Vasquez from various angles and at different times of day. Jaime knew he was exhausted from all the work, the tension, the continuous lack of sleep. Still, there was no doubt in his mind. Oh yes, he knew this man. Knew him well. It had been thirteen years, the camouflage and the beard were gone--but he would never forget Colonel Blanco's eyes.

The Last Supper
December 31, 1999

The senator and his bodyguard, Tonio, were the only guests at Wuchulef for those final days before the great event. A colonelity of their time was spent lounging on the senator's private deck with glasses of Sofía's special fresh-squeezed lemonade. She was never invited. True, during dinner on the first night, Senator Vasquez had warned that he could not escape his governmental responsibilities. There were many letters to write, important phone calls to make, and so on, and so forth.

"Official business," he said, and apologized for being such a poor guest.

"Oh, no, I understand," said Sofía. "If there is any way I can be of service, please let me know."

Thinking it her responsibility to make the extra effort, the following afternoon she brought him a list of the various kinds of imported alcohol that Don Paulo had suggested she purchase. The senator, however, was not much of a drinker, as her father probably knew, which meant an endless supply for him once he arrived.

On the final day before the celebration, just before sunset, Sofía tried convincing the senator to hike the rim trail with her, down inside the famous Mayan head, but he had no interest in that either.

"I used to do a lot of hiking," he said. "Not anymore."

Lit by an orange sun peeking above the eastern ridge, three small boats putter through a sparse morning fog toward the dock. Jake, looking out his bedroom window, shudders, stunned by the depth of his anxiety. Better, he decides, to ignore it, and dubs the first *La Nina*. When Luna climbs out, he gives a sigh of relief. She is such a welcomed sight. A positive sign. Maybe her presence will insure some semblance of peace. Luna turns and lends a hand to the fleshy white old man, William Gast, whose slender middle-aged wife, Marianne, supports him from behind.

A few minutes later comes *La Pinta*. Climbing to the deck is a young woman with a strong grip on her briefcase. Must be the graduate student, Ellen. Following her is a man, or perhaps a woman, in dark grey slacks and a black suede blazer, spiky reddish hair and sunglasses, who Jake guesses to be French Rene. And finally, like the finale he is, comes the tan, robust, Barbeque Larry. For him, Sofía has a hug. She whispers something in his ear. Larry smiles, listens, then kisses her on the cheek.

Last to land is Don Paulo in his custom-built *Santa Maria*, purchased with the compounded interest from his loan to Wuchulef. The boat's actual name, announced in big brass letters across both port and starboard, is *YA MERO*, which in Spanish means (more or less) *ALMOST THERE*. Jake, as usual, sinks at the sight of his father-in-law, and again feels hopeless.

After settling into their respective rooms, the guests disperse. Marianne and William explore the hotel. Ellen gets a fresh papaya *liquado* from the juice bar and goes to the library with her laptop. Luna joins Jake for a hike along the eastern ridge while Barbeque Larry leads Rene down into the Mayan nostril to smoke a joint. Don Paulo, rattled by his curvy four-hour trip from Guatemala City, sidles up to the bar for a Don Julio Real on the rocks. He is accompanied by Sofía, Senator Vasquez, and Tonio, who all drink lemonade.

A simple lunch is served at 1pm. William and Marianne, after a pot of Earl Grey tea, tiptoe past Larry, snoring in a lounge chair, and out onto the rim trail. They walk single file along the cliff, every few steps reminding each other to be careful. At the end of the main trail, William stays up top by the large flat boulder known as 'Table Rock.' Marianne continues past the turnoff to the cave, down beneath the Mayan head's great arching nose, and after a few minutes she waves to him from the sandy beach below. He waves back, delighted, watching as his adventurous wife strips off her clothes and runs naked, squealing, out into the water.

In the kitchen, Aura slices and chops and minces for that night's feast. Appetizers will include stuffed artichokes, papaya chutney, cashew crumpets and a chile-lime jicama. Then will come cream of avocado soup, followed by a Caesar salad. As an entrée, one may chose between quiche Lorraine, roasted rosemary chicken, Larry's grilled rack of lamb, or a mix of the three. On the side will be baby red potatoes, garlic green beans, and four loaves of fresh-baked bread. For dessert, along with organic coffee, the choice will again get difficult: mango custard or chocolate mousse, or, for weight watchers, a *lite* orange sorbet. Naturally, throughout the night will come an endless variety (and copious amounts) of alcohol.

The hotel workers will also get a special treat: a chicken wing, or neck, with their beans and tortillas. Aura sighs and dissects another fowl.

The Xocomil has begun to blow. Out on the trail, William shouts to Marianne that he is going back. She quickly dresses and hurries up to join him.

As the afternoon, and wind, gust toward evening, everyone anticipates the coming night of celebration. Since it is, after all, *The New Millennium*, they must be prepared to party. Luna lights a candle and meditates; Rene smokes a joint; Larry snorts cocaine. He invites Sofia to join him but she declines, sneaking off by herself to pop another percocet. Don Paulo drinks Kahlua and puffs on a Cuban cigar; Jake drinks strong black coffee, William strong black tea; Marianne takes a shower, lies on the bed and masturbates, then falls asleep. Tonio, as usual, sits in the shade and does nothing. . .while Senator Vasquez soaks in his private jacuzzi and wishes he were somewhere else.

Aura is busy all day long taking care of details. By late afternoon, hours before dinner will be served, her whole body aches, her head feels ready to split in half, and her vision goes fuzzy. The world has an unsettling shimmer to it. Nothing looks real. Knowing there will be no rest until this awful party has ended, she has no patience for anyone, or the slightest interest in anything.

But Jaime is flushed with excitement. While others curse the Xocomil, he welcomes it. Honors it. It's as if the strong wind has found a way inside his mind, has given him power. He's been working hard all day, singing to himself and sipping on a pint of aguardiente. Tonight, he knows, will be special. He blocks out his doubtful voices, will not let anything ruin this chance at happiness. When, other than making love to Aura, has he ever he felt this good? The spirits dull his body's aches and enliven him with wonderful thoughts. Thoughts of liberation. Thoughts of revenge. What a perfect time, he's decided, at the turn of a new millennium, to bring an act of justice to the world!

At precisely ten o'clock, as planned, people gather at the main table. Sofía is pleased by the prompt and professional service of her workers. They serve the hor'd'oeuvres without a sound, then somehow know, without her least instruction, the exact moment to clear those plates away and bring the bowls of soup. Ah, the joy of a well-trained staff! Especially Aura, who stands at the kitchen door and directs everything. The girl has done a wonderful job. Maybe she is worth keeping? Perhaps even deserves a raise? *Oh never mind. Nothing I need to think about tonight.* Thanks to the second percocet, Sofía feels her body settling. *Yes indeed, this will be an evening to remember!* She congratulates herself for the weeks of diligent preparation. Everyone is chatting, enjoying the food, the wine, her every chosen detail. She smiles at Larry. In spite of the bothersome Xocomil, he grilled the lamb to perfection. Dessert, she assumes, will be finished well before midnight, leaving plenty of time for aperitifs on the deck, and a toast to the glorious future of Guatemala!

The problems begin at approximately eleven o'clock. Like an omen, the wind rattles the windows. This kind of hellish gale usually comes from the north, making a normal Xocomil seem mild as a purring kitten. It happens once or so a month: the dreaded *Norte*. People have been commenting all night on the strangeness of such a windstorm coming from the south. Tired of the subject, they are ready to talk of anything else. And do. At first a lot of 'Y2K', which no one believes is a problem, yet cannot stop talking about. How utterly boring. Then it gets worse, something about sports. And now who knows what? Perhaps, thinks Sofía, her percocet is wearing off, because she finds it impossible to keep up with the shifting conversation.

Instead, big mistake, she listens to the howling wind. Though nothing is wrong, not really, she feels frightened by it, as if something out there is after her, trying to get in. *Oh my*, she thinks, *what a silly thought.* She looks around the table. It is like seeing these people for the first time. Crazy, she knows it's crazy, but maybe she's not the only one. Maybe it's this evil wind, making everyone think ridiculous things against their will!

Then she thinks something even sillier. . .that someone is deliberately putting these crazy thoughts into her head. She ponders the possibility for several minutes. Cannot get rid of it. *What the hell is wrong with me?* But is that her thought, really, or someone else making her think it? She looks around the table, wondering who, if anyone, is capable of such black magic. Luna is the obvious culprit. The great clairvoyant, hah! She sits there looking innocent, smiling and chatting with the student girl. Is it possible?

No. Sofía cannot bear the thought that such a lowly fraud might have any kind of power over her. No, wait, there must be a better explanation. It makes much more sense that Luna and the rest are under her power--Sofía's power--that she is the one who is reading, and perhaps even controlling, minds. Yes, that must be it.

She reaches for the closest bottle of white wine.

Relax, Sofía tells herself, *this could be fun.*

As if on cue, Larry interrupts William's explanation of his new history curriculum (alternative ways of viewing world events) and mentions the war in Iraq--a world event that, Larry thinks, can only be viewed one way. "Fuckin' Saddam Hussein," he says, "is a problem from any angle."

Sofía looks at Marianne, whose stony expression shows how much she detests the muscle-bound Larry--his dirty blond ponytail and smirky smile. She thinks of the interruption as an attack on her husband. Rather than call the Australian an idiot, however, Sofía hopes for her to keep things civil.

"The world, I'm afraid, is like a bad novel," Marianne says. "A complicated mess."

Sofía smiles at herself. *Well done*, she thinks.

Larry is convinced that both the Gasts have their heads up their asses. *Ah, but how will he put it?* "Complicated," he says, "yes." He widens his eyes at Sofía, as if knowing she's read his mind, then blinks at Marianne with a slight but unmistakable smirk. "Always has been, love."

"Perhaps less complicated in Guatemala," says Senator Vasquez.

Everyone looks at him, as surprised as Sofía.

Less complicated? Huh? It's Jake. She hears him clearly. Her husband knows the senator's reputation, his political connections, and that he must be aware of all the recent assassinations--has perhaps even ordered a few--a silencing of anyone stupid enough to publicly accuse Ríos Montt, or his allies, of war crimes. *Is that,* Jake's thinking, *what he means by 'less complicated'?*

Senator Vasquez says, "Since the amnesty, I mean. Yes, no doubt, we continue to have problems, but things are far better than they were."

No one at the table questions his statement. Nor believes it.

Sofía looks at her father, who seems to have swallowed his tongue, wishing they were among people capable of hearing the truth. He knows the senator is mincing words, but is afraid of embarrassing him. The trouble in Guatemala, her father would love to say, is due to the government's submission to Indian radicalism. Sofía's heard this many times before, and agrees. Something must be wrong for a man like Ríos Montt to be under attack. *Ridiculous!* Don Paulo snorts at what he knows cannot be said and pours himself another glass of tequila. *Why ruin a nice meal with unpalatable facts?*

"Ah, fuck it," says Larry, wiping at his face. "Here we are, at the top of the bloody world, celebrating another thousand years of murderous human history! What a laugh, eh?"

"I believe," Sofía says, "we are here to hope for a better future."

"And I've got a swamp to sell you," he says, matching her unfortunate cliché with one of his own. "Complete with crocodiles."

She gives him a sharp stare, and hopes he can feel it.

"Cheers," says Rene in her deepest, huskiest voice, and clinks Larry's glass like an old pal. The truth is, she also thinks Larry a muscle-bound idiot, and only hangs with him because of his endless supply of high-quality drugs. Sofía has decided, until proven otherwise, that Rene is female. But who cares? More important, this person is a relentless cynic, a danger, squirming beneath a sardonic smile, an insincere compliance, like a finger against a touchy trigger.

For Sofía they are all such hopeless bores. Where is the laughter she expected? Where is the appreciation they should be showing her for inviting them to the most beautiful lake's most elegant hotel on the most important night of the century? Why are they so locked into their own worthless ideas of what matters? Boring boring boring, she thinks, and doesn't give a damn who knows it.

Sofía excuses herself for a trip to the lady's room. Jake knows that means another percocet. He is not fooled by her. Not fooled by anyone. He sips his wine and takes a look around the table. *Wow*, he thinks, suddenly aware he is not alone, that no one else is fooled either. They all see through the pretense, and understand that for some unknown reason (maybe the crazy wind, or the new millennium, or just the high quality booze and drugs) none of them can play the social game and be polite-- everyone saying, or in some way showing, what they really feel.

"Historically speaking," says William, impatient with the ignorant masses, "the world, in fact, *is* less violent." He coughs, his energy fading fast. "Used to be a constant battle everywhere, you know, one tribe ripping apart another, an endless bloody mess and no chance to avoid it."

"Methods have changed," Rene scoffs. "Less bloody on the surface. Easier to justify."

Don Paulo sighs, disgusted, and fills his glass.

"What is different," Senator Vasquez says, "is the influence of modern Christianity. What once was a warring force is now, generally, a source of mediation."

"Seriously?" says Larry.

"Oh, yes, we Christians have changed," the senator says, looking serious as can be. Jake sees it as it is: a humoring of knee-jerk liberalism. "No more stoning non-believers, burning witches, crusading for world dominance, that sort of thing. And now we are allowed to eat meat on Friday, too!"

Vasquez glances around the table, surprised that only Don Paulo appreciates his flippant jab. Jake smiles, then laughs, to let him know he also understands. . .is paying close attention.

"No. . .seriously," the senator continues, his face now genuinely calm and resolute, "in the case of Guatemala, it was the Christian leaders who brought an end to our war."

"Well," Rene says, staring at the senator, "you Christians also started it, so--"

"Pah," snorts Don Paulo, "how can you possibly--"

"Original Sin!" shouts Ellen, the young graduate student.

Everyone looks at her.

Larry says, "What the hell does that mean?"

Bored and restless, Ellen has been drinking steadily throughout the meal--far more than she can handle. Rather than relax her, however, as Jake would expect, the booze has seemed to calcify her intensity. Maybe her dissertation's deadline is getting close. Who knows? Anyway, it's plain to him that she wishes this silly celebration would end. What she needs, she thinks, is a decent night's sleep, a strong cup of coffee, and to get back to work. A good fuck is probably what she needs, but she definitely does not think like that. *Why did I let William talk me into coming? That's what she's thinking. What a waste of valuable time!*

"The lie of Original Sin," she says, her drunken mind flexing for a knock-out punch, "is what Christianity brought to Guatamala."

Sofía returns to a silent table, all eyes riveted on Ellen. Jake winks at his wife's confusion. Aura and Felipa see the lull as an opportunity to take away the dinner plates. Sofía clears her throat and threatens them with her eyes. *Not so fast*, she's saying. *There is no hurry. Yet.*

Sofía smiles and says, "How about some coffee?"

"I hear you are a student." It is Don Paulo, lifting his eyebrows at Ellen. "Of what, I wonder?"

"Religion. My dissertation focuses on how the Bible, and concepts like Original Sin, rationalized the slaughter of indigenous people in Central and South America."

"I see," he says, again reaching for the aged tequila.

Jake holds out his glass. He's finished with wine. His father-in-law frowns, then fills it.

William tries to encourage her. "Will it be a book?"

"I hope so."

"And what," Don Paulo asks with pretend interest, "might it be called?"

"Well, I haven't finished it yet, so--"

"I know," says BBQ Larry, offering up a toast. "Let's call it, *God Bless the Fuckin' Arsholes!*"

A few people moan or shake their heads. Larry laughs and downs his wine.

"What about, *The Fruit of God's Snake-Infested Tree*" sneers Rene, like dangling bait. "Sounds kind of biblical, right?"

"Please," says Don Paulo.

459

"Original Sin," Ellen says, "is a concept constructed to control people through fear."

Senator Vasquez gives her a startled look. "What makes you think that?"

Ah, thinks Jake, Ellen has hit a nerve. The senator's eyes burn like a closely watched fire. Jake doesn't know much about Vasquez, only that he'd been an officer in the army and is now a big-shot politician: In Guatemala, by definition, *an expert at controlling people through fear.* Jake looks at Jaime, who stands against the wall by the kitchen. *Is that how he thinks of me?* Ah, but how to imagine Jaime's thoughts? Forget it. Some things, he realizes, will always be beyond him.

Jaime stands along with the other servants, watching the man now called Senator Vasquez. Though not understanding his English words, Jaime is the only one who knows Colonel Blanco's voice, knows its tricks, its ways of getting people to do whatever he wants. If the devil does exist, there he is in a shiny gray suit. Let him talk, thinks Jaime. Let him enjoy his final moments on this earth.

"The concept of Original Sin," says Rene, "keeps us commoners in line, and feeling guilty, which benefits the ruling class."

"Oh, hooray," says Don Paulo, laughing, "I just love that myth of the ruling class!"

"Well, actually," says William, who then starts coughing and is unable to finish his sentence.

"If there does, indeed, exist a *ruling class*," Don Paulo says, "it is because they were voted into power. It is called democracy."

Rene laughs. "Oh, come on."

"Sorry mates," says Larry. He pulls a rumpled pack of cigarettes from his shirt pocket and shakes them in the air. "I need a break."

"Me too," says Ellen. She nods a quick goodbye and hurries for the stairs as Larry makes his way out to the deck.

"The idea of Original Sin," Luna says, "is the opposite of democracy."

The colonel shows a mock frown. "No, my dear, you are so wrong."

Jaime has no idea what that means, but hears the trickery in Blanco's voice and sees he is trying to fool Señora Luna. *Impossible.*

"Since we are all born with sin," Blanco continues, now with a playful smile, "at least in that we are equal. How could anything be more democratic?"

Rene says, "Democracy, like God, is an illusion."

Don Paulo puffs hard on his cigar, then waves it in the air. "The popular belief in both," he says, "is the general agreement of common people that it is in their best interest to be controlled."

"Huh?" says Señor Jake, who now stares at his father-in-law. To Jaime it looks as if someone has slapped his boss's face. "I believe, *Don Paulo*, that you must be either drunk or just plain ignorant."

The table turns silent again. Jaime wonders what just happened.

"Bueno," says Don Paulo, rising from his chair, "I do believe I've had my fill." He shakes Colonel Blanco's hand and leaves, followed by the weak protests of his daughter.

Señor Jake then turns to the colonel. "I thought we were discussing Original Sin? To be honest, senator, I am skeptical of being presumed guilty before I've done a damn thing to deserve it. Please enlighten me."

"I am a Catholic. For me it is gospel that we humans are flawed beings in a world marked by constant tribulation. I do believe that evil exists. A righteous life is spent avoiding its temptations, and, necessarily, confronting those who do not."

"No one is born with sin," Luna tells him. "Or the right to judge others."

Blanco says, "What, is no one ever to be judged?"

"We are all," she says, "in our original state, innocent. Judgment, like sin, comes later, once our innocence has been taken from us."

Señor Jake starts to speak, then waits when the colonel jumps in: "The innocence you speak of, Luna, is really just selfishness. A baby only knows what it wants. Desire, I am sorry to say, is basic to human nature. It is what the devil ferrets out and feeds on. From our first cry we struggle to get our desires met, and from then on it never ends. People must learn to control their desires in socially acceptable ways. It is a government's duty to make sure they do, and to punish those who don't."

"There you have it," Rene says. "Simple."

"No," Blanco says, "I never said it was--"

"Depends on who's governing, right?"

"Well, yes, it--"

"Seems to me," Rene says, "that the most selfish people in this world end up being the most powerful. Then what?"

"Then. . .what?" Colonel Blanco says. "Is that a serious question?"

"Yes."

"And may I answer?"

"Go ahead."

"Well. . ." he says, "*then*. . .what happens should not be up to us, but Christ Almighty. He is the only one who we can trust to guide us."

Jaime looks at Señor Jake, wondering why he's suddenly gone quiet-- and Luna too--while the colonel is calm and at ease. *This is not how it's supposed to go.*

Sofía's head is throbbing. She's been checking her watch. Midnight is still twenty-six minutes off and she does not want the new era to begin, or the party to end, on such a sour note. "Dessert anyone?"

Marianne smiles politely. "Oh, no, I'm stuffed. Time for us to turn in, right William?"

"I'm with her," he says.

On the other hand, Sofía's thinking, *it might be a good thing if the senator and I celebrate by ourselves.* "Have a good sleep," she says to Marianne. "See you in the morning."

The Gasts nod apologetically, wave goodnight, and weave toward the stairs.

Sofía peruses the remaining guests--a yawning Rene and a bleary-eyed Jake. Her sole concern is Luna, who looks wide-awake and full of herself. A rival, no. A problem, yes.

"In my view," the senator says, "government should align itself with Christian precepts, should guide people beyond their self-indulgent temptations, and toward their higher selves."

Rene makes a kind of snorting sound. "Or at least away from causing any trouble, right."

"Is that a question?" says Vasquez.

"No, that's a fact." She stands, downs the rest of her wine, sets her glass on the table, and marches off in the direction of Larry, outside smoking on the deck. But not before taking a final swing. "Who, I wonder, is more dangerous," she says, and twists around to face the senator, "than the rich bastards who think they're entitled--because they attend church on Sunday--to make rules for everyone else while doing whatever the hell they want?" With a slam of the door she is gone.

Sofía groans. "*Envidia,*" she says, a response meant to dismiss the ignorance of commoners like Luna and Rene, who do not understand civilization's need for strong leadership. . .who are simply *jealous* they

463

don't qualify for the job. *"Asi es la vida,"* she concludes.

"Por lo menos," says the senator, cued by her use of Spanish that he may now speak in their native tongue. *"la vida política, no?"*

Luna rises from her seat with a labored smile. "I'm tired too. Buenas noches."

Vasquez sighs. "I am sorry."

"Sorry?" Luna says. "Why?"

"You do not yet look convinced."

"Well. . .no," she says. "I was wrong."

"Really," says Vasquez, "you've changed your mind?"

"Yes," she says. "I said people are basically *innocent*. That was the wrong word. What your religion fails to see is that we are, by nature, *good*."

Jake laughs, and it takes a few seconds for him stop. "Wait wait wait," he says. "I mean yeah, sure, his religion is a bunch of crap, but--"

"Jake!" says Sofía.

"But your pie-in-the-sky *goodness stuff* smells just as bad. For goodness sakes, Luna, on this original sin thing, the damn Christians may be right! We humans are beyond pitiful, we--"

"Speak for yourself," she says.

"I am, Luna. I am. And what I see is a world over-run by self-serving parasites! Us, I mean. Every one of us. We don't need some elite class of despotic rulers, or imagined enemies, or even the devil to fuck things up. We do fine just by ourselves."

"You don't really believe that."

"No?"

"That's the fear talking, Jake. You should know better."

"Maybe I know things you don't, Luna. Things you can't admit. Our destiny is not enlightenment, *darlin'*, it's self-destruction. That's what the endless wars are about. That's why the planet is dying. Your silly optimism can't stop any of it," he says, then points at the senator, "or his idiotic faith!"

Sofía stands and pounds the table. "Enough Jake! We've had enough! Why don't you and your *darlin'* go finish this by yourselves?"

Luna walks toward the stairs.

Good, thinks Sofía, and focuses hard on Jake, willing him to follow. He looks lost, eyes down, poking with his fork at a cold slice of lamb. *It's all right, honey, go. Go with her. You know you want to.*

She's not surprised when he suddenly gets up and leaves.

Vasquez smiles and returns to speaking Spanish. "Marital difficulties?"

"I'm afraid so, Senator."

"Please, call me Hugo."

"I am sorry you had to witness it, Hugo."

"Believe me, Sofía, I understand how difficult marriage can be."

"Especially with a man like Jake."

"A passionate man."

"A boor."

"Well, perhaps. At least misguided, that is for certain, though I. . .I have to say. . .I believe he's right about the young lady's romance with 'natural goodness.' A seductive idea. Unfortunately, in the real world, there is no such thing."

"Because you killed it, devil!"

Surprised by the loud voice, they swivel their heads to find where it came from.

Sofía knows it is Jaime, who she now sees standing at the entrance to the kitchen. She then spots Tonio rise from his seat by the window. The bodyguard takes a few steps forward, his hand settling above the pistol concealed beneath his coat. Sofía turns and stares at Aura, next to her husband, who looks shocked at his words, as she should be. . .and should stop looking so stupid and to do something!

"Woman and children and babies!" Jaime yells. "You killed them, devil, had them chopped to pieces, and others will soon know it!" Dropping the platter of dessert he was holding, he exits through the double doors. Aura follows close behind.

"Who is that?" Vasquez says.

"It is our. . .our guardián."

"Really? But why is he so. . .what was he saying?"

"I have no idea," Sofía says, and rushes into the kitchen.

At a signal from the senator, Tonio comes to the table. "Take him to my room," says Vasquez. "I'll be there in a few minutes."

"Yes, sir," Tonio says, and goes into the kitchen just as Sofía is coming out.

Sofía holds up her hands as a signal of helplessness, her eyes full of tears. "He won't budge, the stupid little man. Oh, Hugo, I am sorry."

"Never mind," Vasquez says, rising and going to her. He holds her as she cries. Finally, as the embrace begins to feel uncomfortable, he says, "Please, Sofía, come, sit down." When she does, he covers her hand with his. "It is almost midnight. Why let a bit of unpleasantness ruin our evening?" He reaches for the specially ordered Blanc de Blancs and pops the readied cork. Aware that she is also a light drinker, he pours two shallow glasses. Above all, he will stay calm and positive, not show his hostess a trace of worry. "As you said, my dear, we must hope for a better future, yes?"

They clink glasses and drink the champagne down.

Vasquez laughs and pours them another. "Damn good thing a

couple of us are sober."

Sofía laughs too, they drink, and for several minutes he entertains her by listing, as if it were a joke, the many people, now including her guardián, who want him dead. He keeps the stories light and funny. She seems to have relaxed. Then the clock rings midnight.

"There," he says, "we made it." He leans over and kisses her cheek. "Happy New Millennium, dear Sofía, and may all your hopes be realized. Now I need to say goodnight."

"No, Hugo, please." She reaches for the bottle with one hand, his hand with the other.

Monster

Soon as Tonio enters the kitchen, Jaime rushes out the back door. Aura tries to get hold of the bodyguard's shirt. He pushes her away, charges after Jaime, and sees him jump over a short stone wall. A three-quarter moon shows the man running toward the cliffs. Tonio stops, and from his hidden holster grabs a pistol.

Once reaching the rim, Jaime has to slow his pace. It is a narrow path along the upper dome of the great Mayan head--over slabs of intersecting granite--a series of rises, drops, and occasional fissures. The bodyguard seems to be gaining. Jaime isn't sure. The aguardiente fogs his mind. The wind howls. At Table Rock, where the path splits, he cuts left toward the cave. With three turns to go, the moon disappears behind a cloud and he slips, his left knee dragging over the jagged track as he slides to within inches of its edge. A sharp pain shoots from his hip into his lower back. This is not supposed to happen either, but he can't let it stop him. The bodyguard's light flashes on the trail above. Jaime struggles to his feet.

Finally, reaching the cave's entrance, instead of climbing down the ladder Jaime jumps the eight vertical feet. The slippery stone floor comes fast and hard. Wincing at the pain, gulping for breath, he forces his leg to move and scrambles to the back wall, where he squeezes through one of its crannies. He crawls over the small roundish boulder that he dug up yesterday, and hides behind it, dropping into the pocket where it had been. His leg will not stop screaming. He clamps his eyes shut and with both hands covers his mouth.

Tonio pauses at the entrance to the cave. A series of firecrackers go off somewhere in the distance. "Happy New Year," he says, aiming his penlight down at the slick stone floor. Seeing no one, he holds the light between his teeth, but is unwilling to let go of his gun. With just one hand available, he awkwardly descends the ladder. Though he wonders why the floor is damp, he doesn't really care. He shines his light along the craggy wall, moving it slowly from left to right, until he discovers the nostril itself, like a small arched door, with the sparkling lake beyond. He peeks outside and all around--no way to escape--and down below is a drop of thirty or more feet to the jutting chin-like overhang. *Impossible*, he thinks, turning back and lighting up the cave, *so where is that little bastard?*

"Look," Tonio says, "nobody wants any trouble." The place unnerves him, he feels trapped. He only wants to get out of this fucking hole and back to the hotel. "Come on, friend, there's no problem. The senator needs to talk to you, that's all."

He listens for the slightest sound, his pistol raised and ready. *Could be that the pinche Indio attacks me, right? Maybe I'm forced to shoot him, maybe I have no choice.*

He steps forward, his light finding the cranny where Jaime is hiding. It lingers there a moment, then is drawn to a more plausible place, the larger opening that once began the tunnel where young boys climbed to commune with gods. With his gun leading, he ducks inside.

The shaft narrows and twists upward. It is plugged, maybe fifteen feet up, by several fallen boulders. Water drips down from the cracks between them. In a recess just beneath the blockage, something catches his eye.

It is the blue work-shirt that Jaime put there this morning--his extra--which looks just like the one he's wearing now. He left a corner of it dangling over the edge. He also carved a few extra foot-holds so that the bodyguard could not resist climbing the ten feet. . .to see for certain he had been tricked.

On the edge of the final step, Jaime spread a layer of loose gravel. Now, hearing it fall, he lifts himself over the round stone and slips from the cranny. His leg is stiff, is full of darting pain. On all fours, like a crab, he scuttles through the darkness to the ladder.

From the fifth step, Tonio reaches out and grabs the empty shirt. "Cabrón!" he yells, mostly at himself. Hearing *that little bastard* struggle up the ladder, he tries sliding to the ground. The flashlight slips from his hand. His head bashes against a rock. He ignores the dizziness, the blood, and feels his way out of the tunnel. . .then fires twice toward the escaping guardián.

Up and running, Tonio trips and falls. The gun goes off, a bullet piercing his right ankle. He screams; drops the gun; cannot block the tears. "Pinche Indio," he says through his teeth.

Jaime pulls himself up over the edge. Hearing the bodyguard's curse, he knows he's won. He takes the machete from where he hid it by the cave's entrance and with five crisp blows the ladder falls.

Aura had convinced herself that Jaime could outrun the bodyguard. She waits in their hut. It will take awhile for him to go the long way around, first up to the pump station, then down to them. The children were asleep when she arrived, the babysitter nowhere to be seen.

In the distance, toward San Antonio, she hears the sound of firecrackers, and in San Lucas, on the other side of the lake, she sees streams of arcing light. Ah yes, it's midnight, and with the start of a new thousand years the babysitter has gone to celebrate with her friends. Aura knows she should be outraged. What a strange thing that she doesn't care. Jaime will get fired for what he did, and soon they'll be gone from this horrible place forever.

She lies down between Raul and Erica. There is no chance of sleep until he gets home, but at least she can rest. Then the gunshots jolt her upright.

"No, Jaime, no!"

Erica starts crying.

"Mama?" says Raul, rubbing at his eyes.

"You stay here!" Aura says to him. "Stay and wait for Papa, you understand!"

"All right, Mama, all right."

She grabs the flashlight, then takes Erica in her arms, not bothering with a tzute. Minutes later she regrets it. She didn't expect the two-year-old girl to be so fussy, so squirmy. It's almost as if she's trying to get away.

"Stay still!" Aura keeps scolding, moving slowly, carefully, along the rocky path, squeezing Erica tighter.

The moon, like a dented face, beaten and bruised, stares down at them from above the near ridge. Aura's legs go weak. Shivering, she drops to her knees and hugs her daughter, kisses her, strokes her hair. Both are crying now. "I'm sorry, baby. . .I'm. . .so. . .sorry."

Most of the guests run for safety at the sound of bullets. Doors locked, curtains pulled, they hide in bathrooms or closets or under beds.

Luna and Jake hurry to the dining room. Finding Sofía huddled beneath the table, whimpering, Jake crouches down next to her. She looks like a frightened animal trapped in a cage.

"Sofía, what's going on?"

"It's Jaime!" she yells, "your guardián! He threatened Senator Vasquez's life!"

"Jaime would never threaten anyone," says Luna.

"Who asked you?" Sofía says. "What do you know? He accused the senator of horrible things."

"Then it must be true."

"Shut up, you whore! He was your idea, right, so why don't you do something!"

Crying hysterically, Sofía shakes the base of the table.

Jake reaches out for her but she slaps his hand away. He takes hold of her shoulders, twists her toward him and meets her startled eyes.

"Sofía, tell me, where is the senator?"

"In his room."

"And Tonio?"

"I don't know, he. . .he went after Jaime."

"I'll be right back," Jake says to Luna. He bolts for the patio, a shortcut to the cliffs.

Luna says, "Wait, I'm coming with you."

"No!" he yells, slamming the door behind him and running into the night.

Hugo Vasquez, having returned to his room a few minutes after midnight, was not, at first, worried. He fully expected Tonio to bring the guardián and that soon the man would be apologizing. What other choice was there? Without an apology, he would certainly lose his prestigious job, and an Indian could never let that happen.

Not so long ago, the servant would have been shot, no problem at all, no questions asked. Being a good Christian used to mean ridding the country of troublemakers. But times have changed, and Hugo--now a senator, a presidential hopeful--must be willing to forgive the guardián's irrational outburst. That should, at the very least, save the man from ruin and earn his gratitude. Who knows, Hugo thinks, laughing at himself, maybe someday he would even have the poor man's vote!

There are times, like this, when Hugo hates being a politician. . .doing what must be done no matter how distasteful. He sits in his overstuffed chair, listens to distant fireworks, and takes a long deep breath. It is not the first time he's been accused of some horrible act. Such accusations are common since the end of the war, everyone wanting to blame someone else for what happened.

Who knows why this man is so angry? That's his problem.

Simple answers are what people want, only life does not work like that. Followers of Christ know it is not an easy thing to liberate the soul. Devout faith, committed action, and sacrifice--that is the only way. Hard choices are sometimes necessary, and can create enemies.

Vasquez wonders if this guardián is a Christian. Or, even if he isn't, can his grievance be so great that he is unwilling to be reasonable, to hear other points of view? For the Indio's own sake, Hugo hopes not. He does not want any trouble. He wants what is best for everyone. An apology, for a politician, is far less important than a changed mind.

Then come the gunshots. *Dear God, no.* Trying to make sense of them, he assumes that Tonio is trying to frighten the guardián. Perhaps the man decided to keep running? The shots were probably meant to stop him, calm him down, get him to come and talk things through. Still, it was a mistake. One shot maybe, but why three? Tonio does not understand the concept of proportionality. When ordered to bring the Indio back, he should have known not to create a greater problem than before. Now Tonio will need to be publicly reprimanded. Perhaps even fired. What a pity, because he is engaged to Hugo's cousin, Carolina, and Hugo likes him, wants to help him find his way.

Oh, never mind. He can do nothing to stop what has already happened. While confused by the night's strange events, his Kaibil training and intolerance of fear will not allow such unknowns to upset him. He leans back in his chair and reaches for the book on his bedside table. It is an old novel, the supposedly scandalous *El Presidente* by Guatemala's Nobel Laureate, Miguel Asturias. Hugo has been meaning to read it for years. Why not start tonight?

He finds the first sentence:

"Boom, bloom, alum-bright, Lucifer of alunite!"

But he never gets any further than that, his mind carried away by thoughts of his wife and children. And Sofía. Oh yes, he could have had the beautiful woman if he'd wanted. Thank God he is not that kind of man. Though embarrassed by being pushed away, she must realize it was right of him to resist her. It must have been clear how hard he'd struggled to say no.

Hugo feels good he won that battle. Her wanting him is satisfaction enough, a petty conceit he can allow, but nothing more. Rising above such a strong temptation proves his spiritual integrity, and why he should soon lead their great nation.

To succeed, his morality must remain steadfast, must never falter. There will be great obstacles to overcome. There are those who oppose his inevitable rise to power, and, though he joked about it with Sofía, a few of them indeed want him dead. Not just the guerilla extremists, there are also members of the junta who believe his new 'progressive ideas' a danger to their interests. How will he convince them otherwise? Why can't they see that power is not about force, but control of people through their own voluntary consent?

Democracy, yes, that is what Guatemala needs!

The door flies open and Jaime steps inside, clenching a machete, his new clothes torn and filthy, his face drenched with sweat. The two men stare at each other as if from different planets. This is the part that Jaime could never before imagine. His plan was to smile in the devil's face, but he can't.

"What is it you want?" says Colonel Blanco.

"I want your life. . .for all the innocent lives you've taken."

"You think you know me?"

"I know what I need to know."

"You were a guerilla?"

"I was in the army, serving under you."

"When?"

"In Nebaj and Chajul and--"

"No, no," Blanco says, "I was never in Chajul, I--"

"No. . .you didn't need to be. . .you let that butcher Ortiz kill them for you!"

"Wait, I do not understand who you think I--"

Jaime steps forward and raises the machete. "What about Toribio from Acul? Or the whole village of Nentón? Do you remember Nentón?"

"Nentón, yes. . .and there were other places too, of course there were. We were fighting a war, son. Many people died. Soldiers on both sides did terrible things." The colonel stands and faces him. "Lots of us share the blame for that, there is no--"

"Don't move!"

"I did what I believed was right," Blanco says. "I cannot speak for others."

"You speak for yourself! Always for yourself!"

He herds Blanco back through the open French doors and out onto the patio. The moon hangs like a sad face in the starry sky above volcano Atitlán. The night has turned warm, the Xocomil now barely a whisper.

"My problem is how to kill you," Jaime says. "You taught me lots of ways." He points the machete at Blanco's chest, forcing him back against the wrought-iron railing. "My plan was to cut off your head and toss it in the lake. To be fair, I'll first give you a chance to jump."

"Jaime, no!"

It's Luna, he can hear her voice behind him. He turns his head slightly, and in that split-second of distraction Blanco kicks up with his left foot, dislodging the machete.

Both men dive as it clashes to the stone floor. The colonel gets there first, grabbing hold of the handle with his right hand. Jaime climbs onto his back, gripping the forearm that holds the machete.

Luna is standing above them now, screaming, "No, stop it! Stop!"

Blanco struggles to his hands and knees. Jaime yanks on the man's right elbow and they tumble over. The machete flies loose, slides to the edge of the patio, under the railing, over the side.

Jaime lunges at the colonel's throat. They land against a large potted plant, which crashes to the floor. Blanco elbows himself free, tries to get away, but Jaime grabs hold of his leg and again is on top. His whole body aches, but especially his blood-soaked knee. His head is pounding. He battles against a sudden lack of strength, gets his arm around the colonel's neck and squeezes with all his might.

Groaning, Blanco drops back to his stomach. Jaime sees the side of his face: the swollen eye, the fleshy jowls, the soft pink mouth gasping for air.

"Please Jaime!" Luna screams, slapping at his back. "Please, Jaime, please let go!"

Then, to his own surprise, he does. He rolls off, leans against the railing and stares at the colonel, who lies sprawled out on his stomach, eyes closed. Both men are panting. Totally spent.

Jaime feels confused, and ashamed, but somehow knows he cannot kill him. The one person he truly needs to kill, and he just can't do it. Not like this. *But why? Why?* A voice in his head says he's doing the right thing. . .that to kill the colonel would only give the devil what he wants.

Maybe, Jaime thinks, *that's the devil talking, fooling me again, trying to save one of his own. Or maybe I'm just a coward. . .have always been a coward. . .and the*

477

devil knows it.

Luna kneels next to him and holds his head against her shoulder.

"What the hell's going on?" It's Jake, coming through the doorway. His question seems meant for everyone. He lifts the colonel to his feet and walks him back into the room.

Jaime says nothing. His mind, however, will not stay quiet. *It's over*, he keeps thinking. *Over.* He'd hoped that killing the colonel might relieve some of his monstrous guilt, might give his family a reason to respect him, might offer a final chance at life. Now that chance is gone.

"Shhh," whispers Luna, as if hearing his thoughts, "shhh."

It's a loving sound, like his mother used to make when he was a small boy.

"It's all right, Jaime, everything's going to be all right."

No, Mama, I'm sorry, the devil is stronger than me. I can't be with you. For me there will be no heaven. He should tear himself away from Luna's soothing arms, he does not deserve this comfort. Instead, he tucks in closer.

In the room, Hugo lets out a heavy sigh, leans back in his chair and clutches his head. *Now what am I supposed to do?* Where is Calderon, his advisor, when he needs him?

Jake says, "Jaime will be fired, if that makes any difference."

Fired? Only fired? Shot would be more appropriate, but first how nice to pull off the Indio's fingernails! Of course he can't do either--not with all these witnesses--though everyone would understand if the man were arrested for attempted murder. Oh, Christ, what a bother, because that would just draw unwanted attention. Reporters and their petty questions. And what if this Jaime, out of spite, were then to make more problems? As a statesman in the public eye, Vasquez cannot afford to take the chance. But wait. . .wait. . .what if it was Jaime who shot Tonio? Perhaps even killed him? If the Indio did that, no matter what he might say, no one would listen.

"I don't care about your guardián," Hugo says. "Where is Tonio?"

"He's all right," Jake says. "Shot himself in the foot. I sent for a doctor. It's nothing serious."

"Oh, thank God."

"Senator?"

"Yes."

"What will you do to Jaime?"

"I haven't decided. Any suggestions?"

"Well," Jake says, "I suppose you could do the Christian thing and forgive him."

"Hah! But you said that my religion is a bunch of crap. I believe you called me an idiot."

"Yeah. . .well. . .I do hope that I'm wrong, sir."

A woman appears at the door with a baby in her arms. Panting, she puts the child down. "Where is Jaime?" she says, her eyes swollen with tears. Then, as if hiding from the answer, she collapses to the floor, head between her knees, hands over her ears. Jake kneels next to the woman and tries to explain that Jaime is here, he's safe, but her heaping sobs will not allow it. The little girl waddles toward the deck, through the open doors, squealing "Papa! Papa!"

Hugo sees it as a sign. Family, yes. Were it his wife, his daughter, he would do nothing that might cause them any harm.

Jake sees that Erica has changed things. "His girl," he says to Vasquez. "This is his wife. I know the man well, Senator. I know how much he loves his family and--"

"Listen to me," Vasquez says, his eyes intense. "I just want this to be over. No more talk of it to anyone. Ever. If you can promise me that, fine. Problem solved. If not, Jake, everybody will suffer. You understand?"

"Yes," Jake says. It is clear that the threat includes him, and probably Luna too. He is reminded of Captain Reynolds' long-ago threats--at the time forcing him, against his will, to stay quiet about Vietnam. Jake nods at Vasquez's determined stare, reminded of what evil looks like. "I will make him understand, sir. You can be sure he will agree."

Jaime lifts his head when he hears Erica running toward him. Struggling to get up, his bad leg stiffens, a jolt of pain shooting through his lower back. He moans, staggers, and drops to one knee.

Erica stops and takes a step back. Jaime holds out his arms to coax the frightened child forward. Already in an unstable position, however, the movement throws him further off balance and he must brace himself with both hands against the deck. Again he moans.

The little girl, as if realizing it is up to her to make things well, does what she always does when he gets like this. . .slowly inching closer. . .kind of sideways. . .her tiny hands out in front, saying, "Nice monster. . .nice monster."

"Jaime!" screams Aura, running from the bedroom, and soon they are both in his arms, the three of them wrapped together like petals of a broken flower. They are so fragile. So vulnerable. Why then, wonders Jaime, does the colonel look worried?

Luna joins Jake and Vasquez, who watch from inside the room as the baby girl pets her father's head. For Luna it is a healing sight. A blessing.

Glancing at the senator, though, she is struck by his look of deep concern. It is not any sort of sympathy for Jaime and his family, as she expected, but something else, something he sees that has him anxious. "There is no reason," she says, "to fear that man."

"No," says the senator. "No reason at all."

He says it as if he means it, but Luna doesn't trust his words. He could merely be saying that his fear is unreasonable, something he does not understand, which makes it even more frightening. She steps up to Vasquez and looks into his eyes. "So, Senator, does that mean you won't hurt him? You'll leave him alone?"

"Yes. I am not the horrible person you all take me for."

"I hope not," Luna says.

"Come on," Jake says to her, and they walk toward the huddled family.

Luna feels like this is her family too. And Jake's. He may not understand it yet, he's always laughed at her intuitions, but this time feels different. Something crucial has changed. Something finally feels right, feels good, and she's sure it's coming from Jake.

Jaime looks up at them.

Seeing how difficult it is on the poor man's neck, they crouch down beside him.

Jake says, "It seems that you know things you are not supposed to know, am I right?"

Jaime nods, his eyelids pinching back the tears.

"To keep yourself safe," Jake says, "can you pretend you don't?"

"No."

"Listen to me, Jaime. What if it means protecting your wife and children? Can you do it then?"

Luna looks at Jake, bewildered.

"Yes, Señor Jake. If that is what it takes."

Luna, though still confused, understands from Jaime's face that something important is happening. Something that needs to happen. She looks at Aura, who seems to understand it too.

"For now," Jake says, "pretend. Pretend for your family. But just for now, I promise you that. I promise, Jaime, so please, just for now, look at him, standing in the doorway, and nod your head. Good. Good. And I'm nodding at you, see, like the two of us have an agreement. That's it, keep on nodding. Because for now that keeps all of us safe. But when he's gone, Jaime, we'll get you to a protected place, a place where you will be able to tell the truth about whatever it is he did. I want to help you do that, all right? Yes? Good, thank you. . .then we have an agreement. Now you should smile and shake my hand."

Jaime shakes hands with Jake. "I'm sorry, Señor, I cannot smile."

"Oh yes," Jake says, "you can," and puts his hand on Jaime's shoulder.

Luna is not surprised. *This is it,* she thinks. *This is the goodness.*

"I should have told you yesterday, but was sure you'd have quit before the party started."

"What, Señor Jake?"

"Juana called. She wants you to work at La Gloria."

Aura says, "No Señor, I know she wants that, yes, but her husband, the dueño, he won't--"

"Her husband," says Jake. "Yes, that's true, her husband is a problem."

Then comes one of Jake's little boy smiles, making Luna smile too.

"The thing is," he says, "she's gotten other workers on the finca to tell him how they feel. All of them want you back, Jaime. And, Aura, your mother wants you too. Everyone is asking the dueño to change his mind. That is what's happening." Jake looks Jaime straight on. "Juana's idea is for you to go. . .for you and him to talk it out. Say you're sorry and give him a chance to forgive. She says that's all he really wants. Are you too proud for that?"

"No."

Aura watches Jaime's face.

Luna watches her, feeling the young wife's hope, her prayer, that Jaime's softened eyes are saying what she needs to hear. When he smiles, she wraps her arms around his neck and squeezes tight.

Jaime grimaces.

Luna starts crying and squeezes Jake too. Yes, yes, this is her family.

Then it comes clear. It makes perfect sense.

This, she knows, is what Vasquez really fears. . .that it's not just an isolated Indian man he has to worry about. It's them too. It's she and Jake. It's friends like Juana, and others--people who Luna has never met --a whole extended family. From here on out, they will help each other, protect each other. None of them believe there can ever be an easy way through this life. . .but they all, for now at least, feel *lucky*.

"Gracias a Dios," says Jaime.

"Sí" Jake says. "Gracias a Dios."

Glossary (with **accented** phonetic pronunciation)

Important Guatemalan Character Names--in order of appearance:

Manuel	(Mahn-**wel**)
Héctor	(**Ek**-tor)
Consuelo	(Kone-**sway**-low)
Jaime	(**Hi**-may)
Aura	(**Ow**-rah)
Dolores	(Doe-**lor**-es)
Salvador	(Sahl-vah-**dor**)
Raul	(Rah-**ool**)

Important Terms, Things, or Places--in alphabetical order:

Acul (Ah-**kool**) : A village in the Quiché department of Guatemala.

Aguardiente (Ahg-wahr-dee-**en**-tay) :   An alcoholic beverage made of fermented fruit.

Aldea (Ahl-**day**-uh) : A very small village.

Artisano (Ar-tee-**sah**-no) :   A foreign craftsperson who sells on the street.

Atitlán (Ah-teet-**lahn**) : A large volcanic lake in the highlands of Guatemala.

Atole (Ah-**toll**-ay) : A popular festive drink made of mashed corn, spices, and sugar.

Avanzado (Ah-vahn-**sah**-doe) : Advanced.

Cal (**Cahl**) : A liquid made of powdered lime and water.

Callejón (Ka-yay-**hone**) : An alley, or minor pathway through a village.

Cayuco (Ky-**oo**-ko) : A traditional Guatemalan canoe, made of wood.

Caña (**Kahn**-yuh) : Cane bamboo.

Chajul (Chah-**hool**) : A town in the Cuchumatanes Mountains, department of Quiché.

Chalet (Shah-**lay**) : A lakeside property and house, usually of great value.

Chucho (**Choo**-Cho) : A nickname for "dog"

Comal (Ko-**mahl**) : The flat metal plate, used for cooking tortillas.

Comedor (Ko-meh-**door**) : The simplest of Guatemalan restaurants.

Costal (Ko-**stahl**) : A large, durable sack, normally made of plastic mesh.

Corte (**Core**-tay) : A woven skirt worn by Guatemalan indigenous women.

Cuchumatanes (Koo-choo-mah-**tah**-nace) : Large mountain range in North-Western Guatemala.

Cuerda (**Kwair**-duh) : A unit of land measurement, whose definition varies from country to country.

Curandero (Koo-rahn-**day**-ro) : A healer.

Dueño (**Dway**-nyo) : The owner of a business, or householder of a property.

El Norte (El **Nor**-tay) : A common name in Guatemala for The United States of America.

Envídia (En-**vee**-dee-uh) : Envy.

Faja (**Fah**-ha) : A traditional woven belt, used to secure an Indian woman's corte.

Fútbol (**Foote**-bol) : Soccer.

Guardián (Guar-dee-**ahn**) : The caretaker of a chalet, who usually lives on the property.

Guate (**Gwah**-tay) : The common name for Guatemala City.

Guerillero (Gay-ree-**yair**-oh) : A guerilla fighter in Guatemala.

Hospedaje (Ose-bay-**dah**-hay) : A small, cheap, Guatemalan hotel.

Huehuetenango (Way-way-teh-**nang**-go) : A city, and municipal department, in Guatemala.

Huesero (Hway-**sehr**-o) : A shamanic Mayan doctor trained in curing bone-related injuries.

Huipil (Hwee-**peel**) : The traditional hand-woven blouse worn by Indian women.

Ix Chel (Ee-**shell**) : One of the more famous Mayan gods.

Ixil (Ee-**sheel**) : The indigenous Mayan people of the Quiché department.

Jacaltenango (Hah-kahl-teh-**nang**-go) : A town in the Sierra Madre Mountains.

Kaqchikel (Kah-chee-**kel**) : One of the many groups of Indigenous Mayan people.

Maize (My-**ees**) : Corn used to make masa.

Manito (Mah-**knee**-toe) : Little brother.

Masa (**Mah**-sah) : Corn paste used to make tortillas.

Milpa (**Meel**-pah) : A field used only for the cultivation of maize.

Molina (Moe-**lee**-nuh) : The mill where corn is ground into masa.

Naturale (Nah-too-**rah**-lay) : A Spanish word used by Indians when referring to themselves.

Nebaj (Nay-**bahq**) : A town in the Cuchumatanes Mountains, department of Quiché.

Nentón (Nen-**tone**) : A village in the Sierra Madre Mountains.

Ocote (Oh-**ko**-tay) : Strips of resinous pine, used to start fires.

Peone (Pay-**o**-nay) : A peasant day laborer, often poorly paid.

Puja (**Poo**-hah) : A roofing material made of tightly wound grasses.

Profe (**Pro**-fay) : The shortened form of 'Professor'--a title often used for teachers.

Quetzal (Ket-**sahl**) : The national bird of Guatemala. Also the name of its national currency.

Sacapulas (Sah-kah-**poo**-lahs) : A town in the department of Quiché.

Sequestrado (Say-qwess-**trah**-doe) : Abducted, or kidnapped.

Temazcal (Tay-mahs-**kahl**): A traditional Mayan steam room.

Terreño (Teh-**ray**-nyo) : A piece of land.

Todos Santos (**Toe**-dos **Sahn**-tos) : A town in the department of Huehuetenango.

Traje (**Trah**-hay) : The traditional dress of any Guatemalan Indian village.

Tuzukiin (Toot-sue-**keen**) : The Kaqchikel word for penis.

Tzute (**Szoo**-tay) : The traditional Indian wrap used to carry an infant, or whatever.

Tzutuhil (Szoo-too-**heel**) : One of the many groups of Indigenous Mayan people.

Vos (**Vose**) : Spanish slang used between friends, meaning "pal."

Made in the USA
San Bernardino, CA
10 January 2016